BILL MADDEN & MICHAEL RAPPAPORT

A NOVEL OF PRO FOOTBALL

Cover photos courtesy of Earl Shores, originally published in *Full Color Electric Football*, 2015.

First Printing, 2021

ISBN: 978-1-952727-05-4
       978-1-952727-06-1 (epub)

Bill Madden (not the famous sportswriter) and
Michael Rappaport (not the famous actor) have
been friends and collaborators for most of their
adult lives.

This is their first novel.

PROLOGUE

From Fred Reynolds' column, The Washington Evening Tribune, April 4, 1982:

"Talk about futility.

"The Washington Warriors, the North American Football Association's answer to mediocrity (look in the dictionary under mediocre and you'll see their team logo), will hold their annual stockholders' meeting tonight at the Bethesda Holiday Inn.

"That in itself is a rarity in the button-down, everything-all-too-perfect NAFA. When the sainted commissioner -- pause for genuflection toward New Orleans -- strong-armed the old United League into a merger back when you and I still had hair and I could see my shoes without a mirror, he had it written into the league's bylaws that teams would, from that day forward, be operated by one person.

"Only one.

"In other words, no stockholders. That's smart. Stockholders are a pain in the butt.

"However, since Washington had been a publicly owned franchise since

the Association's infancy, and His Most Perfect Holiness knew better than to meddle with that and risk running afoul of Congress (see previous reference to mediocrity), he left our dear Warriors alone.

"Oh, boy, did he leave them alone. While other teams have been encouraged to hire the finest young executive talent, while other teams have been given sweetheart loans to improve their facilities, while other teams have ..."

"You ought to be getting the picture. I'd call the Warriors the bastard stepchild of the NAFA, but I'm not allowed to use the word bastard in a family newspaper.

"Washington has been in the toilet for 31 years, even before His Eminence took charge, but since he came down from the mountain with the stone tablets, things have really been pitiful.

"The Warriors' last winning season was 20 years ago. Over the last eight years, they have averaged a little more than four victories a season, winning 33 and losing 79.

"Folks, if that's what they call the Wide World of Sports, the lovely Cybill Shepherd is at this moment searching frantically for my phone number.

"I don't think I'm compromising national security by telling you things don't look too much better this year, for my love life or for our football team.

"The Warriors have traded away their first three choices in next month's college draft, and the two or three decent football players they do have are on the wrong side of 30 for anyone not planning on running for President.

"To top things off, this year's schedule can be described by only one word -- brutal.

"So where does that leave our beloved Warriors? If you can't answer that question without my help, I'm surprised you've made it this far into the column.

"Tune in tomorrow."

I

"This meeting of the shareholders of the Washington Warriors football franchise of the North American Football Association will come to order."

Franklin Delano Lambert, the chairman of the board of Washington Football Inc., rapped his gavel twice as he surveyed the crowd. It was a steamy night in Washington -- far too warm for spring -- and the conference rooms in the old hotel where the Warriors held their annual meeting had air conditioning that only seemed to work well in January.

Lambert wanted to get the meeting over with quickly and get home so he could enjoy a couple of tall drinks while he watched "Hill Street Blues."

Most of those present for the annual report seemed still to be finding their way to their seats while balancing drinks from the open bar and plates from the buffet.

That's what brings these people here year after year, Lambert thought. Free food and lots of free liquor.

Actually, Lambert found the annual meeting to be a waste of time. He wouldn't even have bothered -- he'd have preferred to mail out an annual report -- except that the team's original charter demanded it. Sometime between April and June of each year, an open meeting of stockholders had to be held at the discretion of the board of directors to review the past season and preview the coming year.

The schedule would be presented, officers would be re-elected and any other business would be handled as quickly as possible.

The board usually held the meeting in April, when interest in football was at its absolute lowest. The meeting often had been held on the opening day of the baseball season or on the evening of the NCAA men's basketball finals.

One year, a grand total of eight stockholders had been in attendance to re-elect the board.

Someone had made a mistake this year, though, which was certainly no surprise considering Washington was far and away the worst-run franchise in the Association. The meeting had been scheduled for a Friday evening when nothing else was happening, and the auditorium was packed.

Lambert knew that would make it more difficult, and the meeting might take longer than the usual hour or so. Whatever happened, he thought, there wouldn't be much interest outside the room in what happened inside.

The board's actions hadn't been questioned in twenty years, and it had been nearly that long since the local papers had bothered to send reporters to cover it. Occasionally there was a short article by a stringer buried in the back pages of the sports section, and once in a while the city's television sportscasters would dismiss the meeting with a single sentence -- usually disparaging -- right after giving the hockey scores.

There was a very good reason for the lack of interest in the team. The Warriors had a long history of ineffectiveness, with more than thirty years of mediocrity since the team had last qualified for the playoffs.

The team struggled along from year to year, rarely quite bad enough to qualify for the first or second draft pick and the real superstars coming out of the college ranks.

When the team had been truly awful, it always seemed that the first draft pick had been traded away a year or two earlier for a player who wasn't even in the league anymore.

The Warriors' stadium, Herbert Hoover Coliseum, was the smallest, most run-down facility in the league, seating only 35,000 and built to accommodate baseball rather than football. At least two thousand of the seats had an obstructed view, but it didn't matter. They hadn't been filled in decades.

Attendance at Warriors games was consistently in the 20,000 to 25,000 range, the lowest attendance of any major football franchise in North America. High-school games in the suburbs drew crowds that rivaled the NAFA franchise downtown.

The last time attendance had pushed the limits of "the Hoove," as local fans referred to the Coliseum, had been twenty years earlier, when legendary coach Bob Brazzatti had come south from New York with a history of brilliance on the field and a promise to build the team into a winner.

He did just that, blending returning Warriors players, rookies and free agents into a team that finished with a 9-5 record and lost a playoff berth on a tiebreaker. For the only time in the history of the franchise, Warriors tickets were in serious demand as fans and media alike looked for greater things in years to come.

Unfortunately, the resurgence never went any further. The fiery Brazzatti was discovered the week before opening day of his second season in a convertible parked off Wisconsin Avenue.

In his company was a bottle of twenty-year-old Scotch and a 16-year-old high school cheerleader who was the daughter of the junior senator from Maryland. They were in the back seat and their clothes were in the front. The coach swore he had been framed, that someone had put something in his drink.

No one listened.

The scandal was swept under the rug, but Brazzatti was secretly dismissed from professional football and banned from the game for life.

A disillusioned Warriors team finished the season 2-12, and attendance quickly returned to normal. Brazzatti had a heart attack and died the week before the final game.

Washington hadn't won more than five games in a season since. Brazzatti had been replaced as general manager by a 23-year-old who had held the exalted position of press liaison and whose only previous management experience had been as assistant manager of a taco stand the summer after his sophomore year of college.

The kid had panicked. He spent the next year trading away draft choices for players who either were past their prime, in possession of talents that no one else could see or somehow seemed jinxed.

A promising young quarterback from Missouri was drafted, signed to a five-year contract and then disappeared two weeks into training camp, never to be heard from again.

Two players obtained from the Boston franchise announced they were in love and planned to be married. Since same-sex marriage was illegal in the U.S., the two players announced they would flip a coin to see which of them would undergo a sex-change operation.

A running back acquired from Montreal retired to run for the Canadian parliament and spend his life working for Quebec separatism. One of the team's few good players, an all-league offensive lineman, moved to Tibet to study under the Dalai Lama.

What few players the Warriors managed to hang onto seemed somehow never to be able to carry the team to anything approaching the near-glory of that one wonderful season. The team struggled from year to dismal year, losing games, players and eventually the hearts of the residents of the Washington area.

The stadium deteriorated more and more each season. It hadn't even been repainted since Eisenhower's first term as president, and it had none of the luxury boxes found in newer facilities, costing the franchise both revenue and local corporate support.

The surrounding neighborhood wasn't much better. Every second house looked like some sort of halfway house for addicts or parolees, making possession of a season ticket more of an invitation to take one's life into one's hands than the status symbol it was in many cities.

The team, however, was not losing money. The NAFA's television contract, which paid each team in excess of $35 million per year, assured each franchise of making a profit even if every ticket for every game remained unsold.

In fact, even the Warriors -- far and away the least profitable team in the league -- were turning a profit of between $35 and $45 million, year in and year out. It was a situation that encouraged little improvement in the management of the franchise.

Each shareholder ended the year with dividends on his stock, and everyone was more or less happy to ignore the fact that every other team in the league turned millions more in profits.

The annual shareholders meeting, then, was usually little more than a charade. There were never any new ideas, never any reasonable suggestions. No major decisions ever were made.

There would occasionally be one or two complaints voiced about the previous season, or the condition of the stadium, but most people who attended would have a few drinks, eat a sandwich or two and leave content in the feeling they had helped to shape the destiny of their favorite sports team.

The board of directors was always re-nominated and re-elected without challenge, and the new board then would re-elect Chairman Lambert by a voice vote. The contracts of the team's general manager and head coach then would be extended.

The general manager then would announce that he and the rest of the front-office staff were engaged in furious planning guaranteed finally to bring success to the long-suffering Warriors and their fans.

Once in a while, when things became truly unbearable, the general manager or coach would be fired and someone new would be hired to rebuild the team. Since the Warriors paid salaries that were roughly half of what the other 23 teams in the NAFA were paying, that talent was usually substandard and the results were disappointing.

Good people stayed a year or two to gain experience and then moved on to other teams. The incompetents stayed forever.

Basically the only thing accomplished by the annual meeting was satisfying the requirements of the charter. Chairman Lambert, who was paid $125,000 a year to do little more than conduct the meeting, was more than happy to oblige.

Lambert sipped at the glass of ice water in front of him on the podium, wishing he could have a real drink. He then cleared his throat and made sure the microphone was adjusted to a proper height and angle.

"As most of you are aware by now," he said in the nasal, patrician accent that had always made him a most ineffective public speaker, "the Association recently suffered a grievous loss with the passing of David Charles, the owner of the Chicago Trojans and one of the founding fathers of the North American Football Association. He was a good man, a strong man, a clever and tenacious operator and yes, even a visionary.

"He was also, as I'm sure many of you in this room know, a close personal friend of mine. It was through his intercession that I was first appointed to this position, and for that I will be eternally grateful. I think it would be altogether fitting to pause here and offer a moment of silence to the memory of David Charles."

Lambert took a step back from the podium, assumed a pose of extreme piety and bowed his head. Most of those in the room obediently did the same, even though David Charles was no more than a name in the paper to them.

After an appropriate amount of time had passed, Lambert stepped back up to the podium, rapped his gavel and proclaimed that the meeting had begun.

At first it went precisely as planned, differing little from previous meetings. From the report of the treasurer to the re-election of the board and the chairman, everything went according to ritual.

The chairman reached into his pocket for his handkerchief and dabbed at his brow as he scanned the agenda. All that remained was his annual State of the Franchise speech and the extension of contracts for the front-office staff.

Lambert took the text of his speech out of his inside pocket. He unfolded a thick sheaf of papers and started to speak.

"Friends, Warrior fans, ladies and gentlemen. Once again it is my pleasure to stand before you and sum up the milestones that made up the previous season."

Lambert could tell from the murmur in the crowd that this would be another speech met with widespread indifference, but he had spent three days writing it, so he pressed onward.

"To be sure, it was not a year marked with the level of success we anticipated at this time last year, but it was not a season devoid of memorable moments."

He stabbed a finger into the air for emphasis, making him look remarkably like a schoolboy trying to tell the teacher he had to leave the room to urinate.

"I think we can take a certain amount of pride in the fact that we won four games last year, an improvement of one hundred percent from the previous season."

He smiled, pausing for applause that never came.

"We came within three points of defeating Miami, the team I'm sure you recall that went all the way to the Championship Bowl. And our quarterback, Battling Buddy Blackwell, in his final year in the Association, passed for more than four thousand yards, a record for most passing yardage by a quarterback with a last-place team."

Lambert smiled at the crowd until he looked around and saw no one smiling back at him. He covered his discomfort by reaching for his glass of water and gulping down half of it before continuing.

"Financially I can report a much rosier picture for last season," he said, chuckling as if he had said something witty. "As reported by the team comptroller, Washington Football Inc., made a profit of $39.2 million last year, which should prove that even in the worst of times on the field, this organization of ours can service its shareholders with the best of them."

He paused again for applause. This time one guy clapped.

"By paying half of that out in dividends, we are able to issue a dividend of $260 per share. While that may not be as large as last year's record $314 per share, it is still a not-inconsiderable return on investment in the present economic climate."

The chairman droned on, losing more and more of his audience with every sentence. He was a tall, reedy man in his mid-sixties who wore a thin mustache that alternately reminded people of Errol Flynn and Adolf Hitler. He had made his fortune thirty years earlier selling an arthritis medicine that was forty-two percent alcohol.

By the time the Food and Drug Administration had gotten around to investigating his product, Lambert had sold out to a group of Texas oilmen looking for a tax write-off, and he had not been in the least concerned when the product had been pulled from the market.

In fact, he always swore that while he had been supervising the production of the remedy, he had never allowed such contamination to occur. His extensive wealth had enabled him to acquire friends with considerable influence, and the matter never was pursued officially.

Eventually one of his childhood friends had become a presidential advisor, and with a good-sized campaign contribution, Lambert had been able to secure an appointment as ambassador to Sri Lanka. While in that position he had managed secretly to build up an export-import firm that increased his fortune even more.

After three years overseas, though, be decided he wanted to return home and he sold his export-import company to a group of Arab oil ministers, returning to Washington and putting in a bid to buy the Washington franchise of the NAFA.

The Warriors had long been an irritant to the league, but the Association was mindful of anything that might endanger its hard-won antitrust exemption and refused to sell to Lambert.

Instead, he was offered the position of chairman of the board and a six-figure salary with the proviso that he do nothing at all. He had managed successfully to accomplish nothing at all for the last fifteen years, and he envisioned doing the same job for the next fifteen.

As chairman, he had been allowed to purchase ten percent of the 1,000,000 shares in the franchise, which earned him well in excess of another few million a year. At the same time, he had a job he truly loved, with a minimum amount of work and a maximum amount of prestige.

He wasn't even required to attend the team's games, which pleased him mightily. Lambert had no great love of football, much preferring to spend Sunday afternoons on his yacht in Chesapeake Bay. In fact, the only effort he had to put forth all year was the preparation and delivery of the speech he was about to finish.

"There is no question that we can hold our heads high indeed in this fiercely competitive marketplace. We have been able to present a true artifact of competition, a football team that, considering our relatively low cash flow, low seating capacity and other factors beyond our control, has done very well indeed."

He looked at his text and saw where he had marked a pause for applause. This time he didn't wait.

"This team represents an impressive achievement, a team in which we can take pride, a team that adds to the richness of life in our beautiful city ..."

"What a crock of shit!"

2

Dave Krause had meant for his muttered comment to be heard only by the man seated next to him. His timing had been off, though, and he had spoken at the precise moment that Lambert had paused for one more sip of water and everyone else in the room had fallen silent.

As a result, Krause's five-word critique of the chairman's speech had been heard by more than half the people in the room, including the chairman, who in response had gagged on his drink and began sputtering.

"I beg your pardon," Lambert had said with an exaggerated sense of patrician outrage as he sloppily mopped the spilled water from the front of his vest.

Dave had tried to pass it off as nothing.

"Uh ... excuse me ... never mind ... just go on with what you were saying."

Lambert wasn't about to let him off the hook that easily, though he later would wish many times that he had.

"Sir, you are no gentleman," he said. "I will not allow these important proceedings to be disrupted in such a crude manner. Please stand up."

"That's hardly necessary."

"I said stand up, sir. I want to see your face when you apologize to me and to everyone else in the room."

"What?"

"I said I wanted to see your face, sir. If you are courageous enough to cast disparaging remarks upon my speech, the least you can do is have similar courage when you stand and apologize for what you said."

Dave stood, but he was more than a little irritated. "Look, sir," he said. "I didn't mean for you to hear ..."

"What is your name, sir?"

"It's David Krause, Mr. Chairman, but I don't think this is worth getting all worked up over."

"Mr. Krause, I will decide what is and isn't worth getting worked up over."

The chairman's manner was starting to annoy Dave. "Look, I didn't mean to disrupt your little speech ..."

"Are you a stockholder in this corporation?"

"Of course," he said. "Why else would I be here?"

"I do not know. You could be an outside agitator sent to disrupt our proceedings."

"Why would anyone want to ..."

"Would you mind telling all of us how many shares of stock you hold?"

"Well ... I have one share."

"One share?" The chairman's face was becoming red as he became more and more exercised. Those who were seated in the front of the room noticed a vein starting to pulse in his temple.

"A man who owns one share in this corporation out of one million has the audacity to pass judgment on my presentation?"

"All right," Dave said, raising his voice a little as he tried to apologize. "I admit I was a little out of line, but I think ..."

"A little out of line? I should say so."

That was too much for Dave. "Listen, Lambert, I wasn't talking to you. I was just talking to the guy next to me. Maybe I was too loud, and I apologize for that, but I have as much right to criticize this team as anyone else."

"Oh, is that what you were trying to do, Mr. Krause?" the chairman asked sarcastically. "And what would cause you to make such a vulgar criticism?"

"Well ... because ..."

Suddenly a third voice interjected itself into the conversation.

"Because it's the God's own truth!"

Dave turned suddenly, surprised by the sudden outburst from the man sitting next to him, a man who now was on his feet.

The chairman sighed angrily. "And who, pray tell, are you, sir?"

"I'm Herbert T. Rojas. I own one share in this lousy team too, and I agree one hundred percent with what my buddy Dave here said."

Lambert sighed.

"In fact," Rojas continued, "I'm just like him and just like a bunch of other clowns who don't bother to come out here because they can't put up with this line of happy horse manure you sling at us every year."

The room was suddenly hushed. The chairman, who for a few seconds had been able to make only gasping noises, finally managed to regain his voice.

"How dare you! How dare you stand there and pass judgment ..."

"And how dare you stand there and act like everything is fine with this god-awful team?" Dave asked.

"I see," the chairman said. "A couple of penny-ante stockholders are trying to tell the rightfully elected officials how to run the franchise. Well, gentlemen, share your exalted opinions with us. What exactly do you think of the Warriors?"

"They suck!" cried Herb.

The chairman was once again reduced to gasping noises. Herb went on, undeterred by the sounds from the podium. "They stink on ice, buddy. The Warriors are a frigging disgrace. They're a joke now and they've been a joke for years and they'll be a joke as long as things keep going on the way they have. And the saddest part of all of it is, they're not even funny. They just suck!"

Dave laughed. "Hey, Herb," he said under his breath. "Don't hold back. Tell us what you really think."

The chairman had regained his voice once again. "I will not be addressed in such a manner by a pair of ... of ... speculators."

He gestured toward two armed security guards standing at the back of the room. "You, and you. Remove these two ... peasants ... so we can continue with our meeting."

"Hold on just a minute," Dave said as the guards made a move toward the two of them. "Maybe it's pretty obvious that you don't give a damn about the team, or about the fans, but I do own a share in this team and so does my buddy. That gives us a right to be here."

The guards stopped about ten feet away and looked at the podium, waiting for further instructions, as Dave continued. "You invited us, or have you forgotten already. Your name was right there on the letter announcing this little get-together. Franklin D. Lambert requests the pleasure of your company ..."

Dave moved toward the aisle, just in case he had to make a quick exit. Herb looked at him quizzically, but he wasn't finished.

"I've been coming to these meetings for twelve years," he said. "And Mr. Rojas, I don't know, maybe as long."

He looked at Herb, who nodded.

"I've known him for the last five years or so, and I'll bet he was coming before that. Every year you tell us the same damn thing. You talk about how successful the team was, despite the lousy record, and you go on and on about how wonderful things are going to be next year. I'll tell you what, I'm pretty damn convinced after twelve years that you don't have a clue what you're talking about."

People around the room were beginning to murmur agreement, and Dave went on.

"We haven't made the playoffs since before John Kennedy was president, we're always making rotten trades so that our best talent winds up playing for other teams and the stupid stadium is falling apart."

"That's a situation we plan to remedy," Lambert interrupted. "As soon as we have sufficient capital."

"Good God!" Herb interjected. "The team made a profit of 39 million dollars last year. Can't we put some of that back into the team?"

The supportive rumble from the crowd was growing. The chairman noticed it, too, and tried to stifle it by raising his voice.

"Sir, there are dividends which must be paid!"

"The hell you say," cried Herb. "This isn't General Motors here, bud. I mean, I really doubt that there are a lot of little old retired ladies living off their stock dividends from the Washington Warriors. They're not going to be eating cat food if you spend a few bucks buying some players."

Dave jumped back in at that point.

"If they are, they should look for better financial advice," he said. "Look, I'd be willing to bet that most of the shareholders are guys just like me, guys who had a few extra bucks to spend once and thought it would be a nice kick to own a piece of the Warriors. Hell, when I get my dividend check every year, I go out and buy myself a nice dinner courtesy of the Washington Warriors."

"And I'd be willing to bet," added Herb, "that nearly everyone in this room would be willing to give up that dinner, or whatever it is they do with their money, if they knew the dollars they were passing up would go toward building a winning team."

He looked around and several of the other stockholders murmured agreement.

"Maybe we could get some players who know which end of the field to run to, or a coach who knows his ass from his elbow, or even a damn coat of paint for the stadium."

Now the crowd was getting really loud. What had been scattered "yeah's" and "good idea's" was becoming a chorus of "damn right!"

"Holy shit!" Herb said as he joined Dave in the aisle. "Do you know what we could do with 39 million dollars? We'd go out and buy us a team that'd go right to the frigging Championship Bowl!"

"Hell!" shouted Dave. "For that kind of money you could buy a whole damn dynasty if you wanted one!"

"Gentlemen, gentlemen," the chairman said as he rapped his gavel for attention. "Are you trying to tell us that you could do a better job of running this team than the current management?"

There was a moment of silence, and suddenly the entire crowd erupted with a single word.

"YES!"

Lambert realized he had erred grievously, and he banged his gavel repeatedly, trying to no avail to restore order. Caught up in the uproar, the crowd shouted its support for Dave and Herb.

"Please, please, gentlemen," the chairman said. "Can we please try to maintain some decorum?"

Even as he said it, though, he realized the one thing he had never expected to happen had happened.

The annual stockholders meeting was out of control.

"What the hell!" came a voice from the crowd. "Let's hire these guys to run the team!"

If the chairman had been expecting anything like this to happen, he would have lined up proxies from the major stockholders who never bothered to attend the meetings.

If the Warriors had been a well-run corporation, that would have been done as a matter of course to guard against the remote possibility of something like this happening.

Luckily for those in the uprising, the management was every bit as inept as the team on the field, and the people in the room -- who controlled approximately seven percent of the stock -- controlled the meeting.

Caught up in the general hysteria, the board of directors passed a resolution authorizing the team to hire Dave Krause and Herb Rojas as co-general managers.

Chairman Lambert abstained.

The board then authorized unlimited authority for them to improve the team as they saw fit.

Chairman Lambert abstained.

Finally, the board passed a resolution forgoing the annual stock dividend and authorizing Dave and Herb to use the money -- the entire 39 million dollars -- to implement their plans.

Chairman Lambert by this time had angrily stalked from the podium in disgust, leaving the proceedings to an assistant. As soon as the meeting had been adjourned, the crowd surged around the new general managers, offering them congratulations, suggestions and support.

Two men volunteered to play for the Warriors. One said he would work for free if he could be the coach. So many people offered to contribute a few extra dollars if they needed it that Dave and Herb lost count. A notary was located, and suddenly standard contracts were being issued and signed.

Within minutes, Dave Krause and Herb Rojas were officially the new general managers of the Washington Warriors.

Formalities concluded, everyone retired to the bar or left for home, looking forward to telling their friends and families that they had taken part in an extraordinary evening.

Unnoticed by the crowd, Stan Pinello, the North American Football Association liaison to the Washington franchise, slipped out the rear exit to make a phone call.

3

Eventually the crowd dwindled down enough that Dave and Herb, who hadn't had to pay for their own drinks all evening, were the only ones remaining in the hotel bar.

"Well," Herb said. "It's nice to finally get a chance to talk to you alone."

"Yeah," Dave said. "All these years we've known each other and we've never really sat down and talked."

The two men had met at the stadium, where they had seats in the same section. They had hit it off as if they'd known each other for years. Dave Krause was forty-six, a management consultant for a northern Virginia firm. He lived in McLean and liked to tell himself he looked a little like Paul Newman, but he knew he didn't resemble anyone in particular.

He still had most of his hair, although it had gone to gray about five years earlier, and he continued to be reasonably successful in fighting off a case of middle-aged spread.

Herb Rojas was younger by two years, but his completely bald head made him look five years older. While Krause gave every indication of being a man who'd be likely to look twice before leaping, Rojas was irrepressible. He owned a bar in Georgetown and he suggested they adjourn there to talk over their new situation.

Half an hour later, they were sitting in a booth in the corner of "Cliches," a moderately successful tavern that was two-thirds empty on this particular night.

"Cliches," Dave said. "Interesting name for a bar."

"It comes in handy," Herb said as he motioned for a waitress to bring them two cups of coffee. "Whatever's just gone out of style in other bars, I pick up for a song and put it in here. I end up with a quaint little gathering place. At least I think that's what the lady from *Washingtonian* magazine called it in her last review."

"A quaint little gathering place?" Mark asked as he glanced around the room at the strange mixture of neon, art deco and green plants. "Well, I guess it all depends on how you define quaint."

"Actually I let my dad handle the decor. He's usually about three years behind the times ... speaking of which ..."

Herb glanced around the bar, looking for someone.

"Laura," he shouted at the waitress.

"Yeah, boss?"

"Where's my dad?"

"Don't know, boss," she said. "He ran out of here right after you phoned."

Herb frowned.

"Your father works here?" Dave asked.

The waitress chose that moment to bring the coffee, and Herb passed one mug across to Dave.

"Yeah," he said. "I let him tend the bar. He enjoys it, and it's good for his social life."

"His social life?"

"Yeah, you wouldn't believe it if you saw the old geezer, but he makes out like a bandit with the women who come in here."

"How old is he?"

Herb thought about that one for a moment. "He just turned sixty-seven."

Dave thought about all the depressing things in the world, and how he'd always thought geriatric sex was one of the worst. He started to say something and then decided against it.

"Shit!"

The voice came from the direction of the door, and everyone turned to see the elder Mr. Rojas come storming through.

"Shit! Shit! Shit!"

"Dad," Herb said. "What the ..."

His father crossed the room and wedged himself into the booth beside his son. He gave Dave a perfunctory glance, but didn't ask who he was.

"I waited up the street at the all-night drugstore for the papers to come out. I bought the Post, the Times and the Tribune and there wasn't a single word about you."

"Maybe they had early deadlines," Dave said.

"Dave Krause, meet my dad," Herb said. "Roy Rojas, Dave Krause."

The elder Rojas eyed him with newfound respect. "So you're the loose cannon who started all this," he said.

"Well," Dave said, lifting his palms. "That's not how I'd have described myself, but I guess it's valid."

"There wasn't anything on the evening news, either."

"Well, dad, I could have told you that. There weren't any cameras at the meeting. I guess the Washington area is going to have to wait until tomorrow to find out what happened."

Roy Rojas was definitely excited. He told them he'd been thinking of ways to improve the team ever since he'd learned his son would be in a position of authority, and he was eager to share those ideas with the two men who would be running things.

"Not so fast, sir," Dave said.

"Hey, there's not much time. We've got a lot to do to turn this team around."

"We, dad?"

"Herbert, my boy. You're the fruit of my loins. When have you ever known your father not to help you with your projects? Remember that science project we did in sixth grade?"

"Yeah, dad," Herb said. "We built a dinosaur that my teacher said looked like Groucho Marx."

"So?"

"Dad, I flunked science that year."

"Yeah, but it was a great-looking dinosaur."

Dave held up a hand to end the exchange. "All that I'm trying to say is that we're going to have to go in there tomorrow and find a way to back out of this."

Both Rojas men answered at once. "You're kidding!"

Dave shook his head. "Think about it," he said. "You're a bartender. I'm

a management consultant. I know how to design systems. Ask me about
flow charts or chains of command and no problem. Ask me how to trade
for a linebacker and you've lost me."

"Hey," Herb said. "How hard can it be?"

This time it was Dave's turn. "You're kidding."

"Not at all," he said. "We're both fans. We've both been season-ticket
holders for what seems like forever. We can do it."

"You guys are naturals," Roy said.

"This isn't a hamburger stand we're talking about," Dave said. "This is a
multi-million dollar corporation, a professional sports franchise."

"Well, sort of," Herb said.

"Yeah," Roy chimed in. "Don't forget it's still the Warriors we're talking
about."

"That's right," Herb said. "Nobody's going to expect much."

Dave wasn't convinced. "Look, the last thing the team needs is guys like
us coming in off the street and running the team. You think four and twelve
was bad? We could go oh and sixteen."

"No way," Roy said. "I know Herb knows more about football than those
guys they've had running things. He buys every one of those preseason
magazines and he listens to all the talk shows. You guys could bring real
football back to Washington."

That brought out a little of Herb's own skepticism. "Pop, this is a different
era. They play football differently now than they did in your day. They've
got computers and specialization. Hell, they've got assistant coaches for
every different position there is."

"So?"

"Bob Polano down in Miami uses plays designed by computers, and he's won four Championship Bowls," Herb said. "How can you go against that?"

Roy shrugged. "I don't know," he said. "It just seems to me like football was more fun back when they were drawing plays on the ground."

"My dad wants to go back to the days when Turk Hopkins was in the Warriors' backfield."

"Go ahead and laugh, Herb," Roy snorted. "But there's never been a more exciting runner than old Turk. Yeah, I wouldn't mind seeing the old Turkster back."

"Mr. Rojas, I think Turk Hopkins died last year."

"Well, I know that. I mean you should get somebody like Turk. There just aren't enough players like that anymore."

They argued back and forth for an hour, and then someone came into the bar with a late edition of the Washington Tribune.

A reporter apparently had received a tip and had thrown together a story in time for the second press run, and the news of Dave and Herb's coup was splashed across the top of the sports page. There hadn't been a picture of Dave available, but the paper had come up with a mug shot of Herb and captioned it "Washington restauranteur."

"God, I hate that picture," Herb said.

"It's not so bad, son."

Herb grinned. "Anyway, it'll be kind of tough to back out now, won't it?"

Dave nodded glumly.

"What time are we going to work, partner?" Herb asked him.

Dave looked at his watch and saw that it was nearly 3 a.m. "Want to meet me down there at eleven?"

"Better make it ten," Herb said. "Got to set a good example on our first day."

4

A thousand miles to the southwest, the day was beginning even earlier than usual. The commissioner of the North American Football Association was always in his office by 7 a.m., even in the offseason.

He usually spent the first two or three hours of his day reading newspapers and magazines and studying the weekly reports turned in by the twenty-four men who were his liaisons to the various NAFA franchises around the country.

He usually didn't meet with anyone before nine or ten in the morning, but on this day there was another man in the office just half an hour after the commissioner arrived in his chauffeur-driven stretch limousine at 4 a.m..

"Let me tell you, Mr. Charles, that I, and the rest of the members of the Association, deeply regret the passing of your father."

"Thank you, Commissioner," Duncan Charles said as he fidgeted in the overstuffed chair across from the giant desk.

Duncan had met the commissioner of the NAFA only once before. He had been ten years old and attending his first Championship Bowl with his father. That had been seventeen years earlier. Duncan had been amazed when he saw the man on television at how little the commissioner had changed, and seeing him in person amplified those feelings.

The commissioner seemed to go on forever without aging. He had been heading the Association for more than a quarter of a century, and had overseen its growth from little more than a mom-and-pop business into a multi-billion dollar enterprise.

The man had to be pushing sixty, but he didn't look a day over thirty-five. His short gray hair was cut stylishly, if a little conservatively, and his six-foot frame still seemed to be carrying the perfect weight.

His smile, which he flashed often and to great effect, looked as if it had come straight from a toothpaste commercial. In every respect, the commissioner of the NAFA appeared to be a confident, intelligent, successful man.

The only thing Duncan couldn't understand was why the commissioner had wanted to meet with him in the middle of the night. The meeting originally had been scheduled for 9 a.m., but Duncan had received a call at his hotel room just before midnight to inform him of the new time for the appointment.

"I apologize for bringing you in so early, Mr. Charles," he said. "But unforeseen developments with one of our franchises last evening necessitated rescheduling my entire day. It was either bring you in early or push our meeting back a day or two."

"No problem, sir."

"Your father and I went back quite a ways, Mr. Charles. As you know, he was one of the founding fathers of the Association."

"Yes, sir. He used to tell ..."

"He was a tough, shrewd operator, your father. He endured much, much more than the average businessman would have. I don't mind telling you it was tough sledding in the early days."

The commissioner came around his desk and perched himself on the corner closest to Duncan. He started speaking in a lower voice with a more conspiratorial tone.

"There are so many stories I could tell you ... Did you know that six franchises folded in the first three years, and that some of the operators had to syphon off money from some of their other businesses to make their payrolls?"

Duncan nodded.

"And of course there were the men like your father. They didn't have other businesses to fall back on, so they really had to bite the bullet. Yes, Duncan, being in the Association in the early days was not always happy Sunday afternoons in the owner's box."

The commissioner stood and smiled.

"But the strong ones persevered, Mr. Charles, because they knew they were onto something that was going to be the biggest thing ever, the sport of professional football."

"Yes, Commissioner."

The commissioner nodded, very pleased with Duncan's apparent cooperation.

"Of course," he said as he returned to his seat behind his desk. "I didn't call you all the way down here to New Orleans to rehash old war stories, did I, Mr. Charles?"

"No, sir, but it's Duncan."

"Beg pardon?"

"Most everyone I know calls me Duncan, Commissioner," he said, chuckling. "When I hear somebody call me Mr. Charles, I always look around to see if my daddy walked into the room."

"Yes," the commissioner said without a hint of amusement in his voice or his expression. He looked at Duncan as if for the first time. The young man in front of him was large, but had nothing remotely resembling a commanding presence.

Duncan's hair was cut short, in an almost military cut. He was broad-shouldered, but soft-looking, as if he never exercised. He stood about 6-foot-2, but usually didn't stand straight. He had a paunch around his middle and looked to be carrying at least twenty extra pounds.

In addition, he had a weak jawline and he often seemed to have difficulty meeting the eyes of the person he conversed with. He looked exactly like what he was, a spoiled young man who had been born to privilege.

"Of course," the commissioner said. "Anyway, Mr. ... Duncan, I wanted you to know that I was a great admirer of your father. In fact, I always thought of him as my friend, as I was his. And I had tremendous respect for him. Duncan, it was David Charles and men like him who made the Association what it is today -- the premier sporting operation in the world."

"Yes, Commissioner, and ..."

"Not America, Duncan. Not even the Western Hemisphere. The entire world. Are you aware that last season we had the highest per game attendance of any professional sport? That for the tenth year in a row, not a single one of our franchises lost money? That the Championship Bowl last January had the highest television ratings worldwide of any show ... ever?"

"Well, I ..."

"Higher ratings than the World Series, Duncan. Higher than the World Cup. The Stanley Cup. The Davis Cup. The ... what are they calling the basketball playoffs this year?"

"Uh, I don't know, Commissioner."

"Whatever," the commissioner said, dismissing professional basketball with a wave of his hand. "It doesn't matter. Duncan, the point is that last year we outdrew them all. We outdrew every single show on commercial television."

"Even ..." Duncan asked incredulously. "... even the Hulk Hogan/Penny Marshall Christmas Special?"

The Commissioner winced. "Yes, Duncan, even that. And do you know why we were able to do it?"

Duncan shook his head.

"We were able to do it because of the vision and guidance of men like your father," the commissioner said, lowering his voice. "My only hope is that you prove to be cut from the same bolt of cloth."

"Well, I hope so too, Commissioner. In fact, I have some ideas I'd like to ..."

"God!" the commissioner continued, in a voice filled with such distress that Duncan was silenced immediately. "It's hard to believe he's gone."

"Who?"

"Your father, Duncan! It was such a shock! He was such a robust, vital individual!"

"Uh, he was eighty-three, sir ..."

"Yes, but he acted like a man much younger! He was so involved in his franchise! He was at every meeting, every game!"

"Uh, well, he did love his team," Duncan said. He also had liver cancer and phlebitis, Duncan thought to himself, but at least he didn't miss any of the league meetings.

"I think I can safely say ..." the commissioner said, "... that it was his love of our little game that made the Chicago Trojans what they are today, one of the most successful franchises in the North American Football Association."

The commissioner looked Duncan directly in the eye. "Do you know how much profit your franchise made last season, Duncan?"

"Not exactly ..."

"Exactly 54 million, four hundred and eighty-eight thousand, eight hundred and forty-one dollars and five cents." The commissioner seemed to caress each of the words as if they were beautiful women. "After taxes."

Duncan's reaction, a loud gulp and a wide-eyed stare, seemed to please the commissioner. It gave him an opportunity to reflect on his visitor, his newest business associate, the new operator of the Chicago franchise of the North American Football Association.

Duncan Charles had been a question mark to the commissioner, and that had made him uneasy. Unknown quantities made the commissioner nervous, but the moment Duncan had walked into his office, the commissioner knew his worries were over.

This man would be no trouble at all.

His twenty -seven year old visitor sat, as he had since entering the office, with his mouth slightly ajar, staring at the pictures on the walls, mesmerized by the photographs of the great moments in the history of the Association.

There were spectacular catches, spectacular runs for touchdowns and spectacular tackles. Intermingled among all these great moments were photographs of the commissioner. Handing out the Championship Bowl trophy. Shaking hands with players, coaches, movie stars and presidents. There was even one of him with his arm around the Pope.

Duncan was awed to be in the same room with such a great man.

"All told, Duncan," the commissioner said, causing the younger man to shift his attention abruptly. "The Association pulled down a profit of well over two billion dollars last year."

"I had no idea ..."

"Few people do, son," he said. "We try, of course, to keep our figures out of the public domain. After all, the NAFA is a private enterprise, and how much money we make is no one's business but our own."

"Well, I guess so."

"I'm glad you agree with me, Duncan. It's reassuring to speak with someone with a grasp of proper business procedures. And it's because we follow proper business procedures, and give the public what it wants, that we were able to make as much profit as we did. Do you realize, son, that half of our franchises fill their stadiums exclusively from season ticket sales? That most of those franchises have waiting lists of people who would sell their young children for the right to buy our tickets?"

The commissioner forged ahead without waiting for a response. "And we owe our success to men like your father. Dave Charles was a perfect example of the kind of man we want in the Association. He was a man who loved football, a man who like myself dedicated himself to the game. Not for personal gratification, not even for the advancement of the Association, but for the good and greater glory of the game itself."

The commissioner leaned forward on his desk and stared straight into Duncan's eyes. "Above all else, Duncan, he wanted to see the game succeed. He wanted professional football to be the best, most exciting attraction in the sporting world."

"Yes, sir."

"And it is!" The commissioner thrust his finger into the air. "It is, Duncan. Football is everything a fan could ever want. Action! Excitement!

"Look at baseball. Too slow.

"Hockey? Too hard to follow.

"Soccer? Too foreign.

"Basketball?"

"Too black?" Duncan interjected.

The commissioner stared at him coldly. "Too confined," he said. "But football, football has the ultimate, perfect balance. It's a team game dominated by individual accomplishments. It's played on a huge field, but played a single yard at a time. There's action every thirty seconds, as regular as clockwork."

He paused for a moment, but only to catch his breath. "And your average fan likes that, Duncan. He likes to know there's enough time between plays to go get a beer or even visit the toilet, unlike baseball, where something could happen at any time, or hockey, where the action hardly ever stops."

Now the commissioner was on his feet, pacing about the room and gesturing, looking for all the world like a football coach giving a halftime talk to his team.

"And football has so many of what I call the pure moments of sport," he said. "The long pass falling into the receiver's arms, just out of reach of the defender. The kickoff returned ninety-five yards for a touchdown."

By this time, the commissioner was acting out every action as he described it.

"The quarterback trapped behind the line and thrown to the turf on third down. The lone runner, bulling his way through a wall of defenders. How could a person who cares at all about competition not get involved? How could anyone be apathetic? How could a fan not love this beautiful game?"

The commissioner slumped back into his chair, exhausted. Duncan sat opposite him and stared, almost paralyzed in amazement. He had never seen the commissioner in such an agitated state, and he doubted anyone else had, either.

In public, the commissioner always was the picture of control. His voice rarely rose or fell and his face never revealed the slightest emotion.

He had weathered twenty-eight years in his position, including some extremely difficult times and more than a few boom years. Few could remember him ever altering his manner for any reason.

There had been challenges from two rival leagues, both of which ended in failure. There had been a merger with a third, two player strikes and Congressional hearings in which the commissioner had singlehandedly convinced lawmakers that the NAFA deserved an antitrust exemption that enabled the league to hold player salaries far below those of the other professional sports.

There had been numerous lawsuits, not to mention the quadrennial negotiations with the television networks. The commissioner had always gotten exactly what he wanted and he had never been anything but calm.

Yet, to impress the newest member of the Association with his love for the game, the commissioner had violated his entire image and had made an emotional wreck of himself.

Duncan was more than impressed. He was overwhelmed. There was a lump as big as a baseball in his throat, and tears started to well up in his eyes. Had he the nerve, Duncan would have run around the desk and embraced the man.

Images of his father started coming back to him. From birth, David Charles had tried to instill the same dedication in his son. Duncan had been two years old when his father had taken him to his first Trojans game. He had been three when he received his first helmet and shoulder pads.

Any affection for any other game, be it baseball or checkers, was ridiculed until it disappeared. Football was to be the only sport for David Charles' son. His bedroom had been filled with posters, photographs and autographed uniform jerseys that reflected the glory of the Chicago Trojans.

The curtains, sheets and comforter on his bed had all been decorated with the team insignia. Even as an adult, he still slept in a single bed on a newer set of those same sheets.

By the time Duncan started school, he was spending almost every free moment playing football on a full-length field built behind the Charles estate an hour north of the city. Sometimes he played with his father, but more often it was the family's servants who were his teammates and opponents.

Every male servant who worked on the Charles estate was a former player, and all of them knew part of their job was to regale young Duncan with stories of the Association. Occasionally a game would be organized with some boys from school. Duncan Charles always played quarterback.

It never quite worked. Duncan never developed the skills, the coordination or the physical stamina needed to play football. That didn't prevent him from making every team he ever tried out for. It helped a lot that his father was always generous with equipment and tickets, and often brought Trojans players to practices to impress the coaches and the other kids.

Duncan sat on the bench in youth leagues, in junior high and for the first three years of high school. Finally, when he was a senior, he got into a game. His father had pressured the coach to play him, and he played the second half of a blowout in the final game of the season.

He got in at wide receiver, and the quarterback had instructions to throw to him whenever possible. Twelve passes came Duncan's way and he dropped every one of them.

For all intents and purposes, that marked the end of Duncan's playing days. It was three weeks before his father spoke to him, and when he finally broke the silence his tone was cold and pragmatic.

"Well," David Charles had said. "If you can't play the goddamned game, you had sure as hell better get used to working in the front office."

The whole direction of Duncan's life changed after that. The games and practices behind the mansion were no more. Instead, Duncan started spending every afternoon at the Trojans' offices, watching every aspect of the operation.

He was forced upon the coaching staff, the general manager, the operations manager, the public relations staff and the sales staff. He even spent a few Sunday afternoons every fall in the broadcast booth, watching Charley Dunahey and Chuck Lindsey do the radio broadcast until one day he worked up the courage to ask a question.

Not wanting to be abrupt, he had crept up timidly behind Dunahey and tapped him on the shoulder, which so startled the announcer that he spun around and shouted at Duncan, and the rest of the radio audience, "Who the fuck are you?"

By the very next weekend, Dunahey was selling refrigerators in Dubuque.

Duncan remained unaffected by all this, aware only that he was being groomed someday to take over the Chicago franchise of the NAFA, a prospect that thrilled him beyond all reason. He lived for the summers he worked for the team while he attended Northwestern University as a business major.

And while he had many friends, attended every important party and dance and pledged the best fraternity on campus, above all else he was aware that he would one day own the Trojans.

Everyone else was aware of this, too, which explained his many friends, his invitations and his acceptance into the fraternity. Duncan's father was very generous with season passes and company vehicles.

The day after he received his degree, Duncan had gone to work full-time for his father. David Charles wasn't one to start his son in a cushy job. He put Duncan to work as a ticket agent, where he showed an immediate aptitude for counting out correct change.

After four years with the team, Duncan was still a ticket agent. Then his father died and left him the team.

Two days after the funeral, he had been called down to meet with the commissioner at his office in New Orleans.

"So, what I want you to understand, Duncan, is the fact that the Association is made up of men such as myself, and your father, who would rather die than dishonor the game, great men who would stop at nothing to be certain football endures and prospers."

Duncan didn't know what to say in response to the commissioner calling himself a great man, so he just smiled.

"And I hope you understand what it takes to be a member of the most exclusive fraternity in the free world, the North American Football Association."

Duncan was almost in ecstasy. "Oh, yes, Commissioner, I do!"

"Very good, Duncan. And I also want you to realize that there are certain standards we feel must be upheld, and the Association goes to great pains to see that those standards are maintained. We want nothing but a quality operation in Chicago, or anywhere else for that matter."

"I understand, sir."

"Of course, I always feel it necessary to personally meet every new franchise operator as soon as possible, although out of respect for your late father I couldn't call you down here until after the funeral. I trust, by the way, that there will be no problems with the will, no prolonged probate battles, things of that nature?"

"Oh, no sir. I'm the only one named in my father's will. You see, my mother died when I was seven and my father never remarried. He always used to say he was married to his team ..."

"We're aware of that, Duncan, plus the fact that you are an only child ... an orphan of the storm, so to speak."

The commissioner chuckled and Duncan smiled. "And," he continued, "at least we're secure in knowing who'll be calling the shots in Chicago. By the way, our preliminary report indicates ..."

Duncan sat up straight in his chair. "Preliminary report?"

"Why, of course. We always have the investigative committee work up a report on prospective franchise operators ..."

"Investigative committee?"

"Yes, Duncan," the commissioner said in his smoothest voice. "After all, we can't let just any fool off the street come in and take over an NAFA franchise. No, we carefully screen every possible operator thoroughly to be sure they measure up to the Association's standards."

Noting the dismayed look that had swept over the younger man's face, the commissioner moved to his side and put a comforting hand on Duncan's shoulder.

"Don't worry, son," he said. "I'm sure that considering your lineage and your experience with the operation ... In fact, that was what I was about to discuss with you. I understand you have been working in the front office for the last four years."

"That's right, sir. I'm in the ticket office."

"Oh, box office manager! Excellent. Very good experience."

"Uh, no, Commissioner. I wasn't the manager. I worked in Group Sales."

"You what?"

"Group Sales," he said. "I was a ticket agent for Group Sales. You know, a Boy Scout troop wants seats together, the Kiwanis are coming in from Peoria, those things."

"Let me get this straight, Duncan. For the last four years you've been counting out tickets?"

"And mailing them, sir. You see, my father believed I should work my way up through the ranks ..."

"Excuse me for being a touch indelicate here, Duncan, but that doesn't appear to be the wisest choice for the future operator of the franchise. Especially at his advanced age, I would have thought he'd want to move you along a bit faster."

"Well, sir, I guess he didn't think he was going to die."

"I suppose I know what you mean, Duncan. Still, I can't help but think it would have been better for you to have started in something like player development or even public relations."

Duncan giggled slightly. It made him sound almost effeminate, and the commissioner winced a little.

"My father used to say that if you're going to sell something, you ought to know what it is."

"Please," the commissioner said, looking unamused. "Please do me the honor of not speaking in riddles, Duncan."

"Yes, sir. My father used to say that the only thing we had to sell was tickets, so I'd better learn everything there was to learn about tickets."

"That isn't necessarily so, Duncan. You are selling the Chicago Trojans and the game of football as well."

Duncan shook his head. "My father said that was your job and that all we had to do was move the tickets," he said, emphasizing his father's quote with a grand sweep of his hands.

The commissioner laughed, a small, humorless sound that resembled, more than anything else, a dog's bark.

"Yes, Duncan, perhaps that is so. Whatever the case, I'm glad we had this little chat, if only because it reinforces a decision we had made earlier."

Duncan leaned forward, an anxious tone creeping into his voice. "What decision is that, Commissioner?"

The commissioner paused, folding his hands on the desk in front of him. "Duncan, we feel you are going to need some help for a while, especially considering your relative lack of experience in operating a franchise ..."

"Commissioner, I graduated from college!"

"I'm well aware of that, Duncan, but even the finest university education could not possibly familiarize you with all the aspects of running a sports franchise. Believe me, you are not alone in this. Virtually every new operator we accept into the Association is terribly unfamiliar with his franchise."

"But ..."

"That is the reason we assign a liaison man to each franchise, one whose purpose is to advise the owner on how to properly run his business and still maintain the standards of the Association."

"Huh?"

"Our liaison usually doesn't get too deeply involved in the day-to-day operations. He serves in more of an advisory capacity, but taking your inexperience into consideration, I've decided to assign you our very best man -- Ray Martini."

The commissioner leaned across his desk and pressed a switch on his intercom. "Beverly, is Ray here yet? Good, send him in."

"Commissioner, I really do appreciate your concern, but I'd like the chance to ..."

Ray Martini entered the room at that moment, and the commissioner came to his feet to greet him. "Hello, Ray."

"Mornin', Commissioner."

Duncan turned to look at the man who had just joined them. Martini looked more like a Texas oilman than the Longhorn fullback he had been twenty-three years ago. He stood six-three and still looked to be somewhere close to his playing weight of 220 pounds.

And unlike many other former football players Duncan had met, Martini had not allowed it to turn to fat. It was obvious that he still worked out regularly. He looked like a man in his early thirties, even though Duncan knew he had to be at least ten years older than that.

His face was one cliche-plagued sportswriters liked to say had been "etched from granite," and newspaper reports still referred to him as "rock-jawed Ray Martini." His steel-blue eyes had the power to burn right through people, making them feel weak and insignificant with a single glance.

It was a power he had used all through his career, first against opposing defensive linemen and then with his own teammates after he was elevated to player-coach of the Dallas Cougars. He had stayed in that position for three seasons, until he realized he was becoming a liability as a player.

Then, with the dispatch that was to become his trademark, he put himself on waivers.

He stayed on as head coach for another five years and then spent seven more as general manager. During his tenure, the Cougars won five division titles and three Championship Bowls. He left Dallas at the invitation of the commissioner, and the franchise quickly sunk back into mediocrity.

The commissioner sent him to Houston as a league liaison, and the Lonestars became a powerhouse almost overnight. He was known around the Association as a miracle worker.

"Ray, this is the young man I told you about," the commissioner said. "I'd like you to meet Duncan Charles."

"Hi, kid," Martini said. "I'm looking forward to working with you. Your dad was a pretty special guy."

Martini gripped Duncan's hand and shook it vigorously. His handshake was strongly masculine without being bonecrushing, but Martini had nothing to prove to the younger man. Duncan knew that the man standing across from him could break him in half without raising a sweat.

"Please to meet you, Mr. Martini."

"None of that, kid," he said, smiling. "Just call me Ray."

"All right," he said shyly. "Ray."

"Duncan, try and think of Ray as an advisor, or perhaps a teacher. Forget the fact that we pay his salary. Remember instead that Ray was once the general manager of our Dallas franchise. Also, I'm sure I don't have to remind you of the success Bobby Blanton has had in Houston with Ray as his liaison."

"Yeah, kid. I was so good in Houston that they won four Championship Bowls there. Then they got tired of the Lonestars winning and they yanked me out of there and brought me into the office here."

"That's right, Ray," the commissioner said brightly. "We didn't want our Texas franchises to have all the good fortune. Here at the Association headquarters, or up in Chicago with you, we get the chance to spread some of that expertise around."

Martini winked at Duncan. "Yeah, just like cow flop, kid."

Duncan laughed.

"Actually, kid, the only way they got me to leave Texas was to promise me the commissioner's job."

"All in good time, Ray. All in good time."

"You know, kid," Martini said to Duncan with a wink. "I could do this guy's job with my hands tied behind my back."

The commissioner chuckled, Martini smiled and Duncan admired the spirit of camaraderie between the two men. He found himself wanting to make these men his friends, but he didn't know exactly how. He decided to try and get into the spirit of the moment.

"Ray, I know a lot of people who think you could do the commissioner's job," he said eagerly.

Both the commissioner and Martini stiffened and fixed him with cold, almost sinister stares.

"Not in this office," the commissioner said.

"That's for certain, sir," Martini added. "There's nobody in the world, myself included, who could fill your shoes."

Now that Duncan had been put in his place, Martini changed the subject. "Listen, kid, why don't we cut loose from this stuffy place and have some lunch? You all through with him, Commissioner?"

The commissioner nodded absent-mindedly. "For now, Ray. One more thing, Duncan, and then I'll let you two go."

He stood and looked Duncan straight in the eye. "Duncan, I'm leaving you with a man of great experience, one of the finest men I've ever had the privilege of knowing. I expect you to value his advice and take it to heart."

Duncan nodded.

"From now on, unless something horrendous occurs, you won't be dealing with me directly except at Association meetings. I can't spend my time working with the individual franchise operators on a day-to-day basis anymore. My job, as your father so aptly put it, is to sell the game of football."

Duncan nodded.

"And yours is to sell the tickets, something Ray is very good at doing. I have the utmost confidence in this man's judgment and abilities, so anything he tells you, you consider it as coming directly from me. Understand?"

Duncan managed not to gulp. "Yes, sir. I do."

"Believe me, Duncan, it's better this way. It's in both our best interests. The more successful the Trojans are, the more successful the Association is. And that works both ways."

"I understand, Commissioner."

The Commissioner smiled, but it was a smile that never touched his eyes. "Ray, you take good care of this boy. I have a feeling he's going to be a real hot property."

"You can count on me, Commissioner," Martini said.

The commissioner turned and offered Duncan his hand.

"Thank you for coming this morning, Duncan. I'm looking forward to having you with us."

"I'm looking forward to being a part of it all, Commissioner. Thanks for everything."

The commissioner released Duncan's hand and turned to Martini.

"Ray, could I speak alone with you for a moment before you leave?"

"Sure, Commissioner. I'll meet you outside, kid."

Martini closed the door behind Duncan as he left the room.

"Did you give him the whole treatment, Commissioner?"

"Every bit of it, Ray. He ate it up. I don't think young Mr. Charles will be giving us any problems at all."

"So we can go ahead as planned?"

"Full speed ahead, Ray. We're right on schedule."

5

Dave and Herb had decided they would meet at Cliches and drive to the Warriors' downtown headquarters together.

Neither of them had managed to get more than a few hours sleep, but they figured a few cups of coffee and a lot of adrenalin would get them through their first day as general managers of the team.

"The way I see it, people probably expect us to last about a month," Herb said as he guided his year-old Lexus through the mid-morning traffic. "So they're not going to give us a whole lot of help."

"They? Who are they?"

"The Board. They're not going to give us anything they don't have to. They want to see us fall on our faces, and we've got to prove we can put together a winning team. By the way, did you come up with any ideas?"

"Well," Dave said. "We did say something about painting the stadium. That might be a good place to start."

Herb stared at him. "How about after that?"

"Well, somehow we've got to start putting together a team. I haven't really thought much about how.”

“I have,” Herb said.

“Care to share your thoughts with me?”

“All right,” he said. “The first thing we need is a coach. A solid, no-nonsense coach who plays straight-up-the-field football, no frills, ten yards at a time. A tough coach who can motivate players.”

“Go on.”

“That’ll be the easy part. In fact, I’ve already got someone in mind. It’s getting players that’ll be tough, but the way I see it, there are a lot of guys out there who can play the game. I’m talking about guys who gave it up because they didn’t want to sit on the bench behind some kid.”

Dave nodded as Herb continued.

“Guys who quit because they got a good business deal. Maybe even guys who quit because they thought they were sick of playing football and now they wish they could come back. All we’ve got to do is convince those guys to play for the Warriors.”

“Herb, most guys like that are too old to play.”

“Maybe so, but the fact we’re bringing them in will show people we mean business, and when the fans in this town get behind us, there’ll be no stopping us.”

“This town wouldn’t support the team if we gave away free tickets and got the team to the Championship Bowl.”

“That’s where you’re wrong, Dave. Nobody’s ever really given this city a chance. You can’t expect people to pay $35 for tickets to see a team that wins three or four games a year.”

“I don’t know,” Dave said.

"If that's the way you feel about it, then why do you go to the stockholders' meetings?"

"They serve a great buffet."

Herb saw he wasn't getting anywhere, so he turned his attention to traffic and didn't say anything for the remainder of the drive. They parked the car and went straight to their new offices, which had yet to be vacated by their predecessor.

Wally Breakfield wasn't happy and he let them know it as he packed his personal belongings into a box on the floor.

"This is insanity!" he said as he slammed his desk set into the box. "How could you possibly have conned those people into giving you my job? Why, I have been in professional football for thirty-five years. They can't be serious about firing me for two boobs off the street."

"Hey, bud," Herb said. "Lighten up. I guess people didn't think three or four wins a year was enough for a lifetime contract. By the way, doesn't that stationery you're packing belong to the team?"

Breakfield reddened, but didn't move to put the paper back. "I thought I might use it to write out my resume," he said. "Although I doubt that a man of my reputation will be out of the game for long. As soon as people learn that I'm available ..."

"A general manager who couldn't produce a winning season in twelve years," Dave said, dryly. "If I were you, I wouldn't hold my breath waiting for the phone to ring."

"I resent that remark, Mr. Krause, and I will thank you to keep your uneducated opinions to yourself. The GM can control only so much. After all, if I had been able to make the moves I wanted to make, I would have had the team in the Championship Bowl by now. Why, just three years ago ..."

It appeared that Breakfield was just getting started, so Dave ducked out of the room on the pretext of locating the restroom. He bumped into a tall, angular man in a gray three-piece suit and horned-rim glasses.

"Good morning, Mr. Krause," the man said. "I'm Stanley Pinello, the Association liaison man."

"Liaison man?"

"Yes. The North American Football Association assigns one man to every franchise to act as an advisor, so to speak. In your case, I would imagine you would appreciate as much help from us as you could possibly get."

"Well, I do have Mr. Rojas."

Pinello laughed humorlessly. "I see that more of a case of the bland leading the blind, sir."

Dave figured Pinello wasn't far wrong, but he wasn't about to agree with him. There was something about Pinello he didn't like, something he had distrusted from the moment of their all-too-fortuitous meeting, and he told himself to go very carefully with this man.

"Thank you for your very generous offer, Mr. Pinello."

"It's not an offer, Mr. Krause. It's my job."

"Well, right now my job is to get myself situated and figure out what's going on around here," Dave said. "And I can't do that until Mr. Breakfield vacates his office. You wouldn't want to help him pack, would you?"

Pinello sniffed. "Certainly not. I'm an executive. I don't do menial labor."

"Then why don't we put a lid on the small talk for now, Pinello? Herb and I will get together with you as soon as we need you."

Pinello fixed him with an icy stare. "Very well, Mr. Krause," he said, turning on his heel and walking away.

Herb chose that moment to make his own escape from Breakfield's office. As the door opened and closed, Dave heard a brief snatch of a diatribe about how no one in Washington appreciated all that Wally Breakfield had done for the team.

"Whew!" Herb said. "That guy's a real piece of work."

"Did you manage to jolly him along at all? We need the office if we're going to get started."

"I think it'll be a couple more hours before he gets it out of his system. I'm not sure he even realizes we're not still in there listening to him. Why don't we get some lunch?"

Dave grabbed a team roster from one of the secretaries and he and Herb headed for the cafeteria. Most of the lower-echelon employees seemed to be very happy to see them and they were greeted effusively by janitors, secretaries and office boys.

Most of the other employees, from the team's comptroller to the public relations man, seemed to view them as something someone had tracked in on the bottom of their shoes.

Dave knew they would have to earn their respect, and he was glad he hadn't been named to the job of general manager alone. At least he would have Herb around for conversation.

They had agreed that the top priority was hiring a coach, and Dave picked at his salad for a while before broaching the subject. "Herb, you told me earlier you had someone in mind to coach the team."

Herb took a big bite out of his cheeseburger. Some mayonnaise was dribbling out of the side of his mouth, and he grabbed a napkin and dabbed at it before answering. "Yeah," he said. "I've got a real good idea."

"Well, who is it?"

"Ben Kennedy."

Dave was stunned. "The Iron Irishman? Is he still alive? I thought I read somewhere that he died."

Herb shook his head. "He's coaching semipro somewhere in the south. I've got my dad checking for me."

"Semipro?"

"Dave, he's a natural. He never had a losing season, and he plays the kind of football this team needs to play -- solid, no-frills stuff."

"But Herb, he was a drunk! He knocked his players around! They've got a union now, and they kind of frown on that stuff."

"Nobody ever proved that assault charge," Herb said. "And anyway, I read a newspaper article a buddy of mine sent me a couple of years ago. He was down in Macon, Georgia, then. Now he's coaching semipro ball and he's supposed to have cleaned himself up. There's a rumor he's born again."

"But his style of football is dead. Hell, he probably still thinks of the forward pass as a last resort."

"I admit he's a little old-fashioned, but he's just the kind of coach we'll need for the old guys we're going to sign up. Ben Kennedy loves older players and they love him. It's the smartass rookies who always gave him trouble."

"But ..."

"That brings me to my next point. We don't have much talent on the roster, and we've only got three picks in the draft. Maybe we won't win many more games, but I think people will come out and pay to see players like Jimmy Gardner, Lester Phillips, Tony Ross, Roxy Reese ..."

Dave was horrified. "Those guys have all got to be forty years old!"

Herb shook his head. "Just Gardner. The rest of them are in their late thirties, except for Ross. He's only 33."

"There's got to be another way to do it. Maybe we could go into the free-agent market."

"Nope. The Association makes you give up your draft choices as compensation, and we don't have any draft choices to give up."

"What about signing guys from little tiny colleges that nobody ever heard of?"

"We might find one or two guys that way, Dave, but I wouldn't count on it. The Association's got a central scouting service, and they get a look at nearly every player in the country."

"There's bound to be a couple they missed."

Herb looked unconvinced. "We'll see. Why don't you check the out-of-town papers, the little community weeklies. Look for anyone the scouts might have missed. I'll go ahead and make up a list of older players we might be interested in signing."

"Then what?" Dave asked. "We take off around the country trying to sign these players?"

"Precisely."

6

Ordinarily the commissioner was the picture of serenity, especially when everyone around him seemed to be panicking.

Not this afternoon, though.

This afternoon he was angry.

"All right, Pinello," he said. "I gave you twenty-four hours. What have you been able to find out about these gentlemen who are causing such a stir in Washington?"

Stan Pinello pulled a file folder out of his calfskin briefcase, opened the folder and began reading from a typed report.

"Herbert Taylor Rojas. Age forty-four. White, of a Spanish heritage long since diluted. He owns a bar in Georgetown that is moderately successful. Reported an income of $56,544 dollars before taxes last year. We have a copy of his tax return."

"Good work, Pinello."

"He's divorced with no children. His ex-wife lives in South Carolina. She's remarried, and never had to file a grievance against him for nonpayment of alimony. He's never been arrested. Served two years in the Army, including a year in Vietnam. Has no outstanding debts of an unusual nature. Drinks, but not to excess. I have more if you want it."

"What about the other one?" the commissioner asked.

Pinello pulled out another folder, adjusted his glasses and began reading.

"David Alan Krause. Age forty-six. White, Anglo-Saxon heritage. Also divorced, with one child, a fifteen-year-old daughter. He lives in McLean, Virginia. The wife and daughter live in Falls Church. Krause was a management consultant for Reeves, Henderson and Dugan in Arlington. Resigned this morning when they wouldn't give him a leave of absence."

"Isn't that a shame," the commissioner said, making it clear by his tone that it was no shame at all.

"Krause made $77,620 last year, and we have his tax return, too. Worked for the same company for 22 years. He was in the Air Force and was in Vietnam at the same time Rojas was."

"That's interesting," the commissioner said.

Pinello couldn't imagine what was interesting about it, but he knew better than to contradict his boss.

"Let's see," the commissioner said. "Both divorced, both in the military at the same time ..."

"I neglected to mention that they both went to the University of Maryland, although they were two years apart."

"Really?" the commissioner asked. "Were they homosexual lovers?"

"Not that I could tell."

"Damn. Well, maybe they know some homos."

"I don't think so, sir," Pinello said. "These reports show no shady associations whatsoever."

"Pinello, were you born yesterday? You said Rojas owned a bar. Well, that's a seedy business. Surely there have to be some shady relationships somewhere."

"We checked, Commissioner. We really did. Rojas has got a clean operation that's geared toward an older crowd. No mob payoffs, no protection. They don't even have rock and roll songs on the jukebox."

"Damn it, I want some smut on those guys!" the commissioner said. "Maybe they're cheating on their taxes."

"We've seen their 1040's for the last five years, sir, and there's nothing at all out of the ordinary. Both of them have been audited in the last two years and neither one of them had any problems at all."

The commissioner sighed. "That's just wonderful, Pinello. The two remaining saints in the country just happen to show up at that particular meeting and take over one of our franchises. By the way, Pinello, exactly what did happen at that meeting? You were there, weren't you?"

"Of course I was there, Commissioner. It's exactly what I told you the other day. Krause made a remark to his friend and Chairman Lambert overhead it and challenged him. Rojas got into the argument and the two of them got the crowd riled up and ..."

"Yes, yes, yes," the commissioner said with a wave of his hand. "And the rest is history. Where exactly were you during this little palace coup, Pinello?"

"In the back of the room, sir. I don't really see where I could have done anything, though. After all, you've told me many times that I'm supposed to keep a low profile."

"I would have thought that extraordinary circumstances such as this might have called for extraordinary measures."

"Now, Commissioner, I couldn't have just gotten up and taken over the meeting. And who would have predicted it would have turned out the way it did?"

The commissioner fixed him with a steely stare. "Perhaps, Mr. Pinello. Perhaps. By the way, where was my dear friend Mr. Lambert during all of this?"

"He was doing his best to keep a lid on things, sir, but I'm sure you're aware he's not exactly the most dynamic leader we have in the Association."

"First chance we get when this is settled, I want Lambert out on his fat ass," the commissioner said. Then he paused and thought for a moment. "No, better yet, you go back to Washington and tell that old buffoon he's out on his ass if anything like this ever happens again."

Pinello nodded.

"One thing I've always said," the commissioner said. "Nothing adds more to a man's backbone than a healthy dose of fear."

Pinello knew from personal experience that that was true. "Certainly, Commissioner. I'll tell him the first time I see him."

"You do that. Now, tell me. Where do we stand with Washington? Are they in any position to upset this year's plan?"

"No, sir. They don't have a draft pick before the fourth round, and I had just about convinced Breakfield to trade that one away when all this happened. They have only two other picks, in the eighth and eleventh rounds.

"As for talent already on the payroll," Pinello added, chuckling. "You know what kind of a team they had last season? Well, they're all a year older now."

The commissioner smiled for the first time since the beginning of their conversation. "Tell me, Pinello, what are these gentlemen planning to do with our Washington franchise?"

"I don't know just yet, sir. They didn't have time to talk with me yesterday, but I'm working on finding out."

"You had better, Pinello. You have managed to do a fairly credible job in the past, and I would hate for a black mark to wind up on your record."

Stan Pinello had been an employee of the North American Football Association for nearly ten years. He had heard the commissioner use that tone of voice with him and with others a number of times, and it never failed to send cold chills down his spine.

"No, sir," he said quickly. "You don't have a thing to worry about. In fact, this might even turn out to be a plus for us."

"How might that be?"

"Well," Pinello added, lowering his voice conspiratorially. "These guys could screw things up so badly that Washington could be out of the picture for years."

"Perhaps," the commissioner said thoughtfully. "But I would still sleep a little better at night if you could come up with some information that would give us some additional leverage with these, ah, gentlemen."

"I'll try, commissioner."

"You do that. I simply do not like having anything unmanageable in the system. Keep digging, Pinello, and let me know what you find. Otherwise, I want you to go back to Washington and carry on as if things were perfectly normal."

"Yes, sir. I'll be in touch."

7

Duncan Charles had dreamed of the day he would be running the Trojans, but he had never imagined it would be so much fun. All he had ever known was drudgery. As a player, his existence had consisted of tackling drills, wind sprints and bench polishing. As a ticket agent it had been computer printouts and complaining customers with bad breath.

Now, as the president and board chairman of Chicago Football Inc., Duncan was learning what it was like to be one of the most popular men in the city. Everyone wanted him to speak at luncheons or banquets.

Every committee in the city seemed to want him as an honorary member, from the Committee to Preserve Antique Fire Stations to the Committee for Disturbed Veterans of the Indian Wars.

Duncan accepted every offer.

He had dozens of employees who seemed to have little to do but wait for him to make decisions, which he did with a vengeance. All he did was make decisions. Not a detail escaped his attention. He changed the number of stripes on the sleeves of the team's uniforms. He decided to renew the radio contract. He ordered new cushions for the seats in the luxury boxes at Daley Stadium.

He was certain he was reaching his potential as a decision-maker. Now he had come to the point where his powers would be put to the test. It was time for contract negotiations, and Duncan relished the challenge.

"All right, Ray," he said. "Let's get right to it. The general manager. He's doing a good job, isn't he?"

"Sure, kid. Leland is doing a heck of a job."

"Then it's settled. We'll keep him. Should I give him a raise?"

"Seems like the right thing to do."

"OK. Leland stays and he gets a ten percent raise. How about Coach Williams? He seems to know what he's doing. Do the players respect him?"

"Sure, kid. They love him."

"Then it's settled. He stays, and what the hell, let's give him a ten percent raise, too."

"Good idea, kid. Wouldn't want to have any jealousy popping up."

"How about his assistants?"

"Kid, why don't you let Leland and Williams handle that?"

"That makes sense, Ray. After all, they are his assistants. Now how many player contracts do we have coming up for renewal this year?"

Martini gave Duncan a look, a look he had come to recognize as a prelude to a lecture. "Kid, usually it's the general manager who handles that end of things."

"Really?" Duncan was disappointed.

"Yeah. Usually Leland meets with the players' agents or lawyers and they work out the details. It's easier to keep the payroll under control that way."

"But, Ray, I remember my father used to get his picture in the papers all the time, announcing he'd just signed ..."

Martini sighed. "Kid, you don't think your dad spent the whole day talking to some lineman's agent, do you? Hell, those kind of guys, the GM doesn't even talk to most of the time. He lets the player personnel guy handle it."

"Oh," Duncan said, reacting as if Martini had taken away one of his favorite toys. "You mean I won't be doing any of the negotiating at all?"

"Well, maybe if guys like Rudy Mann or Whip Johnson, you know, some of the key players, if they start giving us a hard time, then you can get into it."

"But those guys are already signed, Ray. Dad took care of that months ago."

"There's always next season," Martini said. "Remember that every contract ends sooner or later."

"That's true, Ray, and maybe it's better that I don't get involved with the big money players right away," Duncan said, brightening a little. "Who knows? I might end up giving them too much of a raise, right?"

Duncan laughed at his self-deprecating wit. Martini laughed, too. "Right, kid."

"How about we go get some lunch, Ray?"

"Sounds good, kid. I've got some things I've been needing to tell you about."

Duncan had expected Ray Martini to take him to a restaurant where the only choices were the size and thickness of the steak, so he was pleasantly surprised to find himself guided expertly past the maitre'd of Chicago's finest French restaurant.

"Mr. Martini. Good afternoon. Will you want your usual table?"

"If it's open, Francois."

"Of course."

Francois turned and led them to what Duncan assumed must be Martini's regular table. They seated themselves at the table near a window and Martini asked for the wine list.

After the maitre'd had left, Martini leaned forward to speak to Duncan. "Recognize him?"

"Who?"

"The maitre'd. Francois."

"No," Duncan said. "Who is he?"

"Well, when he played for New York eight years ago, he called himself Franky Carlton."

"The defensive back?"

"The one and only."

Duncan was amazed, and his sense of wonder lasted halfway through the salad course.

"Ray?" he asked as he lifted a forkful of lettuce to his mouth. "Didn't you say there was something you wanted to talk to me about?"

"Yeah, kid. I did."

"And?"

"And I got off the phone with the commissioner this morning. He told me he thought you were finally ready to hear about the System."

"The what?"

"The System."

"All right, Ray. Shoot."

"Sit back, kid," he said. "I'll have to give you a little background first."

Duncan returned to his salad as Ray began telling his story. "It goes back to the early days of the Association," he said. "When the commissioner was first elected, way back in the early sixties, the Association was falling apart. The operators were at each other's throats, raiding each other's rosters and selling franchises right and left. Then there was the United League to contend with."

Duncan nodded.

"For a while there, back around 1958, it looked as though the UFL might take us over. Their teams were outbidding ours for all the top college talent and our players were getting old and tired."

"I remember," Duncan said. "My dad was really worried he'd lose all his best players."

"That's right, but the commissioner took care of it. First he talked all the operators into cooperating and sharing the television money. That shored up the weaker franchises. Then he talked the UFL into merging and I'll be damned if he didn't get the best part of the deal."

Duncan smiled.

"Of course, I was back in high school then," Martini said.

"I was little then," Duncan said. "I remember when my father used to tell me stories about those days, he used to tell me how amazed he was that the commissioner was able to pull it off, getting everything under his office and keeping the television contract. He even got the UFL to dump its teams in Cleveland and Oakland."

"He knew those two cities would die," Martini said. "Don't ask me how, kid, but he knew those two towns wouldn't support a team, and damned if he wasn't right. Look at what's happened to other sports in those towns -- straight into the toilet."

Duncan nodded.

"And nobody in either city, except for a couple of newspaper idiots, has ever made any serious noise about getting new teams in there," Martini added. "He knew it, just like he knew Birmingham and Vancouver, two little pissant towns, would make it."

Martini paused for a sip of wine. "He plops big-time football into those two and it goes over like cow chips in a fertilizer shortage. Everyone else said go into Seattle or Tampa, Buffalo even, but the commissioner knew Birmingham and Vancouver would make it. Now they're two of our best cities."

"Well, Vancouver getting into the Championship Bowl in its third year didn't hurt things any."

"Yeah," Martini said. "He was right about that, too."

"Right about what?"

"Everyone was saying it was too soon for Vancouver, that people wouldn't take it seriously, but he decided they should make the playoffs and, God bless him, he was right."

Duncan was really flustered now. "Ray, I don't understand."

"Well, kid, that's what I'm here to tell you about."

"Huh?"

"Here we go, kid," he said. "Hang onto your hat. The first thing that you've got to understand is that the North American Football Association in many ways resembles the game it promotes. Like the commissioner says, this is a team game dominated by individual achievements."

Duncan nodded.

"The Association is made up of twenty-four franchises, and from year to year, some are better than others. Some, like New York and Los Angeles, get more press coverage because of the cities they're in. Others, like Philadelphia or Miami, have such good operations year after year that they get a little more attention than say, Toronto or Washington.

"But no matter how good a team is, or how much attention it gets, no one team overshadows the Association. No matter how good a team is, it is only one-twenty-fourth of the entire operation. Each franchise operator knows that only eight of the twenty-four teams will earn spots in the playoffs and only two of them will make it to the Championship Bowl. But the essence of the Association is that no team wins without the efforts of every other team."

Duncan was more than a little confused by the direction the conversation was taking. "But every team tries to win, don't they, Ray?"

"Kid, every player on every team busts his butt to win, but I'm not talking about the players. The players are not members of the Association. They are the employees. The members, the operators of our twenty-four franchises, have all pledged themselves to work together to promote the prosperity of the Association. They work together by accepting the System."

"What exactly are you getting at, Ray?"

"You'll understand when I'm finished, kid, but I have to lay the groundwork here, so bear with me. The franchise operators accept the System because they know that by doing so, they all will make more money. The commissioner told you that not a single team lost money last season, right?"

"Right, but ..."

"That was because of the System. And that's the real beauty of the System, kid. Nobody ever loses. Think about it. You never hear any of the operators complaining that this team should be broken up or that team is a joke, because all of them are successful no matter who wins or loses. Every one of them makes money, piles and piles of money. No matter who ends up winning the Championship Bowl."

Duncan nodded.

"It wasn't like that before the System, kid. Back in the early days, the New York Comets used to take all the marbles every year because they had the best television contract, the biggest market in the country, the best stadium and the power of the New York media behind them. So they made lots of money and spent lots of money. They signed every good player they could get their hands on. One season, fifteen of the twenty-two college All-Americans signed with the Comets."

"I remember reading about that," Duncan said.

"For Chrissakes, kid, they even put some players under contract who weren't good enough to make their team, just to keep them away from other teams. So naturally New York made it to the Championship Bowl every year. Even though they didn't win it every year, a lot of people around the country got tired of seeing them in it all the time."

"Ray, are you trying ..."

"Hang on, kid. It gets better. The Comets finally had a perfect season. They went 14-0 and won the Bowl, 45-3. That was our worst year ever. The network was ready to drop us. We weren't doing dick for ratings anywhere outside of New York and New Jersey. At least three of our franchises filed the preliminary papers to declare bankruptcy, and then old Judge Davis, the last commissioner, dropped dead."

"Uh huh."

"At first we couldn't get anyone who even wanted to take his place, but the commissioner came out of nowhere -- remember, he was the public relations guy for Philadelphia -- and talked the more solvent teams into ponying up some cash to keep things going another year. He also got New York to loosen up and trade away a few players. After all, what's the use of being the best if everybody else is dying?"

Duncan nodded, but he was starting to feel a little uneasy and he didn't know exactly why.

"Anyway, Pittsburgh came out of nowhere that year and won the Bowl with a bunch of nobodies. We had our best year ever. Fans were fired up all over the country. Then along comes the United League the next year and starts raiding our rosters. Who did they hit the hardest?"

"New York and Pittsburgh?"

"Right on the money, kid. Our two best teams went straight into the dumper. We only signed the kids the UFL didn't want. Disaster, right?"

"Ah, right."

"Wrong. We had an even better year. St. Louis won the championship and attendance and profits nearly doubled. The United League was one of the best things that ever happened to us."

"Then why the merger?"

"Two reasons. First, player salaries were getting too high. We didn't want that, and neither did those old boys over at the United League. Second, the networks wanted the merger. Hell, kid, they begged us for it. You wouldn't remember it, but the United League was about to go under when they made that sweetheart deal with FBC. If it hadn't have been for the television money, their paychecks would have bounced. So naturally when it came time to renegotiate our own contract, all the commissioner had to do was waltz in to ABS and tell them he could deliver a merger. They creamed."

Martini laughed. "Hell, those idiots thought dealing with one league would save them money. The funny thing was, two years after the merger, when we negotiated with all three networks, we ended up with twice as much money as both leagues had made combined."

The thought of that coup seemed to please Martini immensely and he reflected on it for a moment before continuing.

"Anyway, kid, just before the merger we commissioned a survey to find out what fans wanted to see, They wanted touchdowns. None of these 3-0 games that the old league used to have. They wanted 35-34. They wanted to see passing. None of this two yards and a cloud of dust crap. And most of all, they wanted to see the little guys whip up on the big guys. Not all the time, but you remember that old expression about on any given Sunday ..."

"... any team can beat any other team, right, Ray?"

"That's the one, kid. Well, people wanted to believe that. So we let them."

"You let them?"

"Hell, yes. We made them believe it. Because we developed the System."

"Ray, I'm still not following you. What exactly is the System?"

"Every year we commission a secret survey and find out what the country wants to see. What teams should play each other, who they want to see have good years, things like that. Then we feed all that information into our computer and it decides which two teams should make it to the Championship Bowl."

"And then?"

"Then we put those teams into the Championship Bowl."

Martini had said it so matter of factly that Duncan almost laughed, until he realized Martini hadn't meant it as a joke. He wasn't even smiling. Duncan suddenly realized what he was hearing was the truth.

"You mean it's all fixed?"

Martini didn't flinch. "We prefer to think of it as being programmed for maximum audience enjoyment," he said smoothly.

"It's dishonest? A fraud?"

Martini gestured to Duncan to keep his voice down. "Is it, kid? There's no deception involved. We're giving the public exactly what it wants, and the proof is right there in the computer, in the survey data."

"What about the fans who go to the stadiums to root, thinking their teams have a chance to win?"

"Every team has a chance, kid. If not this year, then next year. And in the meantime we offer all those fans a quality entertainment product. What more could anyone have a right to expect for their money?"

Duncan Charles didn't know what to think. He slumped back in his chair and drained his water glass.

"Look, I know it's a surprise, but if you take the time and think things through, you'll see how much more sense it makes than if it were every man for himself. Do you want the NAFA to be like baseball, where .250 hitters make three million dollars?"

Duncan shook his head.

"Or like pro hockey, where the owners can't even get a network television contract?"

Duncan shook his head again.

"With the System, we all cooperate. Everyone prospers, and the men who take the biggest financial risk make the most money. Here's how it works. The computer does all the work. It decides which teams will make the playoffs and then sets up the scenario. It decides, for example, that my old team, the Houston Lonestars, might need a record of ten and four. Then it sets up the games and their outcomes accordingly. After that we let the officials take over."

"The officials?"

"They control the action for us," Martini said patiently.

"They what?"

"They receive instructions right before the game on who is to win and whether the game is supposed to be close. Through the use of penalties, measurements and instant replay, they tilt the game in the direction we want it to go. But only if it's necessary."

Duncan frowned.

 "Look, kid, let's say you're playing Philadelphia and the computer says you're supposed to win a tight game. If Chicago has the momentum, if you've got the game wrapped up, the officials just stay out of things. But let's say you're up by two and the Bulldogs are driving for a game-winning field goal in the last minute."

"Yeah? What could they do?"

"Well, the refs might call an illegal motion penalty, or a pass interference, or maybe even holding. You've probably noticed that a lot of drives run out of steam because of penalties. Chances are some of those penalties were called to keep the game in order."

"It's just the refs, then?"

Martini nodded.

"The players, the coaches, they aren't in on this?"

"Are you kidding me? We have enough trouble keeping them in line as it is. Hell, kid, not even all of the operators know about the System. Granted, most of them do, because a lot of them have served on the Committee at one time or another."

"Committee?"

"The Executive Policy Committee. Six franchise operators plus the commissioner. They get together right before the June Association meeting to discuss the survey results. Usually they just take a voice vote to accept them, but occasionally they might make a slight adjustment."

"Like the commissioner wanting Vancouver in the playoffs."

"Exactly, kid," Martini said, smiling. "Most of the time, though, they just accept the results. After all, why pay a million a year for a fan survey if you're going to jack around with what it tells you?"

Duncan was overwhelmed by it all. It had seemed repugnant to him at first, but he was beginning to see the value of the System. As Martini had laid it out for him, it seemed very impressive. In fact, it was simplicity bordering on genius.

"Just one thing, Ray," he asked. "Why are you telling me all this now?"

"Because the commissioner didn't want to wait any longer to fill the vacancy on the Committee. We want you to take your dad's place as one of the men running the Association."

Duncan was shocked. He had to bite his lip to keep from screaming out loud. My father? My father was in on this? He found it almost impossible to comprehend. Suddenly his mouth was dry.

"Could I have a drink, Ray?"

"Sure, kid." Martini gestured for a waiter and within seconds one was at his elbow. "What'll it be, kid?"

Duncan sighed. "Scotch and Dr. Pepper."

Martini winced a little. The waiter seemed to blanch, but regained his composure quickly.

"We don't have any Dr. Pepper, Mr. Martini," he said in a low voice. "We only have Coca Cola and Seven-Up."

Ray reached into his wallet and pulled out a fifty-dollar bill. "I'd appreciate it if you'd send someone down the street to get some, then," he said.

"Certainly, sir."

When the drink came, Duncan downed half of it in one gulp. The odd concoction seemed to help relax him. "Ray, do you mean my father was on the Committee? My father fixed football games?"

"Your dad was one of the original members, kid. He was the first operator the commissioner talked to about the System."

All of a sudden Duncan Charles wanted nothing more than to get out. All of a sudden he hated Ray Martini, the commissioner, the North American Football Association and his own father.

All of a sudden he wanted nothing more than to go home, turn out all the lights and curl up in his single bed with the Chicago Trojans sheets.

Martini took that moment to touch his arm gently. "Kid, you knew your dad better than anyone. He loved football. He would never have been a part of anything that hurt the game. Neither would any of us. We all love football -- that's why we have the System. It makes the game almost perfect and absolutely irresistible. And the more popular the game is, the better off we all are. Right?"

Duncan didn't answer. He couldn't answer. He grabbed for his drink again and downed the other half. Martini signaled to the waiter to bring another one and the drink appeared almost magically.

"Are you all right, kid?"

"Yeah, sure, Ray. I'm fine. I'm just having trouble collecting my thoughts on all of this."

"Sure, kid. It's a lot to digest in one gulp."

"How has this stayed secret, Ray? How come none of this ever leaked out?"

"Who would tell? Certainly not any of the franchise operators. They've got investments to protect and they know it's for the good of the game. Anybody we don't trust, anybody we think is too rah-rah, we just don't tell them about it."

Duncan nodded.

"That's what I've been trying to explain to you. We present a product, a spectacle if you will, that the public wants to see. We give people games that provide the maximum amount of pleasure and excitement. We give people heroes. What in the hell is wrong with that?"

"Well ... nothing, I guess."

"That's right, nothing. And every franchise in the Association benefits from it in the form of increased revenue and increased profits. Just like any other well-run business enterprise. Remember, kid, we're all in this together. Look at what's happened since we put in the System. Look at your own team. When was the last time the Trojans lost money?"

"I don't know exactly."

"Well, I do. I looked it up before we came over here. It was forty years ago. Every single year since then, Chicago Football Inc., has shown a hefty profit. And how many times have you made the playoffs in that time?"

Duncan thought for a moment. "Twice."

"That's right. Twice. And both times you lost in the first round. So we have nearly forty years of uninterrupted prosperity with only two playoff teams. During a lot of those years -- most of the 1970s, in fact -- you had one of the worst teams in the league, a team that was legendary for its incompetence."

"I wouldn't put it exactly that way, Ray."

"Oh?" Martini raised an eyebrow quizzically. "In 1977, your team was 1-13. How would you describe that?"

"We lost a lot of close games that year."

"That's right, kid. You lost one game when your field goal kicker missed the ball completely on a 24-yard attempt. Do you remember what he did kick?"

Duncan nodded sadly. "I think so."

"I remember too. He kicked the holder in the balls."

"Yeah."

Martini shook his head. "They were awful, but no matter how badly the Trojans did, no matter how tough the rest of the Association was, you sold out almost every game. You sold a lot of programs and hot dogs. Your radio and television ratings remained high. That's the System, kid. And speaking of the System, I've got some great news for you."

"What's that?" Duncan asked hopefully.

"This year the Chicago Trojans, your Chicago Trojans, are going to be a Cinderella team."

"Cinderella team? What's that?"

"Every year the computer picks a team, sometimes two or three, that the public feels sorry for. These are the underdog teams. Maybe they used to be good but haven't had any success in a while. Maybe they're recent expansion teams."

"Like Vancouver?"

"Whatever. But through advantageous scheduling and some good trades, the teams we select as Cinderella teams come out of the pack to be playoff contenders. Sometimes, about once every ten or twelve years, a Cinderella team makes it all the way to the Championship Bowl."

"And?" Duncan was starting to get excited.

Martini nodded, smiling. "This year the Trojans are going to go to the Championship Bowl."

Duncan felt like a small child about to open his presents on Christmas morning. "My team? My Trojans in the Championship Bowl? That's great, Ray. Are we going to win?"

"We'll have to wait and see on that. The Championship Bowl is an open game."

"You mean it's not fixed?"

"Arranged, kid. Arranged. But no, it's not arranged. Not even a hint. By that time, the two most popular teams in the league have made it and we're going to get tremendous television ratings no matter who wins. The Championship Bowl is played straight."

"Wait a minute, Ray. How are we going to make it? We've got a sore-armed quarterback, a gimpy fullback who will probably retire before training camp and the second-worst defense in the league."

"That's all true, but Phoenix is going to trade you Brig McHenry to play quarterback, there'll be a couple of good defensive players on the waiver wire and you're going to draft Willis Waller."

Duncan seemed awed. "The Willis Waller?"

"The walking one and only, kid. Willis Waller, the Morris Trophy winner the last two years. The best college running back in the last twenty years, the kind of superstar player you can build a dynasty around."

"But how, Ray? We have the third pick in the draft. Willis Waller will be gone by then."

"Nope," Martini said, smiling. "Haven't you been reading the papers? All of a sudden everybody's real high on that defensive end from East Tennessee State."

"Barry Kline?"

"That's the one. He's going to be the very first player picked. Cincinnati's next, and they've got more running backs than they need, so they'll go for a quarterback."

"Like Rudy Leighton from Texas?"

"You do keep up with things, don't you, kid?" Duncan smiled at the praise. "That's going to leave the best running back in the country signed, sealed and gift-wrapped for the Chicago Trojans. Your Chicago Trojans."

Duncan's initial feelings of revulsion had turned into complete, utter gratitude. All the time he had been growing up, he remembered his father's one regret had been the Trojans' failure ever to make it into the Championship Bowl. Anything that could put his beloved team into the title game was fine with Duncan.

He did still have a few more questions, though, and he sipped on his third Scotch and Dr. Pepper as he framed them.

"All those other teams, Ray. The ones that will be trading with us and the ones that decide not to draft Waller, do they know about the System?"

"Like I said, kid, not all of them. But all of them have a liaison like me who makes some pretty heavyweight suggestions."

"What would happen if an operator decided not to take the liaison's advice?"

"Well, it's no big deal," Martini said softly. "It's only advice. But a liaison offers his suggestions with the idea that they are intended to promote the welfare of the game. Any operator who isn't interested in the welfare of the game is a fool, and we don't allow fools to operate Association franchises."

"You mean you'd take someone's team away from them?"

"Not necessarily, but it has been known to happen. And there are other, less drastic, things the Association can do to make someone, shall we say, see the light. Things like giving a team a schedule of away games that's very expensive to travel to."

"You mean like a lot of trips to California for an eastern team?"

"Right, kid. The schedule is all part of the System. The Trojans, for example, will play mostly weak teams in their non-division games this year. Teams like Washington and Kansas City. And no two Cinderella teams ever play each other in the regular season."

"That makes sense," Duncan said.

"I think you've got it all now. That's the whole thing. Do you understand now why we need the System, and why it has to remain a secret?"

"Oh, yes, Ray. It was a little tough to digest at first, but I understand completely now."

Martini smiled. "That's good, kid, because the commissioner wasn't just blowing smoke up your butt when he said you were joining the most exclusive fraternity in the world."

"No?"

"It's easier to become a member of the College of Cardinals than it is to get into our little club. That's why we like to do things a certain way, and why we have to be absolutely sure of the men who operate our franchises."

Duncan nodded eagerly. "I'm your boy, er, man, Ray."

Great, Martini thought to himself. Now all I've got to do is tell the commissioner that we have to adjust this year's survey so that Chicago gets into the Championship Bowl.

8

Dave and Herb had expected Benjamin Aloysius Kennedy's office to be a memorial to the man's career. A coach who had enjoyed fifteen consecutive winning seasons, six division titles and two Championship Bowl victories, they assumed, would have at least a few mementoes sitting around.

There probably would be trophies of important victories at the various levels of the game, or pictures of happy teams carrying their coach off the field.

At the very least, they had expected to see Ben Kennedy seated behind a massive desk that allowed him to dominate the room and all in it.

There wasn't anything like that. Instead, they found a spare, soulless office that looked as if it was being occupied by an accountant. There was one window that overlooked the practice field, a simple metal desk, a filing cabinet, a bookcase with a few books about football and a picture of the commissioner in a cheap plastic frame.

One thing they had imagined accurately, though. With or without the assistance of props, Ben Kennedy dominated the room.

"Coach Kennedy, I'm Dave Krause," Dave said, extending his hand. "And this is Herbert Rojas."

Kennedy stared at him and motioned that the two men should sit in the folding chairs opposite the desk. He didn't offer his hand, and after a few embarrassing moments, Dave took his hand back and wiped it on his jacket.

"I know who you gentlemen are," he said. "Please be so kind as to state your business without a lot of meaningless amenities."

"Thanks for seeing us, Coach," Herb said. "By the way, do you mind if I call you Ben?"

Kennedy stared at him coldly. "I certainly do mind, Mr. Rojas. Familiarity is too easily granted in this world. You may call me Coach, or even Mr. Kennedy, but my first name is reserved for my friends and family."

"Jesus!" Herb said.

"No, Mr. Rojas. Jesus was our Savior. I am only a football coach, although I like to think I have had some positive effect on the lives of young men, just as Our Lord did."

It was the first time in their short acquaintance that Dave had seen Herb at a loss for words, so he stepped into the breach.

"Coach Kennedy, I think you might be aware ..."

"... why you two gentlemen are here? Yes, I think so. You want me to be the head coach of the Washington Warriors. You have a cockeyed plan to staff a professional football team with old has-beens who might have one good season of football left in them and with rookies the Association scouts somehow have overlooked. To add further to the totally ludicrous nature of your plan, you intend to coax a winning season from this team."

"You make it sound so ..."

"... unbelievable? It is unbelievable," Kennedy said. "In fact, Mr. Krause, I believe it has little chance of succeeding."

Dave started to rise from his seat.

"But ..."

Ben Kennedy's booming voice made him sit back down.

"But if there is a single man on God's green earth who can take this bizarre plan and make it work, it is I. I will take it."

"The coaching job?"

"Yes," he said. "I accept it for what it is, a chance to return to the coaching ranks of professional football. It is an opportunity to prove to that gentleman ..." Kennedy jerked his thumb angrily at the photograph on the wall. "... that I can still win."

"I was going to ask you about that," Dave said.

"There is no deep dark secret, Mr. Krause. That man ran me out of professional football. He damaged my reputation so badly that I could not function in any sports setting for long, such was the controversy he created around me. Every move I made, every action I took was under such extreme scrutiny that I found it impossible to do the one job the Lord gave me a special aptitude for -- coaching football."

Dave nodded.

"That is why you see me in this office today," Kennedy added. "In a situation devoid of pressure, so as to build back my energy to the level necessary to perform my tasks as a head coach, while at the same time overcoming the stigma that the actions of that gentleman attached to my name."

"Not to mention the stigma of a few hundred long nights with the bottle," Herb said dryly, regretting the statement almost as soon as it left his mouth.

Ben Kennedy didn't react angrily, though. In fact, he barely reacted at all. "Mr. Rojas, a few years ago I would have ordered you, in no uncertain terms and with many words of four letters, out of my office."

"Yeah?"

"There would have been a distinct possibility that you would have gone directly from this office to the nearest emergency room. You will notice that I did not react that way, though. This is not to say your statement did not arouse my anger, or that I do not deserve an apology."

"I'm sorry, Coach," Herb mumbled.

"Your apology is accepted, Mr. Rojas. I admit there were a number of times in the past -- times when I was under severe pressure -- when I overindulged, but if I had imbibed as much alcohol as that gentleman said I did, my liver would be under examination at a medical school, the rest of my body would be buried six feet beneath the earth and my soul would be with the Lord."

Dave didn't know what to say, so he just smiled.

"Any drinking problems I ever had are long past," Kennedy said. "You deserve to know that since you will be signing my paychecks. My propensity to overindulge in alcohol is simply one more aspect of my personality that I have overcome through sheer strength of will, the support of my wife and my faith in the Lord."

"That's great, Coach," Herb said.

"Have you been born again, Mr. Rojas?"

"Nope. I got it right the first time."

"Coach, I don't want to interrupt you," Dave said as he tried to rescue Herb.

"Then please try not to do so, Mr. Krause."

"But," Dave went on, undeterred. "I'd like you to familiarize yourself with our plan of attack."

"No, Mr. Krause, any plan of attack you might have had is now moot. I will be in charge of all football decisions. You have shown your wisdom by hiring me, and I will reward you by molding a winning team for you."

"But, Coach ..."

"I will explain myself once, Mr. Rojas," Kennedy said. "Any time either of you ever have a question, all you must do is ask. I will answer any of your questions. And any time you decide you do not like the way I am doing things, all you must do is terminate me."

"Huh?"

"The fact is, all the players we will be signing will have some sort of severe deficiency in their abilities. They will be too old, or too slow, or too stupid to play the type of football practiced in the Association today. Instead, they will have to play simple, old-fashioned, ten-yards-at-a-time football."

"It's not pretty," Herb said. "But it works."

"It is pretty, Mr. Rojas. Successful football is a beautiful thing."

Lord, Dave thought, Herb can't win even when he agrees with this guy.

"Of course," Herb said meekly.

Very good, Herb, Dave thought. Just agree with the man and then keep your mouth shut.

"Now, gentlemen, I assume your next step will be to beat the bushes for the talent you intend to sign for me."

"Yes," Dave said. "This was the first stop on a long trip for both of us."

"May I assume you would like me to scour the semi-pro leagues I've been working in for players of professional quality?"

"We had hoped ..."

"There are not very many who fit that description, Mr. Krause. Most of the players at this level are too slow, too small or too stupid to play professionally. That is why they call these leagues semi-pro."

"But you know of a few ..."

"Yes, Mr. Rojas. I know of a very few who might have a chance. I will invite them to our training camp."

"That's great," Herb said. "But don't be too picky. Right now we need all the players who can get our hands on. They can't be that much slower or smaller or stupider than the players we've already got."

"Please, Mr. Rojas. I think you might be surprised at the talent you do have. All that may be required is a bit of motivation. I will provide that motivation."

"Now, Coach," Dave said. "All we have to get you to do is sign a contract with Washington Football Inc."

"No contract."

"No contract?"

"I have never signed a contract and I never intend to."

"Why not?"

"I do not believe in contracts," Kennedy said. "You accept me for what I am -- a very good football coach. If I fail to be what I promise to be, you have the right to discharge me. And if I become less than content with the situation at any time, I have the option of resigning. As long as we understand each other, I do not see where a contract is necessary."

Dave shrugged. "All right, then."

"A simple handshake will suffice."

Dave shook Kennedy's hand, and the coach then turned to Herb and shook his hand as well.

"Welcome aboard, Coach."

"Thank you, Mr. Rojas."

With negotiations out of the way, Ben Kennedy began pacing around the room. "I will hire the coaching staff. I will design the offense and the defense. I will call the plays."

"Well," Herb said. "I certainly hadn't planned on calling them."

"That is quite possibly the first intelligent remark you have made since you entered this office, Mr. Rojas."

Herb grinned.

"Don't get cocky. Even a blind pig finds a truffle once in a while," Dave said drily.

"Precisely, Mr. Krause. Now if we win, the credit is mine."

"And if we lose?"

"Mr. Rojas, losing has never been a part of my plans. I want a check for ten thousand dollars tomorrow and ten thousand dollars a month after that."

"Uh, Coach ..."

"Yes, Mr. Krause?"

"That's $120,000 a year."

"I am familiar with simple mathematical functions, Mr. Krause. Is there some problem with that? Are you insolvent?"

"No, not at all. It's just that there isn't a head coach in the Association making less than three times that. I think the average head coach is making a million a year."

"I am familiar with the going rate for wages in my profession," Kennedy said.

"Then why ..."

"Mr. Krause, men who are underpaid are more highly motivated to improve themselves."

Herb stifled a smile.

"I will also be doing quite a bit of traveling, and I expect that any and all expenses I incur will be covered by the team."

"We'll have a corporate credit card issued for you this week," Dave said. "I'll have it expressed down to you from Washington."

Kennedy nodded. "If I see a player I think can help our team, I want to be able to sign him on the spot with no questions asked. And do not worry, gentlemen, my reputation does not include looseness with other people's money."

"Fine."

"Anyone I sign will be worth at least twice as much as I offer him. You will receive reports daily, if that is possible, apprising you of any progress I have made. I want to be able to send any player I sign to camp immediately."

"We'll have the facility in Oxon Hill open by the beginning of the week."

"Excellent," Kennedy said. "I will be there by the first week in July, and we will begin training camp as soon as I get there. I will send you a list of players that I think we might be able to select with our draft choices. I will leave the drafting of them to you. I have serious doubts that any rookies we might be able to get can help us anyway."

"Yeah," Herb said. "Especially the rookies we can get on the fourth, eighth and eleventh rounds."

Kennedy nodded. "Cuts will be my decision alone. If there are any decisions you wish to have an input into, I will listen, but I will have the final word on all football matters."

"Understood," Dave said.

"And if you do not agree ..."

"I know," Herb said. "We can give you the gate."

"That is correct, Mr. Rojas. Now who are some of these has-beens you are thinking of signing?"

"Well ..."

"Tony Ross is in Charlotte," Kennedy said. "Reginald Reese is in California ..."

"Roxy Reese?"

"I believe Reginald is actually his name. Now I assume you are looking for a quarterback."

"Well, we've got Brian Rider coming back, but we'd like to sign a good, strong backup."

"I want you to get in touch with Jimmy Gardner."

"Uh, Coach, we had thought about Gardner, but he's forty years old," Herb said.

"He may actually be forty-one, Mr. Krause. In fact, he is fat, he is lazy and he is a bum who would rather drink than work."

"Sounds like a winner to me," Herb said.

"He is a winner, Mr. Rojas. I neglected to mention that he doesn't have much of an arm left, but he was the best leader I ever saw on a football field and I suspect with the proper motivation he could be again."

"Where ..."

"Gardner is somewhere in the south," Kennedy said. "Arkansas, I believe. He is supposed to be pursuing a career in the entertainment industry as a country and western singer. I will save him from that and make him a quarterback again."

Herb grunted. "Any other easy jobs you want us to do for you, Coach?"

"Mr. Rojas, I could not help but notice that you have the unfortunate habit of saying the wrong thing at the wrong time. Have you had this problem since childhood?"

Herb seemed to shrink back into his chair, and Dave tried to redirect the coach's attention.

"Well, Coach Kennedy, I think that just about takes care of everything."

"One more thing, Mr. Krause."

"Yes?"

"I would like to congratulate you on your wisdom and judgment in being able to recognize the best possible coach for your football team."

Later, after they had left Kennedy's office, Herb muttered to Dave, "Do you think that was his way of saying thanks?"

"I doubt it."

9

The little club looked seedy from the outside, and much to Herb's dismay, it was just as run-down on the inside. It was located on the outskirts of Buffalo Nickel, Arkansas, a town of four hundred people on a good day.

It had taken Herb two flights to get to Fayetteville and a three-hour drive in a rental car to get to Buffalo Nickel, the town where Jimmy Gardner reportedly was performing. It appeared from the half-filled parking lot that only a few of the local residents had ever heard of, much less been to, the club Herb had located.

He guided his rented Monte Carlo into the dirt-covered, deeply rutted parking lot right between two pickup trucks with University of Arkansas bumper stickers. He looked around at the collection of old cars, pickup trucks and motorcycles in the lot and sighed.

When he walked through the doorway into the bar, he saw fifteen or twenty customers, none of whom seemed very interested in the entertainment that had been advertised on the sign outside.

THE SUNNY SIDE INN

GIRLS! GIRLS! GIRLS!

Topless!! Bottomless!!

Continuous action!

Featuring the Fabulous

Belle Starr Monroe!

Cheri Lynn Lovechild!

Jennifer and her Furry Friends!

AND MORE!

In much smaller letters at the bottom of the placard, Herb read the rest of the program:

"Music by former pro quarterback Jimmy Joe Gardner and his Stone Mountain Boys."

Herb looked around the room and noticed Jimmy Gardner sitting on the stage behind a chicken-wire buffer. The former Championship Bowl quarterback was struggling through a song that, if the customers had anything to say about it, would be his last one.

"All right, now," Gardner said. "I'd like to perform an old Hank Williams tune for you good people."

"Oh, no! Not Hank!"

"Shut the fuck up, Gardner!"

"Sit down and bring on the girls!"

Gee, Herb thought, they really love this guy. He looked around the establishment with a critically experienced eye. It wasn't the type of bar he'd have chosen to own, but he couldn't help but notice the bartender.

The man passing out bottles of domestic beer was a large, burly man who looked as if he had recently completed a meal of nails and small plumbing tools. The smile on his face looked fairly genuine, though, and Herb caught his attention as he sat at the bar.

"Howdy, stranger. What'll it be?"

"Beer, thanks."

The man unscrewed the top off a bottle of Budweiser and put it in front of Herb. "Need a glass?"

Herb shook his head. "This is fine. Say, buddy, is that the famous Jimmy Gardner playing up there?"

"In all his glory. Who wants to know?"

"Oh, just curious. Don't get me wrong, friend, but that's got to be the worst version of a Hank Williams song I've ever heard. Do you pay him to do that?"

"Yeah," the man said, grimacing. "I'm paying him. I'm paying him one hell of a lot of money, considering the return I'm getting on my investment. Say, you don't run a club, do you?"

"Not like this one," Herb said.

"Yeah, well, there aren't many like this one. I was just going to give you some free advice if you had a club."

"What's that?"

"I'd tell you to stay away from Gardner. He can't sing a lick. He can't play. His jokes are older than Adam's off ox and he'll drink up your profits for the week in one night. Dang, buddy, he's the only guy I've seen who can scare customers out of a strip joint."

"I'll keep that in mind, chief."

Gardner finished his song to a chorus of boos. "Now," he said into the microphone. "I'd like to do a little song by my old friend Willie Nelson ..."

"No!" shouted a large man in a plaid work shirt at the precise moment a beer bottle exploded against the screen that protected Gardner from his adoring fans. "Anything but Willie Nelson!"

Herb folded a five-dollar bill between his first two fingers and slid it across the bar toward the bartender.

"Say, chief, do you think you could give my old buddy Jimmy a message?"

"Yeah, sure," he said, palming the bill with a grace that belied his size. "You want to talk to him?"

"Sure," Herb said. "As soon as he's finished."

"No sweat," the bartender said. "You can stick a fork in old Jimmy. He's done. Hey, Gardner!"

Gardner looked over angrily. "Dammit, asshole, how many times have I told you ..." Gardner paused momentarily as he dodged the spray from a pitcher of beer that someone had thrown against the screen. "... don't interrupt me when I'm singing!"

"Is that what you call it?" someone shouted from the crowd.

"Gardner, get your fat ass down here!" the bartender shouted. "This old boy wants to talk to you."

The break in the music seemed to shake the audience out of its stupor.

"Yeah, cut the crap! Let's see some girls!"

"We want the women!"

"Get the hell off the stage, Gardner!"

The bartender moved quickly to give his customers what they wanted. In fact, he moved so quickly that Herb thought momentarily about offering him a contract to play linebacker for the Warriors.

"All right, boys," he said. "Keep it quiet!"

He shouted to someone backstage. "Jenny, get your tiny little ass out here! Gardner, off the stage!"

"The hell you say," Gardner said. "I've got six more songs to do. I'm going to finish my set."

The prospect of hearing Gardner sing six more songs seemed to stir the sparse crowd toward open, violent revolution, and there was movement toward the stage. Herb looked around for the nearest exit.

"Goddamnit, Gardner! Get the fuck off the stage!" shouted one man who was wearing a Delco baseball cap and at least three days growth of beard. "You're a worse singer than you were a quarterback."

That infuriated Gardner. "Damn, buddy. Now you're getting mean. I was the best fucking quarterback in the league!"

"Yeah," the guy said. "About a hundred years ago."

Other members of the crowd joined in.

"We want to see some titties!"

"Yeah, and not yours, Gardner!"

That brought a laugh from the crowd, which gave Gardner a chance to escape from the stage with his pride at least half-intact. He was followed closely by the bartender, who apparently was making sure the quarterback didn't change his mind.

Finally a bored-looking redhead ambled onto the stage, with two small dogs following her.

"Hi, y'all," she said. "I'm Jennifer and these are my furry friends."

Herb found himself wondering exactly how the dogs fit into the act, but the bartender chose that moment to bring Gardner over to him.

"Jimmy," he said. "This is that old boy I was tellin' you about. He said he wants to talk to you."

"About a job," Herb mumbled, extending his hand.

"You got a job for me?" Gardner asked, accepting the offered handshake with a hand that seemed to Herb surprisingly soft and small.

"Could be, Jimmy. I'm Herb Rojas. I'm one of the new general managers of the Washington Warriors."

Herb studied Gardner's eyes, looking for just the reaction he got when he mentioned the football team. Gardner's eyes had flashed for only a short moment, but Herb knew he was on the right track.

"Buy you a beer, Jimmy?"

"Sure, that sounds good. The Warriors, huh?"

"Yep," Herb said. "We need a quarterback."

"And what, you want me to recommend a few friends or something? I haven't been seeing much pro football the last couple of years. Too busy building my singing career."

Well, Herb thought. I might as well come right out and say it. "No, Jimmy. We want you."

The bartender dropped Gardner's beer on his foot.

"Now will you look at that," Gardner said, laughing. "Jeez Louise, Eddie, you been tending bar long? Good thing you're not on the Lonestars, they'd make you carry a mug everywhere you go for a week so you'd never fumble again."

"Sorry," he said. "I'll get another one. Hey, buddy, you serious? You want

Gardner here to play football?"

"Well, do you want him to keep playing here?"

"I'll get that beer."

"Listen, Mr. Rojas," Gardner said. "I've got to be honest with you. I haven't played football in three years."

"Four, counting your last season on the bench in Denver."

"And I'm thirty-nine years old."

"Forty."

"Well, actually forty-one," Gardner admitted. "I shaved a year off my age when I started college."

"Smart move."

"Anyway, that's all over now. I'm a country star. I've got a record album out and I've been on stage at the Opry."

Herb was not impressed. "Yeah, Jimbo, I remember that album. What'd they call it -- Championship Country by the Championship Quarterback. It sold five thousand copies, all to Houston fans. Last time I saw it was in the three-for-a-dollar rack in K-Mart. Kids were using it for frisbees."

"Hey!"

"And as far as the Opry goes, you presented an award. They never let you near a guitar or a microphone."

"Sounds like you've done a little bit of homework," Gardner said, sipping his beer.

"That I have, Jimmy. Your record company cut you loose six months ago and no one's picked you up. You were dropped by your agent, and nobody in Nashville will return your calls."

"Yeah, well, I've got a little work to do before ..."

"It won't help, Jimbo. The word is out. Nobody's going to touch you as a singer. That former NAFA quarterback routine doesn't make it anymore and you've been away from the game too long to catch on as an announcer. Let's face it, Jimmy. If you don't have a lot of money put back, you'll be selling your blood and sleeping in doorways within two years."

Gardner glared at him silently, and Herb was afraid for a moment he had overplayed his hand. He paused for a moment and then changed his tack.

"Look, Jimmy," he said softly. "Nashville might not want you, the television people might not want you, but we want you. We need a quarterback with experience. We're going to have a lot of kids on this team, and they're going to need someone to look up to. We need a leader, Jimmy. Last I heard, you were a leader."

"Look at me," Gardner said. "You think I could take that kind of pounding?"

Herb laughed. "Jimmy, we've got our starting quarterback. Brian Rider's our man. He's young enough to be your son."

"He might be," Gardner drawled. "I've been with some ladies in my day."

"So I heard. We just need you to back Rider up and work with him on fundamentals."

"Rider's not a bad kid. He's got potential."

"I thought you said you weren't watching football these days."

"Yeah, well, there's nothing else to do on a Sunday afternoon back here in the sticks," Gardner said.

"So, are you interested?"

"I don't know, man. You did say Washington, didn't you?"

"Yeah."

"Washington's a sinkhole! Guys go there and disappear. It's the fucking Bermuda Triangle of football!"

"And what's this place?" Herb asked, gesturing toward the stage, where Jennifer had divested herself of her clothes while her dogs were doing what comes naturally to canines.

"Yeah, well ..." Gardner thought of another argument. "You know I made forty-five thousand my last year in Denver."

"Jimmy, you made thirty-five thousand, but we'll pay you twice that if you sign with us."

"Seventy thousand dollars?"

The bartender grinned. "Damn, Gardner. You can pay your bar tab."

Gardner took a deep breath. "Look. Mr. Rojas, let's be honest here. This is going to take a lot of effort. I'm not in the best of shape. I'll have to get back into training. I'll have to work!"

"Jimmy, how much work can it be? You were one of the greats. I'll bet you could pick up a ball right now and throw a perfect bomb."

Gardner shook his head. "Naw, no chance of that. I tried. Last week. It was just a little pickup game, and naturally they wanted me to play quarterback."

Herb nodded. "Naturally."

"Well, I tried to throw deep and I couldn't. No more than thirty yards."

Herb was dismayed. "How accurate were you?"

"Hell, I was as sharp as ever, but by the next morning I could hardly move."

"Jimmy, it's not like we're asking you to play four quarters. After all, we've got Rider. You wouldn't play more than five or ten minutes a game, max."

Gardner nodded.

"One more thing, Jimmy. You come highly recommended."

"What?"

"Ben Kennedy specifically asked for you."

"The Iron Irishman?"

"Yeah. He's going to be our coach."

"Well, buddy, I think I'll pass this one up. No way do I play for that crazy motherfucker!"

"Why not?"

"He's a crazy old bastard, a Simon Legree! That man doesn't know the meaning of the word fun. His idea of a good time is catching somebody out during bed check."

"He's changed."

"Yeah, I heard. He found the Lord. I'll tell you, that's a scary combination. Ben Kennedy and Jesus."

"He's still a football genius."

"Anyway," Gardner said. "I want to call my own plays. There's no way Ben Kennedy is going to let his quarterback call the plays."

"He's not stupid. He'll let you call the plays if you can prove you're better at it than he is." Herb didn't know if that was true, but it certainly sounded good.

Gardner grunted. "Nobody in this world is a better play caller than Ben

Kennedy."

"Then what are we arguing about?"

Herb could feel it. He almost had Gardner turned around. He felt like he needed just one more thing to close the sale. "Let's face it, Jimmy. You're scared. You're old and fat and you're scared. You're forty-one years old, you can't throw the long ball and you run like an old lady with polio. But dammit, you're a football player. You played fourteen years in the NAFA and you won two Championship Bowls."

He paused for the big finish.

"Think about this, Jimmy. We're going all around the country, talking to guys like you. Guys the Association gave up on, guys who might have another year or two of football left in them. Guys with something to prove. We're going to build a team out of comeback stories and yours is going to be the one at the top of the list."

He knew he had him. Gardner knew it too, and so did the bartender, who had remained within earshot. Jimmy felt like he should put up a little more of a fight, but it was clear his heart wasn't in it.

"What if it doesn't work out?" he asked. "What if I don't have it anymore?"

"Then you can come back here with seventy thousand dollars," Herb said. "We'll guarantee your salary."

The bartender started to say something, but Herb silently begged him to be quiet. "Listen, Jimmy, I know what you're going through. Sure, you're scared."

"Scared?"

"Maybe you think you've had too many late nights looking at the bottom of a bottle. Too many girls you'll never remember. How the hell are you going to find out if you don't try?"

He stared at Gardner, who sighed loudly. "OK, bubba, you've got yourself a backup quarterback."

Herb stood up, tossed a twenty on the bar to cover the cost of the beer. "I'm at the Best Western," he said. "We'll leave at 9 tomorrow morning."

Gardner nodded. "I'll be there," he said.

"I know you will."

Herb turned and headed for the exit just as a totally nude Jennifer was throwing a bucket of water on her dogs in an attempt to cool them off.

"Hey, Rojas!"

He turned back to look at Jimmy.

"Like hell I'm scared!"

Herb grinned at Gardner. "See you in the morning."

10

Over the next ten days, Herb traveled back and forth across the country, running down every name on their list of recently retired players. At the same time, Dave was contacting names of the list of players they had put together who had never been given a chance.

His list was a lot shorter, and much less disappointing. Most of the men Dave reached had kept themselves in shape, hoping for one more invitation to a big-league training camp. He signed nine of them to free-agent, make-good contracts and invited them to Oxon Hill.

Herb, on the other hand, was constantly amazed and dismayed at the sight of men, only a few years removed from the game, who had allowed themselves to get fat and flabby.

Except for Joe Richards.

Herb was amazed at the sight of the man, who had retired five years earlier in his prime -- at the age of only twenty-six. Richards had been an all-Association safety, and his departure from the game had been a big surprise to everyone.

Reporters had tried hard to learn the reason an all-pro had walked away from a six-figure salary, but they weren't able to get anything out of

Richards. He had disappeared into northern Idaho, and Herb tracked him down in a little town near Spokane.

As he sat on a sofa in Richards' living room, he found himself staring at the man. Richards wasn't carrying an extra pound and he still moved around the room with the same grace and agility he had shown while playing for San Francisco's last championship team.

He accepted the offer of an iced tea, and Richards brought him his drink in a tall glass that sparkled with cleanliness.

"So, Mr. Rojas, I see you and your friend have been shaking things up in Washington."

Herb sipped from his glass. "Then I assume you know why I'm here, Mr. Richards."

Richards nodded. "Please call me Joe."

"Thank you, Joe."

"Yes, Mr. Rojas, I know why you're here. You want me to play for your team."

"Right. How about it?"

"That won't be possible, Mr. Rojas."

"Excuse me?"

"I'm sorry, Mr. Rojas, but there is no force known to God or man strong enough to make me want to return to professional football."

"No disrespect intended, Joe," Herb said. "But aren't you rushing this a little? You haven't even heard what we would be willing to offer."

"I don't need to hear anything. There's nothing you could say or do that would make me want to play again. You could offer me a million dollars and I'd still say the same thing."

"Why? You can't possibly be making as much money at whatever it is you're doing. By the way, what is it you're doing?"

"Political organizing, Mr. Rojas."

"Huh?"

"Money simply isn't as important to me as it once was."

"Why?"

"It's worth almost any amount of money not to have to take showers with them again."

"Them?"

Richards seemed as if he was slipping into a reverie as he told his story. "I used to bring my own towels with me. The way they hand out towels in a locker room, you never know who used it before you, and no matter how hard you wash it, no matter how much soap and bleach you use, once one of them has used it, you can never quite get it clean enough."

"Them?"

Richards looked at Herb carefully, as if debating whether to explain himself. "Negroes, Mr. Rojas. I refuse to shower with Negroes."

Herb winced. This guy was trouble, but he had been an all-league safety. Maybe he was worth one more try. "Perhaps if we offered you private accommodations."

"They were all over the place, speaking their own language, going through their ritualistic handshakes, playing their oversized radios with that rhythmic drivel they call music."

"Maybe we could ..."

"Mr. Rojas, I don't think you're listening."

"There are steps we could take ..."

"I'm not going to sign with you."

"And as far as money goes, how could you turn down ..."

"Mr. Rojas, I can't seem to get through to you."

"We are more than willing ..."

"Dammit, man, I don't want to play football with jungle bunnies."

Herb nodded. "Mr. Richards, I respect your wishes."

"Thank you, Mr. Rojas."

"I wonder if I could ask you one more question, though."

"Certainly."

"You said you were doing political organizing." Richards nodded. "Who for?"

"I am a field organizer for the Aryan Alliance."

"Oh," Herb said in a small voice.

"By the way, Mr. Rojas," Richards said. "Exactly what nationality is the name Rojas?"

Herb hastily made his exit and spent the rest of the afternoon praying that no one else in the entire world ever got wind of that particular conversation.

Two days later he was in Hollywood, trying to land one of the biggest names on their list. Reginald "Roxy" Reese had been one of the greatest running backs in Association history before he had walked away from the game eight years ago at the age of twenty-seven.

In only five years of professional football, he had rushed for nearly eight thousand yards. His best single-season total of 1,887 in his fourth year was a league record that still stood.

He had walked away from the game at his peak as part of a bitter contract dispute with the owner of the Los Angeles franchise, refusing to play for "plantation" wages.

Every year since, there had been stories speculating on Reese's return, but every year since, the season had started and ended without the big running back in uniform.

Dave and Herb had both thought it a lost cause, wondering how they could possibly succeed where all the other teams had failed, but Kennedy had insisted they make the effort.

That was what had brought Herb Rojas to California, and that was what had kept him chasing Roxy Reese around southern California for the better part of two days.

"Look, man, I'm running late," Reese said. "If you wanna talk, you've gotta walk."

What Roxy Reese called walking, most people would call supersonic travel, and just keeping up with him taxed all of Herb's stamina. It was fairly obvious that a thirty-five year old Roxy Reese was still in pretty good condition.

All Herb wanted was half an hour or so to make his pitch, but Reese was setting a blistering pace. If he wasn't making a personal appearance, he was filming a commercial. When he wasn't making deals over lunch, he was making deals over his car phone.

It seemed that wherever Reese went, there was inevitably a camera -- either for a movie, an interview or an episode of his syndicated sports show, "Roxy Reese presents Legends, Legends, Legends."

"Well, Roxy," Herb wheezed in a rare slow moment. "It's good to know you're still in shape. You never stop running."

"Man, I've been runnin' all my life. I wouldn't know how to stop and I wouldn't know what to do if I did."

"Look, when we get to the limo, will you take the phone off the hook, turn down the stereo, roll up the windows and let me talk to you for a few minutes?"

"Sure, my man. Just let me make one phone call."

Reese's "one call" led to another, which led to a meeting in Bel Air, which led to yet another hurried trip to yet another office, which led to a banquet at a Pasadena hotel.

At some point during the evening, Herb lost sight of him in a crowd. He took a taxi back to his hotel and started the whole routine all over again the next morning.

Finally, at 5:30 a.m. on the third day, he was awakened by a call telling him to meet Reese in the hotel coffee shop if he wanted half an hour of uninterrupted time.

Herb brushed his teeth, passed his electric razor over his face a couple of times and washed his face. He knew he looked awful, but he didn't think Reese would mind.

The younger man pushed a cup of coffee across the table to Herb when he sat down. "All right, man. You've got half an hour. Speak your piece."

"Roxy, I would guess by now that you've had someone do a little research for you. I'd guess you know why I'm here."

"Sure," Reese said, grinning. "You're one of those dudes who hijacked the stockholders' meeting in Washington. You're the one who's going around the country signing up old players."

"Well, in a nutshell ..."

"I probably should have told you no right off," he said. "But I figured you'd appreciate the chance to spend a few days with a star like the Rox, not to mention tooling around glamorous Hollywood."

Reese had made the word "Hollywood" into three long, drawn-out syllables, and Herb smiled in spite of himself.

"Thanks, Roxy," he said.

"No problem, man."

"But as much as I appreciate your hospitality, I haven't been able to see much of anything but your dust."

Reese grinned. "Got to keep moving, man."

"But now you're going to hold still long enough for me to make my pitch, right?"

Reese nodded and motioned to Herb that he should speed it up. Herb took a deep breath and started talking. "I've been doing a little research myself," he said. "And I'm convinced of one thing, Roxy. You've got more of a future playing for us than you do out here."

That got Reese's attention quickly. "Say what?"

"That's right. You'd be better off playing football."

Reese looked at him strangely. "It's drugs, right? Some kind of junk that's warped your poor white-bread brain?"

Herb smiled at him, shaking his head.

"Then you've got to be crazy," he said. "What've you been doing the last two days? Look at me! I've got a limo, more babes than I can handle, a mansion in Malibu, a TV show, commercials, movies ..."

"Yeah," Herb said, trying his best to appear less impressed than he was. "That's right now. And maybe even next year, but can you tell me that four years from now you'll still have all that stuff? Sure, you're hot now, but people forget quickly and they're already starting to forget about you."

"Man ..."

"And the longer you're away from the game, the faster they'll forget you. It's already started, hasn't it? New South Airlines dropped you last month, didn't they? And Bronze God Aftershave switched over to that young basketball player."

"Hey, man, both those companies decided to try new campaigns. Is that my fault?"

"I don't know," Herb said. "Maybe if you were a better salesman, they wouldn't have switched. If people forget who you are, you won't be able to sell fur coats to Eskimos."

"I'm still doing Bruiser Jeans."

"For two-thirds the money they paid you last year," Herb said. "Like I told you, I did a little research. And what about your television show? Any new stations pick it up this year? In fact, didn't three of the ones you've got drop you for this season?"

"Yeah," Reese snorted. "Cheyenne, Little Rock and Colorado Springs. Real important markets. Probably wanted to put on another preacher."

"Didn't you go to college at Arkansas A&M, Roxy?"

"Yeah, so what?"

"Hell, if the state you played college ball in is already dumping you, what does that tell you?"

"What's it supposed to tell me?"

"You figure it out," Herb said. "By the way, I understand the producers are bringing in Lisa Sullivan, aren't they?"

"They figure I need a co-host to help me with the women's sports. You know, tennis, swimming, that sort of stuff."

"I tell you, Roxy, it's happening already. This year they bring in a girl, next year they'll bring in a hockey player or a golfer and before you even know what's hit you, you're on your way out the door."

"Who cares about that, anyway? That's just small time. The big bucks come from the movies, and I got half a million for my last one. Don't tell me I've got no future in movies. Anybody offer you half a million bucks lately?"

"Nope, and I don't blame you for taking it, either. But let's look at a little reality, OK?"

Reese nodded. He seemed almost fascinated by what he was hearing.

"Roxy, your pictures are cheap little exploitation movies. They shoot 'em in a month, edit 'em in a week and get 'em out fast. They're in the theatres for two weeks and the video stores a month later. The biggest expense in the budget is your salary."

Reese nodded again.

"And gee, what classics they are. Trouble Man. Riot Man. And my personal favorite, Trouble Man Meets Riot Man."

"Hey, that was a tough one. I had to play two roles."

"I'm surprised you didn't win an Oscar. By the way, where did that picture open?"

"Uh, I don't exactly ..."

"Sure you do, Roxy. Research, research, research. It opened at a drive-in in Dallas, and only there because you used to play for the Cougars."

"Man, get to the point! Your half hour's almost up."

"All right, here it is. I want you to come to Washington and play fullback for the Warriors. All I want is six months of the year. You'll have the other six to make your movies, your commercials and whatever else you want to do."

"You're talking about me going back into football and getting my chops busted."

"I'm talking about getting you back into the spotlight for real," Herb said. "Try this out for size -- Roxy Reese returns to the game he loves, gives up his successful Hollywood career to play football again."

"Shit," Reese said, stretching the word into four syllables.

Herb shook it off. "Look, Roxy, whether or not the Warriors make it to the Championship Bowl, or even the playoffs, we're going to be the biggest story in sports this year. Every reporter in the country will be writing stories about the old men who came back to the game, and you'll be the one they'll all be writing about first."

Reese snorted.

"One year with us and you'll be a real star, not some cheap celebrity only known to the people who go to drive-ins."

"You're a good talker, I'll give you that much."

Herb smiled.

"But I want some time to think about this," Reese said. "I want to talk this over with my agent."

Herb shook his head. "No, Roxy, don't let anyone talk you out of this, and don't even talk to anyone. Just think about it. Just listen to your heart. I want you to come back and play because it's the best thing for you."

Reese stared at him.

"It's Wednesday now," Herb said. "I'll leave a first-class ticket for you at LAX on the Monday morning flight to Washington. Don't worry about money. We'll pay you what you're worth, but don't come back for the bucks. Come back because you love the game."

Reese exhaled loudly. "Shee-it," he said. "Now it's really getting deep in here. Any time I hear a general manager talking to me about loving the game, I reach down and make sure I've still got my wallet."

"I don't want your money, Roxy." Herb looked him in the eye. "I want you to be our fullback."

"Well, man, I'll think about it."

11

With Reese out of the way, Herb got onto yet another flight and crossed the country to Charlotte, North Carolina, in search of Tony Ross. He found him in a car dealership on the north side of the city.

Charlotte was booming, a perfect model of Sun Belt expansion, and Carolina Motors obviously was sharing in the prosperity. The showroom was state-of-the-art, with computer terminals on every salesman's desk and plush chairs and sofas for customers.

Almost before Herb's eyes had scanned the room, a salesman was at his elbow.

"Good afternoon, sir," the blow-dried young man said unctuously. "And what are you looking for today?"

"Just some information."

"Well, then, how about this baby here?" the salesman asked as he guided Herb to one of the new yuppified convertibles. "It's just off the line, and it's a gutsy little four-cylinder that's designed to take you back to the sixties just like that."

"Uh, thanks, but I'm looking for somebody. Tony Ross."

The salesman's mood cooled noticeably. "Tony? That's his desk over there. The messy one."

Herb glanced at Ross' desk. Unlike all the others in the room, which looked as if the cleaning crew had just finished with them, the one belonging to Tony Ross was covered with order forms, phone numbers and other information jotted down on random scraps of paper.

"He's out with a couple of prospects right now. Have a seat. He'll be back any minute."

"Thanks," Herb said. "By the way, just how good a salesman is Tony Ross?"

"Can't you tell?" The salesman's tone was definitely envious. "Listen, he's the best thing that ever happened to this place. People find out they're talking to the famous Tony Ross, the guy who caught 102 passes in a single season, the guy who made The Catch to put Philadelphia in the Championship Bowl ..."

"Yeah?"

"They forget everything else, including the fact that they were only here to look at a car. The last two months, Tony Ross has sold more cars than every other salesman combined."

Herb was confused. "Why are you telling me this?"

"Because I hate the bastard!" the salesman said, venom slipping past his smooth veneer. "I haven't had a decent commission since he got here, and besides ..."

Tony Ross chose that moment to come strolling through the showroom doors, a man and woman in tow who were distinguished only by the starry look in their eyes.

The salesman with Herb muttered, "I can just hear them six months from now. 'Sure, it's a lousy car, honey, but remember who sold it to us?' They'll never get rid of the damn thing."

By Herb's estimate, Ross stood about six-three and he had a definite presence about him. All the great ones seemed to have it. Roxy Reese had, and to a lesser extent, so had Jimmy Gardner. Herb was beginning to feel like he could pick out the former pro football players in any crowd.

Ross still looked to be in reasonably good shape, considering it had been nearly two and a half years since he announced his retirement after the greatest season of what everyone had assumed would be a much longer career. He was starting to develop a bit of a paunch, but he still looked better than any other man in the room.

"Now, Mr. Murphy, why don't you and the little lady" -- he flashed a wink at the man's young wife -- "just sit down here and we'll work up the bill of sale. Wasn't that one sweet little car? How about the way she moved in and out of those curves?"

Ross glanced again at the woman. Herb thought he was being incredibly obvious, but the woman's husband didn't even seem to notice.

The salesman at Herb's side hissed a whisper into his ear. "Will you look at that guy operate! Those people have been coming in here for six months, and not one of us could close a deal with him. Just twenty minutes with Touchdown Tony and the guy's rolling over and begging Ross to scratch his belly."

"Now, Mr. Murphy, how much did you say you were hoping to get for your old Buick?"

The man smiled. "Oh, whatever's fair, Mr. Ross."

The younger salesman took Herb by the arm and directed him away from Ross' desk. "Whatever's fair," he hissed sarcastically. "Of course a fine upstanding young man who played the fine upstanding game of football for the fine upstanding NAFA would never cheat anyone on their trade-in."

"He's good, all right," Herb said.

"Look, mister, do us all a favor. Hire him. I can spot another car dealer a mile away, and take my word for it, you'll be getting yourself one helluva salesman. But hire him, please, before I kill him."

You and what army, Herb thought.

"Please hire him."

Herb expected the man to sink to his knees and throw his arms around his waist.

"Thanks, I think," he said.

"You can wait for him here in the lounge. I'll send him in here as soon as he's finished scratching Mr. Murphy's belly."

He all but pushed Herb into the lounge, which apparently was a shrine to the football career of Tony Ross. It almost took Herb's breath away. There were pictures of Tony running with the football, pictures of him catching the football, pictures of him pouring champagne over various coaches' heads.

One entire wall was a blowup of The Catch, a 45-yard leaping grab that had stunned unbeaten Miami on the final play of the game to put Philadelphia into the Championship Bowl in Ross' rookie season.

There were charts of Ross' career statistics, and in case anyone still hadn't gotten the point, there was a banner hanging from the ceiling.

"Meet former NAFA superstar

"TOUCHDOWN" TONY ROSS

"Now at Carolina Motors"

Ten minutes later, Tony Ross strolled into the room. "Hi," he said. "I'm Tony Ross. And you're ..."

"Herb Rojas," he said, taking the hand offered him.

"Nice to meet you, Herb. How's it going? Well, Jackie told me you were looking for me. You're not with the DA's office, are you?" Ross chuckled nervously.

"No, I'm ..."

"Sorry it took so long, but those folks just wouldn't let me go. They had to talk to Tony Ross, and nobody else would do. She was such a cutie, wasn't she? And sweet on me. I can tell that kind of thing."

Herb nodded as Ross continued his monologue.

"Not that I minded." He winked at Herb. "Those fuzzy ol' sweaters. Whoa! Can't resist 'em, especially the ones that dip down on both sides. So we went out for a test drive, you know, and all three of us were sitting in the front seat. You know that car, there's hardly enough room for two in there, and she was rubbing her leg up against mine. Then her old man had to make a pit stop ..."

"Mr. Ross, why are you telling me this. I mean it's a cute story, but ..."

Ross shrugged. "Just being friendly, that's all."

"Well, I appreciate that. Say, she was built, wasn't she?"

"Just the way I like 'em. Big and round and firm. Just sort of standing up there and defying gravity."

"Must have been one helluva pit stop."

"Yeah, well, he was gone about ten minutes. You know, once them boys get older it takes 'em longer. ... Anyway, you wanted to talk to me about something?"

Herb nodded. "Yeah, I did, but I'm not sure you'd want to give up what you've got here."

"Try me."

"Well, Tony, I'm one of the general managers of the Washington Warriors, and ..."

Herb was interrupted -- and a little shocked -- by a loud whoop of joy from Ross that echoed through the room. "All right!" he said. "I knew it! I knew someone would find me sooner or later!"

Ross was punching his fist into the air and doing a rather awkward-looking dance around the lounge.

Herb grinned. "Is it safe to assume you're glad to see me?"

"Herb, I have been waiting for you for two years. I'm so happy to see you that I could kiss you on the lips! Hot damn!"

Herb was a little confused. "What about all this you've got here? The big commissions? What about big and round and firm, standing up there and defying gravity?"

"Man, the last year I played ball, they paid me $250,000. I'd have to sell every car in Charlotte to make that kind of money."

"What about the, ah, fringe benefits?"

"The ladies? Well, sure, every now and then I get one like today, but mostly it's middle-aged married broads with cellulite looking for one last thrill. I'm used to faster company. You know ... cheerleaders, airline stewardesses, owners' daughters ... you know, table stuff."

"Owners' daughters?"

"Uh, well ... that's not ..."

"Which owner's daughter?"

Ross acted sheepish, but Herb figured he was actually dying to tell him. "Well ... Tracey Cagney."

"Stanley Cagney's girl? Your boss' daughter? The one who looks like ..."

"... like a young Cybill Shepherd." Ross grinned. "Tracey Cagney herself."

"Well," Herb said. "I guess that answers my next question about the sudden retirement."

"Yeah, I was given a choice -- retirement or a lead role in the Vienna Boys Choir."

"Oh."

Ross seemed confused. "You mean you never heard of it? I thought it was all over the Association. Man, I got blacklisted. Nobody would touch me. I couldn't even get anybody to take my friggin' phone calls."

Herb laughed. "Tony, as far as I'm concerned, you can make it with anyone you want as long as you can catch passes as well as you throw them. I don't care who you spend your nights with. All I care about is how long it'll take you to get back into something resembling your own form and how much all this is going to cost me."

"Man, I'd play the games for free."

"For free?"

Ross grinned as if he was about to recite the punchline to an old joke. "Of course, you'll have to pay me a lot to practice."

Herb jumped at the chance to top him. "All right, then," he said. "Keep working here six days a week and just show up for the games."

Ross laughed. "You've got yourself a wideout, man."

12

While Herb had been meeting with the former stars of the NAFA, Dave's job had been more mundane. He had spent his time going from small town to small town, seeing sometimes as many as two or three would-be players a day.

He didn't have to do much convincing. Nearly everyone he talked with still dreamed of a shot at playing in the NAFA, and most of them had stayed in shape waiting for calls only they believed would someday come.

Few of them had jobs that were too good to quit, and Dave was reminded of the line that if you reached a certain age and still had a job that involved wearing a name tag, you might want to think about a career change.

Most were working as salesmen or mechanics.

A couple were gym teachers.

Only two men turned him down. They had married and settled down, and didn't feel they could afford to disrupt their lives. Dave understood, telling them the door would remain open if they changed their minds.

For the most part, though, when he found men who might have a chance to make the team, he found men who wanted desperately to give it a try.

His very last trip, one he had added at the last minute, was to a small town called Bearstown, West Virginia, way up in the Appalachian Mountains. It was the worst trip of all. No airlines flew into Bearstown, and the nearest Amtrak station was an hour away.

Dave didn't like to drive in the mountains all that much, but he rented a car and drove up from Charleston.

Only three hundred people lived in Bearstown, and Dave figured every one of them must be in the high school gymnasium that Saturday evening. The sign outside had advertised "World Championship Wrestling Tonite," but Bearstown looked to be as unlikely a place as there ever could be for anything affecting the entire world to be decided.

"You a cop?" the bouncer outside the dressing room asked Dave during the performance.

"No."

"Private detective?"

"No."

"Skip tracer?"

"Not hardly," Dave said. "Look, what's with all the questions?"

"It's for your own protection, buddy. Last guy who came in to see the Adonis boys was trying to collect an old hotel bill and, well, things got a little messy."

"Messy?"

"Romeo Adonis threw the guy out of a second-story window. Good thing it was summer and they'd filled the pool."

Dave swallowed hard. He certainly hadn't expected this part of his job to involve potential physical danger.

"Don't worry, buddy. They ought to be in a pretty good mood tonight. They're gonna win."

"Do they get real upset when they lose?"

"Nah, not really. Mostly they get upset when somebody double crosses 'em. Like last week, when they were fighting the Blues Brothers -- Ronnie and Jessie Blue -- and the script said the Adonis boys were gonna win. The Blues thought they were supposed to win, though, and it got a little ..."

"Messy?"

"Yeah, messy."

"Lots of blood in the ring, huh?"

"Nope, the dressing room," the bouncer said. "The Blues boys decided to quit wrestling and go back to being prison guards. Well, they should have known better. The Adonis Brothers don't like to get messed with."

"So it seems."

"They should be finished in a few minutes. Just sit right here and wait."

"Any suggestions for dealing with them?"

"Yeah. Smile a lot and don't make any real sudden moves."

"I'll remember that."

Dave had learned of the Amazing Adonis Brothers from a friend who subscribed to every wrestling magazine published. Alphonse Adonis and his brother Romeo were the headliners of the Appalachian Worldwide Professional Championship Wrestling Association. Their press releases said they weighed in at 385 pounds each, and they reportedly stood six-eight in their stocking feet.

Bearstown was their hometown, and they had made such a name for themselves in the tiny mountain community that they had been recruited to play defensive line for West Virginia Technical College, thirty miles away.

The day they left for college was the first time either of them ever had been outside their home county. It was the first time Romeo had worn shoes.

In their one season of college football, they had become the most feared linemen in the history of the Mountain Community College Conference. Unfortunately, neither ever had developed even rudimentary academic skills, and no amount of tutoring and coaching was able to raise their grade-point average above a combined zero point zero.

With only one season of college football -- at a very small college -- they never received the exposure necessary to be noticed by the scouts of the North American Football Association.

They had managed, however, to catch the attention of Carmine "Little Remo" Romano, the commissioner/owner/promoter of the Appalachian Worldwide Professional Championship Wrestling Association, who could recognize a potentially great tag team when he saw one.

The Adonis Brothers, too proud to return home as failures and all too susceptible to a sales pitch, signed on to wrestle.

The voice seemed to boom down from the clouds. "You the guy wants to talk to us?"

Dave sat up with a start. The twin behemoths standing in front of him were managing to block out most of the light and air in the room.

"Uh, yes," he said, smiling and slowly extending his hand. "I'm Dave Krause and I'm with the Washington Warriors."

"The Warriors?" asked Romeo.

"You mean the football team?" asked Alphonse.

Dave made a mental note to restrict his conversation to words of two syllables or less.

"What do you want to talk to us about?"

"Well, guys ... by the way, which one of you is which?"

"I'm Romeo," the mountain on the left said. "He's Alphonse."

"I let Romeo do most of the talking," the mountain on the right said. "Mom said he's the one who got the brains."

Dave tried not to think about what it must be like to be the less intelligent Adonis brother.

"Do you want to talk to us about football?" Romeo asked. "We used to play football."

"We played defense."

"On the line."

"We used to tackle the quarterback."

"All the time."

"Uh, yeah," Dave said. "Listen, Alphonse ..."

"I'm Romeo. He's Alphonse. The ugly one."

"Hey," Alphonse said. "Play fair!"

"Boys, how would you like to get paid to tackle the quarterback?"

"Like in school?"

"Yeah," Dave said. "Only better. You won't have to go to classes."

"Classes?" Alphonse seemed confused.

"Never mind. We'll pay you to play football."

"We haven't played for a long time," Romeo said.

"Maybe we forgot how," Alphonse added.

"Nah," Dave said. "It's got to be something you never forget, like riding a bicycle."

"We never had a bicycle. We were too big."

"Yeah, we played football."

"Our daddy used to tell us to learn how to play football," Romeo said. "He told us we couldn't work in the mines because we were too big. He said we'd never be too big to play football."

Amazing, Dave thought. They both look like Hulk Hogan and talk like Peewee Herman. "Your father sounds like a very wise man."

"He was a dope," Alphonse said.

"Yeah," Romeo said. "Do we look like we're playing football now?"

13

Duncan Charles was beginning to become bored with his job as president of the Chicago Trojans. To his mind, he was accomplishing nothing at all.

He had signed no free agent superstars. He had been involved with no negotiations with agents or the players they represented. He had not even been able to send ripples of terror through the community by threatening to move the team thousands of miles away.

Every time he found something to complain about in his contract with the city of Chicago, the city fathers bent over backwards to make him happy. In the space of a month, they had leveled two city blocks near Daley Stadium to expand the parking lots, they had cut the amusement tax in half so that Duncan could coax more profits from ticket sales and they had promised to build him a new stadium within three years.

His new stadium would be built at a cost of three hundred million dollars, and would not be shared with either of the city's baseball teams. It would have a dome, state-of-the-art luxury boxes, and best of all, it wouldn't cost the team a dime to build.

The Trojans would be allowed to rent the stadium, which would be named after David Charles, for one dollar a year.

All that that had succeeded in doing was making Duncan even more miserable. What was the use of owning a football team if he couldn't get his name in the papers?

He took some small consolation in the fact that the box office was running at peak efficiency. Ticket orders were being filled faster and with fewer errors.

The Trojans had the smoothest-running box office in the entire Association.

"Well, congratulations, kid," Martini said, strolling into his office. "The box office just set another record. They filled a twenty-five ticket order for a Kiwanis group in Evanston in fifty-three seconds."

"Terrific," Duncan said drily.

"Look, don't get sarcastic with me. I happen to think those folks in that office are doing one hell of a job. It's something you should be proud of."

"Yeah, sure."

"By the way, did you get a call from Willie Arbuckle in Kansas City?"

Duncan thought for a minute. "Oh, yeah. He wanted to trade me Chico Coleman for a couple of draft choices and cash."

"Well, good. I'm glad that's all arranged."

"Oh, nothing's arranged, Ray. I turned him down~."

Ray Martini jumped to his feet. "You did what!?"

Duncan shrank back in his chair. "He wanted two of my draft choices, Ray."

"Are you nuts? Chico Coleman's just about the best running back in that division!"

"Yeah, but you told me I'm getting Willis Waller in the draft. What do I
need with two running backs?"

Martini slapped his forehead, an action Duncan had previously seen only
in Saturday morning cartoons. "Duncan. Kid. Listen to me now," he said
in calm, measured tones, as if he were lecturing a particularly slow child.
"Willis Waller is a scatback. A finesse runner. He dances around the defense
looking for openings, and once he gets into the open he's hell on wheels."

"Uh huh?"

"Chico Coleman is a big, nasty fullback who knocks people down so they'll
stay down, and Waller's going to need that kind of blocking. Capische?"

Duncan nodded.

"Plus, when it's third and goal at the one, you're gonna need a guy like
Chico Coleman to bull his way into the end zone. He'll make Waller twice
the runner he is. Jeez, kid, you're being offered a dream backfield and you
turn it down?"

"Ray, he wanted money, too. A lot of money."

"A hundred thousand, right?"

"Right."

"Kid, you'll spend more than that on the asphalt in the parking lot. You're
being offered a fullback for tip money."

"Well," Duncan said, a little edgily. "It is my team, isn't it?"

Martini sighed. "Of course it's your team," he said after a suitable pause.
"I'm just trying to help you get to the Championship Bowl. Remember
what I told you that people were going to be offering you some sweetheart
deals?"

"You mean this is one of them?"

Martini threw up his hands in disgust. "They're all going to be those kind of deals! Any time somebody in the Association calls you with a deal, remember that."

"Uh oh."

"Yeah," Martini said sarcastically. "Uh oh."

"What am I going to do now, Ray? I screwed it up. Now we won't go to the Championship Bowl."

Martini smiled. This was the Duncan Charles he knew he could handle. "Kid?"

"Yeah, Ray?"

"I think I might be able to straighten things out. Would you like me to call Willie and see if he'll still make the deal?"

"Would you, Ray?"

Martini leaned across Duncan's desk and pushed the button on the intercom. "Patty, get me Willie Arbuckle in Kansas City."

"Gosh, Ray," Duncan said, getting up from his desk to allow Martini to sit down and conduct his business. "I'm sorry. I just didn't know ..."

"That's OK, kid," Martini said. He sounded almost friendly again, and he resisted the temptation to reach out and muss Duncan's hair as if he were a small child. "No harm done, I think. But you've got to ... Willie! Hi! Ray Martini in Chicago."

He pushed a button to put the call on the speakerphone so that Duncan could hear the entire conversation, and Willie Arbuckle's voice boomed through the room.

"Ray, you old reprobate! I had a feeling I'd be hearing from you. Say, what the hell you got going on up there? That boy told me he didn't want to make the deal."

"I'm sorry, Willie, but you know how hard it is to get used to the ways of the Association. Duncan's just a little new at it, that's all. Anyway, we do want the deal, Willie."

"Fine, Ray, but tell your boy that next time I might not be so patient. I can't spend my valuable time wet-nursing little boys on the Association's procedures."

"I understand, Willie, and I appreciate your patience. Now tell me, what kind of draft choices were we talking about with this deal?"

"Well, Ray, Frank here suggested that a fifth-rounder this year and a second next year would be suitable."

"Sounds fine from this end. Frankie's a good liaison, and I've never known him to make a bad deal in his life."

"Yeah," Arbuckle said. "He's a crafty ol' boy, all right."

"He sure is. By the way, say hello to him from me, the next time you see him. So we're set?"

"I'll have Chico on the plane tomorrow. My best to Lisa."

"Great. Thanks, Willie."

Martini replaced the phone in the cradle.

"Who's Lisa, Ray?"

"Lisa's my wife, kid."

"I didn't know you were married."

"Yeah, she's been putting up with me for eighteen years."

Duncan hugged himself and rocked back on the sofa. "I'd really like to meet her sometime."

Martini sighed. Wonderful, he thought, I just get him the dream backfield and he wants to meet my wife. "Sure, kid."

With the draft only two weeks away, Duncan was starting to get excited. He made up charts predicting who every team would draft and what the acquisitions would do to their rosters.

He plotted contingencies and made mock trades. He was enjoying himself more than he had since he'd been part of a Strat-o-Matic league as a child.

"This is fun, Ray," he said.

"Yeah, kid. Fun."

"Can we make some more trades? Can we? Can we?"

Martini sat on the edge of his desk. His face clouded over with what Duncan was coming to think of as "The Look," and Duncan knew he had made another mistake.

"I wish I didn't have to keep going over this every other week, Duncan, but you seem to be kind of a slow learner. You will make trades when the System says you will make trades and not a moment before."

Duncan nodded glumly.

"I've told you before that you are not to initiate any trades. People are going to call and offer you sweetheart deals and you are going to accept them."

"All right, Ray."

"Until that happens, you will sit in your big office and collect your paycheck, which, I might remind you, is a pretty good little paycheck."

"It pays my bills."

"You're goddamn right it pays your bills," Martini said. "It's a great little paycheck and you know why? Because the Association knows what it's doing. You start getting your nose in things and you might screw up the System!"

"You and that stupid System! Washington's signing up players left and right! They're always getting their names in the papers! Look at this!"

He handed Martini a copy of The Sporting News, folded open to a story titled, "What's Up In Washington?"

"Look at that, Ray," he said. "They're writing about those guys in Washington and they're not even the owners. I haven't seen any stories about me yet. Are you telling me those guys are part of the System?"

"All I can say is the commissioner wouldn't be letting them do what they're doing if it would mess up the System. Look, kid, you'll be making trades. Big ones."

"Really, Ray?"

"Really. You'll be talking on the phone so much you'll think the receiver's a part of your damn ear. People are going to call you up and offer you trades and you're going to accept them. All you've got to do is say yes. It's all part of the System."

14

Herb wasn't overly familiar with television studios. He'd been in the audience of a children's show once, watching nervously as an orange-haired man in a clown suit performed various forms of emotional abuse on hyperactive children.

He knew the single local station in Lukhardt, North Carolina, wouldn't have the equipment or facilities of any of the Washington, D.C., stations, but he was still surprised to find a studio only slightly larger than the living room of his own home.

There were only two cameras, and one of them was sitting unused off at the side. The other was focused on a tiny set in front of a light blue curtain, and upon the two men and one middle-aged woman sitting behind the set.

"Well, Linda, that's an interesting story about the All-County Bakeoff. Now, with the sports news, here's the former all-Association defensive back with the Denver Mountaineers, Scott Trent."

"Thanks, Larry. Hello, anybody. It was another exciting day in Lukhardt today as the Jesse Helms High School baseball team held tryouts ..."

Herb was doubly surprised by Trent's performance. He remembered the former Mountaineer's style on the field as one of grace and flashiness.

Trent had been known throughout the Association as a player who played to the crowd, waving and pointing, flashing a toothy grin when the cameras were focused on him and generally testifying to the fact that he was one of the most dashing players anywhere and he knew it.

As a sportscaster, he was quite the opposite. Where his off-the-field wardrobe had been both striking and glamorous, it now consisted of a navy blue blazer, a white shirt, a navy blue tie and, Herb assumed, gray slacks. Where once he had possessed a personality that filled entire rooms, now he seemed as charismatic as a loaf of white bread.

He spoke in a clear voice, almost a monotone, as if he were reading the script phonetically. In short, Scott Trent was boring.

The newscast finally ended with a story about an old man who had dug a moat around his house and probably would have preferred not to be interviewed. The anchorman nodded at Trent, who collected his script and walked off the set.

"Mr. Trent?"

"Yeah? Look, I'm not giving autographs."

"I'm not taking any," Herb said. "I'm Herb Rojas and I work for the Washington Warriors. Can I get a minute or two of your time?"

"Well, I'm in kind of a hurry," Trent said. "I'm on my way out to the girls' softball tournament at the YWCA, but you can ride along if you want."

Trent was full of surprises, Herb thought as he opened the passenger door of a Geo Metro.

"Scott, is this your car?"

"Yeah, man."

"What happened to the Mercedes with the fur upholstery?"

Trent laughed. "It's kind of hard to keep up the payments on a machine like that when they're paying you three hundred dollars a week. Anyway, there's nobody in Lukhardt who can even spell Mercedes, much less fix one."

Trent flashed a smile, much like the ones Herb recalled from the old days. There's that old Scott Trent style, he thought. Why doesn't it show up in the studio?

"Uh, Scott ..."

"Yeah?"

"Those were some real interesting stories you did in there, and far be it from me to criticize, but did you know you forgot to give about two-thirds of the baseball scores?"

"I didn't forget. I just didn't give them."

"Why not?"

"Nobody around here gives a damn about anything that doesn't happen around here, and I give 'em what they want."

"Little League scores."

"Uh huh, that's right, and tryouts at the high school and softball tournaments."

"But ..."

"Hey, man, when it's football season they care about the North Carolina colleges, and how the Atlanta team in the Association's doing, but mostly they'd rather see how little Johnny Johnson pitched a two-hitter for Helms High."

Herb noticed a certain tone in Trent's voice. "You don't much like these people around here, do you?"

"Let's just say they lack a certain level of sophistication and leave it at that."

"Then why bother?"

"Hey, man. I've gotta eat."

"You can't eat much on three hundred a week."

"Yeah, well, that's just for now."

"It doesn't have to be. You can make ten times that much playing football."

"I was wondering when you were going to get around to that."

"You know who I am, then?"

"Sure, man. I read the Sporting News. And what makes you think I can come back?"

"Your record. You were one helluva safety, and you don't look like you've lost too much."

"I only retired six months ago."

"Yeah, well, I've seen a lot of guys who didn't take even that long to go down the tubes."

"Listen, Herb, do me a favor and cut to the chase here."

"Sure, Scott, if you'll stop acting like I'm trying to steal your wallet."

"You are, sort of."

"Huh?"

"You're asking me to give up the career I've been working toward all my life and go back to something I didn't really enjoy all that much."

"Lukhardt, North Carolina, is what you've been working toward all your life?"

"Well, not Lukhardt, but ever since I was a little kid, I wanted to be on television. I happened to grow up with the ability to play football, but I always figured that playing football was the easiest way to break into television anyway. Look at Gifford, Summerall, Dierdorf. All of those guys used to play football."

"But giving Little League scores ..."

"It's a start. I've got it all planned out. I stay here a year, maybe two. Get to know the ropes, get comfortable with the camera. Then I work my way up to a bigger station, say in Charlotte or Raleigh. Eventually I'll make it to Washington or New York."

"But you could be in Washington right now," Herb said. "You could work part-time at one of the stations, and maybe do a little radio show on the side."

"Yeah, right, when I'm not getting my clock cleaned for the Warriors. No, thanks. I've had enough of all that. Look, there's no way I can miss. I used to be a football hero, and when they heard I was ready to quit and go into television, this place jumped at the chance to get me. They didn't even ask for an audition tape like the others."

"I take it you're turning me down."

"Listen, pal, I've got it made here. Why should I bother getting my neck broken for a pitiful team like the Warriors?"

"So that's a no."

"Definitely. No."

Dave wasn't having much more success on his most recent trip, either, and when he checked in with his office, he found that his ex-wife had called at least ten times.

Talking with Muriel was right behind root canal work on his list of pleasurable experiences, but he knew if he didn't return her call, she'd never leave the secretaries alone.

His daughter Kim answered the phone. "Hi, daddy!"

"Hello, sugar. How's my princess?"

"Oh, just terrific. Where are you calling from? It sounds far away."

"Somewhere in Alabama. It's a town named after somebody's mule, or maybe it was a Civil War battle, I'm not exactly sure which."

"Alabama? That's gross!"

"That's pretty much what I thought, but there was supposed to be a kid down here who was a pretty good defensive tackle."

"Hey, daddy, I've been telling all the kids at school that you'll be able to give us free tickets and take us to the games and let us meet all those really fly guys you've been signing up ..."

"Sure, sweetheart. Can we talk about all that later? Is your mom there? She's been trying to get in touch with me."

"Oh, sure," Kim said. "I'll get her. See you when you get home?"

"First thing, sugar. Now let me talk to your mom."

"Sure, daddy." Kim didn't put the receiver down before screaming "MOM!" so loudly Dave thought he was in danger of permanent hearing loss. While he was pondering what a wonderful connection it was, his ex-wife came to the phone.

"Hello, David."

Great, he thought. She only calls me David when she's really steamed.

"Muriel, I got your messages."

"I've been calling you for three days."

"I just got the messages today," he said.

"Yes, well, where is the check?"

"The check?"

"Your child support check for June?"

He tried to remember if he had mailed it, and decided he probably had been too wrapped up in the Warriors to remember.

"Look, Muriel," he said in a conciliatory tone. "I might have forgotten. I've been out on the road, talking to a lot of people. I've had a lot on my mind."

"I've got a lot on my mind, too, David. Like paying for your daughter's braces, like paying for her private school, like ... Well, like a lot of things. It's expensive to raise a teenage girl these days. I'm not fortunate enough to go gallivanting off around the country, staying in hotels and living on expense accounts."

"Muriel, it isn't like it's been some sort of pleasure cruise."

"Right."

"Seriously. Do you want to know what I did today?"

"Not really."

"I drove into some little town named after a mule that's no more than a gas station at an intersection where I have to find some kid who played at the high school two years ago. I'm lucky enough to find the kid pumping gas at the very same station, but I'm unlucky that he's consumed such large quantities of beer that he's got a gut the size of the late Junior Samples."

He paused to catch his breath.

"Anyway, all I get from him is directions to this other little pissant town that's big enough to have a motel that I assure you the Hiltons and Marriotts are not fighting to add to their chains ..."

He heard a cough that he knew didn't belong to his ex-wife.

"Well, it's true, dammit, and get off this line!"

He heard a click as the switchboard operator hung up.

"David, I will not be spoken to ..."

"Not you, Muriel," he said, sighing. "Anyway, yesterday I was in some other little pissant town asking about a defensive back named Murphy. He was a pretty good player who went off to Atlanta to try out for the Aces, but they said he couldn't play anymore. When I asked them why, they said he had a sex-change operation and was working in a beauty shop. Yeah, Muriel, it's been a helluva trip."

"I don't care, David. I really do not care. All I am concerned about is you fulfilling your obligations to your daughter. That child support check should have been here a week ago. I am waiting and waiting and waiting and ..."

"Dammit, Muriel! Hold on a minute. It's not like you've had to haul me into court or anything. Has the check ever been late before this -- in eight years?"

"Well, no."

"It's a little late this time," he said. "I'm sorry. I've had to concentrate on so many things lately that I forgot. I'll call the bank tomorrow and ask them to move the money into your account."

"What are you doing flying all over the place anyway? You haven't visited your daughter once since you took the job."

"I know ..."

"And what makes you think you know how to run a football team, anyway? No one around here thinks you're doing a good job. None of the papers think you've signed anybody decent, and everyone's asking why you don't hire somebody who knows that they're doing."

"Muriel, you don't read the sports section. Do you?"

"I can't help it," she said, almost in tears. "All these people keep shoving it under my nose. I go to work and some wise guy has put the paper on my desk and there's a column saying the Warriors are being run by the Three Stooges."

"The Three ..."

"David, what kind of self-image is your daughter going to have if people think her father runs around poking people in the eyes and hitting them over the head with hammers?"

Dave honestly had no answer for that one.

"Anyway, Muriel, I'm not flying around. I'm driving a rented Hyundai. Have you ever driven a rented Hyundai through Alabama?"

"Alabama? That's gross!"

15

Stan Pinello was getting used to frequent flights from Washington to New Orleans. It seemed that the commissioner wanted to be kept up to date on everything the Warriors were doing, and he didn't like to hear bad news over the phone.

"Pinello, I can read the papers," he said. "Tell me something I don't already know."

"Commissioner, there really isn't much to tell. Rojas has been wandering all around the country signing up a bunch of old ..."

"Is there a chance that any of these players they've signed are still under contract to other teams?"

"Unfortunately, no. All the men they've signed have been given their unconditional releases and have all passed through onto the Retired -- No Contract list."

"Damn! I never thought that would come back to haunt us. We used to hold rights to players with one team in perpetuity, but when the players started making noises about free agency and lawsuits, we threw them that as a bone. Of course, the only players who could be free agents were the ones too old to play anymore."

"Well, Commissioner, all the owners know the rules. They're not supposed to put a player on that list unless they're sure he can't play the game anymore."

"Do Mr. Krause and Mr. Rojas know that, Pinello? Have you made them aware of that small fact?"

"Well, not exactly" Pinello said. "They haven't been in their offices lately."

"Then who in God's name is running that team?"

"Uh, Rojas' father."

"His father?"

"Yes, sir. Roy Rojas. Sixty-six years old. Semi-retired. Works as a bartender in his son's bar ..."

"I don't want the man's life story, Pinello. I want to know what the hell he's doing running one of my franchises."

"They hired him as an executive assistant."

"Can they do that?"

Pinello knew the commissioner didn't really expect an answer to that question. "Actually, sir, he isn't doing a whole lot. Mostly he's having the stadium repainted and he's redecorating the executive offices. ... Commissioner, I wouldn't let him do anything that might hurt the Association."

"I certainly hope you are telling me the truth, Pinello. I'm sure you know what a critical year this is for the Association. We go into negotiations with the television networks this coming winter, and I want us to go in with the momentum of the most exciting season in the history of the game."

"I'm well aware of that, sir."

"It's all been worked out, Pinello, and we're expecting public enthusiasm to reach fever pitch."

"Well, sir, the study I commissioned isn't quite finished, but the preliminary report I received just before I left to come down here says that the changes that have occurred with the Warriors should have, at the very worst, a minimal effect on the System."

The commissioner glared at him. "I don't want them to have any effect on the System."

"Well, in that regard we're very lucky they're in the Liberty Conference East. Even with the players they've signed, they don't stand a chance of challenging Miami or Pittsburgh or Atlanta. They might beat out Boston, but at least in the report I have, the best they should be able to do is four victories and a tie for fourth place."

The commissioner relaxed a little and even managed a smile. "Only four victories?"

"That's right."

"Hell, they won four games last year. Are you trying to tell me they'll be no better than they were last year?"

"That's right, sir."

"Well, then I suppose we can let them keep it up. The antics of those gentlemen have gotten the Association a lot of free publicity at what is traditionally a slow time of year. But, Pinello ..." The commissioner swung his chair around and pointed at him. "... you had better make absolutely certain the situation doesn't get out of hand."

"All right, sir."

"I don't care if you have to move in with those guys. I don't care if you have to become Mr. Rojas' homosexual lover. Whatever it takes. I want to be informed of their every move."

Pinello wasn't gay, and it took only a moment's thought for him to decide that if he were he wouldn't be attracted to Herb Rojas. If there was one thing he knew, though, it was that the commissioner's orders were to be obeyed.

"Yes, sir," he said. "Whatever it takes."

He leaned conspiratorially on the corner of the commissioner's desk. "You know, sir, this might not turn out to be such a bad thing. There's been a bit of a groundswell of interest in the team. Their season ticket sales are up slightly and they have been getting a lot of media attention. I can't see how this could help but strengthen the franchise."

"That franchise," the commissioner said in such an icy voice that Pinello jumped off the desk and stood up straight, "was doing just fine the way it was. I have no intention of sacrificing the System, and all the carefully laid plans of this Association, so that ..."

The buzzing of the intercom interrupted him. "Yes?" he said.

"Excuse me, Commissioner, but you have an emergency call from John Levitt in Philadelphia."

"Oh, damn!" he said, picking up the phone. "What can it be this time? ... Hello, Levitt, what ... What? ... Holy Mother of God!"

The commissioner's face, despite his best efforts to the contrary, had gone ashen.

"Sweet Jesus, Pinello! Stanley Cagney just dropped dead!"

16

Stanley Cagney had amazed nearly everyone he met. People had constantly guessed his age as late forties or early fifties, and he always was amused to note their reaction when they learned he was sixty-eight.

They were even more amazed when he told them that he consumed immense amounts of alcohol, smoked three packs of cigarettes a day, never dieted or exercised and stayed out late nearly every night.

His doctors, who had warned him repeatedly about the cumulative effects of the abuse he was putting his body through, were the only ones left unsurprised when Stanley Cagney pulled the ultimate shocker on everyone and died.

Cagney was not married. He had left his wife thirty years ago. He had no brothers or sisters and only one surviving relative. When Stanley Cagney, the operator of the Philadelphia franchise of the NAFA, died, he left everything he owned to his daughter Tracey.

Tracey Cagney, age thirty-two, stood at the open grave watching as the mourners tossed in the traditional handful of dirt. She couldn't help but think how stupid a tradition it was to have people toss dirt into a hole in the ground.

The commissioner paid his respects and then came over to stand at her side. "Miss Cagney, first let me tell you what a tragic loss the passing of your father has meant to me and the other members of the Association."

"Thank you, Commissioner," she said, peering out from under her veil. It was the first time in her life Tracey had worn a veil, and she couldn't help but think what a stupid idea it was.

Even dressed in black mourning clothes, Tracey Cagney was a strikingly beautiful woman. In fact, the commissioner couldn't believe that his old friend Stanley could possibly have contributed half the genetic makeup of this tall, blonde-haired, full-breasted woman.

Perhaps she is adopted, he told himself. Perhaps she is masquerading as his child. Perhaps this incredible-looking woman has no claim at all on his estate.

The commissioner shuddered. Stop thinking irrationally. Insane thoughts for an insane situation, he thought. The first female franchise operator in the history of the Association.

"Miss Cagney?"

"Yes, Commissioner?"

"I would appreciate it if you could come down to New Orleans at your earliest convenience. There are a few things I would like to discuss with you."

She didn't ask why they couldn't just go have a beer and talk whatever it was over now. One didn't "have a beer" with the commissioner. One obeyed the Great Man's bidding.

"That's fine, Commissioner," she said. "I'll be in your office Tuesday."

A hundred miles to the south, Dave, Herb and Roy were meeting for the first time since Dave and Herb had left on what the Washington papers were calling "Gulliver's Travels."

"Well," Herb said. "Where do we start?"

"You guys have certainly raised a ruckus, that's for sure."

"Dad, a couple of stories in the paper doesn't necessarily qualify as a ruckus."

"Well," Roy said. "There hasn't been much in the papers, but on that guy Reynolds' radio show, that's all anybody wants to talk about."

"Roy, the Warriors are all anybody ever talks about on that show," Dave said. "Who'd you get, Herb?"

The younger Rojas checked his list.

"Jimmy Gardner and Tony Ross will be here," he said. "Scott Trent and Joe Richards were definite nos, and I've got a good feeling about Roxy Reese."

"Yeah?"

"Yeah," he said. "I think we'll see Mr. Reginald Reese. I've also got Billy Chadwick, Robinson Williams and Joe Stansberry."

"Not bad," Dave said.

"How about you?"

Dave shrugged. "I signed eleven guys, but I'll be surprised if half of them can make our team. There's two that you've got to see to believe."

"Who?"

"Alphonse and Romeo Adonis. The Amazing Adonis Brothers."

Roy snorted. "They sound like pro wrestlers."

"That's because they are pro wrestlers," Dave said. "But they are awesome physical specimens."

"Sounds interesting," Herb said. "So let's see, we've added maybe a dozen guys between us."

"Yeah, most of them out of shape and in no condition to survive a pro football training camp."

Roy broke into the conversation. "Don't forget our three draft picks. If we can come up with three solid players there, that'll make a total of fifteen additions to the team."

"That's not enough," Dave said.

Roy grinned. "You guys weren't the only ones who were busy," he said. "While you guys were running all around the country, I was doing a little constructive work myself."

"Yeah, dad, and by the way, the office looks great."

"Thanks, but that's not what I meant. I signed some players."

"You what?" Herb asked.

"Which part of that didn't you understand, Herb? Read your daddy's lips. I -- signed -- some -- players."

"Roy?" Dave asked cautiously. "Exactly who are these players you signed for our football team?"

"What you guys don't realize is that people are really fired up around here," Roy said. "I've had people calling me up every day and asking for tryouts."

"And you signed them?"

"Of course not. What do you take me for? I did tell them to come on out and try out, though. It's only fair."

"Open tryouts? Dad ..."

"And then I got in touch with a few people that you bright boys didn't think about and they all said they'd love to play for us."

"Like who, Roy?"

"Well, there's Bobo Anderson, Harry ..."

"You mean Bobo Anderson, Jr., right, dad?"

"Bobo has a son?" Roy asked.

Dave was stunned. "You signed the Bobo Anderson. The Hall of Fame defensive end?"

"Yeah," Roy said. "And Harry Yates, Big Bull Jefferson, Marty Simmons, Pete Reyanovich, Bubba Garenski ..."

"Oh my God, dad, you signed a bunch of old men!"

"Not that old," Roy said. "They're out on the field practicing now."

"Dear Lord in heaven!" Dave cried as he and Herb rushed to the window and looked out at the field. They were all out there in uniform, grunting, panting and wheezing as they tried to get up and down the field.

"Did any of the papers send a photographer today?" Herb asked.

"Now those guys," Roy said proudly, "were players! I remember Harry Yates taking the ball and running down the field ..." He pantomimed a broken-field run. "... back in the days before they had all those pads and helmets."

"Broken limbs," Herb said. "Broken limbs and brain damage."

Dave turned away from the window.

"Did they leave their walkers in the dressing room?" he asked drily. "Roy, these are old, old men. The average age must be fifty-five. We'll be lucky if half of them don't drop dead in the first practice."

"No problem. These guys all kept in shape."

"I can see it now," Herb said. "The papers won't even have to write a story. They'll just send a photographer and he'll take a picture of Big Bull Jefferson staggering down the field. Maybe a little caption under it -- Warriors sign new blood."

"We're going to be the laughing stocks of the league," Dave said.

"Actually, we already are," Herb said.

"Now wait a minute," Roy said. "You guys are getting all upset and I don't think I did anything so terrible."

"No," Herb said. "You just went out and signed up a bunch of guys who are going to have strokes on the field."

"Can you imagine the look on Ben Kennedy's face when he sees these guys?"

"I think Kennedy and Yates went to school together," Herb said.

"Maybe we can call them technical advisors."

Roy wasn't finished, though. "The old guys weren't the only ones I signed," he said. "There were a bunch of young guys who showed up. Guys like Buck Wilson."

"Roy, you didn't sign Buck Wilson."

"Yeah. He's only twenty-seven and he used to be a terrific linebacker."

"Dad, he's also a terrific junkie."

"And a terrific ex-convict."

"Oh, Jesus," Herb said. "Pinello is going to shit a brick."

"No problem. Wilson told me he doesn't do drugs anymore. He said he's been clean for close to two years now."

"Yeah, right."

"He wouldn't lie to me."

"Dad, get real. You probably still believe in the Easter Bunny if you believe that."

"Wait a minute, Herb," Dave said. "Maybe he is clean. I've seen it happen, and if he has kicked it, I seem to remember he was an outstanding linebacker."

"One of the best, but you know the league won't let him play."

"They might. They've been doing a lot of commercials lately about guys rehabilitating themselves."

"All right," Herb said. "Let's talk to him. And if he's really clean, and if he really wants to come back, we'll let him."

"And Roy, since you're so damn persuasive, we'll let you talk to Coach Kennedy about him."

"No problem," Roy said. "And while I'm at it, I'll talk to him about Bobo Anderson."

"Don't press your luck, dad."

The first thing Dave noticed about Buck Wilson was that he didn't look any the worse for wear. He had been a marvelous physical specimen for the two years he had played for the St. Louis Archers.

By the halfway point of his rookie year, he was already recognized as one of the best outside linebackers in the Association. In his second season he was selected as the top defensive player in the league.

It all started to fall apart shortly after that, though. After the second year of his four-year contract, he attempted to renegotiate. When the Archers turned him down, he refused to report to training camp. His walkout only lasted three weeks, but it was enough to turn public opinion against him.

The week before St. Louis opened the season, Wilson was stopped for a routine traffic violation. The highway patrol officer found unlicensed weapons, a large supply of cocaine and two fifteen-year-old girls in the car.

Wilson was in prison before the next Championship Bowl. He served three years before gaining parole under a new program designed to rehabilitate non-violent criminals.

Now he was sitting across the desk from Dave, wearing an expensive suit and a scowl.

"So, Buck, how are things these days?"

"Fine," Wilson said, looking evasively around the room.

"I just wanted to have a few words with you."

"Sure. Shoot."

"I just wanted to get to know you. Just wanted to see how you feel about, well, things."

"Drugs."

"Excuse me?"

"You want to know if I'm still on drugs. You want to know if this big buck nigga is still a junkie."

"Well ..."

"Look, I already told the geezer I'm off the stuff. What does it take to convince you people? I just want to play football."

"Really?"

"What do you mean, really? Damn, man, if I didn't want to play, I wouldn't be here."

"Buck, you're here because you know this team is the only one in the league that would even think about letting you try out."

"Yeah, well, so what?" Wilson said belligerently. "You need some defense and I'm it. I've been out of the league three years while I was in jail, and I worked out every fucking day of that three years. I've got something to prove!"

Wilson was standing now, jabbing his finger toward Dave to make his point. "Like I said, my man, I've got something to prove."

"What's that?"

"That I was the best, man. The one and only, absolute best linebacker in the world."

"You talk a good game, Buck. But I want to make sure you're serious. I mean, if we sign you, we will be making a substantial investment in you."

"It'll be worth it," Wilson muttered.

"It had better be."

"Man, if you had eleven Buck Wilsons out there, nobody'd ever score a point on you."

Dave smiled. "One more thing before you go. Most of the players on this team will be allowed to screw up once. In my mind, everybody deserves a second chance. Not you, though. If we sign you, the first time you slide back into your old habits, the first time I hear anything about you and drugs, you're history."

Wilson nodded curtly and then turned on his heel and left the room.

17

"Thank you, Miss Cagney, for coming here today."

The commissioner smiled his standard smile, the one that never touched his eyes, as he looked across the desk at the new operator of the Philadelphia Bulldogs. Tracey Cagney was dressed in a conservative black dress, as befitting her mourning for her father, but the commissioner noted that it didn't hide her spectacular figure.

All of a sudden the room seemed warmer, and the commissioner stifled an impulse to reach for his handkerchief and mop his brow.

"You're welcome, Commissioner," she said, crossing her left knee over her right. The commissioner almost moaned when he saw her legs. "All things considered, I felt it would be best to get this meeting out of the way so that we could resolve any problems you might have quickly."

"Well, Miss Cagney, there don't have to be any problems ..."

"If there weren't any problems, Commissioner, then what am I doing in New Orleans? Why the command performance?"

The commissioner smiled. "It's hardly a command performance. I only asked you to come at your convenience, Tracey."

"Excuse me, Commissioner. I don't think you know me well enough to call me Tracey."

The commissioner stiffened. "Very well, Miss Cagney. As I was saying to you in Philadelphia, all that I asked was that you come down at your convenience."

"Forgive me for correcting you, sir, but I believe you said I should come see you at my earliest convenience."

He nodded. "Whatever. The fact is that you are here and we can have our little conversation."

She motioned for him to continue.

"All right then, Miss Cagney, I understand your father left no provisions in his will for the transference of the franchise."

"English, please, Commissioner."

"He left no instructions for selling the team."

"He had no intention of selling the team, Commissioner. He left everything to me, as he always intended to do. I am the sole owner of the Philadelphia Bulldogs."

The commissioner smiled somewhat paternally. "Not exactly, Miss Cagney."

She shot him a questioning look.

"The Association owns the team. Your father, and every other franchise operator in the North American Football Association, leases the right to run their franchise."

"Are you telling me I don't own my team?"

"Technically that is correct. Now of course, as the sole heir to your father's estate, you have inherited the license to operate Philadelphia Football Inc. Of course you may continue to do so until such time as the Association decides otherwise~."

"And why on earth would that happen?"

"There are several possibilities, Miss Cagney. If we found you were operating the franchise in such a way as to damage the integrity of the Association. or if you weren't upholding the standards of the Association, or if our investigation were to turn up any sordid facts concerning your character ..."

"Investigation?"

"A formality, Miss Cagney, strictly a formality. Our security staff performs investigations on every prospective operator in the Association in order to satisfy our bylaws. Unless there is some sordid or vile episode in your past, there should be no problem here."

"Then there will be no problem," Stacey said coldly.

"That's good then, and of course John Levitt will be present to assist you."

"I was under the impression that my league liaison was nothing more than an advisor."

The commissioner smiled. Tracey Cagney was beginning to hate that smile. "Normally that is so, but with your relative inexperience in running a franchise, we feel it would be better if Mr. Levitt involved himself more on a day-to-day basis."

"Need I point out to you, Commissioner, that the Bulldogs already have a highly competent front-office staff. I mean, we are the current league champions."

"That is certainly true, but I knew your father well and he was extremely involved in the operation of his franchise. Mr. Levitt informed me that your father was personally involved in virtually every decision, and we feel it would ease your transition if Mr. Levitt stepped in and took your father's place."

"That dog won't hunt, Commissioner."

"Excuse me, Miss Cagney?"

"I should have been more clear," she said, her brown eyes flashing with a look her father had come to know well. "What I meant to say was no."

"No? I'm not sure I understand."

"What part of the word don't you understand, Commissioner? I'll explain. My father was devoted to nothing more than enjoying himself every waking hour. He stayed out all night, he slept until early afternoon and he spent a maximum of two hours a day in the office. That's it, Commissioner."

"Really?"

"That's right. Two hours a day. He came in, signed whatever papers the general manager gave him and then left. That's how my father ran his team."

"What are you trying to tell me, Miss Cagney?"

"I'm telling you that I have a very capable staff and that I do not need any interference from you, from Mr. Levitt or from anyone else."

The commissioner's tone was frigid. "I do not interfere, Miss Cagney. My office does not interfere, nor do my liaisons. The Association has certain interests that must be protected. There are goals that must be reached and standards that must be maintained."

"Goals?"

"It is the responsibility of each of the men I assign to the franchises to advise each of the operators how best to uphold those standards and goals. Mr. Levitt will protect you from the pitfalls that most certainly will arise and he will help you avoid possible violations of policy. He is not going to run your franchise."

"You're damn right he's not," she said in an equally icy tone.

"Miss Cagney, your father worked closely with Mr. Levitt for nine years, nine good years for the Bulldogs, and ..."

"Don't try to kid a kidder, Commissioner. I know how long they worked together and I know exactly what my father thought of Mr. Levitt. He told me. In fact, my father told me everything about the team and the Association."

The commissioner was appalled. Stanley Cagney had been one of the Association's insiders. He had helped to formulate the System and had been a charter member of the policy committee.

"Everything?" he asked.

Tracey smiled sweetly. "Yes, Commissioner, everything. My father taught me everything he knew about every aspect of running a team in the North American Football Association. I know personnel, I know public relations and I know the ins and outs of the politics of the league."

In spite of himself, the commissioner was impressed. He couldn't help remembering the last time he had a new operator in his office, and he compared the confident, competent Tracey Cagney with the inept Duncan Charles. If only she wasn't a woman, he thought.

There was no way he could come right out and ask her about the System. So he inquired obliquely, "And how do you think the Bulldogs will do this season?"

Tracey smiled her sweetest smile. "We plan to win the Championship Bowl."

The commissioner wanted to believe Stanley Cagney had not broken his sacred vow to keep the System secret. He wanted to believe that the beautiful young woman sitting across the desk from him wasn't privy to all the deepest secrets of the Association. He had known Cagney a long time, and he was relatively confident the System was still a secret.

He stood and extended his hand. "I think this has been a very productive conversation, Miss Cagney. We've managed to get some things out in the open and I think we have a better understanding of each other now. And please, please be assured we have only the best interests of your franchise at heart."

"Commissioner, may I speak freely?"

He wasn't sure he wanted to hear what she had to say, but he nodded.

"If I may be blunt, I'm getting pretty damned tired of the attitude you and your associates seem to have toward me. I'm not sure exactly what the problem is, but I think I can make a pretty good guess."

"Please, go on."

"You've never had a woman running one of your teams before and I'm certain that makes you uncomfortable. I'm sure you think I'm going to go out and change the team colors to puce and mauve, or that I'll draft players because they have cute asses. Well, above all else, I am my father's daughter, and you never had a better man in this league than Stanley Cagney."

In spite of himself, the commissioner found himself nodding agreement.

"And just like my father, I am planning on keeping Philadelphia at the very top of the league."

"Miss Cagney, I have no doubts as to your intentions. I am sure you want what is best for your franchise, which I believe had a profit of more than 68 million dollars last year."

"Sixty-eight million, eight hundred eighty-two thousand and six dollars, to be exact," she said.

"That's right," he said, impressed in spite of himself. "And I'm sure you want to make as much or more this year. But the Association is about more than just money. The Association is about a love of the game, about people who are truly devoted to football."

"Spare me, Commissioner. I've heard your little speech from my father."

The commissioner felt a stirring of rage, but he brought himself quickly under control. He was amazed to realize what he was feeling. A part of him wanted to throw Tracey Cagney out of his office and another part wanted to rip her clothes off and ravish her on his office floor.

Being a man with a reputation for prudence, he did neither. Instead, he shook her hand and she left his office. Five minutes later, John Levitt came in for instructions.

"That one's a hellion, isn't she, Commissioner? Just like her old man."

The commissioner nodded grimly. "I knew how to control her father. I don't think anyone in the world has ever controlled that young woman."

He sighed.

"And to think I thought this would be an easy year. To think I thought this was the kind of season I would just breeze right through."

18

There were already nearly a hundred would-be football players at the Washington Warriors' Oxon Hill training camp, with more arriving every day.

It seemed that every other able-bodied man within a hundred miles of the camp thought he could play professional football, and Roy Rojas' invitation to open tryouts had sounded the siren call.

Most realized right away that they were not up to the task. Some others left after a few days of grueling drills, while still others managed to make it through a full week before reaching the same conclusion and packing their bags.

Whatever the case, Benjamin Kennedy gave each man the same opportunity to prove himself, and each time he decided to cut a player, he spoke with that man individually and explained why the man wasn't good enough to play for the Warriors.

The result was a handful of unknown players who earned free agent contracts, and a large number of eighteen-hour workdays for Kennedy and his assistant coaches.

It was still four weeks until the July 1st opening of camp, and a week before the Association's annual draft of college players, but Kennedy was already in midseason form. He worked with the hopefuls from eight until four and then went into sessions with his coaches that lasted all evening and into the night.

He awakened at 6 a.m., and was in the dining room for breakfast when the first tired players dragged themselves in from the dormitory.

Breakfast always meant an informal team meeting, and that always meant a speech from the Iron Irishman.

"You are here again today, each and every one of you, from the twelve-year veteran to the young man named ..." Kennedy consulted his clipboard. "... Lester Brown who came in off the street yesterday evening, you are here to learn to play the game of football at a higher level than you have ever played it before."

Someone yawned.

"There is only one man in the world you have to impress -- me. You do not have to impress the reporters, or the photographers, or the pretty boys from the television stations. You are not here to make an impression upon these people ..."

"How about that lady reporter who keeps coming into the locker room?" quipped a young man with a beard from somewhere in the back of the room.

He received nothing more for his effort than an angry glare from the coach, silence from the other players and a mental note from Herb to buy the man a plane ticket home as quickly as possible.

"You are here," the coach continued, "to convince me that you have sufficient desire and talent to play some football for the Washington Warriors of the North American Football Association. The general managers -- Mr. Rojas and Mr. Krause -- will not be selecting this team. The press will not select this team, try though they may. Your mothers and fathers will not select this team."

Kennedy passed a stern glance over every seat in the cafeteria. "Gentlemen, I will select this team."

He paused only briefly before continuing. "I am looking for men who can block. I am looking for men who can catch, who can throw, who can run, who can tackle and who will do what I ask of them one hundred percent of the time.

"Some of you have played football before. A few of you have played for me. Some of you have tried to make it in this league and have failed. Many of you will have the same experience. Some of you already have decided that you cannot make it and are staying only for the free food and lodging. Some have already left. Good for them. They were not up to the challenges to their bodies and minds and they recognized their limitations.

"They are smarter and more courageous than those of you who are still fooling yourselves into believing you can play professional football."

As he said that, he selected certain members of his audience and looked them square in the face. Herb made several further mental notes concerning plane tickets.

"Gentlemen, I do not care one whit what you have done in the past," Kennedy said. "My only concern is your performance on the field today and tomorrow. All you have to do is prove to me you are football players."

Ben Kennedy sat down and looked solemnly at his clipboard. When they realized he was finished, the players dispersed to their various position meetings.

"Morning, Coach."

"Good morning, Mr. Rojas," Kennedy said without looking up from his clipboard.

"That was a pretty impressive speech, Coach. Do you give the same one every day?"

Kennedy looked up and spoke as if he were instructing a less-than-intelligent child. "No, Mr. Rojas, I do not. Were I to give the same speech every morning, I would have the men who have been here more than one day falling over unconscious with boredom."

"Well, I thought it was terrific. Knute Rockne would have been proud of you."

"I have no intention of aping the late Mr. Rockne," Kennedy said with obvious disgust.

Herb let that statement lie there for a few moments. "You don't like me much, do you, Coach?"

"I do not dislike you, Mr. Rojas, but I find you to be a loudmouthed, smart-alecky know-it-all who has convinced himself he can run a football team. A man who has convinced his friends they could do the same and now is trying to muddle through the process of mangling a valuable business on the strength of his personality. I do not dislike you, Mr. Rojas, but I certainly do not respect you."

"Now, Coach ..."

"If you were as smart as you believe yourself to be, you would have gone out and hired someone who knows a football from a soccer ball to run this team!"

"We were given a mandate to ..."

"Spare me the lecture, Mr. Rojas. I have read the minutes of the stockholders' meeting, and it is painfully obvious to me that you and Mr. Krause worked the crowd into a frenzy so that you could gain control of the team, for what reason I do not know, by promising to make contenders of the Washington Warriors."

"But ..."

"What have you accomplished so far?"

"We painted the stadium."

"Yes, I will give you credit for that," Kennedy said. "You painted the stadium a beautiful shade of blue, but what else have you done? You rounded up a collection of misfits and no-talents, men trying to recapture their long-forgotten youth, men who are generally as unfit a combination of untalented people as have ever set foot on a football field."

"Well, we signed ..."

"An old drunk of a quarterback, a playboy wide receiver and a couple of gorillas with single-digit IQ's."

"And Buck Wilson."

That stopped him. Ben Kennedy stared at Herb with such malevolence that Herb was certain he could feel two holes being burned through his skull.

"Buck Wilson? The drug addict? The convict?"

"Ex-drug addict. Ex-convict."

"Are those the depths we have lowered ourselves to, that we are now scouring the jails and the mental institutions for football players?"

Mental institutions? Herb wondered if there might be a source of talent they had overlooked.

"Buck Wilson served his time, Coach. He cleaned himself up and we are giving him no more of a chance than we gave you!"

Herb was almost shouting, but the coach responded in a much lower voice that was more in the nature of a growl.

"Do not ever use that line of argument with me, young man. You came to me. You asked me to coach this team and I agreed. Had you not done so, I am certain that sooner or later someone else would have."

"The hell they would! Do you know the kind of stink it raised with the Association when we filed the announcement of your hiring? Do you know how hard they looked for a way to make us take it back?"

"And you defended me, at great personal sacrifice, against the wolves howling at your door."

Herb nodded.

"Well," Kennedy said with frosty sarcasm, "thank you very much for entrusting me with this mess. Since I am probably the only man alive who can make some sense of this situation, I really don't think you had any choice."

"Jesus!"

"Mr. Rojas, I have asked you before not to take the name of our Savior in vain."

"Sorry," Herb said. "But if this situation is so fucked up, then why don't you quit?"

"Perhaps I will. I cannot in all honesty say I am happy with the way things have turned out."

"Oh, cut the crap, you old fart!"

Herb expected an angry reply. Instead, the coach stared silently at him for a few moments. "If you will excuse me, Mr. Rojas, I have a practice to conduct."

"What about Wilson?"

His emotion spent, Kennedy seemed almost indifferent. "I suppose he is no worse than the other men out there. We shall see."

"You'll let him try out, then?"

"I will allow it. I assume that you have already signed the man to a contract."

"Well, yes."

"Then send him to me, Mr. Rojas, and I will try to make a football player of him."

19

Fred Reynolds' column, The Washington Tribune, April 24:

"It's that time of year again.

"Tomorrow marks the day that the North American Football Association holds its annual college draft, and it's hard not to wonder why our local Washington Warriors even bother to attend. As in years before, the Warriors will sit and watch while the 23 other teams in the Association grab all the decent talent.

"Our illustrious general managers, Messrs. Krause and Rojas, have done their homework and they have a list of players they would like to draft, players who would fill some of the potholes on this team.

"The problem is, their predecessor, Wally Breakstone, traded away Washington's first two picks to Pittsburgh two years ago. In case you've forgotten who brought such a high price, does the name Bobby 'Batman' Brannigan ring your bell?

"I thought not. I'll help refresh your memory. Brannigan was a pretty good little running back at LSU and he showed a little spark with the Pistols. As soon as the Warriors traded for him, he racked up his knee and decided to pursue a less dangerous occupation.

"One could chalk it up to Washington's traditional disastrous luck with trades and draft picks, but the fact of the matter is that a healthy Brannigan was never worth the price the Warriors paid.

"Deals like that are becoming a Washington tradition, just like the Cherry Blossom Parade, and they have left Krause and Rojas with three picks -- a fourth, an eighth and an 11th-rounder.

"Don't ask me how the previous administration managed to trade their 12th-rounder to someone, but it's gone.

"With the three choices they have, they will be looking for offensive linemen and defensive backs. They desperately need a running back, but they've got more chance of Brannigan making a comeback than they do of getting someone this year.

"I do have one bit of unsolicited advice for my new friends. Draft a linebacker, because this reporter's Association sources tell him there's no way convict/all-star Buck Wilson will be allowed on the field this year.

"The official word out of Cajun-land is that Wilson is under investigation, but my guess is the commissioner will be playing linebacker for our Warriors before Wilson does.

"So wish our boys luck.

"They'll need it. Actually what they need is a miracle, but we should settle for luck."

Dave lowered his newspaper. "He's right, you know."

"Who?" Herb asked.

"The newspaper guy. Reynolds. We are in need of a miracle."

"Well," Herb drawled, chewing on a piece of toast. "I don't have any miracles left. If I ever had any, I used them up on that young thing I spent the night with last night."

"Terrific, Herb. That's all we needed, you going out and getting your joint lubed while the rest of us tried to figure out who we could draft. ... What are you smiling about, Roy?"

"Nothing," he said. "Just smiling."

"Hey," Herb said. "We are in New Orleans, courtesy of the NAFA. Why not take advantage of it?"

"You could take advantage of it some other time," Dave said. "We need to plan our strategy."

"I can give you our strategy in one sentence. What we need is a real ballbuster of a draft choice. Something nobody's expecting. Something that'll have everybody from every city in the league muttering to themselves."

"Any idea?" Dave asked drily.

Herb shook his head. "Not yet, but I'm working on it. How about you?"

"I've got a couple of leads, but nothing like you're talking about."

"Hey," Roy said. "You dug up those Adonis boys. Maybe lightning will strike twice."

"Yeah, sure," Dave said, not sounding or feeling as if he believed it would.

"I've got an idea."

"What's that, dad?"

"Well, I was thinking, boys ..." Roy stole a piece of toast off his son's plate. "We've still got lots of money left. Maybe we can buy a first-round draft choice."

Herb groaned. "Dad, that's got to be the dumbest idea I've ever heard. Nobody in this league sells first-round draft choices. You build franchises around first-round picks."

Roy seemed hurt at the ridicule. "Well, I didn't think it was so dumb, and besides, what do we have to lose?"

"Everybody in the league will be laughing at us, that's what," Herb said.

"Uh, Herb ..." Dave smiled a little. "They've been laughing at us ever since we took over. Don't be so tough on your old man."

"Aw, he keeps coming up with these screwball ideas ..."

"He's just trying to help."

"Hey, would you guys stop talking about me as if I'm not here?"

"So what should we do, Dave? Have him start calling every other team in the league? Start at the top of the list and ..."

"Why not?"

Herb didn't have an answer for that.

"I mean, Herb, it couldn't hurt, and it would keep him out of our hair while we're getting ready for the session. Hey, what do we have to lose?"

Herb shrugged.

"All right, then," Dave said to Roy. "Go ahead and start calling people and see what happens."

"You've got it, boys. And what should I do once I've got one? Should I keep trying and get us two or three?"

Herb started to say something, but Dave stopped him. "Uh, Roy," he said. "One should be enough. We don't want to spend all our money today."

While the Washington brain trust was conferring in the coffee shop, Duncan Charles was eating breakfast in his room on the thirty-fifth floor.

The hotel kitchen hadn't had the Froot Loops he had requested, so he had settled for a breakfast of corn flakes with sliced-up bananas and milk, with a glass of orange juice on the side.

"OK, kid, this is your chance to shine."

"Really, Ray?" Duncan asked as he gulped down another spoonful of cereal.

"Really. There'll be pictures of you standing making your pick. There'll be stories about the wizard deals you make. There'll be all sorts of interviews …"

"Wizard deals?"

"Yeah, kid. I'm not going to tell you all the details. I don't want to spoil the surprise, but let's just say you're going to be getting a pretty important phone call this morning."

"What'll I do?" Duncan sounded almost alarmed.

Martini shrugged. "Just say yes."

Duncan wanted to clap his hands with delight, but he summoned up a little dignity. After all, he didn't want a picture like that ending up in the Chicago papers.

At 9 a.m., Central Daylight Time, the commissioner stepped to the podium and declared the North American Football Association's annual draft of college players to be open.

At 9:01 a.m., Jackson Weatherby, the operator of the Pittsburgh Pistols, stood at his table and announced to the assemblage and to the reporters and photographers in the back of the room that his team's selection -- the first one in the draft -- was defensive end Barry Kline of East Tennessee State.

The national cable audience was treated to film footage of Kline, a six-foot-six, 285-pounder, injuring three different quarterbacks in a game with Memphis State.

A particularly unctuous announcer asked Kline a number of questions that could be answered by "yes" or "no," and one of the network's woman reporters provided an interview with Kline's mother, a woman who seemed to resemble Ma Barker.

By the time the network came out of commercial, the commissioner was back at the podium to introduce Cincinnati with the second pick. At 9:14 a.m., Dr. Ralph Pierson, the multi-millionaire chiropractor who operated the Cincinnati Goldstars, announced that his team's first choice of the draft would be quarterback Rudy Leighton of Texas.

There was another break while fans at home saw footage of the flamboyant Leighton. This time there was an interview with his girlfriend, a live interview in which the girl, a Texas cheerleader, was bleeped seven times for obscenities.

After another seemingly endless series of commercials, Duncan Charles of the Chicago Trojans stepped up to his microphone at 9:28 a.m.

"Is this thing on?" Duncan asked, tapping the microphone and causing feedback to shriek throughout the room. "Oops."

"Go ahead, kid," Martini hissed at him.

"OK, Ray." Duncan cleared his throat. "The Chicago Trojans have traded their first-round choice to the Washington Warriors."

"What!?" shouted Ray Martini.

"What!?" shouted the commissioner.

"WHAT!?" shouted the assembled reporters and photographers.

Dave Krause stepped to the microphone in the middle of all the tumult. "The Washington Warriors," he said, a lot more calmly than he felt, "select Willis Waller of Carlson College."

The commissioner called for a short recess.

Ray Martini grabbed Duncan by the shoulders and steered him forcefully into the nearest men's room.

"But, Ray, I don't have to go to the bathroom yet ..."

Martini pushed him up against one of the stalls. "What in God's name did you do out there, kid? Just tell me, what in the hell did you do?"

Duncan smiled. "Isn't it great, Ray? Isn't this terrific? Boy, it's just like you said it would be. I was on television and all those photographers were taking my picture."

"Fun? Fun?" Martini was practically screaming. A man who had entered the restroom and started unzipping his pants quickly changed his mind and left. "You call trading away the best running back in the country fun? Do you laugh at hangings, kid?"

"Ray, what's the problem? You told me ..."

"Did I tell you to give away the best runner in the country?"

"Ray, calm down ..."

"Calm down? You just screwed up the whole damned season and you're telling me to calm down? You're lucky I'm a pacifist. If I weren't, I'd probably tear your spleen out."

The one thing that precluded the possibility of that happening was the appearance of Stan Pinello. "Ray, I've been looking for you."

"Hello, Stan," Martini said, breathing deeply and trying to get his temper under control. "Would you like to be an accomplice to a murder?"

Pinello looked coldly at Duncan Charles, who was starting to become alarmed.

"Let's wait a few minutes on that, Ray. The commissioner wants to see me, you and laughing boy in his suite right away. He might want to do the deed himself."

If the insiders were confounded by the inexplicable move, the contingent from Washington was enjoying its finest hour. In full view of the media, the other operators and the national cable audience, Dave, Herb and Roy were jumping around and hugging each other.

They had developed an impromptu cheer of "Waller! Waller! Washington!" and they were repeating it to the point of nausea.

The reporters pressed in with shouts of their own.

"Guys, how did you do it?"

"Will you keep him or trade him?"

"Have you talked money yet?"

"Hold it, everybody," Herb said. "We're still trying to catch our breath ourselves. We'll be glad to answer all your questions, but how about asking them one at a time?"

One reporter didn't agree. "Why? There's three of you," he said, but most of the others settled down to await their respective chance at the biggest story of the day.

"How did you manage to trade with Chicago for the draft pick?" asked an older writer who actually had a press card tucked into the brim of his fedora. "And what did you trade?"

"We didn't trade anything!" shouted Roy Rojas. "We bought it!"

"You what?"

"Cash on the barrelhead. We gave Chicago ..."

"Uh, Roy ..."

"Yeah, dad. Let's keep the numbers out of it."

"How did you do it?"

"Well, sir," Roy said, surprising the reporter, who was used to hearing less respectful forms of address from his interview subjects. "We decided the only way we were going to get a decent draft choice was to go out and buy one."

The reporter nodded incredulously as he tried to write down every word.

"So first thing this morning, I went to my room and got on the phone. I started with the first pick and called Pittsburgh. They said no, and then Cincinnati said no. They both laughed at me, but when I got to Chicago ..."

"Willis Waller!" Herb shouted triumphantly, punching his fist into the air.

The commissioner was considerably less pleased as the group assembled in his suite. "Gentlemen, I want some answers and I want them now. We have approximately twenty minutes before we have to go back downstairs and resume the draft, so make it quick."

Pinello spoke first. "Commissioner, I had no idea what was going on between Washington and Chicago. I wasn't even around when ..."

"Why doesn't that surprise me, Mr. Pinello?"

"Uh, Commissioner ..."

"Never mind, Pinello. Now, Mr. Charles ..."

"Commissioner, it's Duncan. My daddy was ..."

"Mister Charles, I could not possibly care less at this moment what you like to be called, but you do appear to be the instigator of this particular fiasco. Perhaps you could find it in your heart to relate to me the events that led up to this little incident."

He smiled coldly. Martini just stood there grimly, and Pinello actually shuddered. He had seen that particular smile before.

"Well, Commissioner, I was in my room this morning just waiting to go downstairs when I got this phone call, just like Ray said I would ..."

"Ray ..."

Martini shook his head. "Later, Commissioner."

The commissioner nodded. "Please continue, Mr. Charles."

"Anyway, it was that guy Rojas. The old one. He told me he was with the Warriors, and he knew I was busy, but he asked if he could have a minute to talk about a deal with me."

"Go on."

"Why is everybody mad at me?" Duncan asked, looking at the three unsmiling faces. "I just did what I was told ..."

"Go on, Mr. Charles."

"Well, this guy said he wanted to talk to me about a deal, and Ray had told me somebody was going to call, so I told him to go ahead. He told me he was authorized to buy my first-round draft choice and asked me how much I wanted for it."

Duncan grinned. "I got a hundred thousand dollars."

Martini practically hit the ceiling. "A hundred thousand dollars! You sold Willis Waller to Washington for a lousy hundred thousand dollars?"

"Mr. Martini, the price of the transaction is of no particular importance at this time. Carry on, Mr. Charles."

"Well, he told me that was an awful lot of money, but if that was what I wanted ..." Duncan grinned again. "You bet that was what I wanted. That was how much we had to give Kansas City in that Chico Coleman deal, and now I've got my money back."

"Please stay on the subject."

"Sorry, Commissioner. Anyway, he said he'd bring an agreement up to my room, and he did, and I signed it and then ..." Duncan reacted almost like a cartoon character. Later Martini would almost swear he had seen a little light bulb flash above Duncan Charles' head. "This wasn't supposed to happen, was it?"

"That's right, Mr. Charles."

"Ray, you said I was going to get Waller! They weren't supposed to draft him!"

"They weren't, kid. In fact, they couldn't until you let them."

"Oh, no," Duncan said, slumping into a chair, his head in his hands.

"Well, gentlemen," the commissioner said, ignoring Duncan and focusing his attention on Martini and Pinello. "We have a situation before us. What, if anything, can we do about it?"

"I'm not sure we can do anything," Pinello said. "Unless you'd like to consider the possibility of having him ..." Pinello glanced at Duncan. "... declared mentally incompetent."

The commissioner glanced at Duncan for a moment as if considering the possibility. Then he shook his head.

"Ray, how about you?"

"Commissioner, Washington drafted the kid in front of God and everybody. We can't just take him away."

"What about violations of the league bylaws? Surely there is something illegal about selling a draft choice."

"It happens all the time, Commissioner," Martini said. "Usually teams trade their picks for players or for other draft choices, but there's nothing anywhere in the rules that says a team can't sell its draft choices outright.

I should know, Commissioner. I helped revise those rules four years ago."

"So did I, Mr. Martini. So did Mr. Pinello, in fact. Make a note of this so that we can amend those rules after this season to make sure nothing like this ever happens again."

"Commissioner?"

"Yes, Mr. Pinello?"

"I have an idea. Maybe we could get someone down there to Georgia to talk with Waller. Maybe he could demand such a large contract that Washington wouldn't be able to sign him."

Martini shook his head. "Won't work, Stan. Association rules say once a player is drafted, he belongs to the team that drafted him until they don't want him anymore. When Waller dies, God will have to bargain with Washington for his soul unless they decide to set him free."

"All that is beside the point, gentlemen. Unless Mr. Pinello can come up with some obscure rule we've all forgotten in the next ten minutes, it looks as if we are stuck with this unfortunate event."

The commissioner gazed coldly at Duncan Charles. "And Mr. Charles, might I have a moment of your ever-so-short attention span to tell you something?"

Duncan looked up for the first time since he had stopped talking. "Certainly, Commissioner."

"Mr. Charles, for the rest of this meeting, and for the rest of the season if that is at all possible, I do not want you to leave Mr. Martini's side. I do not want you to make a move without his permission. I do not want you to urinate without clearing it with him first. Do I make myself perfectly clear?"

Duncan gulped. Then he nodded, and the commissioner dismissed all three men with a wave of his hand.

20

For most of the rest of the day, Dave and Herb took turns monitoring the proceedings while Roy spent his time talking with reporters. He stopped by from time to time, only to find out that the fourth round was still a long way off and the NAFA's draft meeting was pretty boring if you didn't have draft choices.

No one connected with the Association spoke to them. Hardly anyone even looked their way. Had they not pulled off what reporters were calling the "coup of the decade," they might have felt like pariahs.

The commissioner had returned to the podium at the end of the recess, looking as cool as ever. He made no allusion at all to the interruption.

"The next selection belongs to the Birmingham Smashers," was all he said, and Garry Henderson, the operator of that team, stood and announced his team had selected Terry Fitzgerald, an offensive lineman from Notre Dame.

Finally, late that afternoon, after most of the reporters had left for the restaurants and bars, the Warriors' fourth-round pick came around.

Dave stood and made the pick. "The Washington Warriors select tight end George Greenblatt of William Peace University."

"I'm sorry," said the commissioner's secretary, Liz Granger, who had been given control of the meeting as soon as the media had departed. "What was that pick?"

"George Greenblatt," Dave said. "Tight end. William Peace."

"But that's a business school."

"Yes, ma'am, but they play football."

The commissioner's secretary shrugged. "Very well, then. If that's what you want. The Warriors select George Greenblatt."

Elsewhere in the hotel, Herb was learning just how wonderful it would be to own a football team. Tracey Cagney's suite of rooms made the room Herb had look like a broom closet. There was a deep pile carpet on the floor, a full kitchen which he was sure she wasn't using, a big screen television with two video recorders and a fully stocked bar.

There was also a large picture window that provided the room's inhabitants with a breathtaking view of New Orleans, with the NAFA's Championship Bowl Stadium in the foreground. Herb decided he would do whatever it took to spend time in this room, even if it meant allowing Tracey Cagney to adopt him.

"Hello, Mr. Rojas. Thanks for coming by."

"Well, you said you wanted to talk to someone from the Warriors, and Dave's busy making our fourth-round pick. That made it either me or my dad."

"May I call you Herb?"

Lady, he thought, you can call me slimy axle grease if it makes you happy. "Sure," he said.

"And you'll call me Tracey."

Herb nodded.

"May I fix you a drink, Herb?"

"A beer would be great."

"Is Heineken all right?"

Herb nodded. Tracey moved to the bar, took a bottle of beer out of the small refrigerator and poured the contents into a frosted mug. Herb was convinced he had died and gone to heaven.

"Miss ... Tracey," Herb said, sipping from his beer. "I'm sure you didn't call me up here just to buy me a drink. Would it be terribly rude of me to ask what you've got on your mind?"

"Of course," she said, smiling warmly. "You probably already know. After all, you run a football team. I own a football team, and I thought we could do some business."

Tracey Cagney ran her tongue across her lips and Herb could feel a vein throbbing in his forehead. Please, he prayed silently, not a stroke. Not now.

"You've made some pretty interesting deals recently."

"Such as?"

"Well, you signed Tony Ross. How is he working out?"

"He's only been in camp a couple of weeks but he certainly seems to be getting back some of his old form."

"That's interesting. What would it take for you to give up Mr. Ross?"

"You mean trade him?"

"Trade him, sell him, whatever."

Herb could have cried. He had somehow hoped against hope that Tracey

Cagney had found him so personally appealing that she had invited him to her room to seduce him, but her interest in Ross chased any thoughts of sex from his mind.

He thought he knew what she wanted now, but he figured he'd play along and find out for sure. "Is Tony Ross that important to you, Tracey?"

"Oh, very. I'd pay almost any price to have him on my team. He was a great receiver."

"Baloney, lady."

"I'm sorry, Herb. I'm not sure I understand."

"Oh, you understand. I understand. You want to trade for him and then bury him."

"I'm sure I don't know what you mean," she said, her tone noticeably cooler now.

"Tracey, I've talked with the guy. I know exactly what happened between you two."

"Oh, you do, do you?"

"Yep, he told me the whole story, and I have a feeling it would please you to no end to get Tony Ross on your team and make him sit out the rest of the season."

"Not just the season, Mr. Rojas," Tracey said, venom dripping from her voice. "The rest of his career."

"Isn't that a pretty rotten way to treat a guy?"

"Oh, is it?" Her eyes were flashing with anger now. "I'm sure Tony told you my father cut him from the team because he seduced me, but I'm sure he didn't tell you I was the one who told my father to cut him, to cut him so hard and so far no one would ever hear of him again."

"Really?"

"Yes, and it would have worked, if you and your friend hadn't happened along. So now I'm willing to pay the price, whatever it takes, to finish the job."

"Isn't that carrying revenge a little too far?"

"It's worth it, Rojas. Tony Ross lied to me. He told me he loved me, and all he was doing was using me. I was his ultimate conquest, the daughter of his boss. Do you know what he called me?"

Herb shook his head.

"He said I was table stuff."

That's right, Herb thought. That's what he told me.

"It would definitely be worth it, Rojas. It would be an even better punishment for him than keeping him out of the league, to have him on the sidelines, so close to the action and yet so far away from it. God, yes, it would be worth it."

"Seems like an awful waste of talent to me."

"Rojas, my team is lousy with talent. Name your price."

"All right," he said. "We'll take Joe Bell, Sandy Tate and Luther Richardson."

Tracey smiled. "My starting quarterback and my two best wide receivers."

"Oh, yes, and a hundred thousand dollars to make up for what we gave Chicago today."

"You probably think I'm going to say no, Rojas. You probably think that's too much to pay for revenge, but I've got two other good quarterbacks, and receivers are a dime a dozen in this league. And a hundred thousand dollars? That's a joke. Is that what you want?"

Herb nodded.

"Deal, Mr. Rojas."

It came as no surprise to anyone when the commissioner vetoed the deal the next day, citing the oft-quoted rule of "fair balance" in trades. The only surprise to anyone was how much pleasure he seemed to take from his action.

Herb and Dave had never expected the deal to go through. They had other concerns, like signing their first-round draft pick.

21

"Hey, Willis," the reporter shouted. "How does it feel to be in the NAFA?"

"Great!" shouted Waller's father.

"How does it feel to be drafted by Washington?" a radio reporter asked, shoving a microphone forward.

George Waller was not quite as loud. "They'll do."

"What about money?"

"Have you talked contract yet?"

"When are you going up there?"

"We'll let the lawyers handle that," the elder Waller said. Willis had yet to say a word.

The impromptu press conference was taking place on the front porch of the Waller home in suburban Atlanta. It was obvious to all present that George and Willis Waller were father and son. Both were solid-looking and muscular and both carried themselves with a quiet dignity.

One reporter suggested that the elder Waller would have made a fine running back, and another replied that with the Warriors' penchant for signing geriatric players, they might try to sign him, too.

Willis' agent had decided it would be best to emphasize his humble beginnings, so the conference had been set up on the porch, showing all of America that the nation's best runner was the son of a former Atlanta police officer.

The single-story, two-bedroom house was a little run down and in need of a fresh coat of paint, but the agent felt it would help reinforce the image of poverty he was trying to orchestrate.

Besides, no one had lived in the house since the summer after Willis Waller's senior year of high school. That was when one of the hottest recruiting battles ever had raged around the talented young back, and Carlton College had decided he was the missing link to a national championship.

The alumni were more than willing to make Waller and his family happy. One alumnus sold the Waller family a beautiful downtown Atlanta condominium for one hundred dollars, and another made George Waller his chief of security at seventy-five thousand dollars a year.

Willis was given a summer job where he spent four hours a week watching other men load appliances onto trucks. For that he was paid two hundred dollars every week. He drove a convertible owned by the dean and he purchased gas for it with the coach's credit card.

Contrary to popular belief, though, Willis attended most of his classes, except for creative writing, which he detested. He took most of his own exams and achieved a B-plus average on his own merits. He was anything but stupid, and he had a degree in business management to prove it.

One thing his professors had definitely taught Willis Waller was on which side the bread was buttered.

"Any more questions, guys?"

"Yeah, Willis, what'll you do if they don't offer you enough?"

He didn't bother to answer that one. He just smiled.

With that question, the press conference was finished and the reporters packed up and left. Willis, with his father and his agent, went into the house and stood in the empty living room.

"Are they gone yet?" George Waller asked. "Can we get out of this shithole and go home?"

"Give it a few more minutes," the agent said. "You can never tell when some of those guys are still hanging around."

The three men stood around and made small talk before sneaking out the back door, climbing into the agent's Cadillac and heading back downtown.

"All right, Hank," George Waller said to the agent. "Why don't you tell us what the fuck happened. You told me my boy was going to Cincinnati or Chicago."

"Well, my sources ..."

"Sources!" Willis snorted. "Pretty damn lousy sources if you ask me. Jeez, Washington!"

"Well, they've been doing some interesting things."

"Interesting, my butt," George said. "They're not going to make the playoffs, are they? They're not even going to have a winning season. You told me it was all set, that my boy would be on a playoff team his first year. Are you telling us Washington is a playoff team?"

"I think it's safe to say that any team that acquired a back of Willis' talents could easily be considered a playoff team."

"Bullshit!" Willis said. "I can't run unless there's somebody blocking for me, and Washington's line blocks like a bunch of old ladies!"

"They drafted a couple of linemen ..."

"Yeah," Willis snorted. "I know who they drafted. Last-round linemen to block for a first-round runner. They won't be able to keep a stray dog out of the backfield."

"Son, maybe we should wait and see what happens."

"Yeah, Willis. There isn't a whole lot we can do now that you've been drafted. The Warriors have the rights to you, and unless they trade you, which doesn't seem at all likely, you either play for them or you play in Europe."

"Europe?"

"Well, there's talk of someone starting a league over there next year."

"Fuck that noise".

"That's what I thought you'd say," the agent said.

"If they want me, they're going to have to pay me."

"They know that. I spoke with a Mr. Krause this morning and he appears to be willing to pay almost any price to get you into a Warriors uniform."

22

"Is this George Greenblatt?"

"Speaking."

"George, this is Herb Rojas. I work for the Washington Warriors football team. In case you haven't heard the news yet, we drafted you yesterday to play for our team."

"Yes, sir. I know. Thank you."

Herb had expected a little more. He didn't know if Greenblatt would shout or simply overflow with gratitude. He hadn't expected this, though. Greenblatt's voice was completely devoid of emotion.

"Uh, you're welcome, George, but perhaps it's the Warriors who should be thanking you. After all, we expect you to accomplish a lot for us. Now, rookie camp doesn't open for another two and a half weeks, but if you'd like to come up a little earlier to get into shape ..."

"I'm already in shape, Mr. Rojas."

"That's good. Then you should have no problem at all ..."

"I've been in shape all my life."

"Terrific, then ..."

"I've never been in better shape ..."

"That's wonderful ..."

"... to do the work of William Peace Lippmann."

Herb nearly dropped the phone. "I beg your pardon?" he asked, hoping Greenblatt was joking with him.

"I said I have never been in better shape to do the work of ..."

"William Peace Lippmann."

"Yes," Greenblatt said. "I am leaving for Micronesia in two weeks."

"Micro-whatia?"

"Micronesia. Mr. Lippmann is building a resort there, and I have been chosen to serve."

"Chosen to serve?"

"Yes, Mr. Rojas. We will be bringing the wonders of the free-market system to the heathen masses of the South Sea Islands."

"George, do you realize who I am?"

"Certainly, sir. You are Herbert Rojas and you work for the Washington Warriors."

"That's right, George. The Washington Warriors of the North American Football Association," he said, drawing out the last four words in case George had misunderstood him previously.

"Yes."

"Do you understand that what I'm offering you is a chance to play professional football?"

"Yes, and thank you very much, but I have been chosen ..."

"I know, to go to Micronesia, to turn the heathen masses into yuppies."

"That isn't exactly the way I would have chosen to say it, but the gist of what you say seems correct."

"And you're leaving in two weeks."

"Yes."

Herb sighed loudly. "Look, George, is there a motel there in town? A hotel? A tiny little boarding house that rents rooms to traveling salesmen?"

"We have a five-star hotel right here on campus, so that the captains of world industry can stay in comfort when they visit our campus."

"Fine. Stay right where you are. Don't leave town. Don't leave the campus. Heck, don't even leave your room. Send out for meals if you have to, but wait for me. I'll be on the next flight down. We have to talk."

"I have to stay here. We don't leave for Micronesia for ..."

"... two weeks. I know."

The town of Lippmann seemed to exist for one purpose -- as the headquarters of William Peace Lippmann Enterprises.

Lippmann's story was a classic example of the American dream. As his own biographer had written, he had grown up in a lower-middle class family in Constance, Alabama.

He had earned his first dollar by picking up pop bottles at construction sites, and he had built the largest paper route in the state by the age of 12.

He bought his first stock certificates at age 14, and he worked his way through college by holding a variety of jobs, ranging from encyclopedia salesman to itinerant minister.

He got in early on the boom in television evangelism, and for a short time in the early 1980s, his hour-long show was a worthy rival to the Falwells, Swaggarts and Bakkers at the very pinnacle of the religion industry.

Lippmann had a flamboyant evangelical style that had fit in well with the radio broadcasts he had started early in his career, and he had a brilliant business sense that gave him the ability to surround himself with talented people.

His business manager had been a vice president at General Motors, and the man who directed his television broadcasts had won four Emmy awards before going to work for Lippmann.

Lippmann's instincts were so good that he managed to get out of the religion business a full year before the scandals hit, and he embraced big business with all the enthusiasm of a zealot.

The stocks he had bought forty years earlier had split time after time, until they represented a huge block of shares in an aerospace company.

The value of his empire, which included radio and television stations, hotels, a regional airline and an amusement park, was estimated at $850 million, and most financial people thought that was a very conservative estimate.

The small towns of Constance and nearby Hester Bluff had long since ceased to exist. Both had been incorporated into the thriving metropolis of Lippmann, a city of ninety-five thousand in northwestern Alabama.

Herb looked out the window of the left side of the airliner and saw the city. Dave was gripping the armrests beside his seat and not noticing much of anything.

"This is your captain speaking. We'd like to thank you for flying Peace Airlines. We'll be landing at Lippmann International Airport in approximately five minutes so we'd like you to fasten your seat belts at this time. Should you encounter any difficulty during our landing, our flight attendants are here to assist you. Thank you for flying with us, and may Peace be with you."

"Nice touch, the part about peace," Herb whispered to Dave.

Dave Krause didn't seem to notice. He hated to fly, always had and always would. He had never become accustomed to the surge of power as the airplane left the ground, or his feeling of complete helplessness as it descended.

While others gazed out the windows and looked down upon the earth with awe or wonder, he was filled with fear and disgust.

He had always felt he would rather have a small tooth or a large internal organ removed than fly anywhere, but Herb had convinced him his help would be necessary to sell George Greenblatt on the idea of playing professional football.

"Herb, are you sure this is the only way into this town?"

"Yes, Dave," Herb said, a little impatiently. "There are no buses or trains that stop here, and it would have taken too long to drive from Washington. What's the matter, anyway? You've flown before."

"Only when it was absolutely necessary."

"Just think of this as one of those times."

"You could have brought your dad. He'd appreciate it."

"Yeah, but he'd sit there and goo and gush and act like an idiot. This kid's a strange case. He seems to worship businessmen. If he sees two reasonable adults in business suits who aren't shouting lunatics, I think he'll be impressed. I hope so, anyway."

"This had better be worth it. I'd hate to think I put myself through this for nothing."

"It won't be easy, I know that. The kid is going to need some convincing. Let's just hope God is on our side."

"Herb, I wish you'd choose some other time to blaspheme. Oh, Lord, we're going down!"

Two hours later, Dave and Herb were sitting on a sofa in the lobby of the hotel across the street from William Peace University. George Greenblatt was sitting facing them, and he looked like Norman Rockwell's idea of a football player. Tall, blue-eyed and square-shouldered. A jaw that seemed chiseled from stone and a firm, steady handshake.

He towered over both Dave and Herb, and appeared to be carrying at least two hundred and fifty pounds on his six-foot-five frame. The general managers of the Washington Warriors knew they were in the presence of a man who had been born to play professional football.

"I want to thank you gentlemen for coming all the way to Alabama to talk to me," Greenblatt said. "But I really don't see that there is anything I can do for you."

"Let us be the judge of that, George," Herb said.

"Very well."

"Could we just sit and talk for a while?"

The hotel was impressive, the equal of any Herb had seen at any resort. The furniture was brand new and expensive, and there were signed and numbered Leroy Niemann prints on the walls. There were also, much to Herb's discomfort, no ashtrays.

"Is it all right if I smoke, George?"

"Yes," Greenblatt said. "You are a businessman. You can do whatever you like."

He snapped his finger and a bellhop came running up with an ashtray for

Herb.

"Thanks," Herb said, lighting his cigarette.

"George, I think it's pretty accurate that we want you to play football for us," Dave said. "In fact, that's why we drafted you."

"I understand, Mr. Krause, and I am honored that you did, but I have another, more important commitment. I am to do Mr. Lippmann's work in Micronesia."

"How committed are you to this?"

"Mr. Rojas, there are countless millions of people in this world who have never heard of the free-market system, who have no idea at all of the joy and beauty it can bring into their lives, as it has mine. I want to be the one to share it with them, a soldier in the war against Socialism."

"George, you can do that anytime. You're still a young man. You can play football for eight or ten years and still have twenty, thirty, God knows how many years to spread the word."

"That's precisely it, Mr. Rojas. Only God knows how much time I have left. You may well be speaking the truth. I might have decades left in my life, but just the same, the Lord could call me to be with him tomorrow, or next week, or next year."

"But he might not."

"I'm not willing to take the chance. Now is the time. I am in top form. I am young, healthy and ready to stand up to the rigors of life in remote areas. Big business is a young man's profession, much the same as football."

"But George," Dave asked. "Could you be content, twenty years from now, realizing you passed up a chance to play professional football?"

"Very easily."

Herb leaned forward. "George, let's cut the crap here. Is it money? We've got the bucks. What do you want, a car? We'll get you a car. Is it the babes? We'll get you women."

Greenblatt looked as if Herb had slapped him. "I will forgive you your transgression, because I know you are not familiar with my work and cannot understand. I have no time for women now. I have only eight years to make my first billion dollars."

"So that's it, isn't it, George?" Herb asked. "You feel like you owe it to Lippmann, right?"

"That's not it at all."

"Sure it is. William Peace Lippmann. The man who owns your heart and soul."

"No, Mr. Rojas," Greenblatt said calmly. "They belong to a much greater power, the glorious free-market system, the system that has provided a higher standard of living for our nation than for any other nation in the history of mankind."

Dave chose that moment to intercede.

"All right, come on, Herb. This is a lost cause. Mr. Greenblatt, I want to commend you. I have never met a man braver than you, a man who is willing to give up what surely would have been a successful career in the North American Football Association to do what his heart tells him to do."

"Thank you, Mr. Krause."

Dave nodded. "You're giving up the money, the glory, the fun of the game. You did have fun playing football, didn't you, George?"

"Yes, I did," he said, a wistful look on his face. "I enjoyed playing football very much, but those days are behind me now. I am filled with the vigor of a new challenge, the joy of spreading the word of Mr. Lippmann to the masses. When he told me he had selected me to serve in Micronesia, it was the happiest day of my life."

"Mr. Lippmann selected you?"

"That's correct, Mr. Krause."

"You mean you didn't choose to serve in the field?"

"Well, not specifically, but I was aware that I would be used to extend the Lippmann empire in some way."

Dave stood up suddenly. "Thank you, George. This has been a most enlightening discussion."

"Dave, what ..."

"Come on, Herb. Let's leave Mr. Greenblatt here. He is obviously a very dedicated gentleman."

"Thank you, Mr. Krause. Mr. Rojas. I'm glad you understand. By the way, gentlemen, when I informed Mr. Lippmann that you were coming here to speak with me, he asked that I send you to his office before you left."

Dave smiled. "Why doesn't that surprise me? Thank you, George."

Lippmann's inner office on the top floor of the hotel was far more plush than the lounge. The sofas against the walls were deeper and newer, and Lippmann's desk was a marble slab atop an oak body.

"It's pretty obvious we were talking to the wrong guy," Dave whispered to Herb as they waited for Lippmann to finish a phone call.

"Whatever. It's worth it just to see this office."

It looked as if it belonged to the chairman of the board of a Fortune 500 corporation, which is exactly what Lippmann Enterprises would be if it continued its phenomenal growth for another decade. The Picasso on the wall wasn't a print, it was an original, and the wall behind the desk was a series of picture windows that gave Lippmann a panoramic view of the school and the town.

William Peace Lippmann fit right in. He was an imposing figure, a man in his early fifties who looked considerably younger. In fact, he looked as if he could have played for the Warriors not so many years ago. His suit had been tailored on London's Saville Row and it hung perfectly on his broad shoulders. A diamond stickpin kept his tie in place and there were matching cufflinks peeking out from the sleeves of his jacket.

His complexion spoke either of vacations in the tropics or of long hours under a sun lamp.

Lippmann chose that moment to hang up the phone, and motioned to Dave to say something.

"Mr. Lippmann, we'd like to thank you for taking time out from your busy schedule to speak with us."

Lippmann smiled warmly. "No problem at all, gentlemen. I was more than happy to see you."

"I might add, we have been made very welcome at this lovely campus," Dave said.

"That's all very well and good, but how about we cut out the schmoozing here and get down to business."

"If you say so."

"Now let me see if I've got this straight. You drafted my boy Georgie, and you're here to talk him into forgoing his little trip to the South Seas so that he can play football for you."

"In a nutshell," Herb said. "You've got it."

"And after failing with Mr. Greenblatt, you now want me to join with you and help persuade him."

"That's about it."

"Mr. Lippmann, just think of what an accomplishment it would be," Dave said. "To have a professional football player come out of a little school no one ever heard of ..."

Lippmann's face clouded over, and Dave knew he had made a serious error. "I'm sure if you had any idea what you were talking about, you would not have made that statement, Mr. Krause. Perhaps you have never heard of our university, but that would be more a measure of your lack of intelligence than our lack of recognition."

"Oh?"

"I can understand that football executives, being somewhat secluded from the rest of the world, could be unaware of our university, but let me assure you there are many people who know us well."

Dave nodded weakly.

"Look around you, gentlemen. New buildings are going up every day. We receive eighteen thousand applications a year for the two thousand spots in our freshman class. We are managing to raise more than fifty million dollars a year from tax-deductible contributions. That is hardly an indication of a school no one has ever heard of."

"I'm sorry, Mr. Lippmann."

"Apology noted, sir. William Peace University is becoming, if in fact it isn't already, one of the most respected and prominent business universities in the world. And why, you ask?"

Dave hadn't intended to ask, but he figured it was time to keep his mouth shut.

"Because decent people everywhere want to send their children to an institution that will reinforce and uphold the American values they hold dear, as opposed to the state-run, Communist-dominated institutions that decry and destroy those same values."

"Really?"

"We offer a good, well-rounded and I might add, reasonably priced education in an All-American atmosphere. We have no drug problem at this school. We have no racial problems, even though we have students of every race in attendance."

Dave nodded.

"We have no unwed mothers and no abortions. There is no crime, no violence. We have the peaceful serenity one can only obtain through careful adherence to the principles of the free enterprise system."

Dave thought Herb was about to say something, but he fixed him with a hard stare and his friend sat back to listen as Lippmann continued.

"So what do you think of that, Mr. Rojas?"

"It's very impressive."

"You bet your ass it is, and ten years ago, someone came to me and suggested the school should have a football team. Many of my followers were opposed. They asked what business businessmen had being involved with such a violent game."

"What did you say to that."

"I didn't have to say anything. I have always loved football. There is a certain grace, a beauty to the game, and I felt it would help extend our ministry if a team of young, healthy businessmen could play the game as it has never been played before."

Lippmann paused briefly. "I remember how football coaches around the country laughed. They asked what my boys would use for tackles, their stock portfolios? Well, last year we won eight games, and now one of my boys has been drafted by the Association. In two years we play Tennessee and Auburn, and that's when things will really start happening for us."

"I'm impressed," Dave said.

"And having George playing in the NAFA can only help us."

"If we sign him," Herb said.

"You will sign him. I have no doubt about that."

"How can you be so sure, Mr. Lippmann?"

"Because, Mr. Krause, the Washington Warriors will make a tax-free donation to the William Peace Endowment Fund and then George Greenblatt will change his mind."

There it was, right out on the table at last, what Dave knew was coming. He looked over at Herb, took a deep breath and started to say something when Herb beat him to it.

"Like hell we will."

"Uh, Herb, watch your language."

"Don't worry, Mr. Krause. I've heard worse, and Mr. Rojas is not a believer."

"Oh, I'm a believer, all right. I believe that what you're trying to do is extort money from us."

"Herb, that might be a little strong."

Lippmann smiled. "It is a little strong. I think influence-peddling is the term that might more accurately describe it."

"Huh?"

"Gentlemen, I see no point in sugar-coating things. There is only one man on the face of this earth who can convince George Greenblatt to play for you, and you are looking at him."

"I don't know, Mr. Lippmann," Dave said. "He sounded like he really wanted to go to Micronesia."

Lippmann laughed. "That boy will go wherever I tell him to go. If I told him to go to the moon, he'd head down to Florida and wait for the next open seat on the space shuttle. What do you gentlemen take me for? Some little country bumpkin sitting in awe of two slick operators from the big city? Do you really think I would let a boy with that kind of talent waste it in the South Seas?"

"Let's just say I expected better," Dave said.

"What was that, Mr. Krause? I suppose you expected me to give you George Greenblatt out of the goodness of my heart?"

"Something like that."

"My friend, you underestimate me. You have to understand that this is not an inexpensive operation here. Whatever estimates you may have heard about the financial resources available to this corporation, let me assure you that our funds are very rarely enough to sustain such far-reaching programs."

"Not to mention your Mercedes, your Saville Row suits and diamond stickpins ..."

Lippmann smiled. "Mr. Rojas, would you expect me to buy my suits at Walmart or the Men's Wearhouse?"

"I'm sure one hell of a lot of your followers do!"

"Yes, that is true, but my followers look to me for inspiration," Lippmann said. "They look to me to show them how rewarding a love of the almighty dollar can be. The dollar rewards those who follow it, Mr. Rojas, and I am a perfect example of that."

"Uh, Herb. Maybe we're making too big a deal out of this thing."

"Maybe," Herb said angrily. "But there's no way in the world we're going to pay this creep even one dollar. If you do, I'm going to tell Coach Kennedy about it, and if he doesn't care I'll tell the newspapers."

"Gentlemen, gentlemen. I'm a very busy man, and I would prefer you conduct your little squabbles somewhere other than in my office. I must begin my preparations for an upcoming meeting with the chairman of the board of General Motors. If you decide to accept my generous offer, I will be more than happy to speak with you again."

23

Jimmy Gardner looked and felt as though he had been through an alien invasion that utilized anal probes as he limped off the field and into the clubhouse at the Warriors' practice field at Oxon Hill, Maryland. His right eye was swollen almost shut, his left thigh was badly bruised and he felt as if his back was about to go out.

It was becoming apparent that getting back into shape was going to be a bit more difficult than he had thought.

"Oh, Lord!" he cried to no one in particular. "Is practice over, or did I die and go to heaven?"

"Shut up, Jimmy," Tony Ross said. "You want everybody to know what a pussy you are?"

"Eat it, Ross," Gardner said, locating his locker and finding the bench in front of it. He lowered himself painfully to the bench and with no small effort peeled his jersey off and dropped it on the floor.

His chest was covered with welts, and there was a chunk of flesh resembling a small golf divot missing just below his left nipple. Gardner sighed and leaned forward until his head rested against the door of his locker.

"I think I'll die now," he said. "They can just sweep around me and bury me when I start to stink."

"I've got news for you, Jimmy. You stink already."

"Tony?"

"Yeah?"

"How come you look so, well, alive?"

"Because I'm not a fat old man, Jimmy. Because I'm nearly ten years younger than you, and because I'm a slippery wide receiver who doesn't get hit as often as you."

"Oh."

Gardner started thinking about taking off the rest of his uniform and taking a shower. He knew such pleasurable things as dinner, a long bath and eight hours of sleep wouldn't happen until his uniform came off, but he didn't feel particularly motivated.

"Could one of you gentlemen tell me where I can find the coach?"

Jimmy knew that voice. He didn't even have to turn around. There are some men in this world, whether through strength of personality or sheer physical presence, are able to dominate rooms as soon as they enter them.

They stop conversations. They cause heads to turn and jaws to drop. Reginald "Roxy" Reese was one of those men.

Some of the younger players in the locker room started to cluster around Reese like twelve-year-old girls around the latest popular singers, chattering and throwing questions at him.

"Hey, Roxy, you here to play?"

"You gonna help the coach?"

"Roxy, I used to watch you play when I was in high school. Man, you were something!"

"Can I have your autograph?"

Ross decided he had better rescue Reese from his fan club, so he took him by the arm and led him over to Gardner's locker. "Jimmy, if you can find the strength to stand up, I'd like to introduce you to Roxy Reese."

Gardner stood slowly and offered the big man his hand. "Reese, I never thought I'd be glad to meet you."

"Wow!" one of the younger players said. "You mean you two never met?"

Gardner looked in the general direction of the questioner. "We never played in the same conference."

"That's right," Ross said. "But Roxy here kept Jimmy from winning his third Championship Bowl. What was it that day, Roxy? Two hundred yards?"

"Two hundred and seven," Reese said, and the crowd of would-be players reacted with a sigh at the thought that several people among them actually had played in the Championship Bowl.

"That was a long time ago," Gardner said. "A long, long time ago. You here to play, Roxy?"

"We'll see, Jimmy. Just thought I'd come out and see if I wanted to give it a ..."

A voice came from behind them. "You had better decide very quickly, Mr. Reese, if you want to remain on this team."

Benjamin Kennedy was another man who could silence a room with his presence.

24

At the same moment Reese was showing up at Oxon Hill, the Warriors were scheduled to open their negotiating session with Willis Waller and his attorney at the offices in downtown Washington.

Parker T. McMichael IV stood beside his chair at the head of the conference table and cleared his throat.

"Gentlemen," he said. "I do not believe we can delay any further. Mr. Rojas, have you received any word on the whereabouts of your son and Mr. Krause?"

"The last I heard was what I told you an hour ago," Roy said. "Their flight was late leaving Alabama, and a storm delayed them again after their stop in Charlotte. The last I heard, they should have been here by now."

"Well?"

"Well what?" Roy asked. "It's no big deal. If you can't wait any longer, I can speak for them."

"You can?"

"Sure. They've been out of town a lot lately, and I run things while they're gone."

"Yes, but usually the general managers handle ..."

"I have a title, you know. I'm the executive assistant to the general managers. Hey, I know all about signing guys up. A lot of the guys we've got out at camp are guys I signed."

"I wish you'd told us that in the first place," McMichael said. "We could have saved an awful lot of time."

"Now, Parker," Samuel Benton, McMichael's partner, said in his most soothingly professional voice. "There's really nothing to get excited about. We've only lost ..." He checked his watch. "... three and a half hours sitting here. Willis doesn't mind, does he?"

Willis Waller glared at his attorney. "Shit, man. Just get on with it."

"Well, good," Roy said cheerfully. "Why don't you guys start the ball rolling?"

Benton smiled. "That's a pleasantly cooperative attitude."

McMichael took a folder out of his briefcase and glanced at it. "Mr. Rojas, we have done some extensive research, as I'm sure your organization has, and we've developed a proposal based on the estimated value of Willis' services to you and the approximate value of his talents on the open market."

Roy smiled. When he didn't voice any objections, McMichael took it as a signal to continue. "Now Willis is the top running back in the nation ..."

"If you say so. We certainly like him."

"And the Warriors are certainly not the top franchise in the NAFA. The Warriors are one of the few franchises that does not sell out its games. Their games are televised only in Washington, D.C., and Fredericksburg, Virginia. The remainder of the stations that once carried Warrior games -- stations in Baltimore, Richmond, Roanoke and Charlotte -- have switched to games from Philadelphia or Atlanta."

"Well, that'll change ..."

"Perhaps, Mr. Rojas, but we must deal with things as they are. You are not sitting on a hotbed of popularity, and that will diminish Willis' opportunities for outside income. Had Willis been drafted by Chicago, he would have had many more avenues open to him for personal endorsements."

"In Chicago he'd have his own restaurant," Benton said. "In Washington he'll appear at supermarket openings."

"That's not exactly fair," Roy said.

McMichael brushed the objection aside. "Taking all this into consideration, we have come up with a proposal that we feel fairly reflects the type of money Willis should be making."

"And that is?"

"We think it would be very reasonable for Willis to receive a five million dollar signing bonus and a five-year contract worth, let's say, a million dollars a year."

Roy had been writing the figures down as quickly as McMichael said them, adding them up as he went.

"Let's see," he said. "That's ten million dollars for five years." He stared at the notepad as if looking at the figures would change them. When they didn't change, he blew his cheeks out with a huge expulsion of air.

"Whew! That's an awful lot of money ..."

"Yes, Mr. Rojas, but we feel it's a good ..."

"... but if you say it's fair, then we'll have to pay it."

"... starting-off point. What did you say?"

"I said we'd pay it. What else can we do?"

"Uh ... nothing, nothing, that's right. You have to pay it."

"I mean, you've got us over a barrel, right?"

"Exactly, Mr. Rojas, and we certainly appreciate your keen grasp of the subject."

"So if you fellows get me the contract, I'll sign it right now. Even brought my own pen."

"Contract? Sam, where's the contract?"

"Well, it hasn't been writ ... er, finished, yet."

"Boy oh boy, we'll have to do something about that secretary of ours, won't we?"

Benton smiled. "I'm sorry, Mr. Rojas, but we hired her for her looks, not her typing speed. I'm sure you understand."

"Sure," Roy said, grinning. "I always liked the cute ones, too, but I would have thought that, you know, with ten million dollars at stake, you would've been a little better prepared."

"Well, Mr. Rojas," McMichael said. "Let's just say we were caught a little short by the speed of the transaction, so to speak."

"Well, that's the way you do business, isn't it? You tell me what something costs and I decide whether to buy it or not. That's how I bought my car."

"That's right, Mr. Rojas," Benton said as he stifled a grin. "Parker, why don't you take Mr. Rojas and Willis out for a cup of coffee while I get that contract squared away."

"Good idea, Sam. Mr. Rojas, Mr. Waller, care to come with me?"

Roy smiled. "Yeah, a cup of coffee sounds good. Boy, I thought this was going to be tough, but you guys are swell to do business with."

25

Roxy Reese had dreaded this moment ever since he had learned that Benjamin Kennedy was coaching the Warriors.

"Mr. Reese, I must admit I am more than a little surprised to see you here."

"Well, man, I guess I'm a little surprised ..."

"Let us get one thing straight between us right now, Mr. Reese. It is Mister Kennedy. If that makes you uncomfortable, you may call me Coach. I do not answer to 'man.' Is that understood?"

Roxy Reese, a little overwhelmed, merely nodded.

"Now the general managers had informed me that your response to their offer was lukewarm at best ..."

"Well, Coach, you see ..."

"That does not surprise me, really. The soft life, once one has become accustomed to it, is exceedingly hard to walk away from. If you do not mind, I would like to know the last time you worked up a sweat."

"In my last movie."

"Mr. Reese, from my experience, no one really sweats in movies. When your director wants you to sweat, he sends over a man who sprays it on you. What I want to know is, when was the last time you really exercised the muscles of your body? Do you think you could run a mile full-out? A half mile? The length of a football field?"

"Yeah, I ..."

"Should you decide to remain with us, you will find out precisely what your limits are. You will work very, very hard. Ask anyone out there in that locker room. It is excruciating work. A number of the men here are in far worse shape than you, and all of them are working hard. I can say with some degree of certainty that not one of them likes it."

Reese nodded.

"But they are not leaving. They are not giving up. They want to play football and they know the only way is to prove to me that they have worked off the laziness and sloth to which they have become accustomed. Do you know something else, Mr. Reese? They are better athletes and better men, whether they make the team or not, than they ever were before. I am offering you that same satisfaction."

"Yeah," Reese said. "Blood, sweat, toil and tears ..."

Perhaps he appreciated the respect he had gained from Reese, and maybe it was just that he liked the idea of being compared to Winston Churchill. Whatever the reason, Ben Kennedy smiled. It wasn't a warm smile, but Reese felt he had made contact with the man seated behind the desk.

He smiled back.

"Perhaps," Kennedy said. "But when you are through bleeding and sweating, you'll be a better football player than you ever were."

"Coach, I was a pretty fair player."

"No, Mr. Reese, you were more than a pretty fair player. You were the best. The absolute best runner I ever saw on a football field. I used to watch you on television, watch you destroy opposing defenses, and I used to talk to myself. Dear Lord, I thought. What I could do with that man. What I would have given to coach you in those days. But I never had that chance, and you were given to men who pampered you and spoiled you, men who gave in to your every whim and who allowed you to become less of a player than you were meant to be.”

“Hold on a minute, Coach. You’re coming on a little strong here. You’re telling me that you’ll take me, a thirty-five year old man who’s been out of the game for eight years, a man who’s had three knee operations, that you’ll make me into a better player than I was in my prime?”

“Yes.”

“And all I have to do is work hard?”

“Extremely hard,” Kennedy said. “Harder than you have ever worked in your life.”

“What if you fail?”

Kennedy arched an eyebrow at Reese. “I will not be the one who fails, Mr. Reese.”

“What if I get injured?”

“You will mend.”

“What if I don’t like it?”

“You won’t. No one here is enjoying himself, but that is not the purpose of our work together. Everyone here is here for two things -- to learn how to play football and to learn how to win.”

Reese still seemed skeptical. “And you really think you can make me into a better football player?”

“No, Mr. Reese. I cannot make you into anything, but if you decide to join this team and if you follow my instructions, you will make yourself into a better player. It will not be easy, Mr. Reese. In fact it will be damned hard. You have a lot of fat to work off."

"I haven't got an ounce of fat anywhere on me."

"Not on your body, Mr. Reese, but you have fat habits. You think like a fat man, but by the time you are finished here, you will think like a football player."

26

Fred Reynolds' column, The Washington Tribune, May 15:

"Well, Dean and Jerry are at it again.

"Actually, it's probably not fair to compare our favorite local buffoons to that great comedy team of long ago. You see, Martin and Lewis were much funnier. Krause and Rojas, on the other hand, are fast approaching the level of Shakespearean tragedy.

"One would think they would finally learn their lesson. They left that elderly gentleman, Roy Rojas, in charge when they went on their talent search, and he signed up old men who needed walkers to make it up and down the field.

"So what did they do? They went to Alabama and left him in charge again. He promptly threw a $10 million contract at an untested rookie.

"Jesus wept.

"Have they learned yet? What do you think? Once again this week, Messrs. Krause and Rojas are out of town. They are living proof of the old saw that those who do not remember history are doomed to repeat it.

"Once again, Roy Rojas is in charge. Krause and Herbert Rojas are attending the social gathering in New Orleans known as the NAFA's summer meetings.

"As everyone associated with the game knows, little of value ever is accomplished at these meetings. Various committees gather to give final approval to rules changes, and teams get together to discuss trades.

"Of course, since our new general managers took advantage of the hapless Duncan Charles to all but steal the third pick in the recent draft, no one in the league even is speaking to them.

"They should accomplish a lot.

"Not that I blame them for making the trip. The Association picks up the tab -- hotel suites, meals and drinks, entertainment. There are few more enchanting cities than New Orleans.

"Still, perhaps the most interesting thing about the week will be what happens in Washington while they are gone. I cannot help but feel a shiver of fear at the thought of the fort being defended by the elder Mr. Rojas.

"This time I expect him to sell the stadium."

The commissioner stood, lifted his spoon and tapped it against his coffee cup.

"Gentlemen, we have a great deal to cover and not a great deal of time."

The five members of the North American Football Association's policy committee stopped talking among themselves and turned to face the commissioner.

"The first order of business is the membership of this committee. As I'm sure you know, since we last met in January, we have lost two members -- Mr. David Charles of Chicago and Mr. Stanley Cagney of Philadelphia. We have replaced Mr. Charles with his son, Duncan, the new operator of the Chicago franchise."

The commissioner turned with a flourish and faced Duncan. "I hope you will be with us for a long time, Duncan."

Duncan smiled weakly.

"You have made some interesting mistakes since you took control of your franchise, but who among us has never made a mistake? Above all else, you have demonstrated a willingness to accept the guidance and judgment of the Association and to learn from your mistakes."

Duncan smiled again.

"I am beginning to believe you are cut from the same cloth as your father and we are happy to have you as a part of our little group."

"Thank you, Commissioner."

"I wish the same thing could be said for the offspring of our other late colleague." Heads around the table nodded in agreement. "It appears, gentlemen, that Tracey Cagney will bear watching, along with our other problem, the two gentlemen in Washington."

The gentlemen from Washington had spent the week attending the meetings, conferences, seminars and cocktail parties. They were shown new equipment being considered for use in the Association -- new styles of helmets and shoes, a disposable paper uniform that no one found practical and new machines that improved the maintenance of artificial turf.

Dave pointed out that there was little reason for the last, since the Warriors were one of the last remaining teams in the league whose field was natural grass, but Herb was too busy ogling the nubile young things demonstrating the machine.

"Hey, Dave, lighten up," he said. "Maybe we'll put in fake grass next year."

The two of them were enjoying themselves so much that they didn't mind the fact that every other member of the Association treated them as though they didn't exist. No one connected with any of the other franchises had spoken more than two sentences to them all week. No one had called to offer them trades.

No one even said hello to them as they sat in the coffee shop each morning eating breakfast.

"Morning, Dave!" Herb said as he came up behind him and slapped him on the back.

Dave winced as a bite of omelet almost went down his windpipe. "Do that again, Herb, and you'll need an artificial limb."

"My, aren't we in a chipper mood this morning."

"Herb, where have you been? I've been calling your room since seven."

"Sorry, but I just got in. What's for breakfast?"

"Nothing special. Where were you all night?"

"Remember that little redhead we met last night in the bar? She had a friend I hit it off with. You should have been there."

"Why didn't you call me? I would have joined you."

"Hell, I figured you could get your own women. I figured it would hurt your feelings if I had to get you a date."

"I would've gotten over it," Dave said. "You just got greedy."

"Yeah, I guess so ... You mean you didn't get any action?"

"I don't want to talk about it. Herb, did you go to bed with both of them?"

"Dave, a gentleman never tells. I love New Orleans."

"What am I going to do with you?"

"Good morning, gentlemen."

Dave and Herb looked up to see William Peace Lippmann standing over them.

Herb was the first to react. "What the ..."

Dave cut him off with a wave of his hand. "Good morning, Mr. Lippmann. It's such a pleasant surprise to see you again. Won't you sit down and join us?"

"Oh, I only have a minute or two. We're conducting one of our recruitment drives at the Civic Arena this week. You two should attend -- I'm sure you'd find it most uplifting and illuminating."

"I'm sure we would ..."

"What a coincidence," Herb interrupted sarcastically. "That you should happen to schedule something in New Orleans the exact same week the Association has its summer meetings."

"There is no coincidence at all, Mr. Rojas, although you may be loath to admit it. These meetings are scheduled years in advance. In this case, the city fathers presented us with a request last April, requesting that we bring our message of salvation through wealth to this poverty-infested city."

"And you just happened to have an open date this week."

"Precisely."

Herb smiled. "You'll pardon me if I remain a little skeptical. I'm sure you didn't come over here just to pass the time of day."

"As a matter of fact, Mr. Rojas, I did have a specific purpose in seeking you out. Oddly enough, it was to invite you to our meeting this evening. We're featuring a very special speaker, just back from his first visit to the South Seas."

"I wonder who that might be."

"My goodness, Mr. Lippmann," Herb said sarcastically. "How is George ever going to convert the heathen masses if you keep bringing him back to the States?"

"Mr. Rojas, there are heathen masses everywhere."

Herb smiled back while Dave carried on the conversation. "Mr. Lippmann, what purpose would there be in our seeing George again?"

"I only wanted you to see that he was not wasting away in the jungle," Lippmann said, stroking his diamond stickpin. "If anything, gentlemen, he is in even better shape now than he was before he left. He is still young and firmly muscled and now he is tan and robust-looking, as fine a specimen of athleticism as you ever could hope to see."

"You don't have to sell us on the guy," Herb said. "We drafted him. We think he's one helluva ballplayer."

"Remember, Lippmann," Dave said. "You're the one who's keeping George from playing for the Warriors."

"I beg to differ, sir. It was your lack of charity that kept, and still is keeping, George Greenblatt out of the Association."

"Then it'll keep on keeping him out," Herb said.

"Very well," Lippmann said frostily. "That is, of course, your decision. Good day!"

"Well, Herb," Dave said after Lippmann had made his exit. "We still don't have a tight end. Any ideas?"

"Maybe we can do without one."

"Herb ..."

"Yeah, yeah, I know. Well, maybe the tooth fairy will leave one under our pillows."

"I've found worse things under my pillow in the morning."

Upstairs at the policy committee meeting, the commissioner had come to the final item on his agenda.

"As you gentlemen are aware, there have been events taking place in Washington that merit the attention of this committee. I have invited Stan Pinello, the liaison to the Warriors, to give us his thoughts on that situation. Mr. Pinello?"

"Thank you, Commissioner." Pinello consulted his notes and began speaking. "To begin with, despite all the moves they have made in the last two months, the Warriors can be expected to win no more than six games."

Pinello paused to let that information sink in. No one reacted noticeably except the commissioner.

"Six games, Mr. Pinello? Are you absolutely positive?"

"Well, I'd hate to be pinned down on this, but I think six, maybe seven, games is a reasonable ..."

"Seven? Are you telling me the Washington franchise could win half its games?"

Pinello shrank back. "They would still fail to qualify for the playoffs. It will take a nine and five season to earn the runnerup berth in their division this year."

"That's all very well and good, Pinello. But have you done a study of what could happen if Washington were to get every good break imaginable?"

"Commissioner, there's really very little chance of ..."

"Have you done such a study, Pinello?"

"I have an estimate ..."

"And what is that estimate, Pinello?"

He pulled a sheet of paper from his folder and began reading from it. "Should the Washington Warriors have no major injuries, should every game be played under optimum conditions, if Willis Waller and Roxy Reese rush for a total of 1,800 yards between them, if the offensive line holds together and the defensive line exceeds all our expectations, and if their opponents suffer an overly large amount of injuries, there is a chance the Warriors could win nine games."

"Nine games?" The commissioner's voice was dripping with ice. "Are you telling me that team might be one of the eight to qualify for our playoffs?"

"Only if they get every break imaginable."

"Nine games? Pinello, I don't want that team to win four games, much less nine!"

Pinello was near panic. "Just a minute, please, Commissioner. Our study projects a fifty-two percent possibility Washington will win no more than six games, a thirty-seven percent possibility of no more than seven, a ten percent possibility of no more than eight and less than a one percent possibility of nine or more."

"Nine or more?"

"Well ..."

"Or more?"

"Well ..."

"Could Washington win more than nine games?"

"Not a chance, Commissioner. They have no bench strength at all. They're trying out some men who never even played high school ball. And if any of their key players succumb to injury -- Ross, Waller, Reese -- all they have to fall back on is the players they had last year. Realistically, Commissioner, the Warriors will not make the playoffs."

"Are you telling me there is no chance Washington will be in the postseason games?"

Pinello sighed. "Yes, Commissioner, that's what I'm saying. For all intents and purposes, the Washington Warriors are out of the picture."

"Intents and purposes, Pinello?"

"Commissioner, the odds against the Warriors making the playoffs are approximately two hundred to one. You could get rich betting with odds like that."

"I do not bet, Pinello. And I do not care for those odds in the least. The reason we adopted the System was to eliminate the element of chance."

"Commissioner, their chances are so tiny that ..."

"Suppose you are intentionally underestimating those chances, Mr. Pinello. Suppose you have failed to maintain the proper control over the organization and you do not want us to know of your laxity."

Pinello winced.

"Suppose Washington actually has an excellent chance of making the playoffs and you are downplaying it to save your own skin."

"Commissioner," said Pinello in as indignant a tone as he dared. "You know I would never do anything like that. You are more than welcome to check these figures yourself, and if you are able to find any disparity, I will be glad to resign."

The commissioner waved the offer off as if it had not been made. "Pinello, all that matters to me is that Washington fails and fails badly. I want the gentlemen who are running the team to do so poorly they will not be allowed to buy tickets next year, much less run the team. I want them run out of town on the proverbial rail. I want them humiliated so badly that no one will ever even think of doing what they did."

Pinello dared a laugh. "No problem there, Commissioner. I've been reading the papers and listening to the call-in shows, and there aren't many people in Washington who don't think those three are idiots and boobs."

"Let's make sure nothing happens to alter those perceptions, then." The commissioner looked around the table. "Is there anyone here who disagrees with me?"

There never was.

The rest of the week passed all too quickly for Dave and Herb. They attended more sessions and additional demonstrations. They voted on inconsequential issues, but they still were unable to get anything more than the most perfunctory conversations going with any of the other franchise operators.

So they were more than a little surprised when Tracey Cagney walked up to their table in the coffee shop on the last morning of the meetings.

"Hold onto your hat, Dave. A storm approaches."

"Good afternoon, gentlemen."

"My goodness, is it that late already?" Herb asked, gazing dramatically at his watch.

"It is precisely two minutes past twelve, Mr. Rojas."

"Well, so it is. Imagine that."

"Hey, Herb, lay off the lady."

"That's all right, Mr. Krause ... I do assume you are Mr. Krause. Mr. Rojas and I are well acquainted with each other."

"Yeah, right," Herb said.

"Then you must be Miss Cagney. It's good to finally meet you. Herb told me all about your little meeting at the draft."

She smiled a little wryly. "I'm sure he has."

"And I'm sure you'd like to tell me your side of it."

"Nope. Not at all. I couldn't care less what Mr. Rojas told you about what happened, although I would like to talk to you both about that same meeting."

"Really?"

"Really. I'd like to apologize."

"Huh?" Herb couldn't believe it.

"Miss Cagney, why don't you have a seat. Maybe we could order you some lunch."

She shook her head as she sat down. "No thanks, but I will have a cup of coffee."

Dave signaled for the waitress as Tracey kept talking. "As I was saying, I just wanted to apologize for my unprofessional behavior. I didn't handle myself well, and I didn't treat Mr. Rojas with the respect to which a general manager of an NAFA franchise is entitled."

"Gee, thanks," Herb said sarcastically.

"Herb, give the lady a break. Miss Cagney, I certainly appreciate your coming here and apologizing, even if I don't see that you did anything so awful."

She smiled sweetly at him. Herb was disappointed to see the smile was meant only for Dave. "Gentlemen, I am supposed to be running a business and I am expected to behave professionally. The trade that I offered Mr. Rojas was ridiculous and was based on an emotional outburst, and I can only imagine what the commissioner and his cronies said when they heard about it. I wanted revenge and I was wrong. It's a good thing the commissioner vetoed the trade."

"Maybe for you," Herb said. "We would've looked like wizards if he'd let it go through."

"Not necessarily. Every one of those players would have been unhappy in Washington. They might have retired or held out for better contracts. No, it's better this way."

"We accept your apology, Miss Cagney," Dave said.

"Please," she said, smiling sweetly once again. "Call me Tracey."

"All right, Tracey."

"Not you, Mr. Rojas. You may call me Miss Cagney."

Dave stifled a laugh. "As long as you're here, Tracey, maybe you could answer a question for me."

She nodded.

"What's going on around here? Are we lepers or something? Nobody except you will even give us the time of day."

"Can you blame them? You screw up their draft, sign up players everyone wanted out of the league and pay millions to untested rookies. Plus you're getting all sorts of headlines doing it."

"Tracey, they're not very complimentary headlines. And if you read the stories they're connected to, they're even worse."

The waiter brought Tracey's coffee and she lifted it to her mouth and blew on it. It was too hot to drink, so she returned it to the table. "Maybe so, but you are making waves, and there's nothing they hate more in this league than wave-makers."

"We've noticed," Herb said.

"The word's been passed, boys. No one is to do business with you two. No deals. No trades. Not even phone calls. Anybody who even talks to you goes straight to the top of the commissioner's shit list."

"Then why are you here?"

Tracey laughed. "Maybe I'm not in the mood to be a good girl. Maybe I don't like being told who I can talk to. Anyway, the commissioner doesn't like me all that much."

"Because of the deal he vetoed?"

"Among other things. I think some of it is just that I didn't have to be circumcised when I was born."

Dave almost spit up his coffee.

"Wait a minute," Herb said. "As long as you're rebelling, maybe you could do us a little favor."

"Like ..."

"I think I've figured out a way to light a fire under our old friend Billy Lippmann."

"William Peace Lippmann?" Tracey asked. "The financier?"

"Yeah. Now look, you've been seen talking with us. There's enough reporters and Association people around who'll testify to that."

She grimaced. "And they probably will."

"Whatever," Herb said. "Anyway, just make yourself scarce for the next few hours. Then after that, if anybody asks you if you've talked with us about Roger Steele, just say that you haven't got any comment."

"Why would they ask me about my starting tight end?"

Herb shrugged. "Just tell them no comment."

27

"All right, gentlemen," bellowed the voice from the platform high atop the tower. "Give me a mile at top speed and hit the showers!"

Roxy Reese hurt all over. No matter that he'd run a mile after every practice since reporting to camp, it still hurt like the devil. No matter that he was running that mile faster every day, or that he was less and less winded when he finished, Reese still hated the four laps around the quarter-mile track every afternoon.

The mile run wasn't the only thing he didn't like about training camp. He hated it every time Ben Kennedy told him he didn't know how to play football. He despised being told he would have to learn to run all over again. He was sick to death of running straight up the middle, time and again.

It seemed that two-thirds of Kennedy's running plays were designed so that a hole would open either to the left of the center or to his right. Reese was expected either to go through that hole or to block for Willis Waller following him.

And no matter how well he ran the play, the voice would come booming down from the tower telling him to run it one more time.

"What the hell am I running a mile for?" Reese muttered to no one in particular. "Damn field's only a hundred yards long!"

"Aw, Reese, are you at it again?" The voice from behind belonged to Jimmy Gardner. "You're supposed to be one of the leaders of this team, remember?"

"Yeah, Roxy," Tony Ross said as he sprinted past Reese to lead the group heading around on the third lap. "You're supposed to set a good example. These kids are looking up to you."

"Man," Reese said. "This guy's got me doing stuff I've never done before. He's trying to kill me!"

"Hell, Roxy, he's got us all doing stuff we've never done before," Gardner said. "If anybody ever told me I'd be on a team that had a 10 o'clock curfew, I'd have laughed in his face."

"Yep, Jimmy, and if they'd said you'd stick to it along with the rest of us, I'd have laughed too."

"You've got that right, Ross."

"What's a curfew?" asked Romeo Adonis as Gardner and Ross lapped the Adonis brothers.

"That's when they tell you to go to bed, son."

"Nobody tells us when to go to bed," Alphonse said.

"Yeah," Romeo said. "They ask us -- real nice."

"Last team I was on didn't even have a curfew," Gardner said. "The coach figured we were all grown men and we knew how to take care of ourselves. Most nights we'd get in two-thirty, three in the morning and still get up at seven."

"Hey," Ross said. "Didn't that guy get fired when you started the season oh and six?"

"Yeah, but we had one helluva good time."

"Gentlemen, you are lagging behind," boomed the voice from the top of the tower. "Mr. Reese, perhaps you would like to give me two miles?"

"Damn!" Reese said under his breath. "Wish to hell somebody would blow up that tower."

"Yeah," Gardner said. "Who is he anyway, God?"

"No, man," Reese said. "He's Benjamin Kennedy, the lord and master of the plantation, watching over all us poor niggas!"

"I wonder if he ever comes down from that tower," Ross said.

"He's got to, man," Gardner said. "Got to use the facilities."

"Nah," Reese said. "He's probably got a chemical toilet up there."

"Probably has cheerleaders shipped up there at night?"

"For what? Sex?"

"Nah, dictation. He works on his game plans at night."

"Hey," Ross said. "Anybody notice Wade Stephenson wasn't here this morning?"

A hush fell over the group. "Yeah," Gardner said. "Poor son of a bitch was in way over his head."

"Couldn't take it."

"Too far out of shape."

"Too old."

"Whoa!" Gardner shouted. "Stephenson was four years younger than I am!"

"That's right, Jimmy," Reese said.

"Need I remind you, boys, that quarterbacks go on forever? All I've got to do is take two steps back and get rid of the ball."

"As long as you've got linemen," Ross said. "Otherwise you get broken in half by guys like the Adonis brothers."

Gardner shuddered. "Those guys are scary."

"I just thought of something," Reese said. "Just two weeks till the exhibition opener in Toronto."

"Oh, Lord," Gardner said. "Two more weeks of two-a-days!"

"You're moving too slowly, gentlemen," boomed the voice from the tower. "That will cost you four more laps!"

28

The announcement over the hotel's public address system, paging either David Krause or Herbert Rojas, surprised everyone except the gentlemen in question.

"Dave Krause speaking."

"Mr. Krause, is it true what I hear?"

"Why, Mr. Lippmann, I can't possibly answer that question. It's metaphysically impossible for me to know what you hear."

"Don't be coy with me, friend, or I'll cut your balls off and eat them for dinner. Without the fava beans and the nice Chianti."

"That's an appetizing thought."

"I'm sure you're aware of the talk about your proposed trade with Philadelphia for Roger Steele."

Bingo, Dave thought. "Yes, Bill, we've been speaking with Tracey Cagney about him. After all, we still need a tight end."

"I know you need a tight end. That's why you drafted one from me. How

235

could you possibly want to trade for an old man like Steele when you could have George Greenblatt?"

"Come off it, Willy. George isn't in our plans anymore, and he probably wasn't as good as we thought. If George doesn't want to play for us, we don't want him."

"How can you be so foolhardy?"

"Maybe I'm just tired of playing games. I've got an exhibition game in two weeks and I don't have time to worry about whether George Greenblatt would rather play tight end or save the population of Micronesia from poverty and communism."

Lippmann tried to interrupt, but Dave was on a roll. "We're not going to pay you off. We're not going to dance to your tune. Either I sign George Greenblatt today or I find myself another tight end. And I don't think I need to tell you that if I don't sign him, his value to you drops to about zero."

"Just what do you mean, Krause?"

"I guess what I mean to say is that George Greenblatt, South Sea Yuppie, is worth a helluva lot less to you that George Greenblatt, Professional Football Player."

"Are you trying to tell me I would use that boy to make money for my corporation?"

"In a New York minute, Willy."

"My friend, you are sadly mistaken. It is the glorious power of the message, not the messenger, that brings ..."

"Fine. Goodbye."

"Just a moment, sir. Suppose I call your bluff? Suppose I tell you to go ahead and trade for Steele?"

"Thanks for your blessing, Mr. Lippmann."

Dave didn't hang up the phone, though. He held it to his ear and listened to the labored breathing at the other end of the line. "Cards on the table, Lippmann."

More silence, and Dave thought for a moment he might have gone too far.

"All right, Mr. Krause. You've got your tight end."

"You'll talk with him?"

"He'll be in your suite in half an hour," Lippmann said, although Dave was sure he wasn't happy about it.

They returned triumphantly from New Orleans with an ordeal ahead of them. Roy Rojas had agreed to have Dave and Herb appear on Fred Reynolds' radio show, and they went straight from the airport to the studio.

Reynolds told them they would be taking calls from Warrior fans for the first hour of his three-hour show.

"This ought to be good," the reporter said. "Half the people who call in on this show talk about what idiots you are."

"What about the other half?" Herb asked.

"They never heard of you."

"Hope they're the ones who call," Dave muttered.

"I'll bet you do," Reynolds said.

The studio was cramped, barely big enough for two men. With three in the room, and one of them the three-hundred pound Reynolds, Herb was afraid there wouldn't be enough air to go around.

Reynolds' producer signaled to him that they still had ten seconds before airtime, so he cleared his throat and motioned to his guests to be quiet.

"Good evening and welcome to another edition of Sports For You. I'm Fred Reynolds, and we're here every Monday through Friday from seven to ten p.m., taking your calls and rapping about sports."

He paused for a breath.

"Tonight we've got two very special guests, Herbert Rojas and David Krause, the general managers of our own Washington Warriors. Good evening, gentlemen."

"Evening, Fred."

"Hello, Fred."

"Well, guys, you've been running the Warriors for almost two months now, and I'm sure our callers are eager to let you know what they think about the job you're doing. Let's go right to the phones."

Reynolds checked the computer screen in front of him. "All right, line one. Keith from Fairfax. You're on Sports For You."

"Hi, Fred, This is Keith from Fairfax. I'd like to know if Dave and Herb think the Warriors are going to make it to the Championship Bowl this season."

Dave and Herb looked at each other.

"Not a chance in the world," Herb said.

Reynolds was nonplussed. "I must say, I appreciate your honesty, Mr. Rojas, but do you really think that's wise? You're supposed to be trying to build interest in your team, remember?"

"Oh, well. Herb's just a lousy liar."

"Yeah. Listen, Keith. All those years we were listening to this show, the guys running the team would come on and talk about how good the team was going to be and how this was going to be the year the Warriors made it all the way to the Championship Bowl. Then they'd go three and eleven. Well, no more lies. It ain't gonna happen this year, folks."

"It ain't ... isn't?"

"Let's be realistic, Fred," Dave said. "We don't have the talent to beat Miami or Pittsburgh. We probably don't even have as much talent as New York or Boston. Nope, there's no way this team is going to the Bowl."

"But gentlemen, I seem to remember someone getting up at a certain stockholders' meeting and telling us they could bring a winner to Washington."

"We said we could make the team better," Herb said. "And it is better. We've got a coach who knows what he's doing, we painted the stadium and we signed the Morris Trophy winner."

"Yes," Reynolds said sarcastically. "You made Willis Waller, a young rookie who has never played professionally, the highest paid football player in NAFA history."

"Hey," Dave said. "He's going to be a good one."

"Let's hope so."

"Look, Reynolds," Herb said. "Anyone who reads that rag of yours knows you don't like us, but we promised the team would be more interesting to watch and it will be. We're not champions, but we're going to have a helluva good time. When you get right down to it, what more could anyone ask?"

"How about a winning record? Let's go back to the phones. Denise from Alexandria, you're on Sports For You."

"Yeah, Fred. This is Denise from Alexandria ..."

The Toronto stadium was packed for the exhibition opener when the referees called the captains to the fifty-yard line for the toss of the coin.

"Captains Wilson and Gardner of the Washington team, meet captains Lemmon, Wiles, DeJesus, Sanduski and Miller of the Toronto team."

The seven men extended their hands across the fifty.

"Jeez, Jimmy," Bart Wiles said. "What are you doing here? I thought you retired."

"Hey," Lenny Sanduski said. "I thought he was dead."

Gardner just smiled.

"Washington, call the toss."

The referees in the NAFA all had specially minted silver dollars. The head of the coin bore the commissioner's likeness, while the other side had an engraving of the league's stadium in New Orleans.

"I'll take heads," Gardner barked as the referee tossed the coin into the air.

The silver dollar turned over and over until it reached its apex and then dropped to the ground.

"Washington calls heads," the official said. "It is tails. Toronto wins the toss."

Roy Rojas, sitting in the visiting owner's box with his son and Dave, threw up his hands in despair.

"That's it! We're through! It's an omen!"

"What?" Herb asked.

"It's an omen, I tell you! We're sunk! We might as well quit!"

"For crying out loud, Roy. it's only a damn coin toss," Dave said, annoyed they had lost the toss and equally annoyed that Roy was making such a fuss. "The game hasn't even started yet. Try and calm down. At this rate you'll have a heart attack before the first half is over."

"Yeah, dad. Cut the omen stuff."

While they had been discussing the significance of the toss, Timo Brahe, a Hungarian soccer player who had managed to convince Roy he was a cinch to be a star without knowing a word of English, had placed the ball on a tee on the thirty-five yard line.

Brahe stepped three yards back and five to the side and raised his right arm. On the signal from the head linesman, he lowered his arm, stepped up to the ball and with a magnificent sweeping motion kicked the ball seven yards forward and directly out of bounds.

"Nerves," Herb said. "The guy's just nervous. First-game jitters, you know."

The referee picked up the penalty flag he had thrown and stepped off five yards to the thirty. Brahe picked up the ball and squeezed it as if to correct its misguided sense of direction. He held up a finger to test the wind, forgetting that he was in a domed stadium.

Then he placed the ball on the tee at the thirty, stepped three yards back and five to the side and, on the signal from the linesman, stepped forward and kicked it again.

This time it went nine yards forward and directly out of bounds. He did the same thing from the twenty-five and the twenty.

"At least we can't get a safety out of this," Dave whispered to Herb. "After a while it'll be half the distance to the goal."

Roy was still moaning about omens. Finally, with the ball sitting squarely on the fifteen, Brahe managed to keep the ball in bounds, all the way to the twenty-nine. Unfortunately, the Toronto coach had accurately guessed the scope of Brahe's abilities.

He had lined all eleven members of his team on the Washington side of midfield and had pulled all but four linemen, sending seven running backs out to take the kickoff. The ball landed in the arms of rookie running back

Braxton James, who faked to the left, cut back to the right and followed a wall of blockers who had managed to put nine of Washington's eleven players on their backs.

James sailed untouched into the end zone.

"There might be something in that omen stuff," Dave said as Roy smiled smugly.

"Don't look so damn happy, dad. You're the one who signed the lunatic Hungarian."

Roy's lunatic Hungarian was met at the near sideline by Benjamin Kennedy. There had been little or no communication between coach and kicker up to this point. Brahe spoke no English and Kennedy had no knowledge of Hungarian, but the exchange between them didn't require an interpreter.

In fact, not a word passed between the two men.

Brahe approached the coach, who raised his arm to shoulder height and pointed in the direction of the Warriors' locker room. Brahe understood immediately. He took his helmet, left the field and was never heard from until three years later he was elected to the Hungarian parliament.

The first time Washington got the ball, Willis Waller fumbled to set up another Toronto score. The second time the Warriors were on offense, quarterback Brian Rider was sacked twice for a total loss of twenty-three yards.

Toronto got into the end zone quickly after that, using strong runs and quick possession passes. When the Warriors got the ball again, on their first play from scrimmage, Rider was blindsided by the Blues' all-conference defensive end, Chuck Matthews.

Rider made a peculiar squealing noise and fumbled. Matthews scooped the ball up and ran twenty-two yards for yet another Toronto touchdown.

By halftime it was 35-0.

Tony Ross, who had caught the only two passes Rider had been able to complete, came up beside Gardner, who had done nothing but stand beside Kennedy throughout the entire half.

"Jeez, Jimmy," he said, gasping. "Are they that good or are we that bad?"

Gardner laughed. "We're making them look that good. I'm just happy as hell I'm not out there."

With each score, Roy Rojas felt as though he was dying a slow, painful death and he let everyone else know it. Each time a Toronto play gained yardage, each time a Washington play failed, he moaned loudly, beat his fist on the table in front of him or just cursed.

The next box over -- with only a thin partition separating them -- was the press box, and the reporters traveling with the Warriors reacted loudly.

The beat writer for the Times, a florid man of fifty, turned to Fred Reynolds. "If he's going to run this team into the ground, the least he could do is have the good sense to be quiet about it. I'm having trouble sleeping."

Dave and Herb seemed more uncomfortable with Roy's histrionics than they were with the team's performance.

"Come on, dad ... it's only an exhibition game, the first one of the season!"

"Yeah, Roy. It doesn't mean anything. It's just an exhibition."

"I know, boys. I just can't help it. I mean, Toronto's not even that good."

"Well, dad, neither are we, so relax and have another one of those free beers."

"Relax, Roy. It's only halftime. There's still a lot more football left to be played."

"Yeah," Roy said, cheering up a little. "Who knows? We might even score."

In fact, things did get a little better for the Warriors in the second half. Toronto's starters had retired for the evening, and the Blues coach took a long look at a number of rookies and free agents who would never make the team.

The Blues had much less success moving the ball, and Washington finally got something going. Rider started mixing short passes with handoffs to Reese and Waller, and by the end of the third quarter the Warriors had mounted a drive from their own twenty to the Toronto seventeen.

On fourth and two, Ben Kennedy called for his other placekicker. "All right, Mr. Blaylott, it's your turn to show us what you can do."

Needless to say, Norm Blaylott was incredibly nervous. It was his first appearance in a professional game, and he was playing on the same field with men he had admired throughout his childhood. The last thing he wanted to do was embarrass himself.

He wasn't even all that concerned with making the field goal. A close miss would have satisfied him. He just wanted to prove he belonged on the field.

Blaylott concentrated on looking like a calm, collected professional football player. He trotted onto the field with an attitude he assumed looked confident. He accepted the encouraging remarks of his teammates with what he desperately hoped they thought was an air of nonchalance.

He stared at the ground, his arms limp at his side in the same nonchalant manner of every professional placekicker he had viewed on television since he was four years old.

When Brian Rider called the count, took the snap and placed the ball on the turf, Blaylott concentrated on taking firm, confident steps on his approach.

Unfortunately, Blaylott forgot one of the cardinal rules of all sport. He forgot to keep his eye on the ball. Norm Blaylott stepped forward and kicked Rider in the shin. The sound of his shinbone snapping and the ensuing scream were heard in the farthest reaches of the stadium.

Blaylott didn't hear Rider screaming. He didn't see him rolling around on the ground in pain and he didn't notice that the crowd was laughing. All he knew was that he had done the one thing he didn't want to do. He had made a fool out of himself in front of all these people.

All he could think of was what he would tell his father when he called him later that evening. Then he realized that he had never actually kicked the football and that the whistle had not sounded.

In real time, all this took about a second and a half.

An enterprising photographer for the Toronto Bulletin captured that second and a half and got a classic shot of Blaylott standing staring dumbstruck at the ball while Rider rolled around on the ground. It was a photograph picked up by the Associated Press, one that appeared in nearly every sports section in the United States and Canada.

Norm Blaylott reached down and picked up the ball, gingerly, as if it were a foreign object. Not knowing what else to do, he started to run with it. Unfortunately he was surrounded by players who knew exactly what to do, and all of them were wearing Toronto uniforms.

The first one to reach him was three hundred and five pound Eddie Joyner, who hit Blaylott with such force that all the air left his body. The ball also left his grasp and flew straight into the air and into the arms of the second man to reach the scene, linebacker Donald Sussman. He took off for the goal line, seventy-five yards away.

To all but the most devoted fans of the Blues, Sussman was a comical sight as he lumbered down the field. He wasn't graceful or fast, but by the time the Warriors realized who had the ball, he was thirty yards downfield and had worked himself up to full speed. Sussman had never scored a touchdown in his entire career and he wasn't about to be denied now.

When he crossed the goal line, twenty-two seconds later, Toronto had a 42-0 lead.

The Washington players gathered around Rider, who was now in a state of shock from the pain. No one paid any attention to Blaylott as he finally got enough air into his body to breathe again. He crawled off the field without any help.

Benjamin Kennedy intercepted the kicker just before he reached the bench. "Next time, Mr. Blaylott, try to remember it is the ball you are supposed to be kicking."

Blaylott nodded weakly.

One of the first Warriors out to check on Rider was Jimmy Gardner, who needed only one look at the younger quarterback's chalk-white face, contorted with pain, to realize he was now the starting quarterback for the Washington Warriors.

"Oh, shit," Gardner muttered to himself before helping to carry Rider off the field.

As it turned out, Blaylott got a chance to acquit himself somewhat when he kicked a fifty-one yard field goal on the final play of the game to help the Warriors avert a shutout.

Of course, Toronto had scored two more touchdowns -- one on a return of a Gardner interception -- and a field goal.

The game ended with the Blues ahead, 59-3.

This time there was no noise to be silenced when Ben Kennedy walked into the room. He went directly to the chalkboard, took a long look at the team and wrote something on the board.

"Practice, 8 a.m., Monday," Gardner read.

Ben Kennedy turned without saying a word and left the room.

29

"What happened Saturday night, Coach?" Reynolds asked Kennedy at his pre-practice press briefing on Monday.

"We lost, Mr. Reynolds."

"Care to elaborate on that?" the reporter from the Post asked Kennedy. "It's a little hard to build a story around two words."

"Gentlemen, try to keep one thing in mind. Saturday's game was the first one of the exhibition season. We were trying out new players under game conditions and trying to learn their strengths and weaknesses."

"Strengths?"

Kennedy sighed. "We will find some."

"You mean you haven't found any strengths?" Reynolds asked.

"I mean I would not tell you at this point."

The reporter from the Alexandria Gazette, a small suburban paper that sent its lone sportswriter out to practice once a week, had a personnel question. "Have you cut Norm Blaylott yet?"

"We have not cut anyone."

"What about Brian Rider?"

"I am sure you gentlemen have been informed that the X-rays show that Mr. Rider has a fractured shin bone. He will miss at least six weeks and possibly as many as ten weeks. Until that time, Mr. Gardner will be our starting quarterback. We are in the process of signing Lyndon Eaker to back him up."

A hundred yards away, in the locker room, Tony Ross was offering his congratulations to Gardner. "Well, Jimmy. It looks like you're back in the starting lineup."

"On, no, Ross, don't get started with that happy crappy. I ain't a starting quarterback. They signed me for my experience, for my leadership qualities. No way can I be the starter."

"Who else have we got, Jimmy? You think that kid Eaker they're signing's got what it takes to be the starter? Hell, he's just out of some small college down in Mississippi."

"He'll have to learn. Either that or they'll have to trade for a veteran starter."

"You're kidding, right?"

"Heck, no, Rossie. It isn't even that I don't want to do it. I'm just not strong enough anymore. I can't possibly go four quarters. Two, maybe three if I'm lucky. Then I'm in the oxygen tent. They signed me to play no more than five or ten minutes a game, and that's the way I like it."

The coach chose that moment to make his entrance.

"Mr. Gardner, I wonder if I might have a few words with you?"

"Sure, Coach."

"In my office."

30

The Chicago Trojans had lost their first exhibition game and had looked bad doing so. Duncan Charles was not at all happy about it. His team had managed only eight first downs and a mediocre total of two hundred yards of offense against the Pittsburgh Pistols.

Duncan had heard his first boos from the crowd at Daley Memorial Stadium and he was not amused.

"Kid, I shouldn't have to keep telling you this, but exhibition games don't mean squat."

"Aw, Ray, I wanted my first game to be a good one. We looked terrible out there!"

"You didn't look all that bad ..."

"We stunk! We sucked! It was awful!"

"It doesn't matter."

"What do you mean it doesn't matter, Ray? Did you see the papers?"

Duncan fished through the newspapers on his desk and quoted from the headlines. "Same Old Trojan Horses," "Another Chicago Fire." He located a column. "And here's one that really bothers me, Ray. Listen to this one. 'What is Dunkie up to?' Ray, nobody has ever called me Dunkie! I don't like being called Dunkie!"

"Relax, kid. They'll be calling you genius before the season's over."

Duncan wasn't appeased. "Not if we keep going the way we're going! Damn, Ray, we lost, 38-10. At this rate I'll never be as good as my father was."

"Kid, you are damn good. You took in nearly three quarters of a million in parking and concessions."

"Yeah, but ..."

"Look, Duncan," Martini said, putting his arm around the younger man's shoulders. "It's all part of the System. Chicago's going to be the Cinderella team, remember? Well, how can you surprise people if you come out smoking right off the bat?"

"But ..."

"Cinderella teams. Teams that come out of nowhere to take the whole friggin' shooting match. Teams that nobody in their right mind thought would make the playoffs, let alone the Championship Bowl. Teams that somehow manage to catch lightning in a bottle ..."

Martini noticed that Duncan was starting to snap out of his lethargy, so he continued the sales pitch.

"Teams that get something special going, teams that get the players, the coaches, the operator ..." Martini stressed each word at this point. "... on the cover of the Sporting News, Sports Illustrated, and sometimes, once in a while, even Time magazine."

"Time magazine?"

Ray Martini nodded.

Duncan stopped and thought for a moment, picturing what pose he would strike for his cover shot.

"Just trust me. I'm not going to steer you wrong. You'll get to the Championship Bowl."

"But Ray, why did we have to look so bad last night? Those refs threw an awful lot of penalties."

"Hey, kid. The refs have got to get into practice, too."

"Yeah," Duncan said, glumly.

"And so do I."

"You?"

"Sure, me. Who do you think tells the refs when to call their penalties?"

"You do?"

"Damn right. Kid, you're talking to the best damn game caller in the Association. The commissioner told me that himself, and you know that guy isn't overly free with his praise."

"How? ... What? ..."

"It's easy. You must have noticed I didn't sit with you during the game."

"Sure."

"That's because during the game I go to a booth that no one knows about. At least no one except the people who are supposed to know about it."

"Like me?"

"Yeah, like you. I mean, you're on the policy committee, aren't you?"

Duncan grinned proudly. "Yep."

"Now did you notice the guy on the field, the head linesman, the guy with the radio box and the headphones?"

"Sure. He's the guy who announces the penalties for television."

"Yeah, that's what everyone's supposed to think, that all this was just to make things easier for the folks at home. But nobody ever seems to realize those radios can receive instructions, too."

"And they do?"

Martini slammed his fist on the desk. "You bet your ass they do, kid! And you know who's at the other end of that radio?"

"You?"

Martini sat back, a satisfied smile on his face. "Yep, me."

"So you call the shots, Ray?"

"I call the shots. From my little booth that nobody knows about, I run the game. And from a little booth just like it in every stadium in the Association, the liaison man with the home team runs the game."

From the puzzled expression on Duncan's face, Martini knew he would have to give a complete explanation. "Look, kid," he said patiently. "The Association classifies every game, either A, B or C. An A game is one between two teams that are going to make the playoffs. The liaison man keeps complete control over everything. After every play, before the referee resets the play clock, he has to wait for the go-ahead from the man in the booth. He has to be certain that nothing alters the intended outcome of the game as it's been decided by the System. You with me so far?"

Duncan nodded.

"If the wrong team starts to get the upper hand, if it looks as though momentum is swinging the wrong way, I call down to the ref. I tell him we need a holding penalty, or a pass interference, or an offside. It happens on every play, kid. Somebody, somewhere, is holding. And the pass interference rules are so vague that almost anything can be considered interference."

"I've heard that."

"Hey, it's easy. Haven't you ever noticed how a team starts getting a head of steam going and then there's a holding call or an offside and then all of a sudden it's third and forever and all the life's gone out of them?"

"And that's you, Ray?"

"Me and the other liaisons, but I'm the best. Anyway, we watch over the A games like hawks. Now your B games are a little less important. Those are the ones between a playoff team and a non-playoff team. Naturally most of the games are B games. We don't watch them quite so hard, but we make sure we stay in control."

"And what are C games, Ray?"

"Those are the games that don't matter, kid. Some of those games we don't do anything but watch."

"Those are the fun ones, right?"

"Hell, no! I hate just sitting and watching. That's why I was glad when Chicago was picked to be one of the Cinderella teams. Every one of our games will be at least a B game."

"So you'll be controlling all fourteen games?"

Martini shook his head. "You haven't been listening, kid. I only control the home games, the ones here in Chicago. Remember, there's a liaison man with every team and all of them are trained the same. Of course, a lot of them do come to me for advice."

"Because you're the best?"

"You've got it. I'm the best, and now you know all you need to know about the System."

"Except when we're going to win or lose."

"You don't need to know that. Even I don't know that more than a couple of weeks in advance. Look, kid, there were four other owners in that meeting you went to, and you didn't hear any of them asking for details. Did you?"

"Uh, no ..."

"Because they know they don't need to know that. They know how things are going to turn out and they trust the System. It's never let them down before. You should do the same thing. Just sit back, enjoy the ride, collect your money and let the System do all the work. Remember, they're going to remember you forever in this town. You'll be the guy who got the Trojans into the Championship Bowl."

31

"I don't know what my dad's so fired up about, but he wants us right away," Herb said as he stuck his head through the doorway of the office he and Dave shared. "Wanna ride with me down to Cliches?"

What Roy Rojas had waiting for them at the bar was a defensive back, one Scott Trent.

"Why, Scott," Herb said. "Let me be the first to congratulate you. I take it you've worked your way up to one of those Washington stations you were telling me about."

Trent grinned a little sheepishly. "Well, not exactly."

"Oh? Then you're up here to interview?"

"You might say that. I'm here to play for the Warriors."

"Really?" Herb asked, trying to keep from chortling. "My gosh, whatever happened to that carefully plotted career course you told me about? The last time I talked with you, you were about two short steps away from being the next Bob Costas."

"Well, that's kind of on hold for now. I decided it would be good for my career if I came back and played football again, at least for a year or two."

Dave was blunt. "You got fired, right?"

"How did you ..."

"Just a lucky guess. You look like a guy who's unemployed. That and I happened to notice an ad in the Tribune for a sportscaster at your old station."

"All right, guys," Trent said, regrouping and flashing one of the dashing smiles that had made him a crowd favorite in his playing days. "You caught me, dead to rights. Those hicks in that town, they didn't know a good thing when they saw it."

Dave shook his head. "Scott, your ratings were the pits. Word was you could hear the sets being turned off every time you came on."

"Hey!" Trent said. "That's not fair! It wasn't my fault. They didn't do any promotion, their camera crews were a bunch of boobs and the station manager was a sloppy drunk. Now if I'd been with a professional outfit, one that knew what they were doing ..."

"Then why aren't you?" Dave asked. "What are you doing here?"

"I figured it would be a better move if I went back to the game for a while, maybe get on with one of the Washington stations part-time. You know, calling in reports from the practice field, co-hosting the coach's show, that kind of thing."

"Couldn't get another job, huh?"

Trent shook his head. "I can't understand it."

"So," Herb said. "You figured you'd give us a break and come up to Washington?"

"Come on, Herbie," Trent said, slapping him on the back. "Don't make it sound like that. I'm here to play football."

Dave's tone was cold. "Then I suggest you stop sucking up free beer and get your tail out to Oxon Hill. I'll call the coach and tell him you're on the way."

"Now wait a minute, boys. I'm not here for my health. We have to talk contracts, money, options. I'm worth a lot to this team."

"If you make the team," Dave said.

Trent practically spit his beer all over the bar, and Roy reached for a rag. "If I make the team? You've gotta be jacking me!"

"All we do is get players. Ben Kennedy decides who makes the team."

"Aw, guys, you're not telling old Scott here that he won't make the team," Roy said. "As much as we need defensive backs?"

"Uh, dad. Let us handle this ..."

Roy shook his head. "Anyway, I already told him we'd give him anything he wanted. We need this guy bad."

Herb sighed. "All right, dad."

"Scott, just get out to camp," Dave said. "We'll work out the contract with your agent."

"Well, Mr. Krause, my agent's a real busy man these days. I haven't talked to him in a month. Every time I try to call him, he's out somewhere."

"Just get out to the park, Scott. Coach Kennedy will want to talk with you."

Coach Kennedy was, at this moment, otherwise occupied. He leaned back in his chair and looked at the linebacker sitting across from him.

"Mr. Wilson, exactly what is wrong?"

Buck Wilson sighed with relief. From past experience he knew that players who were called into the coach's office immediately after practice were usually not invited to the next practice. Wilson had expected a speech about how difficult the coach's job was, and how tough the decision was, but for the best interest of the team, and so forth and so on ...

"Wrong, Coach?"

"Yes, Mr. Wilson. I would like to know what is bothering you?"

"Bothering me?"

"Mr. Wilson, please do not answer my questions with questions. When you first reported to camp, you displayed a fighting spirit that was, to say the least, impressive. You managed to do a very good job of overcoming my objections. However, your performance in our first exhibition game and in the last couple of practices, has made me wonder if perhaps I was right to object."

He paused and stared at Wilson, who remained impassive.

"Before I make any decision, I wanted to talk with you. I wanted to know if there was one particular problem that was bothering you. Are you having second thoughts about your comeback? Are you having problems with one or more of your girlfriends? Has your pet died?"

"No, Coach. Nothing like that."

"Is it something else, then? Tell me, Mr. Wilson, have you resumed your experimentation with illegal substances?"

"No!" Wilson practically shouted.

"Good. For if you were, I would not hesitate to release you from this organization. And kick your behind from here to Baltimore in the process."

Despite himself, Wilson smiled at the picture of the diminutive coach trying to physically assault him.

"I remind you, Mr. Wilson, that you are here to impress me."

"Yes, Coach."

"And you have not been impressing me the last few days."

"Yes, Coach."

"And you are certain there is no reason for this, no problem that is weighing heavily upon your mind?"

"No, Coach."

"If there were, I would suggest that you share it with me."

"Yes, Coach."

"Barring that, if you felt it was something you couldn't share with me I would advise you to share it with the Lord."

"Yes, Coach."

"Then things will be fine from this point forward?"

Wilson nodded. "Yes, Coach."

"Then that will be all for today, sir."

Dave had been back in his office only about ten minutes when his secretary told him there was a caller on the line, a Miss Cagney from Philadelphia. "Tracey, hi. How are things up north?"

"Fine, Krause. How are things down there in the capital? You keeping Congress from stealing any more of my money?"

Dave laughed. "I'm just trying to put a football team together. How come you're calling? Want to wish me luck this Saturday?"

"Krause, you're going to need a lot more than luck to beat my team."

"Would it surprise you if I said I thought we were going to win the game?"

"Surprise isn't the word for it. It would shock me, stun me and set me back on my heels. Krause, I've seen your game films. What was your score against Toronto, 59-3?"

"Yes, well, I thought I'd say it anyway. I'd be surprised if we even kept the game that close Saturday. From where I sit, the Bulldogs look like the best team in the league. So, did you call only to talk to one of the most charming men in America or did you have some other reason?"

"Please, Krause, you're starting to sound like your idiot friend. Self-effacing humility is a much better approach for you. Actually, I did have a couple of things I wanted to talk with you about. Are you still planning on flying in Friday morning?"

"Yeah, the coach insists we need that extra day and a half in Philadelphia. I'm sure I don't know why."

Tracey laughed. "I live here and I don't know why. Would you like to have dinner with me Friday night? There are a few things I'd like to discuss."

"Such as?"

"Well, I know you've been looking for a receiver to pair with Tony Ross, and I might have one for you."

"Really?"

"Sure. You've heard of Randy Jenkins, right?"

Dave was immediately interested. "The kid who caught sixty passes for you last year?"

"That's the one."

"But he's a helluva receiver. Your number three guy. What's the catch?"

"No catch. We're going toward more of a ball-control type attack, and besides, we've got four other receivers in camp who are better than Jenkins."

Dave tried to envision what it would be like to run a team like Philadelphia, where the biggest problem was finding roster spots and playing time for talented players. He couldn't visualize it.

"What do you want for him? Wait a minute, this isn't another bid for Ross, is it?"

She laughed. "No, I already told you I was wrong about that. And remember, I told you I saw the game films. No, I was just looking for a draft pick."

"How high?"

"A first."

Dave groaned. "How about a second? One of the things people around here hate is that the Warriors trade away their firsts every year."

"Nope. It's got to be a first. And what are you worried about next year for? Aren't you and Rojas on one-year contracts?"

She had a point. If the Warriors didn't win this year, there wouldn't be a next year for the two of them, and Randy Jenkins was an impressive receiver. One thing still bothered him, though.

"This isn't going to make you any friends around the Association, is it, Tracey? What about the commissioner's unofficial edict about not trading with us?"

"If it doesn't bother me, why should it bother you?"

He didn't know, but something bothered him about it. "Can I think about this for a couple of days?"

Tracey laughed. "I don't know. Can you?"

"How about if I let you know Friday night at dinner?"

"Sure. Where are you staying? The Hyatt?"

"No. Herb's dad booked us into a place he used to stay. I don't think he told me the name. Why don't I call you when I get into town."

32

"Oh, Lord."

Dave and Herb stared glumly at the building in front of them. They had known they were in trouble when the chartered airport bus took them past the business district, past theatres and restaurants and into a neighborhood littered with people who looked like they bought their clothes at Army surplus stores.

The Royal Arms Hotel, what was left of it, fit right into the neighborhood it inhabited. It had slipped over the edge from rundown to slum more than a decade ago. Half of the windows were broken or boarded up, the neon sign flickered sporadically and the front steps were covered with trash.

A few feet away from the main entrance, two men were conducting what looked suspiciously like a drug deal. In the alley a few more feet away, a rat was nibbling on some garbage.

Dave groaned. All this place needs is a drunk sleeping in the doorway, he thought.

"Herb, I thought your dad said this was one of the best places in town."

"Maybe we're at the wrong Royal Arms."

"Not a chance, man," the bus driver chimed in. "There's only one Royal Arms in this city and you're looking at it. Man, I heard the Warriors were in trouble, but I didn't think they'd sunk this low!"

"Who said we were in trouble?" Herb asked.

"It's in all the papers up here, man. When they found out you were staying at this place, it was pretty obvious."

"Herb, exactly what did your dad tell you about this place?"

"He said it was a real nice hotel -- friendly, classy. He used to stop here with his father when grandpa came back from the war."

"The war? Which war was your grandfather in, Herb?"

"Korea."

"You mean he hasn't seen this place since he was a little kid?"

"I'm sorry, Dave. I probably should have asked, but he said it was such a great deal. He told me they hadn't raised their rates much since the last time he was here."

"Jeez, Herb, that should have tipped you off right there." Dave turned to the bus driver. "Well, we can't stay here. Take us somewhere else. Anywhere, I don't care. The Sheraton. The Hyatt. Hey, even Motel Six would be better than this!"

"No way, man," the driver said. "Make a few phone calls first. I can't be driving around looking for hotels."

While the players and coaches sat angrily on the two buses, Mark and Herb frantically called hotels from the two working pay phones in the lobby of the Royal Arms.

What they learned was that finding rooms for ninety people on the spur of the moment was much more difficult than finding a single room.

"The Hyatt can take ten of us, but every place else I called is booked solid," Dave said. "There are five conventions in town. Jeez, we're going to wind up sleeping in the train station."

"Or the Royal Arms."

Dave stared at Herb. "Remind me to have someone break one or more of your father's legs." He looked around the lobby of the hotel. "I may do it myself."

***

When Herb showed up at the stadium for Saturday night's exhibition game, Dave was already sitting in the luxury box designated for the visiting franchise operator.

"All right, buddy," Herb said. "What the hell happened to you last night?"

"Hey," Dave said, trying to change the subject. "This is really some setup, isn't it? Real chairs, a bar, a big screen television. It's wild!"

"Answer the question."

"I guess it only goes to show the difference between owning the business and being a hired hand."

"For Chrissakes, Dave, where were you last night?"

"Come on, Herb. You think you're the only guy in the world who ever stays out all night?"

"You didn't have to fight the battle of the roaches all night long."

"Really?" Krause asked. "Who won?"

"They did," Herb said, but before he had a chance to elaborate, Tracey Cagney strolled into the box.

"Hello, Dave," she said warmly. "I really enjoyed ..." Then she noticed Herb. "Oh, good evening, Mr. Rojas."

"Good evening, Miss Cagney. It's so pleasant to see you again. Excuse us for a moment, would you?" he asked as he dragged Dave into the corridor. "Mr. Krause and I have something we need to discuss."

Once they were on the other side of the closed door, Herb looked directly at Dave. "Say it ain't so, Krause."

"Herb, I don't ..."

"Tell me you didn't spend the night with that babe in there."

"Herb, I wouldn't want to be indiscreet ..."

"Holy Mother of God, I hope you're kidding me," Herb said, crossing himself quickly. "I don't think you know what you've gotten yourself into."

"Herb ..."

"That lady is trouble, pal. Trouble with a capital T ..."

"... and that rhymes with P and that stands for pool."

"You're not taking this seriously, Dave."

"You're right. I'm not. I mean, what business is it of anyone else where I spend my nights?"

"Me, for one. The press. The board of directors. That asshole commissioner. What do you think would happen if Stan Pinello found out you were shacking up with the owner of the Philadelphia Bulldogs?"

"Relax, Herb. All right, I spent the night at Tracey's house. House, hell. It's a mansion. But nothing happened."

"Yeah, sure."

"Seriously. I told her about our accommodations and she offered me the use of a guest room. After what you told me about the roaches, I think I made the right choice."

Herb sounded almost disappointed. "You mean you stayed at that girl's house and didn't get her into bed? Lord, Dave, if you're going to get us in trouble, it ought to be because you did something."

"No one saw us, Herb."

"You'd better hope not."

"Look, we're almost ready to make a deal for ..."

"Oh, that's just great! First you wine and dine her and then you make a deal. The commissioner's going to fall all over himself vetoing this one."

"Don't worry, Herb. This one's more a typical Washington deal. She's not giving us a quarterback and two receivers for Tony Ross, if that's what you mean. This is a straight-out, straight-up deal, a player for a draft pick. She wants to give us ..."

"Which draft choice?"

"Well ..."

"Not the first, Dave. Tell me it isn't the first!"

"Well ..."

Herb sighed. "What broken-down player are we getting for our first-round draft pick?"

"Randy Jenkins."

"The wideout?" Dave nodded. "He's not bad. He caught sixty passes last year."

"So I have your approval to make this deal?"

"Sure. Now hadn't you better get back to your young lady?"

It was a particularly hot, humid Saturday night in Philadelphia, and most of the sixty-two thousand people who had paid twenty-five dollars and more for tickets to the exhibition game were dressed in little more than short-sleeved shirts and Bermuda shorts.

In the air-conditioned luxury of the skyboxes, however, Dave and Herb were able to keep their suit jackets on and still worry about catching cold.

Both teams seemed lethargic, and it was apparent that the heat and humidity would play a role in the outcome of the game. The warmups looked as if they were taking place in a swimming pool, and the first half was played much the same way.

Norm Blaylott, now famous beyond his wildest imaginings after injuring Brian Rider, drew a cheer from the crowd when he successfully kicked the ball to the five-yard line on the opening kickoff. Rocky Carlisle, the Bulldogs' all-conference kick return specialist, caught it there and returned it to the Washington forty, where Scott Trent delivered a bruising hit and knocked him out of bounds.

Philadelphia scored a touchdown three plays later, but there was no other scoring for the remainder of the first half. The Bulldog players looked bored, while Washington's offensive players looked badly overmatched.

Defensively, Dave and Herb were beginning to notice some small amount of progress. The Adonis brothers managed to break through the line and tackle quarterback Joe Bell for losses three times, and Bell even fumbled after one of the hits. Scott Trent intercepted a pass and returned it to the Philadelphia twenty.

The heat seemed to bother the Warriors' offensive unit a lot more, though. Jimmy Gardner couldn't get anything going at all. Twice the defense gave him the ball in Bulldog territory, and twice Gardner gave it back with fumbled snaps.

At least, Dave thought as he watched Gardner struggle to his feet after the second fumble, Roy isn't here to make obnoxious noises.

With the Bulldogs leading, 7-0, at halftime, Tracey Cagney stopped by to pay her respects. Before she had a chance to say anything, Herb started gloating over the closeness of the score. "Well, well, Miss Cagney. What's the matter with your boys?"

"I beg your pardon, Mr. Rojas?"

"What's the matter with the great championship team? Your boys can't seem to get it going against the poor little Warriors."

"Uh, Herb ..."

"Cool it, Dave. I'm on a roll."

"Mr. Rojas, my team will win this game. If your team would put up a little more of a battle, they might try a little harder."

"Uh, Tracey ..."

"Look, lady," Herb said. "Our guys aren't exactly a bunch of clowns. They're handling the famous Philadelphia Bulldogs pretty well, if you ask me."

Tracey smiled, but there was little warmth in the expression. It was the type of smile one saw in movies about maniacal scientists and Nazi prison camp commandants.

"Mr. Rojas," she cooed. "I wouldn't pack away the fright wigs and the big red noses just yet."

"Oh, look there," Dave said, trying to change the subject. "The marching band is forming the shape of a Volkswagen. It's a salute to motor vehicles."

Herb wouldn't be deterred. "We'll see about that, lady. I think maybe you've underestimated us. Either that or your team's got no drive. Could be the owner's not the only one who spent the night getting laid."

"Herb!"

"Dave," Tracey said icily. "Exactly what did you tell this ... gentleman?"

"Nothing at all! Just that we were talking about a deal."

"He told me enough."

"Herb, would you shut up and have another beer?"

Herb shook his head angrily. "You may have my buddy wrapped around your little finger, but you're not going to take advantage of the Washington Warriors. No, sir. We've worked our butts off to turn Washington into a winner and you're not going to pussywhip my friend into tearing it apart."

"Herb! That's it!" Dave pointed his finger at Herb. "Outside!"

"Don't bother, Dave. Your friend isn't bothering me." She stared Herb straight in the eye. "I'm too much of an adult to be offended, and too good a businessperson to let your boorish behavior have any effect on our dealings."

"Thanks for understanding," Dave said.

"I will suggest to Mr. Rojas, however, that if he wishes to continue availing himself of my hospitality, he should restrict any further comments to the weather."

"Yes, ma'am," Dave said as Herb remained insolently silent.

"Now I suggest you take advantage of my generosity and have another beer, Mr. Rojas."
Herb didn't say anything, but he returned to his seat and indeed signaled the waiter for another beer. Dave went over to the lady who had finished speaking. "I'm sorry, Tracey. I don't know what got into him."

"A little too much beer, I imagine," she said sarcastically.

"Maybe. I don't know. He doesn't usually lose control of himself like this." She looked at him with disbelief. "No, really. Well, maybe once in a while."

"All right. It's forgotten."

Herb stared straight ahead, pretending he hadn't heard a thing.

The third quarter went much as the first two had. The Bulldogs still weren't trying very hard, but half of their normal effort was enough to keep the Warriors far from their end zone. The Washington defense kept it close, allowing Philadelphia only a long field goal and a 10-0 lead after three periods.

The teams were changing ends for the beginning of the fourth quarter when Ben Kennedy called Gardner aside. The Warriors had just fielded a punt and had the ball on their own forty yard line.

"The time is right for a surprise. Throw the long one."

"Huh?"

"Which part of that sentence did you not understand?"

"Never mind. Coach, you know I haven't been able to throw the ball farther than thirty yards."

Kennedy nodded impatiently. "Mr. Gardner, for all intents and purposes, you are going to be my starting quarterback. I have to know exactly what you can do if I am to design an offense around your talents. I have to know your limits."

"All right, Coach," Gardner said as he headed out onto the field. "But remember, you asked for it."

No one in the huddle said a word when Gardner called the play, although Tony Ross, the intended receiver, shot the quarterback a skeptical glance.

Gardner took the snap, dropped back into the pocket and surveyed the defense as Ross broke downfield. The pass protection held up surprisingly well, but nearly everyone in the stadium wondered why Gardner was taking so long to throw the ball.

Finally, with Ross almost sixty yards away, Gardner reared back and threw the ball as far as he could.

It went thirty yards.

None of Gardner's teammates were in the vicinity of the ball when it dropped from the sky. The only player within reach was Duane Smith, the free safety. He had read the scouting reports and had been certain Ross could not possibly be the primary receiver. Smith was rewarded for his good judgment when the ball dropped into his hands.

With most of the Washington players on the ground, he easily threaded his way through the others and ran untouched into the end zone.

That seemed finally to shake the Bulldogs out of their lethargy, and they scored twice more in the fourth quarter, once on a long drive and once on a breakaway run. By the time the game ended, with the score 31-0 for Philadelphia, most of the fans were in their cars headed home.

Herb brushed off Tracey Cagney's sarcastic comment, muttering, "Way to go, bozos," under his breath as he headed for the locker room.

33

Fred Reynolds' column, The Washington Tribune, August 1:

"The more things change, the more they remain the same.

"I don't remember who the wise man was who coined that particular phrase, and I'm sure he wasn't referring to the Washington Warriors, but it surely does seem to apply.

"If you've been on an island the last few days, you may not know the town is buzzing about another trade. Our buddies in the front office traded their first-round pick in next year's draft for a wide receiver, Randy Jenkins, who wasn't even starting for Philadelphia.

"I thought this was one of the things they based their palace coup d'etat upon, that the fans were tired of seeing the team trade away their first-round picks for other people's rejects.

"Yes, Jenkins is talented. He caught sixty passes in his rookie season, but there's got to be some question how many he'll catch when it's Jimmy Gardner throwing to him instead of all-conference quarterback Joe Bell.

"After all, everyone knows wide receivers are the proverbial dime a dozen. You can even find them selling cars in North Carolina.

"And so, the beautiful Ms. Tracey Cagney seems to have bilked our boys out of their first pick, which should be one of the top picks in the draft if the Warriors win the two or three games I expect them to.

"If you'd seen this trade happen on the street, you'd have called the cops and had them arrest Ms. Cagney for grand theft.

Of course, considering the rather close quarters one of our general managers appeared to be keeping with the lady in question last weekend in the City of Brotherly Love, perhaps we should call the crime rape.

"The way I see it, it's one more example of what happens when you let the inmates run the asylum."

The mood in the locker room was somber when Benjamin Kennedy made his pregame speech. Most of the players present were already thinking about what the coach was telling them.

"... and so, gentlemen, a few more words and then we will take the field. There are sixty-eight of you present at this moment. By this time next week there will be fifty-two and by the week after that, there will be forty-four. For those of you who have trouble with simple arithmetic ..."

Gardner thought he saw coach Kennedy glance at the Adonis brothers, sitting with furrowed brows. "... that means that in two weeks, another twenty-four of you will be gone. Keep that in mind, gentlemen. You are playing for your jobs."

Kennedy paused and cleared his throat. No one moved. "Denver is not one of the stronger teams in the NAFA. They do not have an abundance of talent, and their coaches are not among the most intelligent in the league. We can beat this team, gentlemen. We can beat them by playing good, sound football. We will do it simply and we will do it well."

He looked around and was pleased to see he had the undivided attention of his players and assistant coaches. "No one is to make mistakes tonight. I have been told that mistakes are inevitable, that someone holds or interferes on every play."

Someone nodded and Kennedy glared at him.

"Not on my football team, gentlemen. If you are concentrating and executing properly, you will have no reason to make mistakes. And if you want to be one of the forty-four players who make this football team, you need to know how I feel about mistakes."

Kennedy paused again for emphasis. "I despise them, gentlemen. We have been practicing these plays for more than a month now. You know your jobs. Now go out there and do them."

The game was the Warriors' only home game of the exhibition season. Washington always drew the smallest crowds in the Association, and those crowds were even smaller in the preseason. After losses of 59-3 and 31-0 in the first two exhibition games, Dave wasn't at all surprised to see a crowd of about seventeen thousand in the stands when the Warriors and Denver took the field.

Dave, Herb and Roy didn't want to talk about it, but the three of them were excited by the prospect of their first game of the year at Herbert Hoover Coliseum. The stadium had been freshly painted and most of the potholes in the parking lot had been filled.

An hour before game time, five thousand or so fans were already in the stadium, watching the players begin to warm up.

"Just like we used to do when you were little," Roy said. "Remember, Herb, how we always came early to watch the players get loose?"

"Dad, for crying out loud, it was just last season!"

Herb was in a rotten mood and had been all week. Dave had tried to break through and make his friend feel better, but it appeared that Herb was bound and determined to be irritated and Dave had finally decided to let him.

"He's still mad because you made that trade."

"I am not mad."

"Come on, Herb, you've spoken in one-syllable words all week," Dave said. "All right, so I made a new friend this week."

"You let somebody screw you, and I do mean screw you, out of our first-round draft choice!"

"I thought you liked the trade."

"Yeah, until I saw what Reynolds said."

"Come on, boys ... say, what's going on down there?"

The stadium by this point was still less than half full, but the crowd noise was becoming noticeable. Instead of the usual rumbling, the babbling of thousands of conversations going on at the same time, it appeared a chant was building.

At first it appeared to be nothing more than the crowd priming itself for the game, but as more and more people joined in, Dave realized they were chanting one word over and over again.

"BEER! BEER! BEER! BEER!"

"Now why would they be chanting that?" Dave wondered.

He began scanning the lower stands, trying to figure what was happening. It didn't take him long to realize he didn't see any vendors moving through the aisles. Ne one was selling beer, or hot dogs or cold drinks on what was a hot Washington evening.

"Holy shit!" he said, jumping up and running out of the general manager's box with Herb and Roy following close behind. They ran down the ramp to the concession areas and found them unoccupied. "What the hell?"

"Hey!" shouted a spectator. "There they are!"

They were quickly surrounded by a dozen or so angry fans.

"Where's the beer?"

"Where's the food?"

"I want to buy a program!"

"My little boy wants one of those dolls you put in the back of the car, the ones that the head bobs up and down ..."

"Hey, buddy! My wife's hungry!"

"Herb," Dave said under his breath. "Run out to 7-Eleven and buy a couple thousand six packs."

"Cool down, folks," Roy said. "Just a little miscalculation, that's all. The folks who run the concessions should be here any minute now."

"Yeah, they'll be here in no time," Herb said, grabbing Dave and Roy and heading back to the upper boxes. "Now if you'll excuse us, gentlemen ..."

Once the three of them were back in the press box, Herb turned to his father. "All right, dad, tell me what happened!"

"Uh ..."

"Now, dad. While we're young!"

Dave resisted the temptation to say that it was already too late for that. "Yeah, Roy. What happened?"

"What are you asking me for?"

"Because every time we've left you running things, Roy, you've managed to screw things up royally!"

"Hey, Dave. That's my dad you're talking to!"

"Oh, so you think he didn't ..."

"No," Herb said, sighing. "I know he did something, but he is my dad."

"Herb, I'll bet you fifty dollars the old man forgot to sign a concessions contract."

"I did not."

"Yeah, right."

"Actually, he didn't," Herb said.

Dave had a sinking feeling, a feeling with which he was becoming all too familiar recently. "What does that mean, Herb?"

"Oh, boy," Herb said as he lit a cigarette.

"Herb, did you talk to them?"

"Well ..."

"Herb, what happened?"

"Are we talking about Magruder Entertainments? Are they the people who handle all our concessions?"

"Yeah," Dave said.

"Dave, those are the same guys I deal with at my bar. They distribute Coors. They're crooks, really! They'd rob us blind!"

"And you forgot to call anyone else."

"Yeah," Herb said sheepishly.

"Herb, this may come as a shock to you, but there are thousands of people out there who came to watch the game and probably would appreciate the chance to have a beer and a hot dog."

"Yeah," Roy said. "And what about that guy who wanted the little doll with the head that bobs up and down?"

"All right, all right. But you owe an apology to my dad, Dave."

"You're absolutely right. Roy, I'm sorry. Your son is an incompetent boob."

"Oh, that's all right ..."

"What do you mean, incompetent?"

"Just look around and tell me how many people are out there drinking beer and tell me who's incompetent. Look, get on the phone and call the Magruder folks and tell them to get out here ..."

"It won't work," Roy said.

"What do you mean?"

"I mean it won't work. By the time they get their people rounded up and out here, by the time they get all set up, the game will be over."

"Are you sure?"

"Dave, we run a bar, remember? We know about these things."

"Fine," Dave said. "Then one of you get on the public address system and announce that there won't be any food or drink at this game."

They blamed it on a labor dispute, but that didn't make the fans feel any better. At least half of them left within five minutes after hearing the announcement. It turned out to be the smallest crowd ever to watch a Warriors game.

For those who remained, it was a game which, while something short of spectacular, at least wasn't an embarrassment for the Warriors. The defense was particularly impressive, forcing three Denver turnovers and keeping the Mountaineers bottled up all afternoon. The offense had yet to jell, though, and the score was tied, 0-0, at halftime, even though Roxy

Reese had gained eighty-one yards on twelve carries.

Finally, after Alphonse Adonis sacked Denver quarterback Bobby Beaverman and caused him to fumble at the nine-yard line, the Warriors took the ball in for a touchdown and a 7-0 lead.

That was enough to make Herb finally drop his gloomy outlook, and he joined in the celebration as he, Dave and Roy hopped up and down and hugged each other in their private box. The mood of glee lasted until Herb noticed that Ben Kennedy had not sent the first-string defense onto the field.

"What the hell is he doing?" Herb asked no one in particular. "Where are the Adonis brothers? Where's Buck Wilson? What are Stills and Lopez doing in there? Those guys aren't even going to make the team!"

"Relax, Herb," Roy said.

"Don't tell me to relax, dad! We've got a chance to win a game and Kennedy's putting in a bunch of zeroes!"

"Zeroes?" Dave asked. "I signed those guys, Herb. He's got to look at everyone and he's got cuts to make this week. Leave the coach alone."

Herb settled down until the Warrior defense collapsed and Beaverman completed a long pass over the middle, past the hapless Stills for a touchdown to tie the game. After the kickoff was downed in the end zone, Kennedy kept Gardner and the other offensive starters on the sideline and sent in reserves.

"What!?" shouted Herb.

"Son, calm down ..."

"Give me the phone! Give me the damn phone right this minute!"

"What are you going to do?" Dave asked.

"I'm going to send out for pizza. What do you think I'm going to do? I'm going to call that ...”

“Leave the coach alone, Herb.”

“Like hell I will, dad! Holy ... A fumble! Look at this! Give me the damn phone!”

“No,” Roy said.

“Dad, out of my way!”

Roy shrugged and stepped aside. Herb grabbed for the phone.

“Yes, Mr. Rojas? I assume you must have a very good reason for disturbing me on the sidelines during a game.”

“Coach, what in the hell are you doing?”

“Mr. Rojas ...”

“We need this win, Coach. What in the hell are you doing? Put the starters back in! Now!”

“We have no starters, Mr. Rojas.”

“What?”

“There are no starters on this team until I decide on them, and unless you wish for me to resign at this moment as your coach, you will hang up the phone, place the receiver gently in the cradle and allow me to go about my job.”

“Yes, sir.”

“Thank you, Mr. Rojas.”

Dave and Roy stifled their laughter. In the space of only a few seconds, Herb had been transformed from raving lunatic to choirboy.

"Well," Dave said. "How did that go?"

"I told him what was on my mind."

"And?" Roy asked.

"And he knows where he stands now."

"And so do you. Now you know not to tell the coach how to run his team. So be a good boy and sit there and don't say anything for the rest of the game."

"Yes, dad."

Herb sat quietly for the rest of the game as the Mountaineers scored two more touchdowns and a field goal to win the game, 24-7.

34

No one could remember exactly when Kelly's Bar and Grill had become the unofficial hangout for the Washington Warriors. And once it had, no one knew exactly why it was the Warriors kept coming back, year after year.

Every time camp opened, the returning veterans promised themselves that this would be the year they'd find a better place to drink. Some even tried, but sooner or later all of them drifted back to Kelly's.

When the Warriors had built their training center in Oxon Hill, Maryland, fifteen years earlier, Kelly's had been one of the few places in town that would allow the players to congregate. Most of the owners of local watering holes had grown tired of bottles, windows and occasionally chairs being broken.

They had become weary of the loud arguments and the harassment of the regular patrons that seemed to go hand in hand with allowing professional football players through the door.

Not Kelly's. Seamus Kelly had opened the bar after returning from the Korean War, and even then the Washington Warriors had played an important role in the tavern's success.

Kelly had wanted a place where Warrior fans could gather and watch the games on Sundays. He put in the largest television he could find, a nineteen-inch DuMont, and he papered the walls with posters and photographs depicting the few highlights of the team's history.

Against the odds, and battling the general apathy of the local populace to the team, he made a go of the business by working fourteen-hour days. He did the bookkeeping, stockwork and most of the bartending himself. On most days, his only employee was his wife Nancy, who acted as waitress and greeter and occasionally helped him fix the sandwiches that made up the bill of fare.

Kelly never really got the chance to savor his success. Two years before his beloved team decided to open its training facility in Oxon Hill, just half a mile from his bar, Seamus Kelly dropped dead of heart failure when the Warriors lost a game to the New York Comets on a last-second interception that was returned for a touchdown.

Nancy took it all in stride. She didn't blame the incompetent play of the Warriors for her husband's demise. She even made little jokes about it, claiming truly to be a football widow and saying she had known the one person in town who really did live and die with the Washington Warriors.

None of that served to endear her to her customers. She was a broad, unattractive woman to whom humor seemed to come unnaturally. No one could understand what an affable, outgoing man like Seamus Kelly had seen in her, and the rumor was that she must have been an absolute hellion in bed.

That was sheer conjecture, though. Before Seamus died, no one would approach her out of respect for him and after he was dead, they stayed away out of respect for themselves.

Still, Kelly's had good food, cold beer, reasonable prices and, if you could ignore the bleated commands from the proprietor to keep a lid on it, an atmosphere conducive to drinking beer and talking football.

The Warriors came because those were the only two things they cared about doing after practice, and because all Nancy Kelly asked was that they keep the breakage to a minimum.

"Here you go, guys. Two cheeseburgers, two fries and two big beers. Anything else?" the waitress asked, bending low over the table and offering Tony Ross a generous look down her blouse. "Just let me know."

"No thanks, darlin'," Ross said. "Run a tab for us, will you?"

"Uh, sorry, but Kelly cut off all the credit."

"What?" Gardner snapped.

"Come on, Jimmy, she always does at this time of the year. It's the last week of camp," she said as she popped her bubble gum. "You might not be around later to pay up."

"I can't believe what I'm hearing," Ross said. "Darlin', you're not talking to a couple of snot-nosed rookies here. The man sitting across the table here is the famous Jimmy Joe Gardner, quarterback extraordinaire."

He reached across the table and grabbed Gardner's hand. "Look at this hand," he said. "Two Championship Bowl rings. Men wearing two Championship Bowl rings do not sneak off in the middle of the night without paying their bar bills."

The waitress was unmoved.

"Catch her, Tony. I'll get the next round."

"I don't know if I can trust you, Jimmy," Ross said as he reached for his wallet. "You might not be around tomorrow."

"Just give her the money, dammit! Rossie, what the hell am I always negotiating with you for?"

"Ah, I don't know, Jimmy," Ross said. He handed the waitress a ten and told her to keep the change. "Just comes natural, I guess. Hey, what'd you think of that house out on Central?"

"Oh, I don't know."

"Jeez, Jimmy, you've got to be the most indecisive son of a bitch I've ever met! It's a good thing the coach calls the plays, or we'd never make it out of the huddle! What the hell is wrong with that house?"

"I don't know, Rossie. I just don't want to get stuck with something I might not like later on."

"Then we'll move. Dammit, we're not buying the stupid thing!"

"Tony, it's not that easy."

"Name one thing that's wrong with it, all right? Just one thing!"

"Never mind! The house is fine, OK?"

"Great," Ross said. "You owe me twenty-five hundred dollars."

"I what?"

"I gave the real estate guy five thousand dollars this morning. Security deposit and first month's rent."

"You mean you already signed a lease? Who told you to decide all by yourself, you son of a bitch?"

Ross smiled at Gardner. "Jimmy, we've looked at eighteen houses. I was through looking and I just decided ... Oh, shit!"

"What? What's wrong?"

"Your shadow just walked in."

"Eaker?"

"Yeah, and he spotted us. Here he comes."

Ross waved to him.

"Why'd you do that, Rossie?"

"He waved first. What was I supposed to do, ignore him?"

"Aw, shit. He's gonna come over here and talk all about how good I used to be back in the old days when he was a little kid. I don't need that shit."

"Hey, Jimmy. You weren't that good."

"Yeah, I know, but can I help it if he thinks I was?"

Lyndon Baines Johnson Eaker made it to their table before Ross had a chance to answer. "Hello, Mr. Gardner. Mr. Ross. Would you mind if I join you?"

"Why?" Gardner asked. "Are we coming apart?"

Eaker almost doubled over with laughter. Gardner looked over at Ross, who answered with an eloquent shrug. "Go ahead, kid," Ross said with a wave of his hand. "Have a seat."

"Gosh, thanks, Mr. Ross."

Jimmy Gardner found it impossible to believe he had ever been as young as Lindy Eaker, who, he reminded himself, he would not have to be dealing with if Norm Blaylott had not removed Brian Rider from the active roster. Eaker was twenty-three years old. He always smiled and was always cheerful. He always said "sir" or "ma'am" to those older than him and he had an arm like a rifle.

Unfortunately, he wasn't always in control of that arm, which made him able to throw the ball seventy-five yards downfield but unable to predict where it would go. Time and coaching would probably iron that out, Gardner thought, and then Eaker would be something special.

He had tried out with the Miami Wave the year before, but the Wave already had one quarterback destined for a plaque in the NAFA Hall of Fame and another one who seemed certain to follow the same route someday.

Eaker, with his scattershot arm, didn't survive the first cut. He had spent the previous fall playing semipro ball, where he had been noticed by Ben Kennedy and signed to play in Washington after the injury to Rider.

"Uh, Mr. Gardner, my roommate Randy Jenkins came in with me," Eaker said. "Would you mind terribly if he joined us?"

"Sure, kid. Call him over."

Randy Jenkins had impressed Gardner and nearly everyone else in camp since joining the team from Philadelphia. By his second day of practice it was obvious that he was a threat to Ross for the spot of most talented receiver on the roster.

Unfortunately he was also one step removed from being antisocial. It was inconceivable to Ross that the open and friendly Eaker and the sullen and aloof Jenkins could be friends. Jenkins approached everyone as if he thought they were going to steal his wallet.

"Well, Randy, how's every little thing?" Gardner asked as Jenkins slouched over to the table and signaled for the waitress.

Jenkins glared at Gardner and didn't say a word.

"Look, kid," Ross said.

"Don't call me kid."

"Listen, Randolph ..." Ross said sarcastically. "... I don't know what your problem is."

"My problem, man, is this," Jenkins said. "Where would you rather be, in Philadelphia catching passes for the best team in the league, or in this shithole?"

"Actually, Ross is the wrong guy to be asking that question. He'd much rather be in Philadelphia."

Eaker chimed in. "Mr. Gardner, have I ever told you what a thrill it is to be playing on the same team as you?"

"Yeah, you ..."

"I remember when I was growing up, I used to be a member of your fan club, did I ever tell you that?"

"Well, no ..."

"And I don't even mind not getting to play much, it's such a thrill being on the same field as the old master."

"Old master?" Gardner winced.

Ross came to his rescue. "Lindy, I know you mean well, but Jimmy doesn't really appreciate references to age."

"Thanks a lot, Ross."

"I'm sorry, Mr. Gardner. The last thing I ever want to do is make you uncomfortable. What I mean is, it's really terrific that you've still got almost all of your moves at your age."

"At my ..."

"I'm almost embarrassed to say this, Mr. Gardner, but I know you'll understand. Sometimes, at night, when I'm having trouble getting to sleep, I think about junior high, when I used to watch you play ..."

Even Jenkins had to smile at that one. He thought his roommate had finally gone too far, but Eaker was undeterred. "I used to get down on my knees and say my prayers at night. I asked God to make me as good a football player as the great Jimmy Gardner. And now that I think I'm playing on the same team as you, I don't know why, but it just makes me sleep better."

"That's it!" Gardner stood up quickly. "Come on, Rossie, let's get out of here!"

"Jimmy, it's only nine-fifteen!"

"We've got to get our rest. See you boys tomorrow."

Ross threw a tip down on the table and followed a rapidly moving Jimmy Gardner out of the bar. Once they were out of sight, Jenkins moved closer to Eaker. "Man, what are you doing, sucking up to that old guy like that? What the hell are you doing kissing his ass?"

Eaker leaned back in his chair and sipped from his beer. "Is that what you think I'm doing?"

35

"Daddy, hi!"

"Hi, honey," Dave said as his daughter Kim bounded down the steps toward him. "Hello, Muriel," he said to his ex-wife as she followed slowly behind.

"Oh, daddy, I'm so excited, I've been telling all the kids at school and they are so jealous," she said. "They turned positively green, you know?"

"Green?"

"I mean, they were green when they found out my dad was going to take me to the game here, but to take me up to New York, and to fly up with the team, they were positively insane!"

"I'm glad, honey."

"Well, David, let's get going."

"Let's get ... Muriel, I don't remember telling you this was a trip for three."

"David, you can't possibly imagine that I would let you take my fifteen-year-old daughter to New York City by herself, do you?"

"Muriel, I'm her father," Dave said. "I don't need a chaperone. What do you think I'm going to do, sell our daughter into white slavery?"

"God knows what goes on in New York! I wouldn't know. We were married for nine years and you never took me to New York."

"I wasn't running a football team in those days."

"Whatever the case, either I go with you or Kimberly doesn't go. I will not allow you to take my daughter into the heart of New York City ..."

"For God's sakes, Muriel! We're not going to Harlem! The Comets play in Long Island Stadium. It's no more in the middle of New York than Falls Church is in the middle of Washington."

"I don't care. Either I go or nobody goes."

Dave thought that one over for a moment.

"Come on, daddy. It'll be fun, the three of us together, just like old times."

"Is that what this is all about?"

"What?" Muriel sounded indignant.

"Kim, honey, would you wait in the car?"

"Sure, daddy."

As soon as his daughter was out of earshot, Dave turned angrily to his ex-wife. "You put her up to that, didn't you?"

"I did no such thing!"

"Yeah, right."

"And anyway, you're such a big shot with the team, you can easily get an extra ticket."

"You've thought all this out, haven't you?"

"A little."

"Come on!" Kim shouted from the car. "We're going to be late!"

"Just a minute, honey."

"You'd better decide, David, or she's going to jump right through the windows of the car."

"All right, Muriel. If you insist."

He had always hated one particular smile his ex-wife gave him, and this time was no exception. Oh, boy, he thought. This one's really going to be fun.

The locker room was even quieter than usual before the game. Coach Kennedy didn't give a speech. No one discussed the game plan or compared notes on the opposition, the New York Comets.

Everyone was certain this would finally be the week the Warriors were going to win, and no one wanted to break the spell.

One reason was the opponent. The Comets had been a playoff team the previous two years, but appeared to be on the verge of one of the most rapid descents in the history of the Association. Nine starters had retired from a team that had finished 10-3-1 and three others had been traded for draft choices.

What was left was a collection of rookies and second-year men who would have trouble staying out of the cellar. It was, perhaps, the only team in the Association capable of making the Warriors look good at this point.

But there was more to it than the incompetence of the opposition. There was a feeling among the players that something finally was coming together. The Warriors, at last, were starting to look like a team.

The difference was beginning to show in practice. Passes that had been falling incomplete the week before were being caught. Reese and Waller were slipping through holes that now were being opened by the offensive line. The blocks were more crisp, the tackles more certain.

The players even thought the change had extended to their coach. Kennedy had not criticized anyone at length and had even been seen smiling on occasion. Some thought it was because the most marginal players had been cut and Kennedy now was close to having the team he wanted.

Others didn't look for reasons, choosing to enjoy the less-strenuous workouts and a reduction of the incessant laps around the field at the end of practice.

"They're looking better, Coach," said Roland Keene, Kennedy's long-time assistant who had followed him from job to job for nearly twenty-five years.

"Not enough."

"You don't think they can beat the Comets?"

"Mr. Keene, our old semipro team could probably beat the Comets. You and I could probably beat the Comets. No, we should win, and it will be the worst thing that could happen."

"Why?"

"The Warriors will win, and every media outlet in the city of Washington will be trumpeting the resurgence of the team. And it will last until the opening game."

Kennedy glanced at the clock on the office wall, and he and his assistant stepped out into the locker room. "All right, gentlemen," he said. "It's time to play a football game."

Dave Krause looked around the single owner's box at Long Island Stadium. At least, he thought, I wasn't the only one who brought extra guests. The box was filled almost to the point of bursting, and it was already filled with smoke and other unpleasant odors. The bartender had sent out twice for more ice and people were standing along the back wall.

Herb and Roy each had brought a companion, and the New York franchise operators had brought their entire families. Long Island Stadium was one of the league's oldest, and did not have separate boxes for the home and visiting owners.

It had been a sore spot for years, and the Comets currently were threatening to move to Hartford, Connecticut, or Trenton, New Jersey, if the city of New York didn't build them a new, 90,000-seat stadium with the taxpayers' money.

Dave looked around the crowd and took some comfort in the fact that Stan Pinello was wedged behind a woman bearing a suspicious resemblance to a female comedian who had built her act around her extreme obesity.

Pinello squeezed out from behind the woman and made his way through the crowd. "Good evening, David. And who are these lovely ladies with you?"

"Hello, Pinello. This is my daughter Kim and my former wife Muriel."

"Muriel," Pinello said, taking her hand and bowing slightly. "Why, David, how could you possibly divorce such a lovely young lady?"

Muriel had blushed and giggled, and Dave resisted the urge to say it had been easy.

"Could I get you ladies something? A drink for Muriel, perhaps some lemonade for the youngster?"

"I'll have a gin and tonic," Muriel said.

"A dry martini, shaken but not stirred," Kim said. Pinello blanched for a second and then smiled.

"What a delightful child," he said, giving her a pat on the head that she did her best to avoid.

"Stan is the Association's liaison man with the Warriors," Dave explained.

"Oh?" Muriel had asked, smiling at Pinello. "Does that mean you approve the trades and schedule the games?"

"No, no," Pinello said with a chuckle that sounded to Dave like a wheeze. "Nothing that important. I'm basically a go-between for the Association and the Warriors."

"An advisor?"

"That's right, Muriel."

"How do you like what Dave and his friend have been doing with the team?"

Pinello tried to smile. It didn't quite come off. Dave thought it looked like a baby with a full diaper.

"Well, Muriel, those two are certainly full of surprises, I'll say that much. Look at the time. I've got to be running along."

"Yes, do," Kim said with an air of finality.

"I'll see you all after the game. It was lovely meeting you, Muriel."

"Oh, it's my pleasure, Mr. Pinello."

"Please. It's Stan."

She smiled. "All right, Stan."

"Kim, enjoy the game."

Kim nodded. "So long, Mr. Pinello."

Washington won the toss and took the opening kickoff. Rusty Price, the defensive back Kennedy had tapped for kickoff return duties, fielded the ball at the two and carried it to the thirty, where he was hit and fumbled.

That started a scramble for the ball in which ten different players had it in their grasp at one time or another. The ball reacted as if it were covered with grease, squirting away from one player after another. By the time Price finally fielded the ball again, it was on the fifty yard line.

By the end of the first quarter, Fred Reynolds had taken advantage of his central location in the press box to label the game "The Incompetence Bowl."

It had caught on. Both teams were trying too hard. The Warriors had made only two first downs, the Comets none. There had been three fumbles and two interceptions. The only thing impressive was the punting by Washington's Lou Andrews and New York's Kent Davis.

"Damn, Coach," Gardner said on the sidelines. "It's a real dogfight out there."

"Yes it is, Mr. Gardner, but eventually we will stop making mistakes and that will be the difference."

"Let's hope it happens before Lou's leg gives out."

Kennedy turned to Gardner and fixed him with a stern look. "If you would make a few first downs, Mr. Gardner, the durability of Mr. Andrews' lower extremity would not be in doubt."

36

Eleven hundred miles to the south, the Chicago Trojans were rolling over the Miami Wave, 20-6, at the half. The powerful Wave couldn't seem to put anything together, while the Trojans were enjoying their most consistent performance of the preseason.

Duncan Charles was enjoying himself. "This is great, Ray! Just great! We're beating Miami!"

"Yeah, kid, it's going pretty good. It looks like you might finally have a team out there."

"Ray, I'm sorry I ever doubted you."

"Well, don't get too excited. Miami's a bitch in the second half."

Duncan felt a small tug of fear. "We're not going to lose, are we, Ray? I don't want us to lose!"

"Calm down. You can't expect Miami to roll over and die for you. They're one of the best teams in the Association."

"Come on, Ray! Can't you let us win this one? I thought we were supposed to be a Cinderella team!"

"Not so loud! Jeez, you want the whole damn world to find out about the System?"

"Oh," Duncan said sheepishly as he covered his mouth. "I thought everyone here knew about it."

"Just the operators, kid," Martini said in a low voice. "There's reporters and office help around, too."

"Oops, sorry, Ray."

"Anyway, relax. You're not going to lose."

"Swell!" Duncan shouted, so loud that almost everyone within earshot turned to stare at him.

In New York, Pinello had slipped out of the owner's box and had gone down the hall into the private booth where Abe Lowenthal, the league liaison to the Comets, wasn't even bothering to watch the game.

"Relax, Stan," Lowenthal said. "Have a drink. Before the game I told the boys to call it the way they saw it. They almost didn't know how to handle it."

"It's going to be an awful quick game, then."

"The quicker the better. I've got a date tonight. Hey, if you can hunt somebody up, maybe we can double. I've got a friend who can get Broadway tickets on short notice."

"That's not a bad idea. I might have somebody in mind."

The first half had ended on a Norm Blaylott field goal that put Washington ahead, 3-0, and the second half was more of the same. Neither team moved the ball with any degree of consistency. Finally, on the first play of the fourth quarter, New York scored on a long run by Teddy Denton, a rookie running back from Southern Illinois.

With less than fourteen minutes remaining and the Comets up, 7-3, Ben Kennedy sent his starting offensive unit back into the game.

"It is time for a touchdown, Mr. Gardner," Kennedy said as he gave his quarterback the first two plays.

"I agree, Coach."

"Good. We will start with the twenty-eight pitch. Blue. On two. Then come back with the sixty-two pass."

The play was designed for Roxy Reese to carry the ball around the right end, with Willis Waller running interference. Reese took the pitch from Gardner and sprinted to the right, where Waller had wiped out the cornerback. By the time a linebacker caught up with Reese and knocked him out of bounds, the play had gained thirty-one yards.

Gardner didn't smile when he called the next play. "Sixty-two pass. Red. On One."

Tony Ross made a sharp cut at the twenty, leaving the New York cornerback slipping and sliding. When Ross reached the prearranged spot, the ball was right there. Ross made it to the three before he was tackled, and Reese bulled over for the touchdown on the next play.

Blaylott added the extra point and the Warriors were ahead again, 10-7.

"Well, Coach?"

"Well what, Mr. Gardner?"

"What did you think?"

"I think you did your job." The two men stood in silence for a few seconds, staring at each other. "Was there anything else, Mr. Gardner?"

"No, I guess not."

The Comets weren't about to collapse, though. They drove to the

Washington 11, where they stalled and kicked a field goal to tie the game, 10-10, with six minutes remaining. When the Warriors couldn't move, New York got the ball back at midfield with three minutes to play.

The Comets' quarterback, Teddy Steele, knew he needed about twenty yards to set up a game-winning field goal. After two running plays netted only four yards, Steele dropped back to pass on third down. None of Steele's receivers were open, so he stepped to his left to avoid Romeo Adonis, who had broken through the pocket and was approaching him rapidly.

Unfortunately for Steele, his step to the left took him directly into the path of Alphonse Adonis.

All Steele could remember when he regained consciousness five minutes later was a loud noise, which turned out to be the scream he had made when Alphonse hit him at full speed. He didn't remember losing the ball.

"Pick up the ball, Romeo."

"OK, Alphonse."

Romeo Adonis picked up the ball and began running. Fortunately for the Comets, he was only slightly faster than the proverbial three-legged dog. Two New York players tackled him twenty yards short of the goal line.

That was well within Blaylott's range, though, and he kicked a field goal with nine seconds left to win the game for Washington, 13-10.

Amidst the general celebration by the Washington contingent, Muriel Krause pulled Dave off to the side. "David, would you mind taking Kim home? And could I have my train ticket?"

"What's up, Muriel?"

"Uh, I ran into some old friends ... they offered to take me out and show me New York ... I've never been here, so I figured I should take advantage of it."

"Old friends? Muriel, you don't know anybody up here."

His ex-wife seemed flustered. "It's, uh, an old girlfriend I went to high school with. She's here with her husband, and he works for ... Wait a minute, I don't have to explain myself to you! Just take care of Kim, all right?"

"What about white slavery?"

"No thanks."

Dave was stunned. His ex-wife, perhaps the only woman he had ever met with no sense of humor at all, had tried to make a joke. It wasn't a great joke, true, but it was a start.

"Will you be able to get back to Washington all right?"

"I'll be fine, David. I'm a big girl now. I'll just turn in my ticket for a later train."

"Sure, that's fine. You want us to pick you up at the station?"

"I can take care of myself, David. I'll be all right," she said as she kissed him on the cheek. "On, and congratulations on winning the game."

"Thanks."

Things were not as happy for Duncan Charles in Miami. The home team had taken the second-half kickoff and marched eighty-eight yards for a touchdown, sending the young Chicago owner into a funk. His spirits rallied slightly when his team returned the ensuing kickoff for a touchdown to build its lead back to fourteen points, 27-13.

Chicago maintained that lead until there were four minutes left in the game, when the Wave's Barry Jansen intercepted a pass and ran it in to make it 27-20.

Duncan silently exhorted the clock to move more quickly, and he almost died inside when his team fumbled on its first running play to give Miami the ball back with three minutes left.

"All right," the head linesman heard over his headset. "Let's get out of Miami's way."

Five plays later, Steve Washam skirted left end for a six-yard touchdown run that, with the extra point, tied the score, 27-27. That was how it ended.

"You see, kid," Martini said as the teams shook hands and walked off the field. "Just like I told you. You didn't lose."

"A tie, Ray. A lousy, stinking tie!"

"You're not going to say something about kissing your sister, are you, kid?"

"Ray, it sucks! We were fourteen points ahead with four minutes left!"

"Just goes to show. You can never have too big a lead against Miami. They're too good."

"Ray, you let them be that good!"

"Don't be stupid, kid. Your team played a terrific game, but you couldn't stand up to Miami's pressure. The Wave's a great team. Everyone who knows football knows that. They're the best offensive team in the Association. But you didn't look bad, kid. You scored twenty-seven points."

"So did they, Ray."

"Look, kid. You finished the preseason one, two and one. Not great, but not terrible either. Just about what people would expect from what looks like a mediocre team. Now when your team turns out to be one of the Cinderellas, it'll be more of a surprise."

"Well, I guess ..."

"Just relax. Remember, it's all part of the System."

37

Fred Reynolds' column, The Washington Tribune, September 2:

"Most football teams use the exhibition season to find the answers to questions.

"Not our Washington Warriors. They've used it to create more questions.

"In the past it has been easy to predict the number of victories the Warriors would accumulate in any given year -- just take whatever figure the team's management was promising and divide by two.

"And be satisfied, if not happy, whenever that number turned out to be larger than three.

"Things are different this year. The Warriors' new management, showing a rare glimpse -- at least for them -- of wisdom, hasn't made any outrageous predictions. All the Three Blind Mice have said is that they would provide the Capital City with football they describe as 'fun.'

"Of course, only those who enjoy root canal work could possibly consider the just-completed exhibition season fun.

"Even last weekend's victory over the New York Comets, notable more

for the level of ineptitude than anything else, could not be considered a rollicking good time by anyone other than aficionados of gangland slayings and the Crash of 1929.

"Let's face it, boys and girls. The Warriors are still losers.

"If that's true, then what are these questions yet to be answered?

"The first that comes to mind is how did such supposedly reasonable men as the board of directors allow themselves to be stampeded into turning the team over to Messrs. Rojas and Krause. Along with their friend the elder Mr. Rojas, these three have managed to wreak havoc upon our franchise.

"They have spent millions on players, many of whom did not even make the team. Very little is left of their initial budget, and they weren't helped at all by their ridiculous failure to sign a concessions contract in time for the Denver exhibition game.

"That little fiasco cost the team a quarter of a million dollars and left their cash flow in dire straits.

"In fact, there was a rumor out of Association headquarters this week that the team's paychecks were going to bounce. Happily, that turned out not to be true.

"That leads us to the second question. When will the board realize that they could save a great deal more money by divesting themselves of three salaries? If anyone needs to know to which three salaries I'm referring, they shouldn't be reading this column.

"Perhaps the results of this Sunday's opening game in St. Louis against the Titans will convince the board that the grand experiment with participatory democracy should come to an end."

Tracey Cagney would have preferred nothing more than to be spending the Labor Day weekend at her spacious beach house on Cape Cod, enjoying one of the last beautiful Saturdays of the summer.

Instead, she was standing on her team's sideline and awaiting the commissioner's signal to come to the center of the field to join him for the opening day ceremonies.

Above all else, Tracey knew there were certain duties that had to be fulfilled by the previous season's Championship Bowl winner. One of those duties was playing host to the ceremony that kicked off every season, the returning of the Championship Bowl Trophy to the commissioner.

The great man always awarded the trophy personally on the nationally televised postgame show after the Championship Bowl, and it stayed in the city of the winning team until the start of the next season.

It was a tradition that the winning team served as the home team for the NAFA's Kickoff Bowl, the first of the league's Saturday night games for a national cable audience.

This tradition was one that gave the commissioner great personal enjoyment, and Tracey Cagney knew it would be a slap in the face if she had an employee return the trophy to him on national television.

"Beautiful night, isn't it, Miss Cagney?"

"Don't remind me, Levitt. I should be out at the Cape right now, sipping a pina colada and watching the tide come in."

"Even you don't have the nerve to do that," Levitt said smugly. "Face it, you have to be here."

"I know, Levitt, I know. You don't have to remind me."

She looked at the small, squirrelly looking man standing beside her and wondered how such a person had become liaison to one of the Association's top franchises. Then she answered her own question. Levitt was a devious brown-noser who reportedly had never disagreed with anything the commissioner said.

Then again, she wondered, did anyone in the Association have the courage to refuse the commissioner anything?

Certainly not the networks. All three of them had bargained long and hard for the rights to televise the NAFA and the commissioner had wangled a deal worth one billion dollars a year from them. Two of the networks had agreed to broadcast every Sunday game, no matter how insignificant, to at least the home sites of the teams involved.

The third had cleared three and a half hours every Monday night and had assembled a broadcast team of two former players and an abrasive lawyer.

The commissioner's real coup, many people felt, had been adding cable TV to the package. The nation's top sports channel had anted up three hundred million a year to broadcast a Saturday night game, and the rumor was that the next package would include another network joining for Thursday night games.

Representatives of every network were present in Philadelphia, even though the game would only be carried on cable stations. The commissioner required all of them to take part in the ceremonies to start the season.

At precisely 8 p.m. Saturday, Eastern Daylight Time, the commissioner motioned to Tracey Cagney, who took a deep breath and walked toward him.

Few of the eighty-six thousand people in attendance were close enough to really see what was happening at the center of the field. The commissioner, Tracey Cagney and the various league and network officials were surrounded by reporters, photographers and television cameras.

They could hear the commissioner very well, though, and his sonorous voice boomed over the stadium's public address system to them and to the people listening at home, in their cars and in restaurants and bars all around the country.

"My friends," he said as the crowd cheered. "It's the most wonderful time of year, the beginning of another glorious football season!"

He paused for effect as the cheering got louder.

"As every football fan in the country knows, there is one piece of business we must complete before we can start that season. The Championship Bowl Trophy, the symbol of the single best team in professional football, cannot rest with any one team, because as of now there is no champion in the NAFA. There are only twenty-four teams, all battling for the right to be the best in the world."

The commissioner paused again for more cheers.

"All of those twenty-four have an equal chance at this point, proving once again that competition in the North American Football Association is the purest, most equitable of any organized sport in the civilized world."

More cheering. Then the commissioner signaled for silence.

"If I may, I would like to inject a serious note into our proceedings. I would like to suggest a moment of silence for the memory of the departed franchise operator, the man who brought such glory and honor to the City of Brotherly Love, our dear friend, Stanley Cagney."

He bowed his head as if praying. Tracey Cagney followed suit, as did those at the center of the field, as did every person in the stadium.

I was right, Tracey thought as she glanced around the stadium. No one can say no to the commissioner.

"And now," he said after what he considered a suitable silence. "I would like to turn these proceedings over to the young lady who will continue the great tradition of excellence in this city, the present operator of the Philadelphia franchise of the North American Football Association, Miss Tracey Cagney."

Tracey looked up, surprised and alarmed. She had seen this ceremony dozens of times before and she had never known the commissioner to yield the spotlight to anyone, much less the newest member of the NAFA.

To make matters worse, she was unprepared to make a speech and hated appearing before large crowds.

She smiled weakly. "Thank you, Commissioner, and welcome to the game, everybody!"

The crowd, perhaps sensing her discomfort, roared back an answer.

Tracey rocked back on her heels, not expecting cheers of that volume. She gathered herself and continued. "I just want to say that, as far as I'm concerned, the Bulldogs are still the champions, and we're going to do our damnedest to bring that trophy right back here to Philadelphia, where it belongs!"

The crowd roared even louder than before. Tracey thought she could almost feel the sound.

"Now let's cut the crap and play some football!"

The network executives winced a little at her language, but the crowd obviously loved it. Tracey may have grown up on the Main Line, but she had lived her entire life in Philly and she was one of them. They yelled and cheered, they clapped and stamped their feet and they stood and whistled. Tracey stepped back and glanced over at the commissioner. He smiled slightly and bowed in her direction as she smiled back.

The game itself was an anticlimax. The Bulldogs had no problem with the lowly Calgary Riders, and Tracey Cagney felt a little foolish for not wanting to be in attendance. Her team scored a touchdown on the third play of the game when Sandy Tate took a handoff on a reverse and went sixty-seven yards.

They scored again on their next possession when Joe Bell hit Luther Richardson on a short pass over the middle and Richardson outran the Calgary secondary to the end zone. They slowed down slightly after that, settling for field goals the next two times, but the crowd resisted the tendency to boo.

The Bulldogs rewarded the crowd for its patience by scoring two more touchdowns in the second quarter, taking a 34-0 lead into the halftime intermission. Meanwhile, the Bulldog defense was playing even better, holding Calgary to a total offense of minus eleven yards in the first half.

At one point, Levitt almost allowed himself to feel sorry for the Calgary team. He was tempted to call some penalties to slow down the Philadelphia onslaught, but he remembered that the commissioner was in the stadium and decided it would be better not to deviate at all from his instructions.

He did decide that if the Riders mounted something on their own, he wouldn't stop them. It never happened. Philadelphia scored five more touchdowns in the second half, despite playing only reserves. The Riders were thoroughly humiliated, the 69-0 loss being the worst in the history of the franchise.

They were satisfied simply to escape from Philadelphia without any crippling injuries.

"Good job, Levitt," the commissioner told him as they left the stadium together.

"Thank you, Commissioner. I wonder if I might ask a question."

The commissioner was in an expansive mood. "Why, certainly."

"Thank you. What I wanted to know is why you wanted a blowout. Wasn't it bad for television ratings?"

The commissioner smiled. "That's certainly true, Levitt, but it was only a Saturday game and only a cable audience. People have been complaining the last few years about our drive for parity, so we decided it would be better to show them some real excellence."

"Aha."

"Yes, Levitt," the commissioner said. "This will be a very good year for the Bulldogs, at least until the playoffs."

"Then what happens?"

Ordinarily such a question would have drawn a stern look from the commissioner, but he was in a very good mood and let it pass.

"We'll see, Levitt," he said. "We'll see."

In fact, the commissioner was ecstatic. He was not normally a superstitious man, but the game had been so close to the predicted outcome he could only take it as an omen.

Maybe, he thought, there aren't going to be any more glitches in the System this season.

38

The tradition of playing the opener on Saturday night at the home of the previous season's champion had only been in existence for five years. It seemed a short time to establish a tradition, but no one ever referred to it as such.

Another tradition, one that dated back much further, was the opening game of the Chicago Trojans. The Trojans played in the second-largest stadium in the Association, and rarely were they sent on the road for their first game.

And while Chicago rarely if ever had an empty seat in 100,000-seat Daley Stadium, no one connected with the NAFA was foolish enough to risk losing attendance by having the Trojans open on the road.

"Well, kid, you did a bang-up job."

"I did?"

"Look at those stands," Martini said. "Not an empty seat in the place. You've even got standing room. Hell, I bet you could have had them dangling from the light towers if the city would let you."

"So I did good?"

"Yeah. A real sharp job."

"Thanks, Ray." Duncan Charles leaned forward and spoke to Martini in a conspiratorial voice. "Tell me something. Are we going to win today?"

"You know I can't talk about that."

"Come on, Ray. You can tell me. I own the team, remember? I'm on the Committee. It's not like you're letting me in on some big secret."

"Lay off. I don't want anybody to overhear ..."

"Then whisper it to me," Duncan said, his voice beginning to develop a whiny quality. "Or let's go into the men's room and you can tell me there."

"Kid, I am not going into the men's room with you or anybody else."

"Come on, Ray. I have a right to know. I let you tell me what to do. I let you run the team for me. I let you arrange all the trades, all because of that stupid System! All I want from you is a little information. Is that too much to ask?"

Martini was beginning to get seriously irritated. "Why don't you just sit tight and wait until the end of the game like everyone else?"

"Because everyone else doesn't own the team," Duncan said. "Everyone else doesn't know we're going to be the Cinderella team. And everyone else doesn't know we're going to go to the Championship Bowl."

Ray Martini grabbed Duncan by the elbow and led him out of the owner's box to the corridor outside, pulling him along into a deserted stairway. Then he slammed him up against a wall and started speaking to him in a low voice.

"Now listen to me, you little twerp, and listen real good so I don't ever have to say it again. I'm not going to tell you anything, and if you ever raise your voice to me again, I'll kick your ass from here to Indiana."

Duncan moaned softly.

"If you ever say another word about the System, or the Championship Bowl, or anything else I've told you about, I'll see to it that you're thrown out of the Association so fast your empty head will spin!"

He moved in even closer, his face no more than two inches from Duncan's. "You don't fuck with me, kid! You understand that? You don't fuck with me and you don't fuck with the System!"

Ray Martini didn't wait for an answer. He left Duncan standing in the stairwell, rubbing his injured elbow and wondering where he could find a dry pair of pants.

39

Daniel "Duke" Koontz had played eight years in the Association as a backup quarterback with three different teams before retiring to accept a position with the league. At one point he had even been the backup to a young Jimmy Gardner.

Now pushing fifty and carrying sixty more pounds than he had in his playing days, he was the league liaison for the St. Louis Titans, who were playing host to the Washington Warriors in the season opener for both teams.

First on the agenda on this particular Sunday was the pregame briefing for the officials to give them their instructions for the day. "Gentlemen, this is a C priority game. You won't be hearing much from me, but that doesn't mean I'm going to let it get out of hand."

Kevin Rooney, an insurance salesman in Baton Rouge during the week, was the head linesman and chief of the officiating squad. He did the talking for the rest of the crew.

"Yes, sir, Mr. Koontz."

"Now call only what you need to call, but make sure Washington doesn't get a whole lot of momentum going. If the Warriors do anything marginal, go ahead and call it."

"Yes, Mr. Koontz."

"I'll check back with you at the half."

Three doors down the hall at Gateway Arch Stadium, the Washington players were beginning to wander in. Although the game was not scheduled to begin for another four hours, most of the players were too tense to spend the time in their hotel rooms.

"Mr. Gardner?"

"What is it, Eaker?" Gardner asked without looking up from the shoe he was trying to tie.

"I just wanted to ask ... are you scared?"

"Scared?"

"Well, maybe not scared. But aren't you just a little, you know, nervous?"

Gardner sighed. "Eaker, there isn't a guy in this room who isn't nervous. Yeah, some guys might even be scared. They don't know what's gonna happen. We might get our butts kicked in front of sixty thousand people."

"You, too?"

"Well, I don't think I'll get my butt kicked," Gardner said. "But I'm a little nervous, sure. At least until I get out on the field and get my blood pumping. Then I forget all about it."

"Think that'll happen to me?"

"Sure, Eaker. Look, what's with all the questions?"

"I'm sorry, Mr. Gardner. I just wanted to get a little advice, encouragement even, from somebody who's been through this so many times. I mean, you're probably the bravest man I know, still trying to play football at your age, and if you're nervous, then I guess it's normal."

"Look, Eaker, I'm OK. I'll take care of myself."

Tony Ross had come up to catch the tail end of the conversation. "Say, Jimmy ..."

"What do you want, Ross!?" Gardner almost shouted.

"Lighten up, man. I just wondered if you had an extra shoelace."

"What the hell do you think I am, the damn equipment manager?"

"Never mind, Jimmy."

Eaker chose that moment to make his exit as well. "Uh, thanks, Mr. Gardner, and ... uh, break a leg."

"They say that to actors, you little pissant!" Gardner shouted as Eaker backed away.

"Jeez, Jimmy," Ross said. "What's the problem? Too much coffee? Maybe you ought to switch to a low-sugar diet."

"It isn't too much sugar. It's too much Lyndon Eaker, thank you very much. There's something about that kid that gives me the shivering fits. He's like a fingernail across a blackboard."

"A finger ... Jimmy, that kid's got you scared!"

"Bullshit! He doesn't scare me, but he sure as hell gets on my nerves. He's hanging all over me! Rossie, I've had fan clubs, the press, adoring women who wanted to drape themselves all over my masculine form ..."

Ross snorted, but Gardner ignored him and continued. "I have even had death threats against me from people who didn't want to see me walk onto the field ..."

"Yeah," Ross said. "But they were the fans of your team."

"... but nothing ever has been able to get to me the way that kid and his talk do. Every other sentence he says he's reminding me of how old I am and how good I used to be, and how I'm so brave to still try and play football when I ought to be in an old folks' home."

Ross laughed.

"Tony, am I that far over the hill? Am I trying to do something I can't do any more?"

"I don't know, pal. I'll tell you one thing, though. You've been pushing yourself awful hard these last few days. Seems like you're trying to prove something."

"Yeah, well, maybe I am."

"So that kid does have you scared!"

"Scared my ass! I have never been scared of anything in my life! I've been chased by linemen who weigh more than Coke machines! I've looked down the wrong end of broken beer bottles in joints civilized human beings don't enter without bodyguards! I've made personal appearances on network television and I've never been scared of anything in my entire life!"

"All right!" Ross shouted back. "You're not scared!"

"Damn right I'm not!"

"You're terrified."

"Jeez!" Gardner exclaimed, looking around the room to see if anyone else had witnessed the conversation. "Isn't it time to go out to the field yet?"

Ross grinned. "In about three hours, Jimmy."

"Then," Gardner said, standing and grabbing his playbook, "I am going to go to the john and have myself a good long sitdown so that I can go over the plays and not, I repeat not, be scared!"

While Gardner was trying to calm himself, Dave and Herb were surveying the scene from the top of the stadium.

"Well, Herb, what do you think?"

Rojas looked around the luxury box. "Oh, it's a nine. Nine point five, maybe."

"A nine? You think this is better than Philadelphia?"

"Sure!"

"Herb, the bar was better, the seats were better ..."

"Yeah, and your friend the Dragon Lady greeted us. Did you notice what we ran into on our way in here? All pink and perfumed? She was enough to make this place a ten if it wasn't for the bar."

"Herb ..."

"Yeah, yeah, I know. There are no tens."

It had become a game with them, comparing the various owners' boxes. They had arrived at 9 a.m., too keyed up to sleep, but there had been no one to let them into the stadium. So for two hours they had wandered the downtown neighborhoods.

They were fortunate in that respect. Most of the NAFA's teams played in suburban stadiums that weren't near anything except freeways. St. Louis, though, still played in downtown Gateway Arch Stadium, in the shadow of the famous Gateway to the West. The area was full of shops and theatres, although few of them were open on Sunday mornings.

Herb and Dave did manage to find an open drugstore with a lunch counter, and they killed time by having a big breakfast. They had hoped to find the Washington papers, but the only ones they were able to locate were the New York Times, the Chicago Sun-Times and the St. Louis Post-Dispatch.

Only the local paper had anything about the upcoming game between the Warriors and the Archers, and the St. Louis writer seemed to think the home team would have about as tough a time winning as the Indians had enjoyed at the Little Big Horn.

The stadium finally opened at 11 a.m., four hours before the scheduled kickoff. Dave and Herb had to talk their way in, showing identification to a security guard who had a hard time believing that any NAFA executives would really show up four hours early for a game.

They had gone directly to their luxury box, where Archer employees were still setting the bar up.

Herb turned on the television in the corner of the box and tried to find something worth watching. "Maybe there's something good on," Dave said.

"Sure," Herb said. "Channel Two has the Three Stooges."

Dave grimaced. "Lord, no ..."

With the early games still an hour away, Herb clicked off the television and grabbed one of the newspapers they had brought with them from the drugstore. Dave took another one, and they read every story in the papers, including shipping notices and obituaries.

With the papers strewn around them on the carpet, they decided to go for a walk and check out the surroundings.

They started at the top of the stadium, looking down from the highest seats. From there the field looked no bigger than an average backyard, and Dave knew the fans who would pay twenty dollars for these seats would have to bring binoculars actually to see anything.

After that they checked out the boiler rooms, the locker rooms and the medical room, where the Archers' team doctor was already setting up his X-ray equipment.

Two technicians were trying to impress each other with detailed descriptions of the most gruesome automobile accidents they had ever seen, and Herb could feel the remnants of his breakfast fighting to make a return trip.

Finally they found themselves on the playing field, where the ground crew was still laying down the yardage markers. The St. Louis baseball team had yet to complete its season, so the four-man crew was working around the base paths and pitcher's mound. Dave found it fascinating to watch them work, while Herb, not nearly as enthralled, scanned the stands for early arrivals.

It was Herb who first noticed the lone figure standing at the far end of the field. At first he thought he was mistaken, that surely it wasn't who he thought it was, but as he and Dave moved closer he realized his first impression had been a correct one.

"Hello, Coach."

Benjamin Kennedy seemed surprised to see them. "Oh, good morning, Mr. Rojas. Mr. Krause."

"What are you doing out here so early, Coach?" Herb asked. "Looking for gopher holes?"

Dave expected a sharp retort from the coach, but Kennedy only smiled uncomfortably at Herb's weak attempt at humor.

"Are you ready for the game, Coach?" Dave asked.

Of course he knew it was a stupid question. There would be no excuse for a professional coach not to be ready for a game, and all three of them knew it. No one seemed to know what to say next, though, and Kennedy finally broke what was turning into an uncomfortable silence.

"In case you gentlemen were wondering, I am going over the game in my head. I am studying every play we have and every situation we might possibly encounter."

Dave nodded.

"Sounds like some kind of ritual to me," Herb said.

"Rituals ..." Kennedy said, sounding indignant, "... are for primitive tribes of uneducated natives who have neither the intellectual background nor the sociological training to think things through rationally."

"Sounds like the Adonis brothers to me," Dave muttered.

Kennedy didn't exactly smile, but Dave could tell his remark had amused the coach. He stopped to consider it for a moment, his mouth turning upward slightly at the corners.

"Excuse me, gentlemen. Most times I would suffer your company and answer your inquiries with little or no protest. You are, at least technically, my employers, and there is a certain amount of courtesy and respect due both of you. But these last few hours before the start of a game are moments I reserve for myself. At these times, the only companionship I seek is the Lord."

"I think he's watching the Miami game," Herb quipped.

Dave expected Kennedy to make a scathing comment, but the coach just winced a little.

"All right, Coach," Dave said. "We'll see you later."

They didn't understand why, but both Dave and Herb realized they were no longer quite as antsy after their conversation with Kennedy. They headed back up to the owner's box, suddenly ravenously hungry and eager to take advantage of the St. Louis owner's private dining room for lunch.

40

It was estimated that an audience of nearly thirty million people tuned in to the American Broadcasting System's pregame show, "NAFA Sunday Morning," every weekend during the fall. The show was, as it had been for the last ten years, the most popular sports program in the country.

Part of the reason was Greg Fishbeck, the host and central focus of the program. He was a handsome man with a genial matter and a slightly sarcastic air about him, which some people found annoying but more found endearing.

Fishbeck had perfect hair, perfect teeth, a perfect complexion and a wardrobe donated by a major clothing manufacturer in exchange for a plug at the end of the broadcast.

While other men Fishbeck's age had been knocking themselves silly on the football field, he had spent his college years majoring in broadcasting and minoring in dramatic arts. He had done play-by-play for his college team on a small campus station that could only be heard in the dormitories and fraternity houses.

That had given him the experience and self-confidence upon his graduation to march into the station manager's office at the town's biggest television station. He told the man he was the best sports reporter in the state and he proved it over the next year and a half.

From there it had been a short step to Detroit and then on to the network, where six years of diligent reporting and very little complaining had brought him the prize he had been seeking all along. He was now the Emmy Award-winning host of "NAFA Sunday Morning," and the best-known sports broadcaster since Howard Cosell.

The other three cast members filled specific roles, allowing Fishbeck to be the force that pulled it all together.

The lovely Cathy Dunnison, a former Olympic gymnast and game show hostess, served to add a little pizzazz. Bobby Dutton was a former defensive tackle who brought credibility for those who believed only men who had played or coached in the NAFA really understood the league.

And finally there was Andre O'Connor, the only one of the four for whom broadcasting was only a part-time job. O'Connor was billed as an analyst, but he was on the show because of his international reputation as a high-stakes poker player and all-around gambler.

While everyone connected with the network agreed that Dunnison, Dutton and to some extent even Fishbeck were all replaceable, it was O'Connor's segment, "Andre's Angles," that really drew the ratings.

In fact, O'Connor had such clout that the network had agreed to bankroll any trips he made to Las Vegas or Atlantic City to the tune of $250,000 a year. If he lost, the network picked up the tab. When he won, they split the money, fifty-fifty.

Needless to say, the Association objected to O'Connor vigorously. At one point, the commissioner had threatened to pull the games off ABS if they insisted on using a professional gambler. Whether the Association approved or not, though, everyone knew that nearly $2.5 billion a week was being wagered illegally on professional football.

The network maintained that it was doing the public a service by keeping O'Connor on the air, and both other networks had since added imitators to their own shows.

"Andre's Angles" took up the last five minutes before kickoff, and it was without question the most popular part of the broadcast. In the few minutes between Andre's predictions and the kickoff of the early games, phone lines across the country were jammed as eager bettors called their bookies.

Dave and Herb were no longer members of the betting public, but they decided to stay with familiar habits, so they watched Andre on the television in the owner's box.

"You think your dad's watching back in Washington?"

"Dad hasn't missed Andre since they first put him on the air. When we'd get back from the games, all he ever talked about was what Andre had said was going to happen."

The beer commercial ended, and they turned their attention back to the screen. "Welcome back to NAFA Sunday Morning," Fishbeck said. "We're only a couple of minutes away from taking you out to the stadiums for the early games, and that means it's time for Andre's Angles."

He turned his chair to face the balding, pot-bellied man in the next chair. "Well, Andre, what do we have today to make people rich?"

O'Connor chuckled slightly. "Greg, as usual, the opening games of any season are some of the toughest ones to pick. There are so many undetermined factors that don't become apparent until a few games have been played."

"That's so true, Andre. It always seems like one or two teams come out of nowhere to stage upsets at this time of year."

"Right. Upsets that wouldn't happen later in the season."

"Then again, Andre, what about the games like last night's in Philadelphia? That one really held up to form."

"It sure did. The people who took the Bulldogs and gave the twenty-one points had it covered by halftime, no sweat."

"Why don't we go to the blackboard and see what you've got for us? How about Miami and Kansas City?"

"Greg, as long as Bob Polano is the coach, Miami's going to be one of the truly tough teams in the Association. They've got a front office down there that does a great job evaluating talent and a coaching staff that knows football inside and out. Freddie Morton is the best running back I've seen since Roxy Reese's first time around, and Barton Blanton is probably the best pure passer in the game today."

"How about the Wranglers, Andre?"

"Kansas City? Well, that Chico Coleman trade with Chicago looked like a mistake at the time and it looks even worse now. I look for the Wranglers to drop two or three in the win column from their seven and seven record last year."

"Today's game?"

"Miami by twelve."

"How about Boston and Cincinnati, the Barons and the Goldstars?"

"Greg, Boston may well be the most consistently mediocre franchise in this league. They've finished either seven and seven or six and eight for five years in a row now, but Cincinnati might be the bottom of the barrel aside from Washington."

"How so?"

"The Stars made a couple of good trades in the off-season, but they're going to need a couple more years to put things together. Boston by seven."

"All right, Andre. You mentioned Washington a minute ago, and the Warriors are playing at St. Louis in one of the late games. How about that one?"

"Well, Greg, if there's one team I have to think will make a big turnaround from last year, the Archers would have to be it. They made some absolutely spectacular trades last winter and they picked up some tremendous talent in the draft. I happen to believe they're on the verge of joining the elite. Washington, on the other hand ..."

Andre paused for a moment and then started doing something he had never done in all the years he'd been doing the show. He started laughing.

Fishbeck wasn't sure quite how to respond, so he let O'Connor continue.

"I mean ..." O'Connor wiped his eyes. "I mean ... ha ha ha ha ... Ben Kennedy ... Roxy Reese ... ha ha ha ... Tony Ross ... ha ha ha ... Jimmy ... ha ... Jimmy Gardner ..."

O'Connor collapsed with laughter, and was joined by Fishbeck, who obviously found the idea just as amusing. The entire studio was filled with laughter, from behind the cameras as well as on the set.

Finally, just before they went to commercial, O'Connor collected himself long enough to blurt out, between giggles, "St. Louis ... ha ha ha ... St. Louis by seventeen."

All of a sudden the screen went black. Dave and Herb turned quickly to see Stan Pinello wielding a remote control.

"In case you gentlemen are unaware, the Association does not approve of Mr. O'Connor, or of his appearance on the pregame show. That broadcast is not and will not be tolerated on the premises of a North American Football Association game. I will turn the television back on when the Chicago game begins."

In Chicago, the coin toss had not yet taken place, but Ray Martini was already hard at work, talking over his headset. He was conversing with Mort Latham, instructing the former New York running back, who now ran a Long Island health spa, on the plan for the day's game.

"Mort, the scenario I have in mind calls for a very low-scoring game. Nothing and nothing at the half if we can manage it."

"No problem, Mr. Martini."

"In the fourth quarter, all hell's going to break loose. Chicago will score two, maybe three times."

"Yes, Mr. Martini."

"Let 'em play, but the first time Houston gets anything serious going ..."

"We'll put a stop to it."

"Good, Mort. I know I can depend on you."

"Never let you down before, did I, Mr. Martini?"

"I never expect otherwise, Mort. Now, let's see here. Houston won the toss. Let's make it a good, clean kickoff. You and your boys got your signals all worked out?"

"Yes, sir. We're ready to roll."

Willie Sheraton, Houston's third-year kick returner, fielded the ball on the one yard line. He made a few moves while waiting for his blocking to form. Then, with a sudden burst of speed, he took off for the right sideline. The wall had formed perfectly and Sheraton sailed by the first wave of Trojan tackler and broke into the clear.

"No, no, no!" Martini screamed into his headset. "That's precisely what I didn't want to happen. Mort, let's get a flag on that."

"No problem, Mr. Martini." Latham touched his hand to the front of his shirt. Line judge Forrest Williamson caught the signal and pulled his flag from his back pocket.

Sheraton looked back in disgust from the end zone and watched helplessly as Latham came running up to retrieve the ball. He tossed it to referee Danny Jones, who carried it back to the Houston twenty-two.

Latham made the announcement.

"Illegal block in the back. Number fifty-eight on the receiving team. That's a ten yard penalty."

The flag took the steam out of the Lonestars. After three running plays that netted only four yards, they punted to Chicago. The Trojans ran three plays of their own and kicked it back. It went on that way for most of the first half. The only score of the first thirty minutes came after a long pass by Houston's Steve Sims set up a successful field goal from the twenty.

The half ended with the Lonestars up, 3-0. Duncan Charles sat alone in his private box, his hands folded in his lap, and stared silently at the field.

"This is Greg Fishbeck in New York with the halftime show. For those of you who are watching the Chicago-Houston shootout in the Washington and St. Louis areas, let me remind you we'll be breaking away to your game in time for the opening kickoff. The rest of the country will see the whole game and then get the Sunday Sports Show, where we'll be going out to California, to San Jose State College for the National Bellyflop Championships. Then we'll head back east to Atlantic City for bantamweight boxing ..."

Just as Martini had directed, the Trojans were allowed to come to life in the fourth quarter. They did so with a vengeance. With a series of brilliant plays and spectacular individual performances, Chicago scored two touchdowns and kicked a long field goal. The Trojans' defense, with the help of several strategic flags, stifled Houston at every turn.

The score was 17-3 when the happy Daley Stadium crowd counted down the final seconds, and Duncan Charles wanted desperately to be happy.

His team had won the game, his first as operator of the Chicago franchise. He had proven he could operate the team in the tradition of his late father, but Duncan was neither proud or happy.

He felt he had done nothing to contribute to his team's victory, and his elbow was throbbing from his altercation with Ray Martini before the game.

"Hey, kid, there you are." Duncan flinched as Martini walked up to him. "Hell of a game, right?"

"Yeah, Ray," he said glumly. "Hell of a game."

"Your boys were terrific. I'll bet you're really proud of them."

"Yeah, proud."

Martini smiled. "Come on. I know you're not still upset about that little run-in before the game."

"Well ..."

"Look, I owe you an apology for that."

"Ray, you don't ..."

"No, I do. I was on edge. Opening Day jitters, and I took them out on you. I'm sorry."

Duncan was silent.

"Hey, kid, I don't apologize to everybody."

"All right, Ray. Forget it."

"And after all, we won, didn't we?"

Duncan brightened a little. "Yeah, we did."

"Come on, let's go have a drink. Hell, I'll buy you the biggest steak in town, and since this is Chicago, there ought to be a couple of pretty big ones around."

"All right, Ray. I'm going to let you buy me the biggest steak in town, and the best damn salad and the oldest, most expensive bottle of wine in Cook County."

"Gladly, kid. At least you're letting me make it up to you."

"Make it up ..."

"Yeah, taking it out on you like I did was really stupid. This is a tough job. If I blow it, I don't have to answer to you alone. I've got the commissioner on my back for weeks."

Martini put his arm across Duncan's shoulders and walked him along as they made their way out of the stadium. It was a side of Martini Duncan never had seen before. He had thought of the large man as a bully, a roughneck, someone totally without feelings or fears, but here he was, revealing a tender side and seeking counsel from Duncan.

Almost without thinking, Duncan Charles threw his arm across Martini's shoulders and the two of them walked out of the stadium into the parking lot.

4|

There were no elaborate pregame ceremonies in St. Louis. There were no visiting dignitaries, no legions of reporters. The only camera crew -- from ABS -- was there because it had to be.

"Dave, you've been staring out there forever. What are you expecting, the Goodyear blimp?"

"Just looking at the sky, Herb. Just thinking."

"Looking for an omen?"

"Maybe."

"I'd look somewhere else, buddy. That's a sky that isn't going to rain, but I don't think we're going to see the sun, either." Herb leaned forward, assuming the same pose as his friend beside him. "Just a dull, gray sky."

"Herb, do you ever wonder what the hell we're doing?"

"Sure. All the time. Why not? Everybody else in town is wondering the same thing."

Dave shook his head.

"Hey, buddy. Cheer up. It's almost game time."

Just as Dave had decided he didn't believe in omens, the Warriors promptly lost the coin toss. Ben Kennedy had one final word with his kickoff team, and Norm Blaylott took the field and teed the ball up on the thirty-five yard line.

Blaylott took a deep breath and looked at the referee. When the official blew his whistle, Blaylott took another deep breath and kicked the ball.

Spencer Mills, who had led the Freedom Conference in kick returns last season for Miami before being traded to St. Louis, fielded the ball at the eight. He didn't wait for his blocking to form, but took off immediately up the middle of the field.

Most of the Washington players had looked for a return on one sideline or another, and they promptly overran Mills.

"What the hell?" Norm Blaylott suddenly realized there were only three Warriors between Mills and the goal line and he was one of them. Blaylott couldn't remember if he'd ever made a tackle before, and he hoped desperately that one of the other two players would get to Mills before Mills got to him.

But Mills faked to the left, turned to the right and sent the other two defenders skidding on the artificial surface.

Uh oh, Blaylott thought, it's up to me.

It was a tackle that would be shown on every Hall of Shame show on every little station from coast to coast. No one had ever bothered to tell Norm Blaylott that the worst possible way to tackle a man running full out was to stand squarely in front of him, which was exactly what he did. When Mills reached the spot Blaylott had staked out, the two men collided.

First both men stood straight up and then both men fell down backward.

The next thing Blaylott remembered was the team doctor, the trainer and the rest of the kickoff unit, most of whom he couldn't recognize, gathered around him.

"Norm, Norm, come on, man, wake up!"

"Norm, are you all right?"

"Hell, are you alive?"

"Did ... did ... did I stop him?"

"Stop him? Hell, Norm, you knocked him cold! They're carrying him off the field right now!"

"Oh," Blaylott said a little woozily. "That's nice. Can I stand up now?"

Blaylott tried, but couldn't. Two other players carried him to the sideline, where coach Kennedy stopped them.

"That was a good tackle, Mr. Blaylott. Now go to the locker room. There are X-rays which need to be taken."

"But, Coach ..."

"Mr. Blaylott, you are finished for the day."

Blaylott found he was trying to focus in on three Ben Kennedys, a sight he found more than a little frightening. He summoned up as much courage as he could and addressed his comments to the one on the middle.

"Coach, I can't leave the game! Who'll do the kicking?"

"Mr. Andrews will handle all of the kicking, Mr. Blaylott. Please follow these gentlemen ..."

"But Coach, Lou can't kick field goals."

"Then I suppose we will have to score nothing but touchdowns, Mr. Blaylott."

Blaylott had stopped Mills at the Warriors' forty-nine. The Titans spent the next five minutes moving the ball to the twenty-three, where the Washington defense stiffened. St. Louis was well within the range of Dominic Lazzarro, the Archers' five-foot-four, one hundred and forty-pound placekicker. He put it through the uprights easily, and St. Louis had a 3-0 lead.

"Nothing to worry about," Gardner shouted on the sideline as the kick return team took the field. "It's only three points."

When Rusty Price returned the ball to the nineteen, Gardner grabbed his helmet. "All right, guys," he said as he ran out onto the field. "Time to get our shit together."

The coach called for a series of running plays. First Roxy Reese carried inside, then Willis Waller went outside and Reese took it to the other side. The three plays gained ten and a half yards.

"Man," Reese said in the huddle. "This is hard work."

"Shut the fuck up, Roxy," Gardner said. "Nobody talks in my huddle but me."

Then he called another running play that Jenkins had carried in from the bench. "Draw forty-five. Blue. On One."

Reese broke the draw for ten more yards and Kennedy sent in a pass play. Gardner hit Ross over the middle for another eleven yards, moving the ball across midfield into St. Louis territory.

Reese then gained four yards on an off-tackle play and a sideline pass to Greenblatt gained six more and another first down.

"Borrr --- ring," Pinello complained. "I can hear sets being turned off all over the state."

"I'll tell you what," Herb said. "Just pick up the phone and call down to the coach. Suggest a couple of plays. He really loves ... Damn, will you look at that?!"

Gardner had stepped back into the pocket as if to pass. He didn't throw it, though, and Waller came around behind him, took the ball and started to run.

"The Statue of Liberty?" Dave asked rhetorically. "The damn Statue of Liberty! I haven't seen that play in thirty years!"

"Is that legal?" Pinello asked.

The same thought must have crossed the minds of the eleven St. Louis defenders, most of whom hadn't been born the last time that particular play had been used in an Association game.

The Titans stopped dead in their tracks and watched openmouthed as Waller cut to the outside and took off down the sideline. He scored untouched.

Dave and Herb didn't bother trying to look dignified. They hopped up and down, hugged each other and pounded on the window ledge in front of them. Pinello sat mystified and stared at his college ring.

The celebration came to a screeching halt when Dave and Herb realized that their punter, Lou Andrews, was about to attempt an extra point for the first time in eleven years in the NAFA.

Lindy Eaker set up at the ten. Andrews took two steps back and Eaker called for the snap.

He placed the ball on the ground, spinning the laces in the right direction at the same time as he waited for Andrews to make his run at the ball.

The ball appeared to go straight up into the air when Andrews kicked it. It was the highest extra-point kick anyone ever had seen. Some people claimed to have lost sight of it, while others swore it had been caught in the jet stream!

A few others, likely those who had made the beer concession as successful as it was, claimed they saw the ball hit a duck that was flying over the stadium. Whatever happened, the ball seemed to gather just enough forward momentum to travel the twenty yards to the goal posts. The ball landed directly on the crossbar and bounced in the Warriors' favor.

"You want omens?" Herb asked. "There's your damn omen!"

He and Dave became even less dignified in celebrating the Warriors' 7-3 lead.

They had several more chances to lose their executive dignity as the Warriors rolled to two more touchdowns before halftime. It was more of the same slow style of football that had irritated Pinello, with yards coming three and four at a time. The second touchdown came when Reese went off-tackle from the two and the third was a six-yard pass from Gardner to Greenblatt.

Andrews missed both the extra points, but the half ended with Washington leading, 19-3.

Stan Pinello was livid. Even before the half was over, he slipped out of the Washington box and headed down to the officials' locker room, followed closely by Koontz. When the referees came through the door, Pinello was the first to jump on them.

"What the fuck are you guys doing out there, picking your noses? You didn't call more than two penalties against Washington the whole half!"

"Mr. Pinello, Mr. Koontz told us before the game that we were to call anything that looked like a violation. In our collective judgment, that's exactly what we've done."

"The hell you say!" Pinello shouted in a high whine. "There haven't been any penalties? Those aren't machines out there! They do make mistakes!"

"And when they did ..." the linesman said, "... we called penalties."

"Stan, I've got to stick up for the guys here," Koontz said. "The Warriors were executing pretty well. I didn't see a helluva lot of mistakes out there."

"Executing?" Pinello asked, turning his attention to Koontz. "How about executing a little judgment yourself, Koontz? These guys are supposed to be taking directions from you!"

"Stan, it's a C game. I'm supposed to keep hands off, remember?"

"That doesn't mean sit around with your thumb up your butt, Duke!"

Koontz tried to calm Pinello down, but the Washington liaison wasn't buying. "All I'm saying, Stan, is that I haven't seen the guys miss any calls."

"Then you be the one to talk to the commissioner when he calls and asks why the fuck Washington won this game!"

"Come on, Stan. Those geezers can't possibly hold up for another two quarters!"

"Duke, all I know is that St. Louis is supposed to win by three touchdowns. That means you've got one a helluva lot of ground to make up!"

Head linesman Kevin Rooney spoke up. "Mr. Pinello, need I remind you that you are here as a guest of the Archers and that we are under the direction of Mr. Koontz today?"

"Oh, fuck off!" Pinello said as he stormed out of the room.

In one sense, Duke Koontz was right. The Warriors did seem to tire noticeably in the second half, and Kennedy had to substitute more frequently throughout the third period. Gardner stayed in at quarterback, but Reese and Waller were replaced for one third-quarter drive by Archie London and Harvey Josephson, neither of whom had averaged two yards a carry in the preseason.

Washington didn't move the ball well, but the defense hadn't been on the field all that much in the first half and was relatively well rested. Neither team scored in the third quarter.

Five minutes into the fourth quarter, things started to fall apart for the

Warriors. Scott Trent intercepted a long pass in the end zone only to be flagged for interference. That put the Titans on the one, and quarterback Josh Williams scored on a bootleg run to make it 19-10.

After Washington was stopped and forced to punt, St. Louis got the ball back on its own thirty-one. On the very first place from scrimmage, Williams dropped back to pass. Romeo Adonis sacked him for a twelve-yard loss.

After a quick message from Koontz, Rooney touched his hand to his shirt. The referee threw a flag.

"Roughing the passer. Number sixty-six on the defense. Fifteen yards."

Rooney stepped off the yardage as Romeo Adonis turned to his brother. "I thought we were allowed to do that, Alphonse."

"What, Romeo?"

"Tackle the quarterback."~

"I thought so, too. Maybe we should ask the coach."

"We can't do that. We have to get back to the huddle."

"What should we do, then?"

"I guess we should keep trying to tackle the quarterback, but we'll have to be careful not to hurt him."

The major penalty moved the ball out near midfield, and Williams quickly moved the Titans for another touchdown, which they scored with two minutes to play.

That cut Washington's lead to 19-17, and everyone in the stadium knew the next step would be an onside kick. Kennedy put Price deep as a safety and moved ten other players up to the line of scrimmage.

Lazzarro teed the ball up, stepped back and gave a signal to his teammates.

All ten of them shifted to the right side of the field. The kick was actually more of a push, and it limped along the ground, barely covering the necessary ten yards.

Washington's Danny Jones bent down to pick it up, but it slipped through his legs. Zack Jefferson tried to run with it instead of downing it, and it got past him as well.

Leo Lonergan, the first Archer on the scene, fell on the ball. St. Louis had it just short of midfield with nearly two minutes to be played.

"Gentlemen," Kennedy said as he gathered the defense together. "This is it. We must stop them."

The first three plays netted a first down at the Washington forty as the clock ran down to a minute and twenty seconds. Williams slipped and fell on first down, forcing St. Louis to use a time out.

"Where's the ball?" Trent asked.

"Our forty-three," cornerback Eddie Finley said.

"Got to hold 'em here," Buck Wilson said. "It's second and thirteen, and they're not in field goal range yet."

That took one more play. A screen pass fooled the linebackers, and Wilson didn't catch up with the receiver until the ball was on the Warriors' twenty-five.

The Archers were in field goal range now, and their coach, Dave Wilkins, called for another time out and motioned for Williams to come over to the sideline.

"Let's run it down, Josh," he said. "Lazzarro's real solid from here."

"Coach, we've got plenty of time. I really want a touchdown out of this."

"Well, there's plenty of time. Maybe we can get it close enough for a chip shot. Just be careful. Watch out for those Adonis brothers and don't throw anywhere near Trent."

A draw gained five yards, and Williams threw a pass away with twenty-nine seconds to make it third and five.

Wilkins sent in another play, a deep pass to a back out of the backfield. Isaac Anderson slipped out of the backfield with Buck Wilson shadowing him. Williams saw that Anderson had gained a step on Wilson and he smiled confidently as he lofted the ball toward the flag.

The ball slipped a little coming off his hand. It was thrown to the wrong side, and Anderson stumbled a little trying to turn for it. He never quite fell down, but the pass sailed over his head incomplete.

Carroll Clements, the official nearest to the play, looked at Anderson and then at Rooney, who nodded.

Clements dropped his flag.

"What!?" shouted Wilson. "I never touched him!"

"What!?" shouted Gardner from the sideline.

"What!?" shouted Dave and Herb from the owner's box.

Only Ben Kennedy was silent as the referee announced his call. "Defensive pass interference. Number fifty-six. First down, St. Louis, on the two."

The clock said eleven seconds remained, but the Titans weren't going to take any more chances. Wilkins sent Lazzarro into the game to attempt the field goal, which was little more than an extra point. The Titan kicker didn't even stop to think about it. He checked the area where the ball would be spotted and, after finding it to his satisfaction, got ready to kick.

The holder took the perfect snap and placed it down perfectly. Lazzarro stepped forward to kick the ball when he noticed something large directly in front of him.

It was Romeo Adonis, who had swarmed through the line because his brother had managed to tie up three blockers all by himself. Romeo flattened the holder before Lazzarro had a chance to kick the ball, which squirted off to the side. Lazzarro started after the ball, but by that time, Alphonse Adonis had broken free and was on the loose in the backfield.

That made the St. Louis kicker forget about anything but avoiding possible death or dismemberment.

Buck Wilson fell on the loose ball as time expired. The Warriors had won the game, 19-17.

42

"Welcome back to the Coach's Corner, starring Washington Warriors head coach Benjamin Kennedy. Coach Kennedy's co-host is one of the top sportscasters in the business, Ms. Sally Adler."

Ben Kennedy despised this part of his job. Given the choice, he would have rather been imprisoned than forced to trade banter with Sally Adler once a week.

It wasn't that he disliked Adler, or thought any less of her because of her sex, but Kennedy had grown up in an era when there were no female sportswriters or sportscasters, and talking football with a beautiful blonde was something he was having trouble dealing with.

He knew that making appearances like this came with coaching in the publicity-conscious NAFA, though, and he suffered them without protest as part of the price he paid for being back in the big leagues.

His discomfort came across all too easily, though, and seeing Kennedy squirm was not the chief reason viewers watched the show. It helped that Coach's Corner directly preceded the NAFA's Saturday night game, but even Dave and Herb admitted that the reason they watched was simply to enjoy Sally Adler's tendency toward Spandex tights and low-cut blouses.

"Well, Coach, it's that time of the show when we go over last Sunday's highlights."

Sally put her hand on Kennedy's knee, and the coach jumped noticeably.

"Why don't we just roll the tape and you jump in whenever you feel like it, coach."

"Very well."

They both turned in their chairs to face the large screen behind them.

"Now here's the opening kickoff," Adler said. "Mills takes the ball and there, you can see the coverage break down and Mills breaks into the clear. Coach, you must have been tremendously surprised to see Norm Blaylott make the tackle."

"Yes, I was."

"After all, kickers in this league don't make too many tackles, do they?"

"You are correct, Miss Adler."

"There's the tremendous hit Blaylott put on the runner. Let's look at it in slow motion. Notice how they butt heads and stand each other up? Not exactly your textbook tackle, eh, Coach?"

"No, not exactly."

"But it worked."

"Mr. Blaylott was doing his job."

"In fact, he did his job so well that neither one of them returned to the game. By the way, folks, Norm is fine. There was no serious brain damage and he'll be back on the field tomorrow against the Pittsburgh Pistols. I'll bet you were concerned for a while there, though."

"Yes, we were."

"Head injuries can certainly be tricky, can't they?"

"Yes, Miss Adler. They can."

They watched the Washington touchdowns and most of the St. Louis comeback. As the show neared its end, Dave noticed from backstage that Sally Adler had somehow managed to open another button on her blouse.

Kennedy must be made of stone, he thought. If that was me out there, they'd have to make this show X-rated.

"Coach, next we've got the most controversial play of the game, that pass interference call on the final drive. Here's Anderson making his cut and Buck Wilson taking the fake. Now Anderson's in the clear, as we can see on this isolated closeup. And here's where he stumbles and the pass falls incomplete. Now Coach, I didn't see Wilson anywhere close to him, did you?"

"No," the implacable Kennedy said.

"Then it was obviously a terrible call by the official."

"Please roll the tape again."

"Again?"

"From the beginning."

The technician replayed the tape and Kennedy called for him to stop it.

"Right there," he said.

"There?" Adler asked. "That little bump, that little push was what they called interference?"

"I assume so. It was the only time Mr. Wilson had any physical contact with him."

"But Anderson was barely off the line! The ball wasn't even in the air!"

Coach Kennedy looked at Sally Adler and said in his sternest manner, "Miss Adler, the rules state that if a receiver is bumped, pushed, tripped or otherwise impeded from completing his pass route, it is interference."

"Yes, but that's only if the receiver has traveled five yards past the line of scrimmage." Sally Adler was known for doing her homework.

"That is correct."

"But Coach, Anderson was no more than two yards past the line of scrimmage when that little bump took place."

"In that angle we saw, that's correct."

"Coach, are you going to give us that old excuse about camera angles being deceptive?"

"Yes."

"So you're telling us the zebra made the right call?"

"I am certain the official made what he considered the correct call in that situation."

"Well," Adler said. "It didn't end up mattering anyway, because of what happened on the next play. Let's take a look at the play that ended the game."

There was really nothing either of them could say. The energy, the force with which the Adonis brothers dispensed with the St. Louis line and then went in to crush the play spoke for itself. When the replay was over, they sat in silence for a moment.

"Whew!" Sally Adler finally exclaimed. "I'm just ... spent! That was awesome!"

"Yes, it was."

They went to a series of commercials at that point, and Dave ogled Sally Adler while the makeup person came out to touch her up for the second half of the show.

Ben Kennedy just sat quietly.

"Well, Coach Kennedy," Adler said when they were back on the air. "Tomorrow you've got the Pittsburgh Pistols. They were seven and seven last year, but I don't see that they've made a heck of a lot of improvement. True, they still have Andy Hellmond at quarterback, and he's one of the finer play-callers in the Association."

Kennedy nodded.

"And they've still got halfback Johnny Smith," she continued. "Of course, he's becoming more famous for his underwear commercials than he is for his running. But their defense, well, it's not exactly pitiful, but realistically it's full of holes. They've got two rookie linebackers and a line that didn't have a single sack against Dallas last week."

"They won, though."

"Yes, Coach, they beat the Cougars, 20-10. All things considered, I have a very hard time understanding the Pistols being five-point favorites."

"I would not know, Miss Adler. I do not gamble."

"And even if you did, Coach, I doubt that you'd tell us," she said, leaning over and slapping him on the knee. Kennedy barely resisted the urge to slap her back.

Adler laughed at her own wit and continued. "Well, Coach, are the Warriors ready to play Pittsburgh?"

"Yes."

"All right, then. That's all the time we have tonight. Thanks for tuning in, and be sure to tune in next week when we'll be back on Coach's Corner to talk about the game with the Pistols. Stay tuned for the NAFA Saturday night game, Chicago at Birmingham. Now, for coach Benjamin Kennedy and all the other people who bring you Coach's Corner, this is Sally Adler. Keep 'em flying."

43

Carl Lombard, a former All-America cornerback at the University of Tennessee and the head of the officiating squad for the Warriors' game with Pittsburgh, stood silently while Stan Pinello gave him the instructions for the game.

When Lombard left college, everyone who knew him expected him to have a promising career as a player in the NAFA. He was drafted in the first round by the Atlanta Aces and came into camp with the highest of expectations.

For some reason, though, Lombard was never able to get the hang of the intricate defenses used in the Association. Atlanta kept him on its practice squad for a year and traded him to Kansas City after the season. The Wranglers released him on the final cut.

Tryouts with San Francisco, Denver and Calgary were similarly fruitless, and Lombard finally realized he wasn't going to make it as a player.

Not able to bear the thought of being separated from the game he loved, Lombard did the next best thing. He applied for a job as an official.

He passed the Association's psychological examination with a near-perfect score, the highest mark anyone could remember. He was willing to accept the low pay, the difficult travel and the lack of attention. To the delight of league officials, he immediately saw the beneficial aspects of the System, accepting its existence as a game-saving process, exactly the way it had been explained to him.

In fact, Lombard reveled in the fact that, denied success as a player for so long, he and he alone would be in control of the game.

After only a few games, though, it was apparent to all concerned that Lombard was not going to be the top-notch official everyone had hoped. Instead of a seasoned professional with precise and instant judgment, he became an overzealous, pompous and altogether loathsome individual.

He lusted after the power offered him, calling more penalties than any other official in the league, even more than those ordered by the league liaisons.

Because of this, the games Lombard worked became long, tedious affairs, punctuated by delays as the officiating crews met and tried to decipher Lombard's decisions.

In three seasons as an official, Lombard had fallen from favor quickly. He had initially been assigned to A-level games, but by the middle of his first season he was working B games. By the start of his third season, Lombard was handling nothing but meaningless affairs between non-contenders.

Lombard hated being assigned to C games. There was supposed to be little involvement by either the liaisons or the officials, the idea being to dispense with them as quickly as possible, a concept Pinello was stressing in the strongest of terms.

"... are we clear on that, then? I don't want any hot dogging out there. We've got the Bulldogs game, a national telecast, coming on right after this, and the Association doesn't want any run-over into that game. Do not call any penalties unless I specifically ask for them, or unless something is so obvious you'd be arrested if you didn't call it. Understand, Lombard?"

"Yes, sir," Lombard answered sullenly.

"I mean, if you see a guard reach out, grab a guy by the shoulder pads and throw him down on the ground, I want you to think about calling holding. I want this game over with fast, Lombard. Let's shoot for two hours and forty-five minutes, OK?"

"Yessir, Mr. Pinello."

Pinello was still explaining things to the referees when Herb Rojas headed for the owners' box half an hour before game time. He had spent the past three hours making sure the concessionaires were set for the large crowd that was expected for the Warriors' home opener, and he was still a little preoccupied.

He almost bumped into a woman outside the owners' box, and he immediately turned on the charm. "Well, hi baby ... Muriel?"

Dave Krause's ex-wife was equally surprised to see him. "Oh! Hello, Herb. How are you?"

"Fine, just fine."

"And your father?"

"Oh, he's as happy as a clam. In fact, he's inside right now. Why don't you come in and say hello? Why didn't Dave bring you up?"

Muriel blushed. "I'm not here with David. A ... a friend brought me to the game."

"Funny, Dave didn't say anything about ..."

"David doesn't even know I'm here. I didn't want to, uh, take advantage of his position to get tickets."

"Sure, I understand. Where are you sitting? I'll tell Dave, and then he can ..."

"No!" Muriel seemed almost alarmed at the thought of running into her ex-husband. "I mean no, don't bother David. I'll be honest with you, Herb.

I'm here with a date, and David might get jealous or upset to see me ..."

"Muriel, you've been divorced for eight years. I hardly think Dave's still in the jealous stage."

"Well, it would be uncomfortable for me."

"Yeah, I guess so. Look, are you getting something to eat, or a drink? Let me go inside and get you a cup of coffee."

"Thanks, Herb, but I've really got to get back to my seat. Anyway, isn't the game about to start? Don't you have to get in there?"

"Yeah, I'm with this really cute little ... Well, I won't bore you with details. Let's just say that if we win, I'll be in for one hellacious night."

"Good for you, Herb," Muriel said without smiling. "Well, I've got to go. I'll see you later."

"Yeah, later."

Compared to all the other owners' boxes in the Association, the Warriors' box was truly awful. Maybe it was because the team was community-owned and didn't have one single man in charge. Maybe it was because the team always had run a cut-rate operation.

For whatever reason, the only advantages the people in the private box had over those in the stands were air conditioning and a private restroom.

There was no big screen television, no well-stocked bar and no refrigerator stocked with tasty items. The seats, while a little more comfortable than the wooden benches in the stands, were torn, stained and marred with cigarette burns.

By Dave and Herb's rating system, the owner's box at the Hoove would rate no more than a two.

Not that Roy Rojas noticed. He was having a terrific time and was making sure everyone else knew it.

"This is great!" he shouted, slapping his fist on the arm of his chair. "What a terrific view of the field!"

"It's not that great, Roy," Dave said. "In all the other stadiums, these boxes are on the fifty yard line. This place was built back when they had a baseball team."

"So we have to sit on the thirty. Who cares?"

"Lots of people. Most of the other owners hate this place. You don't see the Pittsburgh folks hanging around here, do you?"

"So what? I'm still having a great time. Hey, isn't that Reynolds over there? The reporter?"

Dave looked over and saw the rotund sportswriter talking with two other men. "Yeah, that's him."

"You mean after all the rotten things he's written about you guys, you let him into the games?"

"We have to, Roy. He's a reporter."

Herb chose that moment to make his entrance. He had caught the tail end of the conversation and as usual, he jumped right in. "Anyway, dad, if you think he's writing bad stuff about us now, you should see what he'd say if we tried to keep him out of the stadium."

Roy noticed someone else. "There's that Sally Adler. Say, she dresses like that in public, too!"

"Sure, dad. You want to meet her?"

"Sure!"

"Well, maybe at halftime. The game's about to start. But let me warn you, dad, don't bother trying anything with her. That broad is one cold fish."

"I take it you tried."

"Roy, you should have seen him. He practically fell all over himself trying to get her to go out with him."

"Well, son, you can't always bat a thousand."

"Terrific, Dave. We're running a football team and my dad's using baseball terms. Anyway, she's not worth the trouble. Believe me. Who knows? Maybe she doesn't like guys."

"Hey. Over there, isn't that Chip Madison from Channel Four? Is he covering the game, too?"

The first half moved even more quickly than Pinello had expected. Pittsburgh took the opening kickoff and used nine minutes of time scoring a touchdown. Washington answered with an eight-minute drive of its own, extending into the second quarter and ending with a two-yard touchdown run by Roxy Reese.

Not a single penalty was called in the entire half, which ended with the score tied, 7-7.

"You're doing very well, Lombard," Pinello said during their halftime meeting. "It looks like you're finally learning how to follow orders. There might be hope for you yet."

Lombard didn't seem pleased with what Pinello had perceived as a compliment.

"I'm just doing what you told me to do," he said non-committally.

"Well, I'm glad you're cooperating. In fact, I'm going to make sure I mention you in my report to the commissioner. I haven't had to correct you once."

"Thank you."

"Now in the second half, you can go ahead and call a few penalties. After all, we don't want people to think you're asleep out there."

"But only if they're obvious."

"Very obvious, Lombard."

"Yes, sir."

There were a few penalties called during the second half, but the pace of the game remained fast. Washington managed to score a touchdown in the third quarter and Pittsburgh scored one with six minutes left in the game.

Neither team did anything spectacular, and time was winding down with the score tied, 14-14.

The Warriors got the ball for the last time with five minutes to play. Using mostly inside running plays by Reese and Waller, with an occasional short pass to keep the defense honest, they moved to the Pistols' twenty-five with just over a minute to play.

Gardner called for a time out and waddled over to the sideline.

"Call thirty-seven red, Mr. Gardner."

"Coach, hear me out. The passes have been working like a charm. Greenblatt's been open every play on this drive."

"I am certain the Pittsburgh coach is aware of that, Mr. Gardner. I consider the risk unacceptable."

Ben Kennedy turned to one of his assistants, effectively terminating the conversation. Gardner stood there, feeling angry and frustrated at the same time. He thought about calling his own play as he trotted back to the huddle, but he knew he would do what the coach said.

"Thirty-seven red. On two."

Stan Pinello was leaving nothing to chance. "OK, Lombard, time for your big moment. Let's have a nice little holding call here to push Washington out of field goal range."

The Warriors were lining up to run the play, and Lombard had yet to respond to Pinello's instruction.

"Lombard, did you hear what I said? Let's have a holding call ... Lombard, are you listening? Goddammit, Lombard, answer me!"

Reese took the handoff from Gardner and drove off-tackle behind a block from Willis Waller. The play broke for nineteen yards and Reese finally was pulled down at the Pittsburgh six. The Pistols had used all their time outs, and couldn't stop Washington from allowing the clock to run down to the final seconds.

Kennedy sent the field-goal unit onto the field as the crowd cheered wildly.

Pinello was still shouting into his headset. "What the hell's going on down there, Lombard? What the fuck are you doing, letting them run the clock down like that? Get a time out, dammit, get a time out!"

Pinello grabbed his binoculars and managed to locate Lombard on the field.

"Holy shit!" he shouted when he saw that the official had his headset off and was tapping it against his palm. Lombard had a disgusted look on his face, as if the apparatus had died on him.

"Oh, no!" Pinello moaned.

Pinello watched helplessly as Lindy Eaker took the snap and made a perfect spot on the thirteen. Norm Blaylott put the ball through the uprights as time expired, giving the Warriors a 17-14 victory and a 2-0 record.

Roy was surprised and disappointed by the lack of excitement in the press box. While he was about to jump out of his skin at the thought of his beloved team winning its first two games, the reporters present were working methodically at their video screens, as if the Washington Warriors won every day.

He was about to say something to Dave and Herb when Fred Reynolds noticed them.

"Gentlemen, gentlemen," the rotund reporter said, causing a few of his colleagues to look up from their stories. "What a rare pleasure. It's such a genuine thrill to have our illustrious general managers and their assistant grace our humble surroundings."

"We don't come in here too much, dad," Herb muttered.

"Why not?"

"Because, sir," Reynolds said. "You happen to be in the most poorly equipped and operated press room in the North American Football Association. Notice the charming color of the walls? Vomit green, the very same color they painted the temporary government buildings during World War II, I might add."

"What does World War II have to do with it?" Dave asked.

"That's probably the last time these walls were painted," the reporter from the Post quipped.

"We're getting around to it," Herb said.

"And the food," Reynolds added. "Yes, this Warriors management team knows how to spend its dollars wisely. Where most of the other organizations understand the value of good publicity and lay out elaborate buffets for the ladies and gentlemen of the media, the Warriors spend that money on washed-up players and untested rookies. Do you know what we had in here today?"

"What?" Roy asked.

"Green roast beef and rancid chili."

"I don't notice you missing a lot of meals, Reynolds," Dave said.

"All I'm saying, Krause, is that other professional sports organizations recognize that we have a job to do and do their best to make our surroundings pleasant, the Washington franchise seems to delight in punishing the fifth estate."

"Yeah," Herb said. "I've noticed you punishing yourself with the free beer, Reynolds."

Reynolds drew himself up to his full height of five-foot-seven. "It helps me forget, sir."

"Wait a minute, guys," Roy said. "Fred has a point."

"Dad, don't bother ..."

"Tell you what, Reynolds. Next time you're up here there'll be a spread like you've never seen before, and it'll all be on me."

"Are you implying, Mr. Rojas, that you might be able to buy my affections in print by feeding me better?"

"No, I just think you've got a point. You guys are our guests and you should be treated like guests."

"Then you are a gentleman, Mr. Rojas," Reynolds said stiffly. "But it will not change my opinion of you and your cohorts. I still believe you are imbeciles."

"Give me a break, Reynolds," Dave said. "The guy's just trying to be nice. Just accept it in the spirit it's offered."

"Very well ... but you guys are still boobs."

"Hey," Herb said. "We're 2-0, aren't we?"

"So were the guys two years ago. They lost five out of the next six and finished up 4-10. You haven't proven anything yet. Win a few more and I might change my mind."

"But don't count on it, right?"

"Right."

"By the way," Roy asked. "Where's Sally? I wanted to meet her."

Reynolds' already sour face became even more distended. "That sleazy little bitch? She's probably still down in the locker room. Probably giving it to Kennedy, getting a new angle on the team, so to speak."

"Hi, guys!" Sally Adler breezed into the press room, causing at least half the reporters to stop typing.

"Hello, Adler," Reynolds said coldly before turning and heading back to his seat.

"What's the matter with him?" Roy asked.

"Who knows?" Adler said. "He doesn't like the idea that a woman can cover football, not to mention do better at it than he does and make more money to boot. And who, might I ask, are you?"

"I'm Herb's father, Roy Rojas."

"Aha, the legendary elder Rojas," she said, touching him lightly on the arm. "Where have they been hiding you?"

"He doesn't get out much," Herb said. "He's got a bad heart."

"Don't listen to him. My heart's in fine shape and so is the rest of me."

"I'll bet," she said, smiling sweetly and causing Roy to wish he were thirty years younger.

"I've been pretty busy. I'm running Herb's bar for him and I've been doing a lot with the team. I'm handling press relations these days."

"Really?"

"Yeah, I think that's where they figure I can do the least damage. Tell me,

Sally. What's with these guys, anyway? We just won. Don't they know it?"

"Roy, these guys are pros. With certain exceptions," she added as she glanced at Reynolds. "They can't afford to let themselves get worked up."

"Yeah, well ..."

"Say, Roy. I'd like to get to know you a little better. There might be an interesting angle in it. Are you doing anything tonight?"

"Well, no."

"Maybe we could have dinner. My treat."

Only Dave noticed the little exchange between Roy and Herb, the triumphant grin on the father's face and the disbelieving look on the son's.

44

The ringing of the phone beside his bed had awakened Pinello at 3 a.m. The commissioner had been upset enough by the Warriors' second victory in as many weeks that he ordered the Warrior liaison to catch the first flight out of National Airport.

Pinello sent his female companion home, threw a few things into an overnight bag and left for the airport. He didn't have to check schedules. He had flown to New Orleans often enough that he had the list of departures from both Washington airports committed to memory.

The first flight out was only half-full, and Pinello wasn't at all surprised to see that Carl Lombard was also among the passengers. They shared a cab from the airport to the commissioner's office, even though either said one word to the other.

"All right, gentlemen. What happened?"

"Commissioner," Pinello said. "It was a simple case of equipment failure."

"Mr. Pinello, if you think for a minute that I brought you down here on a Monday morning, upset my entire day's schedule and spent a large amount of the Association's money just to hear excuses, you are sadly mistaken."

"Yes, sir. But ..."

"Commissioner, he's telling you the truth," Lombard said. "My headset failed. I don't know how it happened, but about halfway through the fourth quarter, it went dead on me. I tried to signal Mr. Pinello, but he must have missed it."

"You lying little shit! I watched you the whole time!"

"Mr. Pinello," the commissioner said. "I would appreciate it if you would try and maintain some sense of decorum in my office."

"Commissioner, the man is lying!"

Lombard wasn't giving up that easily. "You didn't talk to me once the whole first half, Pinello. You told me before the game that it didn't matter all that much, that you wanted a fast game with no penalties."

"I told you to call the ones you were sure of."

"You said to think about calling the ones I was sure of."

"Mr. Pinello, it does seem rather strange that you did not contact Mr. Lombard once in the entire first half."

"Yeah, Pinello. What were you doing, getting a little tootsie?"

"A little ..."

"As a matter of fact, Commissioner, I did see him leave the game with a woman."

"Mr. Pinello?"

"Commissioner, you know me better than that."

"Mr. Pinello, did you have someone up there with you?"

"No!"

The Commissioner paused, staring first at Pinello and then at Lombard. "I thought not. Still, I had to be certain."

"Well, now you are. And what about this lying little piece of scum? What are you going to do about him?"

"For the time being, nothing. I'll have to wait for the report from the lab."

"Report?"

"Yes, Mr. Lombard," the Commissioner said as he turned to face the official. "I had Pinello send the supposedly defective headset to an electronics laboratory."

"You let him break into my locker?"

"Yes, to retrieve Association property."

"Well, I'm not exactly sure what the report will show. I dropped the headset."

"You what?"

"Well, actually I ... kind of ... threw it against the wall."

"You purposely damaged Association property?"

"Well, it was already broken, and I was so angry about it dying on me that I sort of kicked it across the room."

"Mr. Lombard, you realize that the repair or replacement costs of that unit will have to be taken out of your salary?"

"Yes, sir."

"All right, then. You may leave."

Both men got up to go, but the commissioner wasn't finished with Stan

Pinello. "Not you, Pinello. I'd like you to stay a little longer."

"Yes, Commissioner."

After Lombard left, the commissioner turned and stared out his window at the NAFA stadium for at least three minutes before saying anything.

Pinello was beginning to feel very uncomfortable, but he knew there was no point in rushing the commissioner. He would say whatever was on his mind whenever he was ready, and no sooner.

"Mr. Pinello, we have a serious problem," he finally said without turning around.

"Commissioner, I was in control of that game."

The commissioner wheeled quickly. "No, Pinello, you were not! A man in control of that game would never have allowed it to be that close!"

"But the game didn't mean anything, sir. It was a C game, for crying out loud!"

"Every game is important, Mr. Pinello. Are you aware of what our standings look like?"

"Well ..."

"In the Liberty Conference East, Miami and Washington are tied for first place with two wins and no losses. Atlanta and Pittsburgh are one and one, and New York and Boston are both winless. Do you see the point I am making?"

"I think ..."

"Pittsburgh was supposed to be where Washington is, Mr. Pinello. The Pistols are one of our Cinderella teams this year, and already we are having to adjust the System because of what happened yesterday in Washington."

The commissioner stood and started to pace.

"Mr. Pinello, the Washington franchise has had a long and glorious tradition of losing seasons. That has been no accident. When we first started using the System, we asked people which teams they most wanted to see in the Championship Bowl, as I'm sure you know."

Pinello nodded.

"The teams at the top of the list changed every year, Pinello, but the team at the bottom was always the same. Do you know what that team was, Pinello?"

"Washington?"

"Yes, Washington. Needless to say, this aroused our curiosity, so we commissioned a separate survey to find out why. Was it the Washington players they hated? The coaches? Their uniforms? Their helmets?"

"What was it, Commissioner?"

"It was none of those things, Pinello. The reason people didn't like the Warriors was because they were in Washington! Think about it. People hate Washington, D.C., more than they hate Los Angeles or Detroit or Cleveland. They even hate it more than they hate New York. And why is that?"

Pinello shrugged.

"Because Washington is our seat of government, the great omnipotent bureaucracy that takes their money, that makes them wear seat belts and not smoke, that makes them send their children across town to school and then won't let them pray when they get there. Pinello, people love their country, but they hate the government. And where is the government?"

"In Washington."

"Exactly, and so are the Warriors. So not only do people get a thrill when their team wins, they also get an added measure of enjoyment when the rest of the Association walks all over Washington, year after year. It is their measure of revenge.”

The commissioner leaned forward until his face was no more than a foot from Pinello’s.

“It is your job, Mr. Pinello, to make certain the good people of America have their revenge.”

“Because we give the people what they want?”

“Because we don’t want to lose money. Can you imagine what would happen if the Warriors made it to the Championship Bowl? It would be a ratings disaster! We’d be lucky to come in third behind Diff’rent Strokes and Happy Days.”

The commissioner shuddered visibly at that thought.

“Have I impressed upon you the importance of Washington returning to the cellar immediately?”

“Yes, sir.”

“Good, Pinello.”

“Actually, Commissioner, there might be a good side to this.” The commissioner looked at him quizzically. “After two victories to start the season, imagine how people in Washington are going to feel when the Warriors take a nosedive.”

The commissioner smiled. “Make it so, Mr. Pinello.”

NORTH AMERICAN FOOTBALL ASSOCIATION STANDINGS
After Two Weeks of Play

LIBERTY CONFERENCE

East Division	W-L-T	West Division	W-L-T
Miami Wave	2-0-0	Los Angeles Generals	2-0-0
Washington Warriors	2-0-0	San Francisco Kings	2-0-0
Atlanta Aces	1-1-0	Houston Lonestars	1-1-0
Pittsburgh Pistols	1-1-0	Denver Mountaineers	1-1-0
Boston Barons	0-2-0	Calgary Riders	0-2-0
New York Comets	0-2-0	Detroit Crushers	0-2-0

FREEDOM CONFERENCE

East Division	W-L-T	West Division	W-L-T
Philadelphia Bulldogs	2-0-0	Cincinnati GoldStars	2-0-0
Jacksonville Stingers	2-0-0	Dallas Cougars	1-1-0
Chicago Trojans	2-0-0	Minneapolis Stallions	1-1-0
Montreal Mustangs	0-2-0	St. Louis Archers	1-1-0
Toronto Blues	0-2-0	Vancouver Westerners	1-1-0
Birmingham Smashers	0-2-0	Kansas City Wranglers	0-2-0

45

"Hi, I'm Willis Waller, running back for the Washington Warriors. Looking good on the field counts big for me, but looking good off the field is just as important.

"So to make sure I look my best, I take my head down to Earl's House of Hair, where I get the latest, most up-to-date do in the city. So if you want people to notice you like a thirty-yard run, get your head down to Earl's House of Hair on Commonwealth Avenue in Alexandria. ..."

Herb moved to the next chapter on the videotape.

"Hi, I'm Willis Waller, running back for the Washington Warriors. Now I don't have to work on my image. Everybody knows I'm a hard-running, smooth-moving tailback. But maybe you need to work on yours.

"If you do, then get your bad self down to Earl's Mensworld, where they've got all the fly new outfits and all those little extras that go with them. Tired of looking like you just fumbled? Then get down to Earl's Mensworld, on King Street in Alexandria ..."

Herb advanced the machine again.

"Hi, I'm Willis Waller, running back for the Washington Warriors. Hey,

what's the point of watching all the games if all you have to watch them on is a beat-up old black and white that doesn't get half the channels anyway? Especially when you can get down to Earl's Appliance Universe, where you can rent yourself the finest new color televisions.

"There's no money down, no credit check and with Earl's easy payments, you can rent to own and the set can be yours in no time at all. All you've got to do is say, 'Earl, I want to watch Willis in color.' That's Earl's Appliance Universe ..."

Herb put the remote control down and stared at the screen.

"What the hell ..." he and Dave said almost in unison.

"Wait," their visitor said. "There's one more."

He picked up the remote and fast-forwarded it one more time.

"Hi, I'm Willis Waller, running back for the Washington Warriors. I might be a rookie on the field, but I'm a pro when it comes to having a good time, if you know what I mean. Now I don't have any problem getting the company of good-looking young ladies, but maybe you do. Well, your troubles are over.

"Just call Earl's Escort Service. They can fix you up with some of the finest, foxiest young ladies in town, and it won't cost you an arm and a leg. So why sit around the house like you didn't make the final cut? Just call Earl's Escort Service, at 976-GIRL."

Earl Spring walked across the room and removed the disc from the VCR.

"That last one would be shown only on certain cable systems and on closed-circuit television in area hotels," he said. "We're after the business trade. You know, traveling salesmen."

Dave and Herb stared at Spring, who was not the sleazy-looking individual they had expected. The suit he was wearing must have cost at least fifteen hundred dollars, and he spoke with the clipped measured manner of an Ivy League graduate.

"I don't care if it runs in Tijuana," Herb said. "Why are you showing us these commercials?"

"Professional courtesy."

"Forgive me, Mr. Spring," Dave said. "But I've got to admit I'm at somewhat of a loss. I can't understand why you're making such a big thing out of Willis doing endorsements. He hasn't made that much of a name for himself yet. And that doesn't sound like his voice. He doesn't usually talk so much like a ... a ..."

"Like an African-American? We were just tailoring our approach to the market. And Willis might not have made much of an impression with the Tribune or with the Post yet, but have you seen Ebony? They're quite impressed with him."

"So?"

"And with the money you're paying him, he was more than anxious to make a little on the side."

"The money we're paying him!?" Herb sputtered. "He's the highest-paid player on the team! The highest-paid player in the whole damn Association!"

"Yes, yes," Spring said. "But wages in football are far below those paid to baseball or basketball players. Willis was eager to make up the difference."

"So you signed him up?"

"Yes. We have a personal services contract. Anything Willis does outside of football, he does for me."

"Well, congratulations, Mr. Spring," Herb said. "You've got yourself a valuable property there. Use him in good health."

Spring smiled. "I'm glad you feel that way. I do plan on using him. Unless, of course, you'd prefer him not to be working for me."

"Are you suggesting we might want to buy out your contract with Willis?" Dave asked.

"Perhaps."

"And did you have a figure in mind?"

"Two hundred thousand dollars," Spring said calmly.

"Two hundred thousand!?" Herb nearly shouted.

Dave was calmer. "Have a nice life, Mr. Spring."

"I plan to. Did I tell you some of the other ads we're planning? Earl's E-Z Loans, Earl's STD Testing, Earl's Marital Aids, Earl's Adult Books and Novelties ..."

"Mr. Spring, if you're implying we might be embarrassed by all this, you're sadly mistaken. We couldn't care less what Willis does in his spare time."

"I'm glad you're so open-minded, gentlemen," Spring said, fingering his silk tie. "Considering the fact that some of the promotions we plan on doing might involve some element of, shall we say, danger."

"Danger?"

"Yes, Mr. Rojas. Danger. Loss of life, permanent disfigurement, possible career-ending injury. Let's see, there's Earl's Shock Therapy Center, Earl's School of Bungee Jumping, Earl's Institute of Bullfighting ..."

"Bullfighting?"

"Rodeo, too. Those animals can get awfully testy."

"You wouldn't purposefully harm Willis Waller, would you?"

"Of course not, Mr. Krause. Of course not. But there is always an element of risk involved.”

“Mr. Spring, you are amazing.”

“I’m quite rich, too.”

“Well, we’re not going to make you any richer,” Herb said. “Not two hundred thousand dollars worth!”

“Did I mention Earl’s Firing Range?”

“Uh, Herb, the man has a point.”

“In fact, gentlemen, I am a reasonable man. The amount I require is negotiable, as is the form of my compensation. I’d be willing to accept something other than cash in payment.”

“Such as?” Herb asked suspiciously.

“The War Room.”

The War Room was the Washington Warriors’ official souvenir shop. It was a small store on a commercial corner in downtown Washington that wasn’t far from the team’s offices. It was more of a public relations property than a viable business and in fact had not turned a profit in the last twelve years.

To Dave and Herb, it was more of a bother than anything else. They had tried to convince Roy to manage the place, but even he had turned them down.

“You want the War Room?”

“That’s right, Mr. Krause. I want the exclusive franchise to operate the War Room. Of course, I would receive all of the profits from ...”

“There are no profits!” Herb said. “The place is a loser, a dog, a tax writeoff.”

“Then it will be my tax writeoff, gentlemen.”

"And that's all you want?" Dave asked.

"That's it. I'll even pay you for the franchise. One dollar. I would ask you to give it to me, but some money must change hands if I'm to avoid the gift taxes."

"It sounds strange," Herb said.

"I'll sign an agreement to keep it as a souvenir shop as long as there's a team in Washington. And if you decide to hang on to the property, we'll just have to go ahead with our next commercial ..."

"Got a dollar, Earl?"

NORTH AMERICAN FOOTBALL ASSOCIATION STANDINGS
After Four Weeks of Play

LIBERTY CONFERENCE

East Division	W-L-T	West Division	W-L-T
Miami Wave	4-0-0	Houston Lonestars	3-1-0
Washington Warriors	4-0-0	Los Angeles Generals	3-1-0
Pittsburgh Pistols	2-2-0	San Francisco Kings	3-1-0
Atlanta Aces	1-3-0	Denver Mountaineers	2-2-0
Boston Barons	1-3-0	Calgary Riders	1-3-0
New York Comets	0-4-0	Detroit Crushers	0-4-0

FREEDOM CONFERENCE

East Division	W-L-T	West Division	W-L-T
Philadelphia Bulldogs	4-0-0	Cincinnati GoldStars	3-1-0
Chicago Trojans	3-1-0	Dallas Cougars	2-2-0
Jacksonville Stingers	3-1-0	Minneapolis Stallions	2-2-0
Birmingham Smashers	1-3-0	St. Louis Archers	2-2-0
Toronto Blues	1-3-0	Vancouver Westerners	2-2-0
Montreal Mustangs	0-4-0	Kansas City Wranglers	1-3-0

46

Fred Reynolds' column, the Washington Tribune, October 9:

"Pinch me.

"It's certainly as much of a surprise to me as it is to anyone else in this crazy town, but the Washington Warriors are 4-0.

"Undefeated.

"And the government has decided to stop collecting taxes, ministers have stopped preaching against the evils of strong drink and fast women, and Red China has agreed to dismantle all of its missiles.

"Four weeks ago, I'd have said any of the last three things were more likely than the first, but yes, Virginia -- and Maryland, too -- the Warriors are undefeated.

"Who woulda thunk it? Not me, that's for sure.

"Unfortunately, people in this city seem to be incapable of accepting this for what it is -- a pleasant fluke.

"But no, every cab driver in town, at least the three or four who speak

English, and everyone else you run into seem to believe the Warriors are on their way to the Championship Bowl.

"Please, people, keep a few facts in mind. First, Washington has not had a winning season in twenty years and hasn't been in the playoffs since pre-merger days.

"Second, the season lasts fourteen weeks, not four. A lot of players on this team have trouble making it through four quarters. How are they going to make it through fourteen weeks?

"And finally, the team is still being run by the same three men. Messrs. Rojas, Krause and Rojas may be flying high right now, but they're still boobs.

"In short, we're a long way from the Championship Bowl.

"Remember also that the teams Washington has been playing aren't exactly the class of the league, either. They upset a fairly mediocre St. Louis team and then came back to win one from Pittsburgh.

"Two weeks ago they beat Atlanta, a 1-3 team that gave the Warriors all it could handle. That one was only by 27-20, and it took a Scott Trent interception in the end zone to secure victory.

"And yesterday they built a 14-0 lead against the New York Comets, perhaps the worst team anywhere, and what happened? The Comets scored ten points in the fourth quarter and were on the Washington two-yard-line when time expired. Another win, but hardly awe-inspiring.

"Now don't get me wrong, ladies and gentlemen. No one would be more pleased than I if the Warriors were to make it to the playoffs, and if they made it to the Championship Bowl, I would lead the parade down Pennsylvania Avenue.

"I'm just not going to bet the farm on it."

Jimmy Gardner collapsed onto the bench in front of his locker. "Lord, Tony, I feel like I've been rode hard and put up wet."

Ross was unsympathetic. "Cut the cowboy talk, Jimmy. You might be able to fool some of the kids around here, but I happen to know you were born in Darien, Connecticut."

Gardner ignored him. "Tony, when that Rojas fellow came up to me and started waving visions of glory, fame and money under my nose, I really should have stopped and thought twice about it. I might have remembered why I retired. Pain, suffering ..."

"You'd be here anyway. You'd have remembered something even worse than that -- starvation."

"Oh, kiss my ass, Ross. Just pucker up those lips and kiss my rosy, red rectum. God, I'm tired!"

Ross snapped his towel in Gardner's general direction. "Get the ass in question up and moving, Jimbo! We've got things to do tonight."

"Things to do? As in ..."

"As in Cindy and Amy, Gardner. What should I tell poor Amy, that big, bad Jimmy Gardner doesn't want to come out and play with her?"

"Rossie, you didn't do it again, did you?"

"My friend, you have got a date with a body that just won't quit."

"Why do you keep getting all these dates for me, Tony?"

"Because you can't get them for yourself."

"Bullshit, Ross! Bullshit! Jimmy Gardner can get himself a woman any time he wants!"

"Live or inflatable, Jimbo?"

"Excuse me, Mr. Gardner, Mr. Ross ..." George Greenblatt had walked up unnoticed.

"Oh, hi, Georgie," Ross said. "What can we do for you?"

"It's about my meetings, the ones I hold before the games. No one is coming."

"No one?"

"Well, a couple of guys came the first time, but they got such an awful ribbing they never showed up again. It isn't fair, Mr. Ross. I don't mind carrying a heavy load, but I don't think I should have to shoulder all the responsibility for the team's success."

"George, I don't think I understand."

"All right," Greenblatt said. "I told you that I almost went to the South Seas to work for Mr. William Peace Lippmann."

"Yeah," Gardner said.

"Get on with it, Georgie," Ross said gently.

"All right," Gardner said, sighing. "I have offered to teach my teammates how they can maximize their incomes, how they can best prepare for an uncertain economic future. I have given them investment advice, I have offered to put them on allowances and invest the rest of their income for them."

"And?" Gardner asked.

"They laughed in my face. They continue to spend money on fast cars, on women, on alcohol and other substances that give them nothing more than a few hours of pleasure."

"Oh, thank goodness they're not wasting their money," Ross said drily.

"But they are!" Greenblatt wailed plaintively.

"It was a joke, George," Gardner said.

"A joke? Oh, humor."

"That's right, Georgie," Ross said. "Tell us, though. What do you expect us to do for you?"

"You, Mr. Gardner ..." Greenblatt said as he pointed down at the dumbstruck quarterback. "... are the team captain. It is your obligation to require the other players to attend these meetings."

"Require?"

Tony Ross broke in. "Georgie boy, I think you have a mistaken impression of Jimmy's powers as captain. He gets to call the coin toss and talk to the officials. If he tried to make the guys do anything, they'd tell him to take a flying leap."

Gardner shook his head. "Where do you get all these ideas, George?"

"From the writings of Mr. Lippmann, of course."

"And George, exactly what has this Lippmann told you?"

"Well, when I was in the jungles of Micronesia, bringing the blessed free-market system to the heathen masses ..."

Ross made a motion with his hand, indicating that George should speed it up.

"I received an urgent message from Mr. Lippmann, telling me to return to the United States immediately. He told me he had a vision that I should be back here in America spreading the truth through professional football."

"And?"

"And it has been a success. We won our first four games, but unless we begin showing some good sense, we will lose."

"Greenblatt," Gardner said. "Did he really tell you that?"

"I do not lie, Mr. Gardner."

"George, I think the topic deserves serious discussion, but not here in the locker room. I'd like a little time to get my thoughts together. Say, I've got an idea!"

Don't you dare, Ross said to himself. Don't you dare.

"George, Mr. Ross and I were going down to Kelly's. Why don't you join us? We'll have a couple of beers and talk this over."

"I'm sorry, Mr. Gardner. I don't drink beer." Ross breathed a silent sigh of relief. "But if it means we can get this team on the right track, I'll be happy to accompany you."

"Nooooo!"

"What's the matter with Mr. Ross?"

"He just hurts a lot after a hard practice, Georgie." Gardner laughed. "So we'll see you at Kelly's, around seven?"

"I'll be there, Mr. Gardner. And thank you."

"No problem, kid."

As soon as Greenblatt left the room, Ross turned angrily toward Gardner. "What the hell did you do that for?"

"Relax, Rossie. Trust me. That kid's got a problem, and I think I know how to handle it."

"What about our problem? Two luscious young ladies who are not going to take kindly to having our little party expanded by one fanatic yuppie."

"Yeah, well, you'll handle them, Tony," Gardner said, grabbing a towel and heading for the showers. "Just like always."

Gardner and Ross weren't the only ones with a problem. Dave Krause looked at his desk, which was empty. Then he gazed across at Herb, whose desk was equally clean.

When the Warriors had won their first two games, Dave had anticipated being overwhelmed by ticket orders, requests for player appearances and endorsements and other such business he was certain would be too much for the small office staff to handle.

Using his management experience, Dave had figured they needed to hire four new secretaries.

They had found it difficult not to hire sixteen, assaulted as they were by attractive young women who knew a soft job when they saw one. Herb was willing to make his decision based only on the size of the applicants' bustlines. Dave wanted to hold out for rudimentary secretarial skills.

"Whatever you say, Dave. Please promise me you won't hire the old lady with the hairs growing out of the mole. We're going to have to look at them, you know."

They had settled upon four young ladies who, if truth be told, were the four most attractive applicants who actually could type and speak English. What the heck, Dave had thought, we do have to look at them all day.

By the time the Warriors had won game number three, though, it was apparent they had overestimated the workload. There had been a few car dealers and shopping malls that had requested players for appearances, but overall the fans still were lukewarm at best. They laid off two of their new secretaries.

After the fourth victory, the office work had dropped to the point where they had to think about laying off the other two.

"Well, that takes care of Jenny," Dave said to Herb as the girl left the room. "Now get Bridget in here and we'll get this over with."

"Uh, Dave, could we talk about that?"

Dave knew immediately what was on Herb's mind. "Oh, no."

"I really don't think it would be a good idea to let her go."

"Herb, you didn't."

"Didn't what?"

"Didn't make promises to her in the heat of passion. Did you?"

"Well, not exactly in the heat of passion."

"Afterwards?"

Herb shrugged. "What else could I say? Thanks a lot, baby, and by the way, we're getting rid of you?"

"Herb, how many times have I told you not to screw the help? They call that sexual harassment these days."

"How could I resist? She practically attacked me!"

"Yeah, right."

"No, really."

"All right, then. What did you tell her, that her job was safe?"

"Not exactly."

"Herb ..."

"Well, I didn't tell her she wasn't going to be fired."

"No, you told her she was going to be ..."

"... promoted."

"Promoted!"

"Well, I told her I was pleased with her performance ..."

"There's an understatement."

Herb shot him a look before continuing. "... and I said that I thought it would be beneficial to the operation if she was given a more responsible position."

"Like getting your coffee."

"Like administrative assistant."

"Herb, we don't have enough to do to keep the two of us busy! And we've already got your dad on the payroll as an assistant! How are we going to explain another assistant?"

"Dave, who knows?"

"What?"

"I mean seriously, who knows that we don't have anything to do?"

Herb had a point. Dave couldn't offer a reasonable response. No one in town really knew what their jobs consisted of. In fact, after months on the job, even they weren't really certain. They had signed players and a coach, done what they could to improve the stadium and managed to win four games in the process.

"So," Herb said, interrupting Dave's train of thought. "What do you say?"

"I guess I'm just afraid of what'll happen if the press gets wind of this."

"Probably the same thing that'll happen if they find out about you and Tracey Cagney."

"That's different. No one knows about me and Tracey." Dave sighed. "All right, Herb. Bridget can stay."

"What about the promotion?"

"Why not? If she's going to do a useless job, she might as well be well paid for it."

"See how easy that was? You won't regret it. After all, you get to look at her, too."

"Thanks."

"I'll tell you what. I'll buy lunch."

"Fine. Anywhere but your bar. I'd like something other than hamburgers and potato chips, if you don't mind."

Herb affected a hurt look. "Whatever you say, Dave. You pick the place."

He chose an Italian restaurant in the downtown area, one neither of them had been to in a long time. As it turned out, the restaurant had become very popular and there was a line of people waiting to be seated.

The maitre'd wasn't impressed by their august positions with the Warriors, or Herb's reputation as a "fellow restauranteur," and Herb wouldn't let Dave slip the man a twenty.

They put their names on a waiting list, and decided to pass the hour with a short walk through the neighborhood. It wasn't until they turned a corner that they realized they were in the vicinity of the War Room.

"Jeez!" Herb said. "Will you look at that!?"

The War Room was jumping. There was a crowd around the store, and large numbers of people were coming and going where before there had only been the occasional lost tourist.

They decided to check out the store, and they found Earl Spring himself, in a conservative suit, greeting customers at the door.

"Well, Mr. Rojas, Mr. Krause. Welcome to the War Room. What brings you here?"

"We were in the neighborhood," Dave said.

"There was a line at Angelo's," Herb said. "We had some time to kill ... Where did all these people come from?"

"I beg your pardon?"

"These people, Spring! Where did all these people come from?"

"Word of mouth, Herbie. Once people found out about this place, there was no stopping them!"

"But the War Room was always here, and nobody ever came before."

"Well, we've got some special deals now," Spring said. "Anyone who brings us a new customer gets a free poster."

"Of their favorite player?" Dave asked.

Spring shrugged. "If that's what they want. Usually they pick the cheerleader poster."

"Cheerleaders?"

"Here. Take a look."

Spring unrolled a poster of four young ladies who were two steps beyond voluptuous wearing costumes one step of the right side of the local decency ordinances. Herb sucked in his breath sharply.

"Those aren't our cheerleaders!" He turned to Dave. "Are they?"

Dave shook his head. "I don't think so, and I'm sure if they were, you'd have noticed."

Spring laughed. "Well, they could be. We had a few of the real cheerleaders at the photo session, but they weren't, how can I say this, photogenic enough."

He shrugged. "So I hired a few models to fill in."

"A few models ... Isn't that dangerously close to fraud?"

Herb shook his head. "Not necessarily, Dave. Anyway, who cares what the real cheerleaders look like? This poster looks great!"

"It's a big seller, too. The first run was fifty thousand and they were all gone in a week."

"A week," Dave said, obviously impressed.

"The second batch just got here and they're already going fast. Now we're starting to get orders from some of the chains in the area."

"How much is the team making off these?"

"Nothing, Dave."

"Nothing?"

"Remember our deal? I get all the profits, remember?"

"But you're using our logo, our reputation ..."

"Well, in spite of that, we're still making money," Spring said smugly.

"Anyway, Dave. Think of all the free publicity we're getting out of this."

"Here," Spring said. "Let me show you some of the other things we've got going here. Of course there's the usual stuff ... trading cards, pennants, buttons, pen and pencil sets ..."

"Hey," Herb asked. "Have you got any of those little statues? You know, the kind with the heads that bob up and down?"

Dave and Spring both stared at Herb. "For my dad," he said sheepishly.

"He'd love to have one of those things."

"I'll see if I can't order one for you."

"How much?"

"My treat, Mr. Rojas. Here," Spring said, taking a package off a shelf. "Let me show you a little number that's really moving. It's a life-size, inflatable Warrior doll. As you can tell, it comes in two skin tones."

"Two?"

"Well, if you guys sign a Chinaman or an Arab, I'll add others. All anyone has to do is select his or her favorite Warrior, and we add this latex mask of his face."

Spring pointed to a display on the wall. "See, this one is Roxy Reese, and this one is George Greenblatt."

"Clever."

"Thank you. By the way, the dolls are anatomically correct."

"How much are these things?" Dave asked. "And who buys them?"

"They're $39.95," Spring said. "Single women buy most of them, but we've sold a few to men."

Dave and Herb looked at each other for a moment.

"Listen, gentlemen, I'd love to stand around and chat with you," Spring said. "But I do have a business to run. So take your time, look around. Enjoy yourselves."

"Thanks, Spring," Dave said. "But we've got to get going. Angelo's probably got a table waiting for us by now."

"If we're lucky," Herb said.

They pushed their way through the crowd, and Dave was a little disappointed that none of the Warrior fans shopping for souvenirs had recognized them. By the time they made it back to the restaurant, they had only fifteen more minutes to wait before being seated.

They ordered drinks, and then lunch. Herb was silent until Dave asked what was wrong.

"Herb, do you remember any requests coming our way?"

"Requests?"

"Licensing requests from Spring, asking if he could use the team logo on that stuff."

"No," Herb said. "Gee, it seems like he should have, doesn't it?"

"Maybe he asked your dad."

"I doubt it. You know Roy. If something like that had come through him, he'd have been hopping all over us."

"Let's ask him when we get back. And let's check the deal we signed with Spring. Maybe there's some clause we overlooked."

47

The team had been watching game films for nearly three hours. Ben Kennedy was parading up and down in front of the screen, barking out orders to freeze the tape so that he could make his point time and again.

Not a play passed that wasn't shown twice, and some came in for three viewings. Kennedy used his pointer to demonstrate every little flaw, every little mistake a Warrior player had made in the previous week's victory over the New York Comets.

"Damn, Jimmy," Tony Ross whispered to Gardner. "I thought we won that game."

"Stop right there!" Kennedy shouted at the assistant coach who was manning the video recorder. "Mr. Wilson, I was under the impression you were supposed to be covering that man."

"Which one, Coach?"

"The man three steps behind you, sir. The man who would have caught that pass and run for a touchdown had Romeo Adonis not sacked the quarterback."

"He's really laying into Wilson today," Ross said. "What's going on here?"

"I don't know, Rossie, but you've got to admit Wilson didn't have his best game Sunday."

"Maybe. I don't know, I play on the other side and I kind of like it when defensive players screw up."

"Yeah, me too. Keeps the old man from getting on me."

"And you, Mr. Gardner ... Stop the tape! ... Mr. Gardner, is your advancing age affecting your peripheral vision? Were you unaware of Mr. Gullotta in the open?"

"Coach, I hit Ross for a twenty-five yard gain on that play! Gullotta was only a secondary receiver."

"Mr. Gardner, you forced the pass to Ross. Gullotta was the open receiver."

"Yes, sir."

Kennedy motioned to his assistant to start the tape again.

"Jeez," Gardner whispered. "What's gotten into the old man?"

"Relax, Jimmy. He's probably afraid that we're starting to get complacent."

"Get serious, Rossie."

"Well, you know the coach. He's afraid of losing intramural games."

"Silence, gentlemen!" Kennedy thundered in Gardner and Ross' direction. They managed to keep silent for the rest of the session.

48

Dave and Herb returned to their office to find Pinello there, his feet up on Herb's desk, talking to Roy. "Well, gentlemen, welcome back. That was a long lunch. Angelo's must have been very crowded."

"Yeah, we had to wait ... How did you know we went to Angelo's?"

"I told him," Roy said. "How was it?"

"Crowded," Herb said. "We stopped by the War Room."

"Yeah. Spring's really got that place booming."~

"Well," Pinello said smugly. "It just goes to show what can be done with proper management."

Herb ignored the implied dig. "Dad, do you remember a request from Spring to use the logo on stuff?"

"Stuff?"

"T-shirts, posters, inflatable dolls ..."

Pinello stood up. "He's got the dolls in there already?"

"Pinello, you knew about this?"

"Of course I did. Mr. Spring's requests came across my desk and I approved them."

"Now why the hell ..."

"Because I am the Association liaison, Mr. Rojas, and all such requests have to go through the Association."

"You mean Spring doesn't need our approval?"

"Not technically," Pinello said in an extremely patronizing tone. "You see, in actuality, the local team doesn't even own the name Washington Warriors."

"Say what?"

"Let me explain. All trademarks, logos, nicknames and other such things belong to the North American Football Association. All the team owns is the right to operate a franchise in Washington, within very specific guidelines established by the Association."

"But we've had other requests ..."

"Merely a courtesy. More to let you know what's coming out than anything else."

"Let me get this straight," Dave said. "You mean even if we didn't approve of something, it could still come out if the NAFA wanted it?"

"Technically, yes. But rest assured, the Association would never allow something detrimental to the team or the NAFA to be produced."

"Pinello, what do you call anatomically correct inflatable dolls with players' faces on them? Or posters of cheerleaders who aren't really cheerleaders?"

"Those dolls have been very popular in other cities. Especially in San

Francisco, for some reason. People seem to like the idea of having a football player in their own home.”

“Or bed,” Dave said drily.

“Whatever. We don’t ask people what they do with them once they take them home. And of course, the franchises receive a hefty share of the proceeds, which in your case go to Mr. Spring.”

“What about the poster?” Herb asked.

“Mr. Rojas, cheerleader posters are the biggest money-makers in every city in the Association.”

“But they’re not our cheerleaders. And those aren’t their costumes.”

“So a little fabric got lost. Who’ll notice?”

“Who’ll notice?” Dave asked incredulously. “He’s already sold fifty thousand of them!”

“And has anyone called to complain?”

“Well ...”

“As a matter of fact, the only reaction seems to be people wondering why those girls aren’t at the games.”

“Pinello, our cheerleaders are wholesome young women,” Dave said. “They don’t even do cheers. They just sort of stand there and shake their pom poms.”

“Uh, Dave?”

“Yeah, Herb?”

“I hate to admit it, but he’s got a point. Our cheerleaders are, well, boring.”

“Boring?”

"Yeah," Roy chimed in. "And they're not even that young!"

"Now in most of the other franchises," Pinello continued. "They understand the value of entertainment. They hire dancers, women who know how to shake something other than their pom poms, if you catch my drift."

Roy's eyes lit up.

"They've got choreographed routines. They have outfits done by professional designers. Come on, Krause, get with it! Cheerleaders are big right now! They get almost as much publicity as the players. They're on magazine covers, talk shows, movies ..."

"Think about it, Dave!" Herb broke in excitedly. "We'd get a mountain of free publicity out of cheerleader tryouts! We can hire some Broadway choreographer to work out some routines ..."

"I don't know, Herb."

"What's not to know?" Pinello asked. "It's a great idea. There's nothing that sets the media's blood pumping more than a hundred women in skimpy costumes."

Actually, Dave thought, it wasn't really that bad an idea. And the chance to finally get some good publicity didn't hurt, either. "Well," he said. "I guess ..."

"Oh, I almost forgot," Roy said. "Have you ever heard of a Carmine Romano?"

"Not that I know of? Why?"

"He called while you and Herb were at lunch. He didn't leave a number, but he said he'd get back to you."

"Hell," Herb said. "He's probably just some guy who wants Roxy Reese's autograph."

"I'll get a number if he calls again. I've got to get back to work now."

"Work?" Herb asked. "What work?"

"Hey, I've got a desk that's covered with stuff."

"A desk full ..."

"Yeah, I've been pulling my hair out ..."

Oh, Lord, Dave thought. Not again.

"Uh, Roy. Does this have anything to do with the press relations job?"

"What other jobs do I have around here?"

"Roy, all you have to do is write out press passes for the local papers and the visiting reporters ... Roy, have you written out the passes?"

"Well, there were so many, and our press box is pretty small ..."

Dave and Herb broke out of the office and raced down to the room where Roy had a desk. There, strewn all around the top of the desk, were somewhere between fifty and a hundred envelopes.

"Holy shit!" Herb said as he grabbed a stack of letters. "The New York Times, Newsweek, Sports Illustrated, SportsWeek, the Richmond Times-Dispatch, Newsday ..."

"Listen to these," Dave said as he went through another stack. "Inside Sports, the Boston Globe, the Los Angeles Times ..."

Roy chose that moment to walk into his office. "Now you see my problem," he said. "How could I write passes for all those ..."

"It's easy!" Dave said. "You just put your pen in your little hand and write the name on the pass! Look at this! Time magazine, the Denver Post, the Dallas Morning News ..."

"Now, boys. You know how small our press box is. And you know how much it costs to feed reporters. We can't be expected to write out passes for every diddly little paper in the country."

"Dad, these aren't diddly little papers! These are the biggest papers and magazines around, and they want to write about us!"

"That's it," Dave said. "Now we're really screwed! I can just see the headlines -- Warriors Refuse Press Credentials, Warriors Close Press Box, What Are Warriors Hiding?"

"No problem. I'll just take care of them now."

Dave sighed. "We'll have to call all these editors. We'll have to let them know we're not turning them down. It's too late to mail them out now. We'll just have to have them pick them up at the Will Call window on Sunday."

"Let's get to work," Herb said.

49

Jimmy Gardner was working very hard at getting drunk, and Tony Ross was more than happy to provide whatever assistance he could. Gardner and Ross also were working very hard at convincing Cindy and Amy to continue the party at their house. Ross figured they were halfway home when George Greenblatt walked up to their table.

"Hello, Mr. Ross, Mr. Gardner. I hope I'm not interrupting anything here."

"Not at all, Georgie," Gardner said drunkenly. "Not at all. Pull up a seat and park your butt."

"Well, uh," Greenblatt said, looking first at Cindy and then Amy. "I'm not really sure ..."

"Damn, Georgie, they're just girls! Hell, just think of them as guys with tits!"

Greenblatt pulled up a chair and sat between a none-too-pleased Tony Ross and an all-too-pleased Jimmy Gardner. Amy was the first to speak.

"Are you a football player, too?"

"Girls," Gardner piped up. "This is none other than the famous George

Greenblatt, one of the best rookie tight ends in the league and one helluva guy!"

Cindy smiled sweetly at George. "I like rookies."

Gardner leaned forward. "I have a feeling you also like tight ends."

Everyone but Greenblatt howled at Jimmy's joke. George sat politely, unsmiling and watching the four other people at the table.

"Come on, Georgie," Gardner said, slapping Greenblatt's shoulder. "Loosen up a little. This is a party."

"Uh, Mr. Gardner, could we speak in private?"

"You and me?"

"Yes, sir."

Gardner glanced around the table. The girls were giggling and Ross was signaling furtively that he should take Greenblatt somewhere, anywhere.

"OK, Georgie," Gardner said, struggling to his feet. "Let's you and me find some place to have us a little chat."

Gardner picked up his almost-empty mug and steered Greenblatt through the crowd toward two empty stools at the end of the bar.

"Kelly," he said. "A refill over here. What'll you have, Georgie?"

"How about a ginger ale?"

Gardner winced, but covered it quickly. "A ginger ale for my buddy here."

"Keep your panties dry, Gardner," came the booming voice from behind the bar. "It's coming!"

Gardner turned his attention to Greenblatt, who was sitting with an earnest look on his face. "All right, Georgie. You wanted me and you've got me.

What's up?"

"I'm sorry to disturb your evening, Mr. Gardner, but I don't have anyone else to talk to. My parents are dead and I don't have any brothers or sisters. I really haven't made any friends on the team."

"Hey, it can't be as tough as all that."

"No one even talks to me. Every time I come up to someone, they turn away or ignore me ..."

"Maybe they're afraid you're going to start quoting stock prices to them."

Greenblatt looked like a puppy who had been beaten. Almost against his better judgment, Gardner was starting to feel sorry for him.

"I only want to help people," he said. "It's the way Mr. Lippmann trained me."

"Well, then, why don't you call him? Talk it over with him."

"That's a long-distance call, Mr. Gardner. I can't afford it."

"Whoa, Georgie! I know rookies don't make the really big bucks, except for Waller, but the money's still pretty good. I'm sure you can scrape together the money for a lousy phone call."

"Oh, I'm well paid. It's more money than I ever dreamed of making. And Mr. Lippmann has been extremely grateful ..."

"Mr. Lippmann?"

"Yes, he writes to me every week, telling me what a wonderful thing I'm doing by sending him my paycheck."

"Your paycheck? Your whole paycheck? You don't keep any of it for yourself?"

"Well, half of my money goes into the Lippmann Endowment, and he invests most of the rest of it for me. He sends me a little back, enough to go to an occasional movie, or a few sodas here and there. I don't really need the money, Mr. Gardner. I live at the camp and eat all my meals at the training table. Besides, Mr. Lippmann is doing such wonderful things with the money."

Gardner stared at the young man beside him, absolutely not believing what he was hearing.

"Anyway, having spending money doesn't matter to me. The only thing bothering me is the way people treat me."

"Georgie, I'm no Dear Abby. I'm lousy at giving advice, but it seems to me people would appreciate you a little more if you looked at them like people instead of potential accounts."

"I can't help it. I hate seeing people waste their lives and their talents. You don't know how much it bothers me to see you putting that vile substance in your body when you could have invested a dollar and twenty-five cents into a mutual fund instead."

Gardner looked at his beer for a second and then slowly put the mug back on the bar.

"Georgie, I can't tell you -- well, I won't tell you -- how to run your life, just like you can't tell me how to run mine." Gardner hoped his message was getting through. "All I can tell you is that you're a good tight end. If you can just relax, enjoy yourself and concentrate on developing your own talents instead of trying to turn us all into billionaires, you'll be a terrific tight end."

"Well, I suppose I should thank you."

"Don't bother, Georgie. Talk's cheap, and any time you need somebody to talk with, just look up your old quarterback. That's what captains are for."

"Thanks, Mr. Gardner." Greenblatt finished his ginger ale, put his glass on the bar and left the building. Gardner watched him leave and then returned to his table.

"What's the matter with that kid, Jimmy?" Cindy asked. "Is he gay or something?"

"Nah, he's just a fanatic," Gardner said. "He was in training to be yuppie scum, and I don't think he's used to being around women who don't carry briefcases and wear horn-rimmed glasses."

"A yuppie?"

"Yeah. Why?"

"Well," Cindy said. "We've got a friend who'd just love to meet him."

"Meet George?" Gardner was puzzled. "What is she, some kind of freak?"

Cindy and Amy both laughed. "Nothing like that," Amy said. "She just likes challenges."

Anyone who liked challenges wouldn't have enjoyed the Warriors' game with the Vancouver Westerners all that much. It was apparent very early on that the Westerners hadn't come to Washington to play football.

Their quarterback, Drew Melindez, completed only one pass in the first half -- to Washington's Scott Trent -- and Vancouver was never really in the game.

The Warriors scored three touchdowns in the first period, with Roxy Reese, Tony Ross and Nick Gullotta all finding their way into the end zone. Randy Jenkins scored on a seventy-five yard reverse to start the second quarter, and Norm Blaylott beat the halftime gun with a field goal that made it 31-0 at intermission.

Pinello didn't even bother talking to the officials at halftime. He knew the game was over. Pinello had ordered the officials to call more than a dozen penalties on the Warriors in the first two quarters. None had dampened the Warriors' enthusiasm or improved the Comets' performance.

There was no way, Pinello was certain, that the Westerners would come to life, even if he were to have a penalty called on Washington on every play. He spent the rest of the game trying to figure out what he'd tell the commissioner the next day.

Washington scored only once in the second half as Kennedy rested the regulars. Harv Josephson broke a tackle at the line of scrimmage and ran sixty-two yards for a touchdown midway through the third quarter.

Vancouver managed to avoid total humiliation by driving to the one-yard line in the closing seconds and kicking a field goal as time expired.

The Warriors had won their fifth game of the season, 38-3.

In the locker room afterwards, Ross was jumping up and down and pounding Gardner on the shoulder pads. "Tired now, Jimmy?" he shouted.

"Why the hell should I be tired?" Gardner asked. "Nobody touched me all damn day!"

"Now this is the way it's supposed to be," Ross said happily. "Jimbo, we are going to celebrate tonight!"

"I'm with you, buddy."

"Let's make a party out of it."

"Yeah," Gardner said. "We can invite Roxy ... and Willis ... hell, even Eaker ... and Greenblatt."

Ross blanched for a moment, but he was too happy to allow even the prospect of partying with George Greenblatt to dampen his enthusiasm. "Jimmy, I don't care if you invite the Iron Irishman himself!"

50

The newspapers in Philadelphia were on a familiar kick, wondering what was wrong with one of their city's sports teams. Only this time it wasn't the cellar-dwelling baseball team, or the mediocre hockey club. This time it was the undefeated Philadelphia Bulldogs.

It seemed almost a silly question to ask about a team that now had won fourteen consecutive games dating back to the middle of the previous season. It was in fact that long winning streak that had started reporters looking so desperately for a story.

There was simply nothing to write.

The Bulldogs had been dispatching their opponents with machine-like precision. There had been few spectacular plays or outstanding performances. The Bulldogs merely had done what they always did well -- move the football from one end of the field to the other while keeping their opponents from doing the same.

That was the way it always had been. The Bulldogs weren't a team with a history of spectacular catches or pressure field goals. The town had come to expect their victories, boring as they were. And while there were some people who yearned for flashier play, most of the fans were simply happy to have a consistent winner.

The reporters weren't among those happy throngs. A team that won in such boring fashion didn't generate award-winning stories or build newspaper circulation. There were never any conflicts between players and coaches, or between coaches and the front office.

As far as anyone was concerned, the Bulldogs were one big happy team, made up of contented players, brilliant coaches and a smiling owner.

In fact, Stanley Cagney had become known late in life as "Smiling Stan," a man more concerned with his own pleasure than the success of his businesses. But Cagney had known enough to turn his team over to professionals and then not interfere with them.

The Bulldogs won ... and won ... and won some more. Reporters had to be content to write stories that ran under headlines that said, "Bulldogs Win Again."

After victory number five, though, a young columnist for the Dispatch decided it was time for another kind of story. Rudy Lomax had an idea.

"What's the matter with the Bulldogs?

"From time to time in sports, teams become all too accustomed to winning. It becomes second nature -- it becomes an assumption they take for granted.

"When that happens, teams become lazy. They put out only enough effort to win and no more. That apparently has happened to our Philadelphia Bulldogs.

"Look at yesterday's game with Toronto. Everyone knows the Blues are one of the weakest teams in the Association. Yet our mighty 'Dogs, who beat these same Blues, 38-3, just two weeks ago, only managed a 14-10 victory in Toronto this time around.

"Even that victory might not have come about had not the Blues suffered a crippling number of penalties in the fourth quarter, killing their momentum just enough to allow the 'Dogs to come from behind.

"Many of you will be happy with the fact they won. Others will say to leave them alone, that at least they're 5-0. I hope all of you will be singing that same sad tune when this lack of execution, this lack of effort, comes back to haunt the 'Dogs.

"When a truly fine team like Jacksonville comes to town, and uses the 'Dogs' lack of effort to its advantage, what happens then?

"I'll tell you. The bubble breaks, and once the aura of invincibility is gone, they'll lose another game and another, until the dream of another Championship Bowl victory is gone.

"Remember, without motivation, talent is nothing. The 'Dogs had better stop dogging it."

The story mirrored what a lot of people had been thinking, and it swept through the town quickly. Other sportswriters, sensing a bandwagon, jumped on quickly. By the end of the week, every paper within fifty miles of Philadelphia had featured a piece on the sagging attitude of the Philadelphia Bulldogs. Lomax had been invited to appear on every local sports call-in show to further discuss his theory, and the television sportscasters were chiming in with their own commentaries.

The only person who remained silent on the subject was Tracey Cagney.

51

By Sunday, the talk was all over the league, and it almost rivaled the biggest surprise of the year -- the 5-0 start by the lowly Washington Warriors.

"Hi, everybody. I'm Greg Fishbeck, back with more of NAFA Sunday Morning. It's time now for Andre's Angles, and I'm sure a few of you more observant viewers have noticed that Andre isn't here with us in the studio today. That's because he's on the field right now in Washington, and he's going to tell us exactly what's happening down there. Andre?"

"Thanks, Greg, and hello, everybody. Well, it took some time, but there's finally some interest starting to grow in this city for the amazing, unbeaten Washington Warriors. This team normally draws between twenty-five and thirty thousand fans a game, a little more than half of capacity here at Hoover Coliseum."

The camera panned the stands, which were almost full.

"Today's crowd is estimated at better than fifty thousand, which is as close to a sellout as they've had here in nearly two decades. And right now the Warrior cheerleaders are parading around in their new uniforms, getting the crowd worked up to a fever pitch."

The camera showed the cheerleaders in their new, skimpier uniforms. Unfortunately, they were the same old cheerleaders, and they were ill-equipped to wear the sexier costumes. They were trying out their new dance routines as well, but were succeeding only into bumping into each other in the process.

"Andre," Fishbeck asked as he stifled a laugh. "How would you account for this amazing string of success by the Warriors?"

"Well, Greg, something should be said about the remarkable comeback of Roxy Reese, who has rushed for nearly six hundred yards in five games. And something has to be said about a defense, led by the amazing Adonis brothers, that has been fairly stingy. Overall, though, I'd have to attribute their success to one thing -- luck with a capital L."

"So you're saying Washington isn't that good?"

"Definitely, Greg. The Warriors have yet to play Miami, or Philadelphia, or Chicago. They've been fattening up on some of the weaker teams, and that ends today. Houston's a tough club that always plays well on the road. As much as I hate to see this big crowd disappointed, I'll take Houston by six."

Herb Rojas looked out from the owner's box and smiled. "Fifty thousand people," he muttered to himself.

"Did you say something, Herb?" Dave looked up from his newspaper.

"Just looking around. Jeez, I remember when this would have been half a season's attendance. Hey, look. There's Section 38. Did you bring your binoculars?"

Dave handed the glasses to his friend, who started scanning the section. "Yep, there they are. They're all there. There's Jack McKinney, the cabbie."

"I'll bet some people think Cabbie is his last name."

"Well, that's what everybody always called him -- Jack McKinney the cabbie. He brought his kid."

"Zack?"

"Yeah, and Bob Blair is there."

"Old Bubblegut?"

"Yeah," Herb said. "Remember how he used to hate that name?"

"Can you blame him?"

"Yeah, but the name fit so well! He must have put away enough beer and hot dogs for five people."

"Yeah, and you knew when he'd had enough. He'd take off his shirt and start scratching his belly."

"No matter how cold it was. I always wondered why he never caught frostbite."

"With all that anti-freeze in him?"

"Oh, yeah. Listen, I've got an idea. Why don't we go down there and watch the game from our old seats?"

"You're kidding."

"Not at all. We can talk to our buddies, see what they think about the thing we're doing, have a few beers ..." Herb paused when he realized Dave was shaking his head. "Why not?"

"I just wouldn't be comfortable. We'd spend our whole time answering questions, explaining stuff ..."

"Dave, these are our buddies. All they care about is seeing the team win. They should love us, for crying out loud. Their team is finally winning."

"Who are you trying to kid, Herb? We can't go back there. Hell, we're not even fans anymore."

"I don't think ..."

"Every time we watch something happening down there, we think about the trades we made to get those players, or why we kept this guy or cut that guy. We know too much now, and anyway, it's hot down there."

"So that's it. You just don't want to give up the free food and beer and the air-conditioned box."

"That's part of it, but not all of it."

"You're right."

"About the food?"

"About not being a fan any more. So what do you say we have a couple of beers and crank up the air conditioning?"

Dave looked through the glass partition that separated the owner's box from the press area. He noticed Roy Rojas immediately. Roy was standing behind a table at the back of the press box. The table was covered with various cold cuts, cheeses and salads. Off to one side stood two kegs of imported beer.

Roy was supervising two young women as they filled plates for the various writers. At the same time he was carrying on an animated conversation with Sally Adler, who was dressed as seductively as ever.

"Will you look at that old fool?" Herb growled. "Man, he thinks that girl is the greatest thing since canned beer."

Dave smiled as he saw Sally Adler touch Roy's arm lightly. "Looks like she likes him, too."

"So she's got you fooled, too? That is one manipulative lady."

"I don't ..."

"She's using him, can't you see? She's trying to weasel some kind of story out of the old man, that's all, and once she gets it, it's bye bye, Roy. She'll be gone."

"I assume you've spoken to Roy about this."

"Yeah, but you know my dad. He's as stubborn as ... as ..."

"As you?" Herb sputtered a little, but finally smiled. "Look, Herb, it looks like he's having himself a good time, so relax. Let's just sit down and watch the game."

Houston won the toss and elected to receive. The Lonestars started from their own thirty and drove for a touchdown. Quarterback Woody Rollins found receivers for passes under the Warriors' deep zone, and on the eighth play of the drive, he ducked under Romeo Adonis and scrambled six yards for a touchdown.

Ben Kennedy wasn't at all perturbed. "All right, gentlemen," he said as his offensive unit took the field. "It's time to play some football."

The Warriors answered with a touchdown, taking sixteen plays and nine minutes to tie the score. No play on the drive gained more than six yards. There was one twenty-seven yard burst by Willis Waller, but it was erased by a holding penalty.

"Coach, that wasn't holding!" Eaker exclaimed on the sideline.

"I am aware of that, Mr. Eaker."

"Aren't you going to do something? Protest? Yell?"

"There is nothing to protest, Mr. Eaker. I am certain that the official believed he was making the proper call. We will survive."

Eaker decided it wasn't in his best interest to continue the conversation, so he returned to his seat on the bench. When the offense came off the field, Jenkins grabbed the seat next to him.

"I saw you sucking up to the coach a couple of minutes ago," Jenkins said. "First Gardner, now that old man. What the fuck are you doing, Eaker?"

"Yeah, well, I've got to remind him I'm around. Otherwise I'll never get to play."

"Really? And what happened to your little plan? Man, I thought you were going to make Gardner work so hard he'd kill himself."

"Shit, I thought he would. That old man was sweating so much last week I thought he'd keel over on the field."

"Yeah. Who'd have thought somebody that old would actually start to get in shape?"

Eaker shrugged. "Now all I've got to do is make myself indispensable to Kennedy. Eventually he's going to see that Gardner's wearing out."

"Hey, you're already playing some."

"Yeah, I'm holding for Blaylott, and I played the second half last week when we were thirty points ahead. What a challenge."

"Better work fast, my man, because Rider's gonna be healed up before too long, and you know what that means."

While they were talking, the Warriors' defense forced a turnover, and Kennedy called for his offensive unit.

"It means," Jenkins whispered to Eaker as he grabbed his helmet. "Write me from the semi-pros."

The second quarter was more or less a repeat of the first, with Houston scoring a touchdown and Washington answering shortly before halftime. The teams took it to the locker room tied, 14-14.

Stan Pinello was waiting for the officials as they came in off the field.

"Did you get my message?" Pinello had already half-worked himself into a rage. "I seem to remember telling you this game was a B priority. Did that slip your tiny little minds?"

The officials looked at each other.

"Now, boys," Pinello said, practically hissing. "I am certain you are aware there will be hell to pay for all parties involved if Houston doesn't win this one. Now maybe you've been having pity on Washington. Maybe you didn't want to embarrass them in front of their home fans."

The officials stared at him as he ranted on.

"Well, gentlemen, I don't give a flying fuck how you feel. Humiliate them if you have to. Grind their bodies into the turf. The Washington Warriors are going to lose this football game, is that understood?"

He didn't wait for an answer, turning on his heel and stalking out of the locker room. The officials looked at each other again.

"Well?"

"Man, that guy's obviously never been a ref."

"All he wants are penalties."

"Yeah, when I made that one holding call, I thought the crowd was going to have my head."

"You could have picked a better case of holding than that one."

"It was the only one I've seen all day."

"You ought to hear this asshole on the headset," the head linesman said. "He says to give him a holding, or give him a clipping. I don't understand it. This team isn't that good, but they're not making mistakes."

"So what are we going to do?"

"I don't know about you guys," the back judge said. "But I like being an official. If Pinello says shit, I'm gonna squat down right there on the field and give him a big one."

"Not me," the referee said. "If there's nothing there, I'm not making anything up. That crowd wants blood and it's not going to be mine."

"Yeah, well, what if the league finds out you refused to call what the man wanted?"

"Did you hear about that guy Lombard? He fucked up here four weeks ago, and last week they caught him in bed with a fifteen-year-old girl. He swore it was a set-up."

"You don't think the Association ..."

The other officials looked at him. He didn't even bother to finish his question.

"Let's just do what they want," the head linesman said. "If the man wants penalties, we'll give him penalties."

The crowd, sensing a sixth consecutive victory by the Warriors and fortified with a halftime's worth of beer, was even more vocal by the time play resumed.

Washington's Rusty Price took the kickoff two yards deep in the end zone, spotted a seam in the coverage and broke into the clear. Price heard the cheers and was at the Houston thirty sailing toward the end zone when he heard the crowd turn angry and knew it was all for nothing.

"Illegal block. Washington. Number seventy-one."

The crowd, almost in unison, shouted "NO!"

The sudden, unified reaction seemed to startle the officials, and it appeared to some that they were starting to look around nervously as they took the ball back to the Washington twenty and stepped off half the distance to the goal line.

It was the worst thing they could have done. The fans, like angry animals sensing fear, knew they had the referees worried. The sound level doubled and redoubled as nearly every voice in the stadium came in with "NO!

NO! NO!"

The shouting didn't stop when the Washington offense took the field, and Ross had to raise his voice to get Gardner to hear him as they trotted out to the huddle.

"Think they're upset, Jimmy?"

"Yeah, a mite peeved, I'd say."

"Looks like they've got the refs a little on edge."

"Look, Rossie, I don't know about the refs, but I know they've got me a little on edge."

Gardner had to shout to get the play across in the huddle, and the chanting continued as the Warriors took their places at the line of scrimmage. It stopped long enough for the Warriors to get the play off, and Gardner mouthed a silent prayer of thanks.

He backpedaled quickly and saw George Greenblatt breaking free at the thirty. Gardner released the ball and stood back to admire his handiwork.

Just as he watched Greenblatt catch the ball and turn upfield, he felt all the air leave his body as Houston linebacker Ricky Simpson hit him from the blind side and flattened him.

The crowd was momentarily stunned, and one of the officials reached for his flag. The head linesman shook his head, though, and the flag remained pocketed.

Ross ran angrily over to him. "You shit-eating little slob! Don't you know a goddamned roughing the passer penalty when you see one? That was right under your damned nose, you little idiot! What do they have to do, rip his head off?"

The official stared straight ahead. "Play football, Mr. Ross."

Jimmy Gardner finally regained his breath and got to his feet. Ross helped him back to the huddle as the roar of the crowd grew louder and louder. The chant was the same, the ominous "NO! NO! NO!" now filling the stadium. The stands were starting to shake a little as the fans stamped their feet in the same cadence of "NO! NO! NO!"

Running back Archie Johnson brought the next play into the huddle. "Draw to Reese, Jimmy."

Gardner thought for a moment and then called the play. "Thirty-four blue. Draw. On One."

The crowd noise stayed at the same angry level for the next few plays, with the fans mollified only a little by the success the Warriors were having moving the ball. Progress was slow, at times tedious, but the Warriors eventually worked it down to the Houston sixteen.

Kennedy sent in a play designed to yield a score. Greenblatt was to head for the right flag and turn at the last minute, while Ross was to break five yards in front of him. Gardner was surprised to find how open Ross was, and he chuckled to himself as he threw a flat ball toward his receiver.

Free safety Ken Arnold was the only Lonestar in the vicinity, and he made a desperate lunge that only succeeded in cutting Ross' feet out from under him as the pass flew harmlessly over his head. As everyone in the stadium expected, the official in the vicinity dropped his flag.

"Pass interference. Number eighty-eight. Offense."

"What!?" shouted Ross.

"What!?" shouted Gardner.

"WHAT!!?" shouted the crowd.

The official explained the call to Ben Kennedy. "The defensive player had an equal right to the ball. In my opinion, the offensive player interfered."

Kennedy said nothing at all, but the crowd more than made up for his silence. The side behind the Warrior bench began the same chant of "NO!

NO! NO!" On the other side of the stadium, the fans began their own chant of "NO WAY! NO WAY! NO WAY!"

The entire stadium soon picked it up. They were standing again, clapping their hands and stamping their feet in rhythm with each and every syllable. Some started pounding their fists on the arms of their seats. From one corner of the stadium, an even scarier chant began. "KILL THE REFS! KILL THE REFS! KILL THE REFS!"

Soon that cheer, too, spread through the stadium, and it was probably inevitable that some of the more inebriated fans would think about rushing the field. Some of them had been drinking all day, and more than a few were angry enough actually to try and act out the wish.

The security guards stopped most of them before they got anywhere near the field. One or two made it to ground level before they were tackled and taken away.

But one man, who had started all the way on the upper deck, had built up such a head of steam that he bowled over every security man in his path.

Herb noticed him before anyone else.

"Holy shit!" he said, grabbing Dave's arm and pointing him out. The man pushed his way past the last guard and headed directly for his objective, the misguided official who had called the penalty on Ross. The referee was frozen with terror as the huge fat man with no shirt came barreling toward him.

Herb stood and shouted, "No, Bubblegut, No!"

Either Blair didn't hear him or it didn't matter at that point. When he reached the official, he tackled him. Before the security crew was able to pull him off, he had his immense hands around the man's neck and was beating his head against the turf.

It took four men to pull him off, handcuff him and lead him off the field, much to the displeasure of the crowd.

"Herb, isn't there something in the rules about the home team forfeiting a game if the crowd becomes disruptive?"

"I don't know, Dave, but whether there is or not, it'd probably be a good idea to make some sort of announcement to that effect," Herb said as he picked up the phone to call the public address announcer.

Actually, the worst was already over by the time the announcement was made. Blair had managed to do what many in the crowd had wished they could do, and the sight of the referee being carried off the field on a stretcher and Blair being led away in handcuffs seemed to bring everyone back to reality.

Gardner looked at his teammates in the huddle. "Guys, if we don't score now, they're going to be after us instead of the refs."

He called the play, broke the huddle and headed up to the line. The ball was on the twenty-six after the penalty, and the Lonestars were expecting a pass. Kennedy had sent in a pass play, a short out to Jenkins, but Gardner audibled off and called a draw to Waller.

It took everyone completely by surprise and the rookie breezed into the end zone for a touchdown.

Pinello called down for a holding penalty, and the head linesman signaled it to the line judge. The line judge shook his head. The linesman signaled again and the other official once again shook his head violently.

The head linesman didn't dare to make the call himself, so he shrugged and let the play stand.

Washington had a 21-14 lead after Blaylott added the point after, but the game was far from over. Houston came back with a quick field goal and then a touchdown as the third quarter ended with the Lonestars up, 24-21.

Things got worse before they got better. Rusty Price fumbled the ensuing kickoff, and was unable to get anywhere once he recovered it. The Warriors were backed up to their own three.

On the first play of the series, Gardner took the snap, spun around and handed off to no one as Willis Waller rushed by on the wrong side. An offensive lineman bumped Gardner and knocked the ball loose. It bounded into the end zone, and all Gardner could do was dive back and fall on it as three Lonestars fell on him. The safety made it 26-21.

The score stayed that way for ten minutes. Both teams appeared to have given it their best shot and now seemingly were exhausted. Most of the fourth period was played between the thirties, and each team missed a long field goal as time began winding down.

When the two-minute warning sounded, Houston had the ball on its own twenty after Lou Andrews' fifty-eight yard punt had rolled into the end zone.

Coach Kennedy pulled the Adonis brothers aside as the defense headed onto the field.

"Gentlemen, do you know what needs to be done?"

"Yes, Coach," they chorused.

"They are not to get the ball across the line."

"Yes, Coach."

"If you can, make them fumble."

"Yes, Coach."

As it turned out, they didn't have to bother. Rollins stepped up to the line and surveyed the defense as he started to call signals. "Two! Forty-four! Two! Forty-four!"

Rollins looked at his receivers and backs, then shifted his gaze to the center of the line. His eyes fell on Romeo Adonis, who was staring right back at him and making low, growling noises deep in his throat.

"Hut! Hut!" So intent was Rollins upon Romeo Adonis that he completely forgot he had just called for the snap. When the center brought the ball up, Rollins dropped it as if it were a red-hot brick.

Alphonse Adonis saw the ball on the ground and fell on it. Three plays later, Gardner found Jenkins wide open in the end zone. The frightened officials once again ignored Pinello's frantic calls for a penalty, and Norm Blaylott's extra point gave the Warriors their final margin in their biggest victory yet, a 28-26 win over the Houston Lonestars.

Hours after the game had ended and the crowd had gone, Dave and Herb were still in their seats. They weren't sure if they were savoring the victory or were just too tired to move. Next door in the press box, the reporters were working on their stories, and Roy had long since left with Sally Adler.

Neither Herb nor Dave heard the door to their box open.

"Daddy? Are you still in here?"

"Kim? Kim, what are you doing here?"

"I just wanted to say hello. I didn't want to come to the game and not get to see you."

"You were here for the game? Why didn't you tell me?"

"Mom didn't want you to know. She thought you might get upset if you knew she was here with another guy. She'll probably kill me when she finds out I stopped by to see you."

"I won't tell her if you don't."

"Thanks, daddy."

"No problem, babe."

"Hey, kid," Herb said. "What did you think of the game?"

"It was awesome! I never thought I'd see people get so bent, you know."

"Bent?"

Dave shook his head. "Don't bother trying to figure it out, Herb. You'll just make yourself crazy."

"Oh, daddy ..."

"Hey, if the Nazis had teenagers doing codes for them, we'd all be speaking German today."

"Daddy!"

"Sweetheart, hadn't you better get back to your mom? She'll be worrying."

Kim snorted. "She's not worried. She hardly even knows I'm here, she's so wrapped up with this new guy of hers."

"At least she's getting out."

"Yeah, but this guy is really weird! Mom can do so much better."

"Well, I guess after she's had me, every other guy sort of pales in comparison."

Herb laughed. "I see your dad's still a real humble guy, Kim."

At Kelly's, the party was the rowdiest yet, but the proprietor didn't bother stopping it. Even her patrons who didn't like football, who couldn't care less about the Warriors, were getting caught up in the excitement of the moment.

"Kelly!" Gardner shouted. "Break out the imported stuff!"

"Gardner, you moron, you know the only imported stuff I've got here is Canadian beer!"

"That'll do, Kelly my girl, but when we win the Championship Bowl, you'd better have champagne in this place!"

"Hell, Gardner, you win the Championship Bowl and I'll pay for the champagne!"

"All right!" Gardner shouted as he pounded his fist on the table. "We're gonna hold you to that one!"

Kelly pointed to her eyes. "Check these for concern, Gardner."

Buck Wilson pounded Roxy Reese on the back. "Holy shit, Rox-man, we've got ourselves a team! Six and oh!"

"Do that again, Wilson, and I'll break your arm." Wilson noticed that Reese was smiling when he made that remark, but he backed off anyway.

"Hey, did anybody invite the coach?"

More than one voice answered. "Hell, no!"

Tony Ross, feeling absolutely no pain, slurred out a challenge to the rest of the NAFA. "Bring 'em all on ... all of 'em ... Pittsburgh, Miami, Boston ... Bring 'em on."

Gardner slumped back in his chair. "Lord almighty, who'd have thought the Washington Warriors, with yours truly at quarterback, would be undefeated. Six and oh. Hey ..." Gardner looked around the room. "... where's Georgie?"

"Greenblatt? He left early."

"Past his bedtime, right?"

"Sort of," Ross said. "He left with that little number Cindy and Amy introduced to him the other night."

"Whoa! Greenblatt's getting it on? Little Georgie Greenblatt?"

"All night long!"

Gardner laughed. "Give her one for the Warriors, Georgie!"

52

It was a long ride back from Pittsburgh.

Buck Wilson stared out the window, occasionally slamming his fist into the armrest. He had let a sure interception slip through his fingers and into the grasp of the man he was covering, and that man had taken the ball and run for a touchdown.

Scott Trent, who had been caught out of position all day, sat with Rusty Price, who had lost two fumbles on kickoffs. Neither felt much like conversation.

"In the bag, man," Willis Waller said angrily. "I had it in the bag! The hole was there, big enough for a guy in a wheelchair to get through. One step. One step and I was gone!"

"Relax, Willis," Roxy Reese said. "Don't worry about it. You dropped the ball. It happens. Tomorrow in the statistics you'll see Fumble -- Waller. Two weeks from now, nobody'll remember it."

"No one will remember?"

"No, man. No one."

"You mean like no one remembers that time in the playoff game in Kansas City, when you dropped the ball on their nine?"

"Right. No one remem ..."

"And the game at Houston when you dropped that handoff?"

"Well ..."

"And that time in the Championship Bowl ..."

"Willis, do me a favor. Just shut up and stare out the window for a while. Tell me if you see the Grand Canyon."

"But Roxy, we're headed from Pittsburgh to Washington. The Grand Canyon is in Arizona."

"Then I guess you won't be bothering me!" Reese turned on his side and tried to make it look as though he was sleeping.

The only seat that had been left for Lindy Eaker on the flight was beside Norm Blaylott, and Eaker almost would have preferred to stand. Early in the first quarter, with the ball on the twenty-three, Blaylott had been set to kick a field goal. He never got the chance, because Eaker muffed the snap.

Both men had been buried under the Pittsburgh defense. Now Blaylott was limping and not feeling at all sociable towards Lyndon J. Eaker.

That had been the Warriors' only scoring opportunity of the entire game. After that, they didn't cross midfield. Pittsburgh, on the other hand, moved into Washington territory early and often. The final score had been 41-0.

Gardner sighed. "Rossie, you think there's any way we could avoid seeing the coach for the rest of our natural lives?"

"It's not the coach I'm worried about. It's those game films."

"Oh, Lord," Gardner said. "Maybe we'll be lucky and somebody will put a magnet next to those videotapes."

Around Washington, the mood was about as low as it was on the flight. The Warriors' aura of invincibility -- the feeling that somehow, some way, the team would find a way to win -- was gone, and callers on Fred Reynolds' Sunday night radio show seemed heartbroken.

"Hi, this is Fred and you're next."

"Am I on, Fred? ... Yeah, this is Bobby in Silver Spring, and I want to know what happened to the Warriors today. They really sucked!"

"Uh, Bobby, you're not supposed to say 'suck' on the radio."

"Sorry. Well, what happened? They were really bogus!"

"They sure were," Reynolds said with a hint of glee in his voice. "I'm sorry to say that this might have been a better example of the real Washington Warriors. The old players they signed finally seem to be running out of gas."

"So you don't think they're going to make it to the Championship Bowl?"

"Bobby, they might not win another game. Look at their schedule. Two games with Miami, one with Philadelphia and Chicago ..."

"What about Boston and Atlanta? They still play Boston twice, and Boston really su... oops, sorry."

"Boston's no pushover, at least not for a team that seems to be falling apart as quickly as this one is."

"So you don't think they're going to make it to the ..."

"Bobby, I already answered that. Thanks for calling. Hi, this is Fred and you're next on Sports For You."

"Hi, Fred."

"Could you turn down your radio, please?"

"Sure, Fred. This is Mitch from Woodbridge, and I'd like to know if you think the Warriors are going to make it to the Championship Bowl?"

425

53

The commissioner leaned back in his plush chair. His face had a rosy glow and he looked to be very satisfied with life in general and the System in particular.

"Well, Pinello, I'm pleased that we finally are on the road to solving our Washington problem."

"Yes, Commissioner."

"Mr. Davis did a masterful job in that game. He had Washington bottled up all day."

"Yes, Commissioner."

"Why haven't you been able to do that, Pinello? His command of the situation was awesome. You could take a few pages from his book, if you ask me."

"Yes, Commissioner. Burt did a good job."

"I think we can safely say that Washington's days as a winning franchise are drawing to a close."

"Yes, Commissioner."

"I'm glad you agree. Then we can withdraw Washington from our priority list."

"Commissioner, are you sure you want to do that?"

"Absolutely, Mr. Pinello. You can't imagine how much it irritates me to even have to think about that franchise."

"I'm aware ..."

"It hasn't been easy getting things straightened out. Imagine all the excitement about Washington being 6-0. But finally some of the actions we've taken to correct it are starting to bear fruit."

"Actions?"

"Yes, Pinello."

"I wasn't told about any actions."

"You didn't need to know. I've had a couple of my people here in the league office working on some little surprises for our friends in Washington."

"Uh ..."

"Let's just say that Mr. Krause and Mr. Rojas will be relatively busy, shall we say, putting out fires the next few weeks."

Sportswriter Rudy Lomax wasn't putting out fires in Philadelphia. He was doing his best to start one of his own. The Bulldogs were 7-0 and one of only two unbeaten teams in the Association, but Lomax was still hammering away.

He had found a gimmick, and he was riding it for all it was worth, no small accomplishment for a twenty-eight year old reporter who had been in Philadelphia less than two years. He had been given a regular spot on one of the radio call-in shows, and he used that spot constantly to speculate on exactly what was wrong with the Bulldogs.

He already had written an essay for an upcoming issue of Inside Sports, documenting great falls from grace of the past and comparing them to the present situation in Philadelphia. He was given a twice-weekly column in the Dispatch, with his picture at the top.

"Should we let sleeping dogs lie?

"It was nothing more than another exercise in malaise last Sunday as the Bulldogs puttered and stuttered their way through yet another boring victory.

"Perhaps we should be happy that the offense came to life. Last week the 'Dogs squeaked by lowly Kansas City, 13-10, with the help of a defensive touchdown. This week they managed to put a few points on the board -- 28, to be exact.

"Ordinarily, that would be valid cause for celebration. Of course, our boys needed every last one of those points to beat a pathetic Montreal team, which scored 27 points of its own.

"Sure, they had a 28-0 lead at the half, but who were those amateurs wearing Philadelphia uniforms in the second half? Only the total ineptitude of the Mustangs kept them from winning and knocking the 'Dogs off their pedestal.

"One shudders to think what might have happened had the 'Dogs been playing Miami.

"So what do we do? I have to admit I'm stumped. Perhaps the coach should be reminded that he can be removed at any time, or maybe some trades should be made to break up the complacency that's so obvious on this team.

"Maybe what the 'Dogs need is a little hunger. Maybe some of the younger players should start ahead of our superstar slackers. After all, ladies and gentlemen, there are no sacred cows.

"Whatever is to be done, it should be done very soon -- before it's too late."

Tracey Cagney tossed the paper across her desk to her general manager, Ed Bixby.

"Did you see what that little twerp Lomax wrote today?"

Bixby nodded. "Don't take it too seriously, Tracey. All he's trying to do is make a name for himself by stirring up a little controversy. Hey, that's what sells papers."

"I don't know, Ed. Maybe he's got a point. You were at the game. Can you explain that second half? Maybe we are getting complacent."

"Tracey, I've seen this happen dozens of times. Just keep the team going like it has been. After all, we are undefeated."

Tracey Cagney answered in a voice that sent chills down Bixby's spine. "Yes, we are. And we're going to stay that way."

If the fans in Philadelphia were getting a little bored with their unbeaten team, those in Washington acted as if they had no idea what to expect from their own once-beaten Warriors.

In truth, neither did the Warriors.

The smart money around the country was saying that their bubble had burst, that after the lopsided defeat in Pittsburgh, Washington would begin to slide back toward its accustomed position in the standings. The Nevada oddsmakers had opened Miami as a twelve-point favorite, and by game time the odds had risen to fifteen in favor of the powerful Wave.

Andre O'Connor called Miami his lock of the week to win by at least that much, and the first half of the game made him look like a genius. The Wave scored four touchdowns, none of which the Warriors managed to answer.

The Wave's offense simply overwhelmed the Washington defenders with the flashy style of play for which the team had become famous. The third of the four scores came on a triple reserve that caught all eleven defenders chasing the wrong man.

Gardner turned to Kennedy after the fourth score made it 28-0. "They do call it the Wave Upon Wave offense, don't they, coach?"

"And what do they call the defense, Mr. Gardner?"

"How about friggin' good?"

The Warriors did manage to score a field goal just before the half ended when Norm Blaylott kicked a 48-yarder, but the 28-3 score as the teams ran off the field had Stan Pinello thinking the commissioner had, as usual, been right.

He didn't even worry when Washington took the second half kickoff and drove sixty-eight yards for a touchdown, but the score did seem to bring the Washington general managers to life.

"Gee, they really looked different on that drive," Kim Krause said to her father. "What did the coach say to them in the locker room?"

"Oh, I don't know Probably just reminded them about the waiver wire."

"The what?"

"Never mind, Kim."

Pinello called down to the head linesman. "Let Miami get it back on this drive."

Washington didn't give them a chance. With a third and five on the Wave's forty, Miami's Steve Carpenter dropped back to pass. Troy Jones was breaking downfield on a fly pattern, the idea being to get a quick score to take the life out of the Warriors.

Carpenter threw the ball -- right into the arms of Rusty Price.

From that point on, it was Washington's game. The Warriors took possession on their own twelve and moved purposefully down the field for a touchdown. Pinello tried to get penalties called the whole time, but the officials wouldn't cooperate.

"We can't do anything, Mr. Pinello," the head linesman said when they met briefly between the third and fourth quarters. "They're not making mistakes."

"The fuck they're not! You're not catching them, that's all. I've worked plenty of Washington games and there have always been plenty of mistakes in the past."

"With all due respect, sir, the last time that happened, one of our men wound up in the hospital." The linesman paused. "By the way, did he ever regain consciousness?"~

"I don't know and I don't care right now! You just better get off your fat ass and find something to call."

The head linesman had been right. The Warriors weren't as flashy or as talented as Miami, but they were executing perfectly. The referees weren't about to risk another disruption -- or a possible injury -- by calling penalties that weren't there.

There really wasn't much danger of that happening, though. It was as if the fans had spent themselves two weeks early, and besides, everyone in the stands knew Miami was far too good a team actually to lose to the Warriors.

The Warriors hung on, though. They stopped Miami on downs again, and to the disbelief of nearly everyone in the stands, they took over deep in their own territory and drove for another score. Gardner found Greenblatt for a scoring pass with nine minutes left in the game to cut Washington's deficit to 28-24.

That finally seemed to awaken the Wave, and Carpenter responded with a drive that used up nearly seven of the remaining nine minutes. When the officials signaled for the two-minute warning, Miami had a first down on the Washington twenty-four.

"OK, boys," Carpenter said in the huddle. "Here's where we wrap this thing up." He called for a pass into the end zone.

The Adonis brothers had played together for more than ten years, ever since junior high school. They had developed a special type of bond between them, a level of communication they could never have explained to anyone else. It was as if they could read each other's minds. "Romeo?"

"Yeah?"

"Yeah." They knew what needed to be done.

Carpenter took the ball from center and started dropping back into the pocket. At almost the same moment, the three members of the offensive line assigned to keep the Adonis brothers out of the Miami backfield found themselves on the ground gasping for air as nearly eight hundred pounds of angry hillbilly rolled over them.

Alphonse hit Carpenter before he had a chance to set his feet, and Romeo fell on the ball the quarterback so obligingly dropped. The referee signaled the change of possession and the crowd finally came to life.

Romeo stopped Jimmy Gardner as they met on the field. "We got you the ball," he growled. "Do something with it."

It took the Warriors eight plays to score. Gardner used sideline passes and quick hitters to move his team up the field, and with six seconds left, he found Tony Ross in the corner of the end zone to give the Warriors their first lead of the game.

It was a lead they didn't relinquish. Norm Blaylott's squib kickoff was designed to minimize the chance of a long return, and Buck Wilson hit the return man as the gun sounded to end the game.

Washington had beaten Miami, 31-28, to move into a tie for first place.

54

Dave and Herb arrived at their office Monday morning to find George Greenblatt waiting for them.

"Good morning, Mr. Krause. Mr. Rojas."

"Uh, morning, George," Herb said sleepily. "What brings you here this morning? Is there something we can do for you?"

"Yes, there is. I would like you to release me from my contract effective immediately."

That awakened them better and faster than any cup of coffee.

"You what!?" Herb shouted.

"I want you to release me from my contract. I no longer want to play football."

"You can't be serious, George," Dave said. "You can't just throw a pro career down the toilet!"

"Well, yes."

"George, has something happened? Has somebody said or done something that ..."

Herb couldn't stay calm. "Nobody's done a damn thing, Dave! The coach made him run a few too many laps in practice, or maybe he didn't call enough plays for him yesterday. Poor little Georgie got his feelings hurt!"

"It's nothing of the sort. In fact, Coach Kennedy is one of the fairest, most decent men I've ever had the privilege of knowing. I stayed on longer than I intended because of him."

"Then it's money, right?" Herb asked. " A little squeeze play to get more money out of us?"

"George, is it money? Are you trying to tell us you want us to increase your salary ..."

"Mr. Krause, money has nothing to do with it."

"George, I don't understand then. How can you be so calm about throwing away a career a lot of people would kill for?"

"I'm calm, Mr. Krause, because I know for certain I've made the right decision. It's as simple as that."

"Are you sure?"

"Very sure. Mr. Lippmann assured me ..."

"Aha!" Herb shouted.

"Hold on, Herb. George, you've spoken to Lippmann?"

"I discussed it with him, but this is my decision ..."

Dave cut him off with a wave of his hand. "George, would you do me a favor and just sit here for a couple of minutes? Mr. Rojas and I have something we have to take care of. I'll have our assistant, what's her name ..."

"Bridget," Herb said.

"I'll have Bridget bring you a cup of coffee."

"I don't drink coffee."

"Well, then, tea or a soda."

"I don't allow anything stimulating to invade my ..."

"Milk, then," Dave said, a little exasperation sneaking into his voice. "Just tell her what you want," he said as he dragged Herb out of the office with him.

Once they were in the hall, Herb beat Dave to the punch. "You want me to call Lippmann, right?"

"Right, and after your little squeeze gets Georgie what he wants, have her ..."

"My little squeeze?"

"... have her get Kennedy on the phone."

"You think he can talk George out of this?"

Dave shrugged. "I don't know, but it's worth a shot."

He took a deep breath and walked back into his office. Greenblatt still was sitting there, a stricken look on his face. "Well, George, did Bridget give you what you wanted?"

Greenblatt looked wounded. "Is it that obvious, Mr. Krause?"

"Obvious?"

"I knew I couldn't hide it. I've seen it. People look at me differently now. They're staring, pointing me out. I can almost hear them talking. They know I'm a fallen man."

"George, just because we lost a game ..."

"I'm weak, Mr. Krause. I have given in to the base desires of my body, polluting this temple by surrendering to temptations of a physical nature."

"I don't think I'm following you."

"It's this town. This evil, despicable town. This town where moral values are bought and sold, where a man who is good and true and loyal to the teachings of his childhood cannot withstand the pressure and corruption ..."

"Did someone corrupt you?"

"Yes," Greenblatt said, hanging his head.

Dave resisted the urge to laugh and went over to the young man seated before him. "George, it's not that bad. Really. One time is not going to make ..."

"You don't understand at all!"

"Oh, I think I do ..."

"I was weak! I gave in to the most carnal of desires. I have been defiled by wanton pleasure."

"You got laid."

"And it wasn't just one time, either."

"All right, but ..."

"It wasn't even twice. It was again ... and again ... and again. Over and over and over, letting myself use and degrade that poor child who was looking to me for guidance and ..."

"Child?" Dave asked, a little worried now. "How old was she, George?"

Greenblatt seemed confused for a moment. "Oh, nineteen, twenty."

Dave breathed a sigh of relief. "Then she wasn't really a child."

"She might as well have been. She was looking to me for deliverance. The poor thing didn't know what she was doing. She was unaware of the temptations she was presenting me. Her nubile young flesh, soft and supple ..."

"Uh, George ..."

"Firm, round breasts, swaying from side to side ..."

"George ..."

"Strong, muscular thighs ..."

"George! Enough! I get the picture."

"I defiled her, Mr. Krause. And I defiled myself."

"George, don't you think you could work this out here? Why do you have to leave?"

"Mr. Lippmann suggested to me that perhaps it would be better if I returned to the campus for a retreat of sorts."

"A retreat ... George, that reminds me of something. Would you mind sitting here for a moment while I take care of something?"

"Of course ..."

The moment Dave was out the door, he ran full speed to the outer office where Herb and his assistant were on the phones. "Herb, have you got Lippmann yet?"

"They're trying to get him to the phone right now."

"Great. When you've got him on the line, buzz me on the intercom. I'll take the call out here." He turned to Bridget. "What about Coach Kennedy?"

"He's watching films."

"Tell them to get him to the phone. Tell him it's an emergency."

Dave sprinted back to his office. He stopped just outside the door, caught his breath and strolled in calmly. "George, let's look at this retreat thing. Now, I'm not one to deny the value of a little silent meditation, but isn't returning to Alabama a little drastic? I mean, couldn't you meditate here in town, or out at the camp?"

"Mr. Krause, everywhere I look I see temptation. The young child I degraded ..."

"George, would you please stop calling her a child. It makes me nervous."

Greenblatt nodded glumly. "... the young woman I degraded lives in the very town where we practice. I'm weak, and staying would only perpetuate that weakness."

The phone buzzed, and Dave jumped out of his chair. "Just a minute, George! I'll be right back!" He shouted over his shoulder. "Have some more coffee!"

"But I told you I don't drink ..."

Dave ran back to the reception area and grabbed the phone out of Herb's hand before he had a chance to say anything. "Listen, you son of a bitch ..."

"Daddy?"

"Kim, what the hell do you want?"

"Well, don't sound so friendly ..."

"Sorry, baby. I've got a crisis here."

"I just wanted to know," she said, stretching out her words. "If it was all right if I stayed over at your place tonight ..."

"Sure, honey. Fine. I've got to go ..."

"Mom'll bring me over around seven, OK?"

"Yeah, seven. Bye," he said, hanging up the phone. "Next time," he said, glaring at Herb. "Let me know who it is."

Herb shrugged, but Dave didn't see it. He already had started his run back to the office where once again he stopped, took a deep breath and strolled in.

"I just thought of something, George. There are an awful lot of people, young people, around here who look up to you. After all, even considering your shortcomings, you're still a good person. I'm sure it would be a great loss to them if you were to fold up your tent and sneak away."

Dave paused for effect. "After all, if you give in to your failings, instead of overcoming them, then what sort of example would you be setting for those people who are trying to fight their own weaknesses?"

Greenblatt didn't answer, and Dave hoped he was making some small amount of headway. "And what about this young lady you're so concerned about? What is she going to think? She'll probably go further down the same path of degradation ..."

The intercom buzzer interrupted him again, but this time he didn't jump out of his chair. "Excuse me, George," he said almost suavely. "It seems as though it's always something. I'll be right back."

This time Dave didn't run. He walked, forcefully, out to the outer office, letting his anger build with each and every step. By the time he reached the phone, he was ready to scream at Lippmann, but Herb was already doing it for him.

"... You son of a bitch! ... I don't give a rat's ass if you don't like being addressed that way! I'll call you what I damn well please! ... You'd better not hang up on me, Lippmann! ... Yes, he's here."

Herb handed the receiver to Dave.

"Hello, Lippmann," he said through gritted teeth.

"Mr. Krause. So nice to hear a civil tongue."

"Yeah, well, it's not going to stay that way long if you don't do something about Greenblatt."

"George? Why, what seems to be the problem?"

"Come on, Lippmann, you talked to the kid. You put the idea in his head to leave, and ..."

"I beg to differ, Mr. Krause. While it's true that I spoke with the boy, the fact is that he called me seeking guidance, and I would be a poor CEO indeed if I failed to help my subordinates. It was George who was in desperate need of a sympathetic ear, which he obviously could not find there."

"So you told him to come back to you."

"Well, I did suggest that he would be better off in an academic atmosphere."

"He would ..."

"Yes, he would, and he would be a great help to me. George is a young, strong and intelligent boy, and there is much work to be done. Schedules to arrange, people to meet, funds to raise ..."

Lippmann let his voice trail off, and Dave was immediately aware of what he was trying to lay between the lines.

"All right, Lippmann, let's get to the point. How much is this going to cost me?"

"I beg your pardon?"

"I said, how much is this going to cost me?" Herb was shaking his head vigorously, but Dave ignored him.

"In other words, you're asking me what sort of a financial hardship it would cause my organization to be without the services of George Greenblatt?"

"Put it any way you please, Lippmann."

"Well, George does have a certain value to me, especially considering the publicity a former football player could bring ..."

"How much, Lippmann?"

"Let's say half a million would be appropriate."

"Half a million!?" Dave shouted.

"NO!" Herb groaned.

"How about a hundred thousand, Lippmann?"

"You must have misunderstood me, Mr. Krause. The size of your donation to my organization is no longer a matter for negotiation. Or perhaps you do not need me to intervene with George. Perhaps you would like to convince him to stay without my help."

Dave swallowed hard. "All right, Lippmann. You've got your money."

Herb collapsed into a chair, his head in his hands.

"Do I have your word on it, Mr. Krause?"

"Yes, Lippmann."

"Because if you renege on this, it will be very easy for me to convince George that he is desperately needed in Micronesia."

"I understand," Dave said, totally defeated. "Just talk to the boy."

"Very well."

Dave put Lippmann on hold and buzzed his office phone.

"Dave, are you crazy?" Herb asked. "We might not even have half a million to spare."

"What we don't have is a choice. George is one of the best tight ends in the league, and we can't afford to lose him." He buzzed his phone again. "Come on, Georgie," he said. "Pick up the phone."

"Maybe we can trade for a tight end. Or maybe there's one out there somewhere ..."

"Herb, no one's going to trade with us, and it's a little late in the season to be combing the hinterlands ... Why the hell isn't he picking up the phone?"

"Are he sure he knows you're buzzing him?"

"He's not stupid, Herb. Just malleable."

Dave dropped the receiver and sprinted for his office. This time he didn't stop to gather himself, but crashed right through the doorway to find an empty office. George Greenblatt was gone.

The intercom buzzed. "I've got the coach on the line," Bridget said. "What was it you wanted to ask him?"

Dave sighed. "Ask him if he knows where we can find a good tight end."

55

Nick Gullotta had no star quality whatsoever.

He lacked the smooth, quick moves that were typical of wide receivers in the NAFA. He was the Warriors' third receiver behind the talented Tony Ross and Randy Jenkins, and when he was in the game he was used mostly as a decoy. He occasionally drew coverage that might have gone to the prime receivers, and he caught enough passes to keep defenses honest.

Gullotta was comfortable with his position on the team. In his high school days he had been good enough to catch the attention of a few college coaches, and in college he was just good enough to be noticed by Association scouts. Pro coaches appreciated his determination and his willingness to accept a secondary role.

That had been enough to keep him in the league for nine years, with five different teams.

He knew the Warriors probably would be his last team, and that he might already be in the last year of his career. That didn't bother him. He had been taking classes at Georgetown University for the last three years, trying to complete an MBA.

If there was one thing Gullotta had noticed in all his years of football, it was that agents made almost as much as top players.

So he lived with the anonymity. He received attention that was equal to his talents, and that satisfied him. He might once have entertained dreams of superstardom while he was in high school, but he was a reasonable man. He knew he was no superstar.

He was heading up the freeway, trying to figure which of his teammates he could represent, when the police car pulled up behind him and sounded its siren.

"What can I do for you, officer?" Gullotta asked as he got out of his car.

"May I see your license and registration, sir?"

Gullotta reached into his wallet. "How fast was I going?"

"You were clocked at sixty-eight miles an hour, sir."

"Gee, I'm awfully sorry. Have you ever been thinking so hard about something that you just forgot what you were doing?"

The officer smiled weakly. "Of course, sir."

He took the license and registration and walked back to his patrol car.

"One time I even drove right past my exit," Gullotta called to him. He turned and hit his fist on the hood of his car, wondering how much the ticket was going to cost him. He didn't hear the patrol car's doors open, or notice the first officer and his partner jump out with guns drawn.

"All right, Gullotta! Freeze!"

"What!?" he asked, turning around to see the policemen behind their doors, their gun barrels pointed at him.

"Freeze, mister!" Gullotta stood there, his hands in the air. "Now assume the position!"

"Assume the ..." Gullotta muttered.

"Up against the car, scrote!" the second officer said. Gullotta leaned against the car in an imitation of television shows he'd seen as the two officers ran up to him, forced him into a spread-eagle position and frisked him quickly.

"Hey," Gullotta protested. "What's the idea ..."

"Keep a lid on it, hairball!"

"Hey, Gary," the first officer called from the inside of the car. "Lookie, lookie what I found!"

The officer handed a bag half-filled with a white powder to his partner. "Looks like some mighty fine nose candy here. Say, friend, you got any idea where this might have come from?"

"I don't know anything about it," Gullotta said.

"Yeah, I'll bet you don't." He reached for his handcuffs, snapped them over the receiver's wrists and led him toward the patrol car.

Herb was late arriving at the news conference at the police station, and the public information officer already was reading from a prepared statement.

"... and the arrest was made by officers Gary Gordon and Robert Herron ..."

Every reporter in the room had a copy of the statement, which would have seemed to eliminate the necessity of reading it, but the officer went on, undeterred.

"... when the suspect was stopped for a routine traffic violation, his driver's license and automobile registration were fed into our central computer by the officers on the scene and it was found that the suspect had been reported to the county narcotics bureau through the anonymous hotline number available to the public. The suspect had been named as a major distributor and user of illegal narcotics."

Herb was trying to get a copy of the statement, but no one seemed to have an extra one.

"The suspect was apprehended without resistance. He was not under the influence of any controlled subject or of alcohol, as determined by the officers on the scene. The suspect voluntarily agreed to blood tests, and we will have the results of those tests shortly. He was given a body cavity search ..."

Herb winced.

"... when he was brought in for incarceration, and nothing was found. He has been charged with possession of a controlled substance with intent to sell, and is being held without bail in the county detention facility."

"What!?"

The officer looked up. He had been expecting questions, but none of such short duration. Then he noticed that the question had come from Herb. "Gentlemen, we have taken the liberty of inviting a representative of the Washington football team, Mr. Herbert Rose."

"Rojas," Herb muttered as he made his way to the podium.

"Chief, what did you find and how much of it was there?"

"I'm only a lieutenant, Mr. Rojas, but we found high-grade cocaine -- approximately sixteen kilograms of it -- in the glove compartment and trunk of Mr. Gullotta's vehicle."

"Was it in any way concealed?"

"The substance was sealed in plastic bags inside the spare tire. You might say it was concealed."

Some of the reporters began asking their questions.

"Chief, was Gullotta dealing to other members of the team?"

"Chief, do you know who his connection was?"

The lieutenant raised his hand for silence. "The suspect has not yet made a confession, but sixteen kilos of cocaine would be enough to supply a lot of people."

"Wait a minute here!" Herb said. "I would appreciate it if you didn't imply that we're running a team of junkies."

"No one is saying that," the officer said patiently.

"Mr. Rojas, is drug use widespread on the team?"

"Do you use cocaine, Mr. Rojas?"

"No!"

"But you did sign a player with an acknowledged drug problem." That question came from Fred Reynolds, who had slipped into the press conference at the back of the room.

"Wilson's clean."

"You're sure of that?"

"Yes!"

"What about Gullotta? Will the team furnish a lawyer?"

"I'm sure Nick Gullotta can take care of himself. I'll try to talk with him, though."

"Is he off the team?"

"Jeez," Herb said. "The guy's in jail."

56

Dave weaved his way between two lines of tables, carrying a tray with a pitcher of soda and two mugs and trying not too successfully to keep the soda inside the pitcher and off his shirt. He spotted his daughter at the far corner of the restaurant, waving frantically and pointing at a table.

He smiled in response, wishing that someday Kim would pick a table that didn't require a major expedition to reach. "You could have helped me, you know," he said as he deposited the tray and what was left of the soda on the table.

"You looked like you were doing all right. Anyway, that was our deal -- you get the sodas and I get the pizza. By the way, they'll be bringing the pizza in about fifteen minutes.

"Thanks, Kim," he said as he poured sodas for himself and his daughter.

"Anyway, you wouldn't be having these problems if you just had something in the house for me to eat."

"Well, I said I was sorry. It was a rough day."

"That's OK. You just forgot I was coming over."

"That's not true. I remembered."

"Yeah, sure. Right when you heard me ring the doorbell."

Dave grinned. "You're getting too damn smart, you know that? So what made you want to stay over with your old dad?"

"Oh, nothing."

"Right. You just had to spend some time with your dad, like you haven't been seeing enough of me."

"You're getting too damn smart, too."

"Hey, watch the language!"

"Daddy, don't be silly. You should hear how everyone else talks!"

Dave grimaced. "Thanks, but I'd rather not. What is it, baby? Is your mother mad at you?"

"Not really."

"Look, Kim, it's great having you stay over. I don't even mind having to get up at six to take you to Falls Church to school ..."

"You don't have to do that. I'll take a cab."

"The hell you will!"

"Daddy! Watch your language!" She slapped him lightly on the wrist. "Anyway, I can handle it."

"Really? I suppose you take cabs to school every day?"

"Sure, daddy. Mom's new guy pays for it."

"Whoa! Mom's new ... So Muriel's having someone over ..."

Kim looked down sheepishly. "I think I goofed."

"What? She didn't want me to know about ..."

Kim nodded.

"She must have thought I'd be jealous."

"I guess."

"Don't worry, babe. It doesn't bother me at all. In fact, nothing would make me happier than to see your mother get married again."

"Oh, daddy! Yeccch!"

"I have a feeling you don't care for this guy too much."

Kim shook her head. "I can't stand him, daddy. He's so gross. I don't see how you can work with him."

"Work with ..."

"He's always complaining about you, always getting mad and he's got that high, whining voice ..."

Dave nearly gagged on his soda. "High, whining ... Oh, God. Say it isn't so, Kim."

"Yeah, he's always mad about something."

"Kim, would this fellow's name happen to be Stan? Stan Pinello?"

"Yeah, daddy. Don't tell mom I told you, OK?"

"I know. She'll get mad."

"And then she'll tell him, and he'll get mad. And I don't like it when he gets mad."

"Why? Has he hit you?"

"That little dweeb? Are you kidding? I'd deck him!"

Dave was temporarily amused by the idea of his daughter decking Stan Pinello.

"Good Lord," he said. "Pinello and Muriel ... Well, I guess it makes sense."

"Oh, daddy! Yeccch!"

After a very inauspicious start to the week, things settled down somewhat after that. Gullotta stayed in jail, and Greenblatt didn't turn up. Aside from that, it was just another week as the Warriors got ready for their ninth game, a road clash with the lowly Boston Barons.

By Saturday night, Dave was relieved just to sit down and watch "Coach's Corner" with Herb and Roy.

"Good evening, everyone, and welcome to another edition of the Coach's Corner. I'm Sally Adler, with coach Benjamin Kennedy, and our special guest this evening is Warriors quarterback Jimmy Gardner."

The camera pulled back to show the three of them sitting on the set. Sally Adler looked voluptuous and charming, Ben Kennedy looked as uncomfortable as ever and Gardner, hair uncombed and tie slightly askew, looked as if he had just dropped in from out of town.

"Of course," Adler said. "This has been a week that can only be described as turbulent."

"In some ways," Kennedy said drily.

"The Warriors are, at the very least, a team in turmoil. Wouldn't you agree, Jimmy?"

"Well, ma'am, there might be better ways of ..."

"Let's look at the facts. Your starting tight end has disappeared for parts unknown, and one of your wide receivers has been arrested for dealing drugs. In fact, Jimmy, I'd like to ask you if there's a drug problem on the Warriors. How about it?"

Kennedy answered before Gardner had a chance. "Miss Adler, there is no drug problem on the Washington Warriors."

Adler seemed taken slightly aback by the severity of Kennedy's tone. She said nothing, and when Gardner realized the coach wasn't going to say anything else, he jumped into the void.

"I agree with the coach. "There's no big-time drug problem on the team."

Adler worked with the coach every week, and she knew his moods. She decided to change the subject. "Well, then, what about George Greenblatt? Does anyone know where he is?"

"No."

"Sally," Gardner said. "That boy has fallen off the face of the globe. I happen to know the front office has been looking for him night and day, and no one's turned up the slightest trace of that boy."

Herb slammed his fist down on the chair.

"All right," he asked the crowd around the television. "Who's been talking to Gardner?"

"I make it a point not to," Dave said as he signaled to Roy to bring him another beer. "He keeps asking for more money."

"Let's not talk about money, OK?"

Dave looked up from the bar, alarmed. "Not again?"

"Yeah, again. We're tapped."

"Good God!" Roy exclaimed as he brought three beers. "You mean the team's broke again?"

"Something like that," Dave said as he sipped his beer.

"All those millions of dollars gone?"

"Every goddamn penny," Herb said, staring at the television, where Sally Adler had finished with the highlights of the previous week's game and was prepared to discuss the upcoming opponent.

"Coach, all things considered, it's certainly fortunate you've got a weak opponent this week."

"I disagree, Miss Adler."

"In other words, you're going to try and convince us that the Boston Barons are a better team than their record would indicate and that any NAFA team can beat any other team on any given day."

Ben Kennedy nodded.

"Jimmy," she asked, turning slightly and causing her skirt to slide a few more inches up her thigh. "Are you planning anything special for the Barons?"

Gardner didn't realize she was speaking, he was so intent on looking at her legs. When he realized she was asking him a question, all he could say was, "Huh?"

"Is anything special planned for this game?"

"Uh no, ma'am, not really."

"Won't the absence of Greenblatt and Gullotta make a difference in your game plan?"

"Well," Gardner said, regaining his composure. "We really didn't throw to Nick all that much, so it won't matter all that much that he's not there. Now with George gone, it means we won't go to the two tight end-offense all that much, but I think we've got enough talent on the team to overcome it and win."

"Coach," Adler said, turning again and causing her skirt to slide up even further. "Do you agree?"

Kennedy paused before answering, and the director decided that showing any more shots that included Sally Adler's legs might be cause for FCC censure. "Do you agree, Coach?" Adler repeated her question.

"For the most part."

Roy Rojas lowered the sound on the set as the customers in Cliches began drifting away from the television. "Now what I want to know," he said as he leaned over the bar. "Is where nearly forty million dollars has gone."

"It's even more than that, Roy." Dave took a long pull on his beer. "Remember, that's just what we started out with. There's been a lot more than that. Parking, our share of the concessions, local television money ... it's all gone."

"But where?"

"Well, dad," Herb said. "A lot of it went to players who were signed up and never made the team ... I seem to remember some guys whose average age was about fifty that we had to pay off before the press found out we were raiding the old folks' home."

Roy looked sheepishly away from his son and his friend. Herb wasn't finished, though. "Then there was the matter of a five million dollar signing bonus for Willis Waller ..."

"All right, Herb. I think he got the point."

"One more thing, dad. Remember that contract we had to sign with the concessionaires at the last minute? We only got ten percent. Most of the other teams are getting thirty and some of them even get fifty. Hell, last year we got twenty-five percent!"

"But what about attendance? We've had fifty thousand at the last two home games.”

“That money goes directly to the Association,” Herb said. “Then it gets distributed equally among the teams, along with all of the television money. Those checks haven’t arrived yet. By the way, Dave, have you spoken to our friend Pinello about that?”

“I have not spoken with our friend. I’m afraid if I do, he’ll end up without a few teeth.”

“Oh, yeah. Sorry. I’ll talk to Pinello.”

“Come on, Dave,” Roy said. “So the guy’s banging your ex-wife. Big deal. You’re not jealous.”

“I just don’t like the idea of that creep being around my daughter, and whether you believe it or not, I don’t want to see Muriel get hurt ... much.”

“Let’s get back to the money,” Herb said. “It’s got me worried.”

“Well, there really isn’t much more to say ...”

“Except for that thing from the city.”

“What thing from the city?”

“Well, Dave, it seems that the previous general manager of the Washington Warriors neglected to pay the property taxes, sewage bills and other user fees for the past three years. It all came due this week, for which we received a bill for five million, two hundred and fifty-eight thousand dollars.”

“Which you paid,” Roy said.

“Of course I paid it, dad. You think we wanted it all over the papers that the city was suing the Warriors for non-payment? Not that it would hurt our standing with the media. Hell, they couldn’t think any less of us than they already do, but I didn’t see a whole lot of point in giving them more fuel for the fire.”

"Hey," Roy said. "They've let up a little."

"Yeah, they're not talking about running us out of town anymore. Your buddy Sally's been sharpening her claws a little, though."

"Don't take that too seriously. She told me she likes you guys."

"Right. Dad, she's using you ..." Roy Rojas rolled his eyes skyward. "... and don't you give me that look of yours!" Herb said in an exasperated voice. "That bitch wants a story, an inside scoop, that's all."

"You're too tough on her. Seems to me, son, that we need all the friends we can get."

"Yeah, well, keep her happy, Roy." Dave signaled for another beer as Roy grinned.

"Anyway," Herb said. "We managed to make the payroll this week, and the check from the Association should be coming any day now. When I see Pinello, I'll ask him about it."

They flew to Boston the next morning to join the team, which played the Barons in a late-afternoon game. Maybe it was the fact of a road game against a poor team, or maybe it was simply a letdown after the big victory over Miami.

Perhaps it was the events of the week, the loss of Greenblatt and Gullotta, but whatever the reason, the Washington Warriors played like a team that could not have cared less. Had Boston been a good team, it would have been a blowout.

The Warriors' Rusty Price fumbled the opening kickoff twice before finally finding the handle. He was snowed under on the six. From there, the Warriors moved four yards in three plays. Lou Andrews, standing in his own end zone, took the snap and saw eight rushers coming through the line.

He rushed to get his kick away and shanked the ball, which went out of bounds at the Washington nineteen.

The Barons scored on the next play, with Teddy Curran slipping past Buck Wilson and catching a pass in the end zone.

Washington got it together enough to tie the score early in the third period, when Roxy Reese caught a screen pass and raced fifty-seven yards to make it 7-7.

Beyond that, though, the Warriors accomplished nothing.

It was only Boston's basic incompetence and the sterling play of the Adonis brothers that kept the game a low-scoring affair. There was only one other score, a long field goal by the Barons with eight minutes to play.

The Warriors dragged themselves off the field 10-7 losers, their second defeat in nine games.

57

Pinello strolled into the office and threw the afternoon edition of the Tribune onto Herb's desk.

"Congratulations, Herbie," he said, a triumphant tone in his voice. "You made the front page."

He had folded the paper so that Herb couldn't avoid seeing the headlines.

WAR ROOM RAIDED!

Warriors' Souvenir Outlet Actually

Front For Gambling, Drugs, Prostitution:

Team Denies Involvement

Pinello smirked at Herb. "Just another example of the sterling judgment being used by this team's general managers, selling their retail operation to a criminal. Smart thinking, Herbie."

Herb looked disgustedly at Pinello. "Would you get the hell out of my office?"

"In due time, Herbie. In due time. I just want to know what other brilliant moves you and your buddy have in mind for this ... By the way, where is your friend Dave? Shouldn't he be sharing in the glory of this most momentous day in the history of the franchise?"

"Dave took a couple of days off. He said he was going out of town."

"That may well be the best thing that's happened to the team this year," Pinello said sarcastically.

Herb looked at the paper and threw it down.

"You're really enjoying this, aren't you, Pinello?"

Pinello stopped and thought for a moment or two. "Officially, I am appalled. I find it truly unfortunate that the team has made such an embarrassing blunder. While I expect that the Association will investigate the circumstances surrounding these events, I am sure there has been no significant damage done to the reputation of the franchise."

He stopped and smiled coldly.

"Off the record, I couldn't be happier. All year long I've been watching you two boobs and that wreck of an old man of yours muddle your way through, ruining a professional football team. Ignoring my advice, ignoring the Association, just doing whatever you damn well pleased."

"We've won, Pinello. The team is seven and two."

"And you really think you had anything to do with that? The team won in spite of you, Rojas, and now, little by little, piece by piece, it's starting to fall apart. Who's next, Herbie? How much longer will Reese's legs hold out? And Gardner's arm, do you really think it'll last for five more games? Seems to me that kid Eaker is playing more and more every game."

"Yeah, well, Rider should be back in a couple of weeks."

Pinello grinned. "It's no good, Herbie. You're through. The team's going down the tubes, and so, I hear, is Kennedy."

That got Herb's attention. "What about Kennedy?"

"Nothing definite, but I've heard that Kennedy's starting to get a little ... well, unstable."

"Is he drinking?"

"Well, I can't say for certain."

"I'll bet you can't."

"Look, Herbie, I told you that the old guy wasn't right for the Association. I told you he was a bad risk."

"Yeah, you did," Herb said, walking over to the window and gazing out. He couldn't think of anything more to say.

Pinello was just getting started, though. "By the way, what are you going to tell the papers?"

"The truth. Spring offered to buy the store and we sold it to him. Damn! I should have known. I mean, I've been doing business in this town for twelve years. I should know a front when I see one."

"Really?"

"Sorry to disappoint you, Pinello, but I've never run one."

"You sounded like an expert."

"Will you get the hell out of my office?"

"Sure, Herbie." He turned to leave, but then turned back. "By the way, have they found that guy yet?"

"Spring?" Herb shook his head. "Vanished without a trace. Like he never existed. All his places around town are closed up."

"Interesting," Pinello said as he left the room.

Things got worse before they got better, and late that night, Herb dug out a phone number he had gotten earlier in the day. Tracey Cagney rolled over to answer her phone.

"Hello ... Who? Who is this?" She nudged Dave. "Hey, Krause, it's your partner."

"Wha ... Herb? What the hell!?" He grabbed the phone, rubbing his eyes. "Herb, how the hell did you know ... All right, calm down ... Oh, come on, Herb ... You're serious, aren't you? Damn ... When ... All right, I'm on my way. I'll meet you at the hospital ... Oh, three hours, two and a half if I really push it. Right."

He hung up the phone and then jumped out of the bed and reached for his clothes.

"What the hell's going on? Your friend sounded excited."

"Oh, really?" he asked as he stepped into his pants. "How could you tell?"

"Well, he told me, and I quote -- to cut the fucking chatter and put you on the phone ... Hey, are you leaving?"

"I've got to get back," Dave said, throwing on his jacket and heading out the door. "My starting quarterback has been shot in the ass."

It was almost dawn when Dave arrived at the hospital. As much as he had wanted to drive straight through, he had made several stops for coffee. Even with all the caffeine he had put into his system, he was still barely conscious when he pulled off the highway and into the parking lot.

Herb looked as bad as Dave thought he probably looked. He was waiting just outside the lobby, smoking the next to last of a pack of cigarettes.

"Well, it's about time!" he said. "You come by way of Detroit?"

"Easy, Herb, easy. How's Jimmy?"

"He's fine. Hell, he looks like he's even enjoying it."

"What happened?"

"Well, Gardner and ... Listen, I need another cup of coffee. You want one, Dave?"

"No!"

"All right, all right ... Jeez, you look terrible! You want to lie down or something?"

"For Christ's sake, Herb! What the hell happened?"

Herb leaned against the wall and reached for another cigarette. A small man with a mustache and a bow tie walked up to him.

"Excuse me," he said. "What you do in the privacy of your own home is your business, but when you smoke in my personal breathing area, I'm afraid ..."

"Get the fuck out of here before I rip off your head and shit down your neck!" Herb shouted, causing the little man to turn almost as white as the hospital walls. He retreated with blistering speed from the crazy man who obviously needed a cigarette.

"Anyway," Herb said, turning back to Dave. "It seems that Gardner and Ross were out having a good time with these two bimbos. The babes took Ross and Gardner back to their place, and who should walk in but their husbands."

"Oh, boy."

"They started shouting something about messing around with their wives. They said they were tired of big shot football players taking advantage of them, and one of them just happened to have a shotgun with him ..."

"They walked in with a shotgun?"

"Hey, I don't have all the details yet. So anyway, the husbands burst in and Gardner and Ross make a break for the nearest exit, which happens to be the back door. They head for the fence, with the two guys right behind. Ross, being younger and faster, gets to the fence and over it. He's pulling Gardner over the fence when ..."

"Bang."

"Exactly. Well, the shot got the attention of the neighbors, who called the police ..."

"Who arrested the husbands."

"Right. Malicious mischief, assault with a deadly weapon, discharging a firearm within the city limits ..."

"Well, at least they're alive. How's Jimmy?"

"He'll be all right," Herb said. "The doctor said he'd be out of action for a couple of weeks ..."

"A couple of weeks!?"

"Hey, Dave, all things considered ..."

"Yeah, well ..."

"They got all the buckshot out of his ass, and nothing important was hurt."

"Like his arm, his legs."

"He should only miss two games."

"And Ross? How's he?"

"A little shaken up."

"I'll assume he was the one who told you all this."

"Uh, no. Not really ..."

"You got it from the police report, then?"

"Nope, I read it a few minutes ago in the early edition of the paper."

Dave winced. "Already?"

"The reporters were on the scene as fast as the cops. Maybe faster." Herb leaned against the wall, taking a long drag on his cigarette. "Of course, nobody bothered to call us until Ross got around to it."

"Yeah, well, it's not like we're family or anything."

Herb smiled. "God, I'm tired. I've been up all night. Of course, I didn't have to drive back from Philadelphia."

"By the way, how did you know ..."

"Where to find you? I guessed. Pretty good guess, huh?"

"Is it that obvious?"

"That you're making it with Tracey Cagney? I don't think so. I haven't told anyone. Just be careful, OK?"

"Sure ... say, here comes Ross."

Tony Ross, looking not at all the worse for wear, came into the courtyard and walked right up to Dave and Herb.

"Morning, guys," he said breezily. "Been here all night?"

"I have," Herb said. "Looks like I had a little team loyalty, at least."

"Whoa! Hold on there, Herb. The cops questioned me until 3 a.m., so don't act like I just rolled out of bed. By the way, how's Jimmy?"

"All right, I guess. Nothing serious."

"Hey, Tony," Dave asked. "Have you had any discussions with our friends from the press?"

"My phone's been ringing off the hook."

"Great, just what we need. More humiliation."

"Hey, relax. We didn't take a bribe, or kill someone, or join the Ku Klux Klan or the mob. We just got caught fooling around with a couple of married women. Nobody's going to give a damn ... In fact, I'll bet a lot of people are going to get a kick out of it."

"What?"

"Sure," Ross said, grinning. "What's that they say? All the world loves a lover?"

Dave groaned.

58

Bridget was up and walking toward them the minute they walked into the outer office. "Where the hell have you been?"

"Oh, hey, babe," Herb said. "Sorry. I should have called."

"No kidding, big shot. I've been putting out fires for you all morning, and all day yesterday, I might add."

Herb leaned on her desk and turned to Dave.

"You see," he said, gesturing toward Bridget. "You see how they are when they're not getting it regularly?"

Bridget picked up the phone book and slammed it down on Herb's hand. He howled and collapsed to the floor. Dave started to laugh, but Bridget cut him off with a stare.

"And you," she started in on Dave. "Not leaving me any word where you are. People have been calling me for days. I've got reporters calling every five minutes, and there's this creep who showed up yesterday. He hung around waiting for you, smoking some horrible cigar and trying to look down my blouse."

"What was the guy's name?"

She looked at her appointment book. "Romano. He wouldn't tell me what he wanted, but he paced around like a caged dog all day. Watch out for that guy. There's something I don't trust about him."

"All things considered, I don't think that's too much of a surprise," Herb said. Bridget picked up her telephone and brandished it at him. He backed away quickly.

"He's here again. He's waiting in your office."

"Thanks, Bridget," Dave said, steering Herb around the desk and toward the office. "And thanks for keeping an eye on things. Why don't you take the rest of the day off?"

"I planned on it," she said as she covered her keyboard.

"What's the matter with you two?" Dave asked Herb once Bridget had left.

"I don't know. She's a strange broad. She's been asking me all kinds of questions lately, and the other day I found her going through the files in the office."

"Huh?"

"She said she was looking for something, but when I asked her what, she got kind of funny about it."

"You'll never learn, will you, Herb?"

Rojas didn't have a chance to answer, because as soon as they were inside the office, they were confronted by a squat, sweating man with at least three days growth of beard. The man was wearing what had to have been one of the last lime-green leisure suits still in existence outside the Smithsonian.

"Gentlemen," the man said in a loud, rasping voice that had a strange mix of New Jersey and North Carolina accents. "Glad to finally meet you."

"Uh, nice to meet you, er ..." Dave said as he shook the fat man's hand.

"Romano. Carmine Romano. My friends call me Little Remo."

"Glad to meet you, Mr., uh, Remo. What can we do for you?"

"Well ... do you mind if I sit down?"

Neither of them objected, so the man plopped down into a chair and started his story. "I thought I might drop in on you and discuss a little problem we have."

"We?" Dave asked.

"Yes ... By the way, which of you is Mr. Krause?"

Dave raised his hand.

"Then you must be Mr. Rojas." Herb nodded. "Glad to get that straight. Mr. Krause, I believe that you're the one who came to West Virginia and signed my boys."

"Your boys?"

"Maybe I'd better start at the beginning. You see, I am the commissioner and sole owner of the Appalachian Worldwide Professional Championship Wrestling Association."

"Uh oh."

Romano nodded. "You might recall that Alphonse and Romeo Adonis worked for me before you so abruptly snatched them away and put them to work playing professional football."

Herb broke in. "Would you cut the crap and get to it?"

"All right, Mr. Rojas, if you insist. It seems you neglected to inquire as to the conditions of employment of the Adonis brothers before you took them away."

"Romano ..."

"If you had done any sort of checking, you would have soon become cognizant of the fact that those two boys were already under a personal services contract to the Appalachian Worldwide Championship Professional Wrestling Association. In short, they work for me."

"You'll have to forgive me, Mr. Romano. I'll be happy to confess my ignorance. I always thought wrestlers were all free agents, and neither one of them told me anything about having contracts with you."

"That doesn't surprise me. I'm not sure they even remember signing the contracts, but let me assure you that they did."

Herb broke in. "Well, Remo, I'm sure we can work out some sort of arrangement here. The Warriors will be more than happy to purchase their contracts from you."

"Oh, you don't have to do that."

"Really? That's good. But if you don't want money, then what are you doing here? What do you want?"

Romano smiled. "I want the Adonises."

"You what?"

"In fact, I already have them. Last night, when I wasn't able to speak with you, I went out to your facility in Maryland and picked them up."

"How the hell did you do that?" Herb asked, nearly apoplectic.

"I told them they couldn't play football any more," Romano said, smiling. "And they believed me."

Dave and Herb looked at each other.

"They're on their way to Breaker's Crossing, West Virginia. They have a match scheduled for Saturday night."

"I don't believe this!" Dave said. "I've never heard anything so ridiculous in all my life. You snatch those two boys out of professional football and throw them into a wrestling show in some little jerkwater town ..."

"They'll be well taken care of."

"Wonderful," Herb said. "That means you'll feed them."

Romano smiled. "That's quite an accomplishment in itself."

"Don't get cute, Romano," Herb snarled. "You're disgusting, you know that?"

"I'm a businessman, Mr. Rojas, just like you."

"Not even close, Romano."

"Well, it's all a moot point now. All I wanted to do was stop by and pay you the courtesy of informing you of my actions. Unlike others ..." He glanced pointedly at Dave. "... have done."

"Look, Romano," Dave said calmly. "We're all adults here. We know that if I were to pull out my checkbook right now, I would write down any reasonable price you named."

Romano shook his head. "There is no amount of money, Mr. Krause, that could make me give up the Adonis brothers, because there is no way you could pay me what those boys are worth."

That raised both Herb and Dave's eyebrows.

"Do you know what the presence of two former professional football players will do to my gate receipts?"

"Yeah," Herb said. "And how much of that will the Adonis brothers get?"

"About as much as they get of your gate receipts, Mr. Rojas." Romano stood, straightened his clothing and made ready to leave. "Now I have other business to attend to. Good day, gentlemen."

Then he left the room, and so, Dave and Herb decided, did the Warriors' chances.

Of course they were right, at least as far as Sunday's game with the Atlanta Aces was concerned. The only good thing that happened was that Ross had been right about the public's reaction to the incident in which Jimmy Gardner had been injured. Outside of a few isolated protests, there was no outcry for any sort of punishment for the two men.

Indeed, when Gardner hobbled onto the field carrying a donut-shaped cushion, the crowd roared with sympathetic laughter. As for Ross, the fans had always thought of him as a playboy, and he had done nothing but add to his image.

There were banners and posters hanging in the stands attesting to his prowess off the field, and the network cameras stayed away from them all afternoon.

Unfortunately, Ross played as if he had spent the previous night with a number of the young ladies who had hung the banners. His moves were sloppy and slow, and he was constantly dogged by the defensive back assigned to cover him.

His teammates fared little better. The only player who seemed unaffected by the controversy was Norm Blaylott, and the offense only got close enough for him to kick one field goal.

Lindy Eaker seemed intent upon proving just how far he was from being a quality starting quarterback. At first, people blamed his poor performance on nerves, which were to be expected of a rookie quarterback starting his first game.

After a while, though, it became apparent that Eaker was just a bad quarterback. Three different times he turned to the wrong side on a handoff, once fumbling, once having to carry it himself and once handing the ball to an Atlanta defender.

The defender had the presence of mind to thank Eaker and then run for a touchdown.

When he dropped back to pass, he wasn't any better. His arm wasn't all that inaccurate, but he lacked any sort of touch at all. To receivers accustomed to soft, wobbly tosses from Jimmy Gardner, the rocketlike passes of the younger Eaker were anything but welcome.

The ball was bouncing off their chests all afternoon. The only bright spot was that his passes were too hard for the defenders to handle as well, and he threw only one interception.

Atlanta had no such problems. The Aces played capable if uninspired football and cruised to a 24-3 victory. By the end of the game, half the crowd and all of the banners were gone.

It was beginning to look as if the Warriors' bubble had burst, and the toughest part of the schedule loomed ahead. The team was still in position for a wild card playoff berth, but even that could disappear quickly.

NORTH AMERICAN FOOTBALL ASSOCIATION STANDINGS
After Ten Weeks of Play

LIBERTY CONFERENCE

East Division	W-L-T	West Division	W-L-T
Miami Wave	9-1-0	Houston Lonestars	8-2-0
Washington Warriors	7-3-0	Los Angeles Generals	6-4-0
Pittsburgh Pistols	6-4-0	San Francisco Kings	6-4-0
Atlanta Aces	4-6-0	Denver Mountaineers	4-6-0
Boston Barons	3-7-0	Calgary Riders	3-7-0
New York Comets	2-8-0	Detroit Crushers	2-8-0

FREEDOM CONFERENCE

East Division	W-L-T	West Division	W-L-T
Philadelphia Bulldogs	10-0-0	Cincinnati GoldStars	8-2-0
Chicago Trojans	6-4-0	Dallas Cougars	6-4-0
Jacksonville Stingers	6-4-0	Kansas City Wranglers	5-5-0
Birmingham Smashers	3-7-0	St. Louis Archers	5-5-0
Montreal Mustangs	3-7-0	Minneapolis Stallions	3-7-0
Toronto Blues	2-8-0	Vancouver Westerners	3-7-0

<h1 style="text-align:center">59</h1>

In Chicago, everyone was rooting for the Trojans to reach the playoffs, no one more so than Duncan Charles.

He was unable to sleep. He was too tense to go to his office and he wasn't even taking telephone calls. He spent his days in his penthouse, watching television, reading the newspapers, eating ice cream and worrying.

Worrying along with him were Chicago's sportswriters. The Trojans were tied for second place in their division, but they were one loss away from third place and missing the playoffs. That was the way it had been for most of the season.

The Trojans were never really in, but never really out, either. Every time they would get some momentum going, something would happen and they would stumble. Every time that happened, everyone would assume the season was about to go down the tubes and the dream of the playoffs would have to wait yet another year.

Yet somehow the Trojans got it together time after time. They stayed in contention for the second-place playoff spot in the Freedom Conference East.

Duncan had fallen into a daily routine. He would get out of bed and call room service for breakfast. He would read the morning papers while eating and then he'd place a call to Ray Martini. He'd always say the same thing.

"Ray, are we going to make it?"

"Yeah, kid," Martini invariably said. "We're going to make it."

Duncan would then hang up the phone and turn on the television to watch cartoons.

On this particular morning, though, it would take more than a phone call to reassure Duncan Charles. The Trojans had lost to Philadelphia. That wasn't unusual in itself. Every other team that had played the Bulldogs had lost, Rudy Lomax to the contrary, but this one had been particularly disheartening for Trojan fans.

It had come after two convincing victories, 32-10 over Birmingham and 41-9 over Toronto. Finally, everyone assumed, the team that had threatened all season to become a powerhouse was finally putting things together in time for the stretch run.

A 31-13 loss to Philadelphia had changed all that. Suddenly there were stories in the local papers about the imminent collapse of the Chicago Trojans. There were reports of dissension, rumors that half the starting backfield was about to be benched and one unconfirmed report that half of the defensive line had tested positive for an embarrassing social disease.

Local television commentators all featured in-depth reports on the shattered condition of the team, reports that were full of taped replays from the Philadelphia game that made the Trojans look particularly bad.

It was all intended to drum up interest in the team, to increase newspaper sales and build television ratings, but it had an entirely different effect on Duncan Charles. It made him feel as if something had gone terribly wrong with the System.

"It's still in place and it's running like a dream."

"But, Ray, the team looks so bad! And what if all these stories are true?

Ray, is my team falling apart?"

"Kid, I've got a lot of things to do today. I can't be spending all my time holding your hand. If you can't take my word for it, that's your problem."

"I just want to know what's going on," Duncan whined. "You say the System's working, but how can I tell? Can you just give me a little hint or something?"

Martini was rapidly losing his patience. "You know damn well I can't ..."

"Aw, I gotta know! Who would I tell, anyway?"

Martini sighed. "All right, kid, listen good. You're going to lose Sunday to Jacksonville and then you're going to lose to Kansas City. That'll drop you to six and six and you'll be in third place."

"Noooooo!" Duncan moaned.

"Then," Martini continued. "You're going to win against Toronto. That'll put you into a tie for second with Jacksonville. Last game of the season, you play Washington and Jacksonville plays Montreal. If you both win, Jacksonville goes to the playoffs because they did better in the division. If you both lose, the same thing happens."

"Nooooooo!"

"But Jacksonville does not win. They blow it, and you walk all over Washington. The Chicago Trojans win their last two games and squeeze their way into the playoffs. Now is that exciting or is that exciting?"

"But what if something goes wrong, Ray? What if someone on my team gets injured?"

"Kid, you forget. I'm in control. You could put a damn high school team out there and I'd get them into the playoffs. For God's sakes, Duncan, I don't think you've understood a thing I've told you. We've been together all these months and you haven't understood a damn thing!"~

"Now, Ray ..."

"The whole idea behind the System is to give people what they want. People want excitement! They want the playoff races to go down to the wire! How much excitement can you get out of a team that wins a playoff berth four weeks before the season ends? All right, kid. Now do you understand what's going on here?"

"I guess so."

"Now if any of this gets out, there'll be hell to pay, do you understand that, too? I've told you more than anyone outside of me and the Commissioner is supposed to know, and you know damn well we're not going to tell anyone."

"Me, either, Ray. You can count on me."

"I'm going to, Duncan. And I'll have your ass if you let me down."

60

Dave, Herb and Roy were sitting in a booth in the back room of Cliches with their lawyer, Clyde Smith, a somewhat regular patron and occasional drinking partner.

Twenty years earlier, Clyde had marched with civil rights activists while he attended Georgetown Law School. After graduation he had dedicated himself to serving the poor and unfortunate of the District, opening a storefront office in the section of the city that had been burned out during the 1968 riots.

It was an exciting, fulfilling time. He was able to represent those who otherwise would have been lost in the system. He kept poor families from being evicted.

He kept men from losing their jobs because they happened to be black and their employers were white, and he helped companies formed by black entrepreneurs get government contracts.

He was also starving. It took him two and a half years to figure it out, but once American Express had cancelled his card, on the same day the collection agency called to remind him he was three payments behind on his college loans, he was suddenly aware he couldn't make it this way any longer.

He figured he had done enough for the community he'd grown up in, and all he had to show for it was an empty bank account and a bad credit rating. He closed his storefront office and went to work for Levinson, Kelly, Arnold and Vukovich. He specialized in class-action suits and he never looked back.

About a year later he started frequenting Herb's bar, where he became a familiar figure and an off-the-record legal adviser to Herb and his father.

Clyde had been a freewheeling single, cutting an even wider swath than Herb through the women who frequented the bar, right up to the day he met Rose, another regular. They didn't have their wedding in the bar, but Herb had paid for a reception there as part of his duties as Clyde's best man.

Since the wedding, Clyde had cut back on his appearances, but was still available for help and advice in exchange for a couple of drinks.

He looked at the subpoena in his hands.

"Damn! The Grand Jury. I never thought I'd see one of these things again."

"Yeah," Herb said. "Imagine how excited I was to get it."

Roy leaned forward and reached for the document. "Boy, they sure do make it look fancy, don't they? All those curly lines ... looks sort of like something you'd buy at the dime store."

Clyde laughed. "You'd better take it a little more seriously than that, man. I can tell you that Thomas R. Banion means business."

"Sure," Herb said. "But what the hell do they want with us?"

"That's easy to see. Next year the District elects a mayor, and I think our illustrious district attorney is taking advantage of some free publicity to position himself for a run."

"What kind of ..."~

"It'll get everyone's attention. The team is winning, so people are interested. Banion will put the Grand Jury through its paces for two weeks or so, grab some headlines and make a few recommendations. Then it's all over. Any idea what this thing is all about?"

"The War Room, I guess," Dave said. "They'll probably try to dig up some connection between us and the mob."

"Well?"

"Well what, Clyde?"

"Is there any connection?"

Dave looked with disbelief at the lawyer. "What do you think?"

"It doesn't matter what I think. I think that's what they're going to ask you and I think you've got to have an answer to the question."

"All right, the answer is no."

"Got any proof?"

"Proof?" Dave asked. "What the hell do we need proof for? I thought you were innocent until proven guilty in this country."

"Sure. You'll never get convicted of anything or probably even indicted, but they'll sure as hell drag you through the mud. So you do need proof."

"I guess so."

"When do they want you?"

Herb looked at the subpoena. "Monday morning."

"Which one of you is going to go?"

Dave looked at Herb, who shook his head. Dave gave him a "not me" look in return. Before either of them could say anything, Roy piped up. "I'll go."

61

The Philadelphia Bulldogs were the only unbeaten team left in the NAFA with four games still to be played, but Rudy Lomax was still writing stories about the imminent collapse of the team.

Those stories weren't drawing as much attention as they once had, now that the Bulldogs had all but clinched a spot in the playoffs. Still, they were bothering Tracey Cagney, so she called Lomax in for a private conversation.

She didn't bother to stand or come out from behind her desk when he entered the room. She merely indicated a chair in front of the desk. When Lomax sat down, Tracey spoke in a quiet voice.

"Mr. Lomax, don't you think you've exhausted this one particular subject? Isn't it time you started writing about something else?"

Lomax hadn't expected a direct attack, but he was able to tell her no with little difficulty.

Tracey wasn't giving up all that easily, though. "I certainly would appreciate it if you would consider it."

"Are you threatening me, lady?" Tracey said nothing. "I wouldn't do that if I were you. I haven't even scratched the surface of what I know about this team. You don't want to screw around with the press, lady!"

Lomax's voice was rising to an extremely unpleasant pitch. Tracey sat impassively behind her desk, saying nothing.

"For instance, I don't think all the juicy facts about your little affair with Tony Ross ever made the papers. I know he dumped you and I know your late father ran him out of the league. I even know you tried to get him from Washington."

Tracey still didn't react, and that seemed only to anger Lomax more and more.

"Now how much are the dear people of Philadelphia going to think of you as a franchise operator if they find out you tried to trade away your quarterback and two wide receivers for a little revenge?"

Tracey just smiled. Lomax got madder and madder.

"And here's something else, Miss Cagney. I know you're making it with one of the Washington general managers."

She raised an eyebrow but still said nothing.

"I haven't figured out which one yet, whether it's that idiot Rojas or his buddy Krause, but I know it's one of them and it won't be long before I've got names, dates and places."

"So?"

"So don't sit there like Little Miss High and Mighty and tell me what kind of story I should or shouldn't write. You might just get my editor mad enough to let me write the kind of story I've been wanting to write ever since I started on this thing."

Lomax then got to his feet and looked down at Tracey, feeling immensely superior. She thought about her options, looked up and said, "Go ahead, Lomax."

His mouth dropped open. "What?"

"Go ahead," she said, smiling sweetly. "Write your story. See how far you get."

"All right. All right, I will."

"Maybe you should. That will be all, Mr. Lomax."

Once again, Tracey didn't rise. She sat there behind her desk until Lomax left the office. Then she reached for her phone and punched in a number.

Lomax spent the ride back to his office composing his story in his mind. He was certain the news of Tracey Cagney's love affairs would stand the town on its ear, and might even rock the entire NAFA.

He had finished the story and was already starting to think about a feature he could pitch to Sports Illustrated when he breezed into the newsroom.

"Hi, Jack," he said as he logged onto his computer terminal. "Man, have I got a column that'll knock your socks off. It's about Tracey ..."

"Not just now, Rudy."

"Huh? What do you mean?"

"I mean not just now," the editor said. "We need to talk. Then I've got a new assignment for you. I want you to head out to Mountain View High School. The field hockey team is in the regional finals this afternoon."

62

The Warriors had resigned themselves to the fact that Eaker would have to start against Philadelphia. The coaches worked with Gardner and Brian Rider some, but Gardner was still limping and Rider was still a week or two away from being ready to return. So Eaker took most of the snaps, trying to develop the timing in one week that took an entire season to put together.

There was some improvement, but Eaker was still throwing the ball as if he was afraid of it, and passes were still bouncing off the receivers' chests.

The same thing happened on Sunday afternoon. By halftime, Eaker had completed only four of nineteen passes. Reese and Waller were running well enough to keep the game interesting, but once the Bulldogs realized how one-dimensional the Warrior attack was, they put eight and nine men up front to stop the ground game.

Again Norm Blaylott provided all the scoring for the Warriors, kicking two long field goals in the second quarter, but Philadelphia managed two touchdowns in response and led, 14-6, at halftime.

Dave Krause didn't notice much of what was happening on the field. He spent most of the game staring across at the Philadelphia owner's box at Tracey Cagney. She seemed to alternate between businesslike discussions with her subordinates and obvious excitement when her team did something good.

Occasionally she slipped Dave a sly wink, which he did his best to return without anyone noticing. Through it all, whatever the mood, she remained feminine, attractive and totally desirable.

Early in the third quarter, Herb leaned over and whispered to his friend. "She's something, isn't she?"

"Yeah. She certainly is."

"Watch out for her, though."

"What does that mean?"

"One of her assistants told me something. This week she got pissed off at some reporter. He'd been writing some stories that were bugging her. Then she makes a phone call and all of a sudden the guy's on the high school beat."

"No kidding?"

"No kidding. You're moving in the big leagues now, and that's a lady who's used to getting what she wants."

"I know."

"Yeah, well, watch out."

Dave smiled at his friend and then turned back to look at Tracey, who had been watching their conversation.

The second half turned out to be more or less a replay of the first. Washington couldn't generate any offense and the Bulldogs moved the ball almost at will. Blaylott kicked two more field goals and Philadelphia scored two more touchdowns to win the game, 28-12.

When the game had ended, there was the I'm-being-a-good-sport meeting between the owner of the Bulldogs and the Warriors' general managers. When Tracey Cagney shook Dave Krause's hand, he felt a piece of paper. Later, when the stadium was almost empty, Dave stepped over into a corner and opened it.

"Stay in your hotel room. I'll meet you there. I'll make you feel better."

63

"Welcome back, everybody, to the final hour of Sports For You. I'm Fred Reynolds, and joining me in the studio for the final hour is the Honorable Thomas Banion, the district attorney for the District of Columbia. Now as any regular listener knows, we don't normally have guests from outside the world of sports, but Mr. Banion is heading up the investigation into the Warriors and certain events that have happened this season."

"Actually, Fred, my investigation is a little broader than that. We're looking into certain scandalous and questionable practices in the entire sporting establishment. We will be looking at the recruiting practices of colleges, at the seeming discrimination of major league baseball against the Washington area ..."

"That's all well and good, Tom, but so far the only area you've covered is the Warriors. Now without betraying any confidences, could you let us in on some of the skeletons you've found in the Warriors' closet?"

"Fred, it's pretty obvious the Warriors are being run by idiots, but it wasn't until we started our investigation that I realized just how wide-ranging their incompetence has been. Just to illustrate, we invited someone from management to appear before us. They sent Roy Rojas."

"The elder Mr. Rojas? Not Herb Rojas or Dave Krause?"

"One and the same. You would think they would have taken the Grand Jury seriously enough to send someone who knew what was going on."

"In other words, the elder Mr. Rojas was not helpful."

"Let me put it this way. Either Mr. Rojas spent the last seven months with his head in a hole or he was withholding information."

"I was not!" Roy Rojas shouted to Dave, Herb and Clyde as the four of them sat in the bar listening to the radio. "Where does that guy get off saying something like that?"

Herb put his finger to his lips and silenced his father.

"Freedom of speech, my man," Clyde said. "It's an old custom."

Dave laughed, and the four of them turned their concentration once again to the broadcast.

"So what you're saying," Reynolds said. "Is that you feel the Warriors are throwing up a smoke screen."

"Well, it's still too early to tell. A few more days of testimony and we'll know exactly which cards are in whose hands."

"What about their finances?"

"The team is definitely in rocky shape financially. There was a period a few weeks ago when the cash flow was so bad the team almost failed to meet its payroll."

"So they're broke?"

"No. They recently received a seven-figure television check from the league, and that will take care of their short-term problems. But they have been saddled with a very poor concessions contract, one in which they get only ten percent of the proceeds ..."

"As opposed to twenty-five to fifty percent for every other team in the Association."

"That's right, Fred. Anyway, the players and other employees don't have to worry about being embarrassed when they cash their paychecks."

"What about the Earl Spring affair? Was Mr. Rojas helpful at all?"

"Not very. He wasn't involved -- at least he claimed not to be involved -- in the transaction with Mr. Spring."

That was too much for Roy. "Claimed not to be involved!? I didn't know a damn thing about that guy!"

"We know, dad."

"Get out the cross and nails, boys," Clyde said as he reached over and turned off the radio. "The man is out to crucify you."

"Why us, Clyde?" Dave asked. "What does he get out of it?"

"You just heard it, man. The guy's on the radio. He's getting an awful lot of free publicity."

"What about Reynolds?"

"Ratings," Herb said. "Plus it makes him look like a genius for what he was saying about us before the season started."

"Listen, guys," Clyde said as he stood and stretched. "I'd love to stay and listen to you all night long, but I've got things to do tomorrow before I take the old man here downtown."

"You think we should let Roy keep testifying, then?"

"Why not? At least he can't hurt you."

"Will you stop talking about me like I'm not here!?" Roy shouted.

"How much longer you think this'll go on?" Dave asked.

"That's not the question. The question is how much longer you can stand it."

In New Orleans, the commissioner certainly wasn't having any trouble standing it. In fact, he was pleased.

"Sit down, Stan."

Pinello felt so relieved he almost sighed aloud. He had been certain the commissioner had summoned him to New Orleans to chew him out again, but when he saw the ear-to-ear grin on the man's face, he knew it wasn't going to be a difficult session.

"I wanted to congratulate you on your success with Washington," he said, chuckling. "Ironic, isn't it, Stan, that Washington's failures become our successes?"

Pinello nodded.

"I wanted to tell you that after a shaky start, your work this season has been outstanding. Should you manage to maintain this same level of excellence to the end of the season, I can assure you that you will not be unhappy with your compensation. Perhaps even ..." He paused for effect. "... a position will be opening up here in the main office."

Pinello was speechless. Tears welled up in his eyes, and a lump developed in his throat that threatened to cut off his oxygen. He was certain if he tried to speak he would either blubber like a child or pass out on the carpet.

Since neither of those would help him in the commissioner's estimation, he merely smiled, nodded and looked back at him.

"Thanks for coming today, Stan. I'll look forward to hearing from you this Sunday."

"That's ... that's all?"

"Why? Was there something else you wanted to tell me?"

"No, Commissioner. I just assumed that, with you flying me down here and all, I thought there would be something else."

"No, not especially. I was sure that the present situation was due to your work. By the way, are you still involved with Mr. Krause's ex-wife?"

Pinello made a sour face. "Marginally, sir. I've found that she really doesn't have that much to do with Krause. It seemed to upset him a little bit when he found out, but he hasn't said an awful lot to me about it."

"Either our Mr. Krause is an extremely secure individual or a very cold fish."

"Commissioner, I don't think he gives a damn. Except that he did tell me to stay the hell away from his daughter."

"His daughter?" The commissioner lifted an eyebrow. "Hmmm, perhaps we have found Mr. Krause's weakness."

"Uh, sir, I really don't think there'd be much to be gained by attacking him through his kid. And in all honesty, Muriel is about as much fun as root canal work."

"Pinello," the commissioner responded in a lowered tone. "I never suggested that you enjoy yourself with this woman. I suggested you initiate an affair to see what sort of information could be gleaned from her. To that end, obviously, we have not been altogether successful, but I still feel there is a certain value to maintaining the status quo."

"So you want me to beat up his daughter."

The commissioner blanched. "Pinello, we are not monsters. We are businessmen. We don't hurt children. All I want you to do is create a situation where Mr. Krause's concerns are redirected toward his family, rather than his franchise."

"You mean do something like move in with his wife?"

"Very good, Pinello."

"That takes care of Krause. What about Rojas?"

"We're working on it."

64

Tracey Cagney was stunned by the anger in the voice at the other end of the line.

"Thanks loads, Tracey!"

"Dave? What the ..."

"You are one hell of a dealer, you know that? You set me up just like a damn bowling pin!"

"Dave, honey ..."

"Yeah, right! Gonna do us a favor. You're overloaded with receivers. You don't care what the Association says, you're going to trade with us anyway ..."

"Dave, I really don't appreciate getting calls like this. Just tell me, what the hell am I supposed to have done?"

"You traded me a damn junkie, that's what you did!"

"I traded you ... Jenkins?"

"Very good, sweetheart."

"Dave, believe me, I had no idea ..."

"Yeah, sure. The guy was a speed freak!"

"What happened?"

"He collapsed! Right on the practice field! They carried him off, went to his locker to get his clothes and found a damn drugstore! Coke, marijuana, speed ... Anyway, thanks for everything, Tracey. You're a real pal."

"Dave, you've got to believe me. I had no idea the kid was doing drugs. All right, I knew he was a little flaky ..."

"A little flaky? Jeez, that's the understatement of the ..."

"... and yes, he didn't get along too well with the other players, but ..."

"No kidding. Oh, and by the way, Jenkins was also the guy who set up Nick Gullotta."

"Well, there you see. At least you'll get Gullotta back."

"Wonderful," Dave said sarcastically. "I lose one of my starting receivers and get back a decoy. That's just great."

"Look, lover," Tracey said, her voice cold. "Get one thing straight right now. Jenkins might not have been a Boy Scout, but if I'd known he was a doper I'd have run him out of the league. I thought I was doing you a favor! I'll keep that in mind the next time I'm feeling gracious."

The line went dead and Dave was immediately sorry he had even picked up the phone. He didn't have time to sulk long, though. Herb walked into the office with more information.

"Curiouser and curiouser."

Dave looked up. "Wonderful. I scream at a lady and my friend is busy making literary references. What's up, Herbert?"

"It seems our friend Jenkins is confessing his ass off. You know who his main contact was? Earl Spring."

Dave's eyes opened wider.

"I thought you'd like that. And God knows why, but it was Spring who got Jenkins to set up Gullotta."

"Did he say why?"

"Nope. It seems that our little Randy was only following his instructions."

"Maybe that's what made him a good player. A lousy pusher, but a good player."

"It's also apparent that he was trying to supply the team with drugs."

"Any regular customers?"

"You mean players?" Dave nodded. "He won't say. He won't say anything about his deals, and no, he doesn't have any idea where Spring is."

"This all makes me really uncomfortable."

"You mean Wilson?"

"Yeah. What if he's back on drugs?"

Herb shrugged. "No proof of that yet. We've just got to hope he's not. Anyway, there is some good news. Gardner's been cleared to play this Sunday."

"Thank God! What about Rider?"

Herb shook his head. "He's still a couple of weeks away. Probably not until the playoffs."

"The playoffs? Who the hell is thinking about the playoffs now?"

"My dad, for one. It's all he's been talking about, at least until this Grand Jury thing came up."

"He's pretty upset, isn't he?"

Herb sighed. "Yeah, I haven't seen him this worked up in a long time. Even making it with Sally Adler didn't get to him like this."

"Maybe we shouldn't let him go back ..."

"I tried. I told him I'd take his place, but now he says his honor is at stake. They're raking his only son over the coals, and he says he's not going to stand for it."

"Well, at least he doesn't have to go back until next week. Maybe something will come up before then."

The Warriors had slipped to third place in their division, and their performance in the last few games had diminished people's respect for their abilities so much that their home game with fourth-place Boston was an even-money game.

Local fans interest also had dropped off, to the point that Hoover Coliseum was only half-filled on Sunday. The fans who came saw a mediocre game, with no scoring at all in the first half.

Washington still was adjusting to Gardner's return, and Boston was playing pitifully. Neither team crossed midfield in the first two periods.

The only optimistic note was Roxy Reese. He seemed to be carrying the ball on every other play. By the end of the first half he had rushed for nearly seventy yards, but that was nearly seventy percent of the Washington offense.

At the half, Pinello met with the referees.

"You're doing all right out there, gentlemen," he said. "The game seems to be progressing well enough."

"Thanks, Mr. Pinello."

"One thing worries me, though. The way Reese is running, I know he's going to break one. And the way Boston plays, it might be enough to give the Warriors the game."

"Well, we can hardly throw a flag every time he carries the ball."

"You will if I say so."

"Mr. Pinello ..."

"Boys, all I'm saying is that I want Reese stopped, and if Boston can't do it, it's up to us."

"We're only the officials. We can hardly break the man's legs."

"Look, I don't need smart-ass remarks from some two-bit zebra," Pinello said, fixing the man with a stare. "What I need is for you boys to do what I say. If the Warriors aren't going to make any mistakes, then we'll have to let Boston get away with a few."

No one watching the game seemed to notice the reduction in penalties during the third quarter. One of the radio commentators did mention that the game was going by rapidly, but he attributed it to the large number of running plays.

After the Warriors were forced to punt once again late in the third quarter, Gardner went directly to the coach.

"They're killing us, Coach! They're all over Tony and Nick! They've been hitting me late, and will you look at that?"

A Boston defender broke through and tackled punter Lou Andrews long after he had kicked the ball away.

"Hey, Ref!" Gardner yelled. "Where's the flag? What the hell happened to roughing the kicker?"

The official ignored Gardner and Kennedy grabbed his quarterback by the elbow. "Mr. Andrews is fine, Mr. Gardner, and shouting at the officials will do you no good."

"Jesus, Coach, can't you do anything about this? It's like they've got five extra guys on their side!"

"Mr. Gardner, there is little that any coach can do about the quality of the officiating, and I would appreciate it if you would not take the Lord's name in vain."

"Sorry," Gardner said. "But why the hell don't you go out there and tell them ..."

"Need I remind you that non-playing personnel are not allowed to cross the sidelines onto the field of play? And when was the last time you saw an official alter his call because of a protest by a coach?"

Kennedy had a point, but Gardner wasn't in the mood to hear it.

"Save the history lesson, Coach."

Kennedy stiffened, staring down his nose at Gardner. The quarterback stared back with equal determination. Then both men returned their attention to the game.

In the fourth quarter, the Barons opened up with a long drive that finally got them into field-goal range.

Boston set up for the kick from the Warriors' twenty-four, but as the snap was made, the Washington line overwhelmed the blockers. Greg Sisisky, the Barons' quarterback and holder, didn't even bother putting the ball on the ground.

He scooped up the snap, stood and rolled to his right, where he saw Leroy Barrett, one of his receivers, breaking unnoticed toward the end zone. It was a simple toss, and Barrett caught it at the three and strolled across the goal line. The Barons added the point after for a 7-0 lead with ten minutes remaining.

The Warriors couldn't move the ball from their own thirty, with Gardner throwing three straight incomplete passes under a big pass rush.

"I've had it!" he shouted at the coach as he came off the field, slinging his helmet away. "We're getting murdered out there, and the refs are standing around with their thumbs up their butts!"

"Very well, Mr. Gardner. Just say the word and I will replace you with Mr. Eaker."

Once again Gardner and Kennedy tried to stare each other down, and this time Gardner broke.

"No, I guess not," he said, going over and retrieving his helmet.

"By the way, Mr. Gardner, there will be a one hundred dollar fine for throwing your helmet."

Gardner gritted his teeth. "I'll send you a check."

Kennedy smiled and turned back to the game.

Lou Andrews took the snap at his own fifteen. With the Barons looking to set up a punt return, he had little pressure. Andrews stepped forward and kicked a high, towering punt that seemed to hang in midair for twenty seconds. Les Warren, Boston's deep safety, had to backpedal all the way to his own twenty to locate the ball as it finally started to fall to earth.

In postgame interviews Warren would say, again and again, that he had lost the ball in the sun. The ball bounced off his helmet and flew straight up in the air. Dennis Chennelle, the first Warrior downfield, caught the ball on the fly and ran untouched into the end zone. Blaylott added the extra point and the score was tied, 7-7.

The Washington defense was exhausted, but the Boston offense was every bit as tired. The Barons managed to grind out a few first downs, but they bogged down at the Washington forty-eight, and with three minutes to play, they had to kick the ball.

The punt was nearly perfect, a high, soaring spiral that hit on the four and kicked toward the sideline. It bounced out of bounds just before the flag marking the corner of the end zone. The referee spotted it five inches from the goal line.

"Oh, shit!" Gardner said as he reached for his helmet. He had three minutes remaining, and more than ninety-nine yards to cover.

Boston was in a prevent defense, looking to keep the Warrior receivers from sneaking downfield for big gains. Kennedy crossed them up by calling six straight running plays. Reese took it four times, Waller once and Ross once on a reverse.

Each time they ran, the Barons were thinking pass, and when Ross went twenty yards on an end-around, the ball was at the Boston thirty-two with thirty seconds to play. Gardner mentally added the distance, and he knew a forty-nine yard field goal would be at the outer limit of Blaylott's range.

The Warriors had one time out remaining, so Gardner thought he could run two more plays. Kennedy sent in a pass play, figuring the Barons would finally look for the run. They didn't, though, and Gardner checked off at the line of scrimmage.

He called a sweep to the near side, with Reese carrying the ball for the thirty-fifth time in the game.

Even before he got the ball, Reese knew it would be tough to make anything. One of the outside linebackers had diagnosed the play perfectly, and Reese decided just to get to the sidelines and stop the clock. With two defenders trying to keep him in bounds, Reese put on an extra burst of speed as he raced to the sideline, straight at the timekeeper.

The sideline official had looked down momentarily, checking his electronically controlled stopwatch. When he glanced back up, Reese was directly on top of him. There wasn't any time to move, and even if there had been, the timekeeper was frozen in fear.

He didn't move an inch as Reese plowed into him, followed seconds later by both defenders. Out of training and habit, the timekeeper managed to stop the clock the moment he saw Reese step out of bounds.

A split-second later, as Reese hit him, the timekeeper heard a frightening sound, the sound of a large bone being snapped in two. For a moment he wondered if it was his bone, but he didn't feel any pain in his legs.

Roxy Reese did. He felt so much pain that he blacked out. The television men caught every second of it, with Reese motionless on the ground and the trainers rushing to his side, offering smelling salts and cradling the damaged leg.

The television announcers were properly sympathetic. "Boy, Hank, you really hate to see that happen."

"You're telling me, Chuck. He's probably all right, though. It's probably just a pulled muscle or a cramp. They'll take him off the field for some X-rays and next week he'll be as good as new," the announcer said as the camera caught a shot of two men coming out, carrying a stretcher.

"Anyway, Hank, it doesn't look like a knee, and that's good news for the Warriors ... While there's a break in the action, let's go back to Greg Fishbeck in our New York studio. He's got an update on that exciting contest in Atlanta between the Aces and the Miami Wave."

Two minutes later, the New York control room contacted the director on the scene in Washington. He signaled his assistant on the sidelines, who signaled the timekeeper, who signaled that play could resume.

With twelve seconds remaining, the Warriors lined up for a forty-nine yard field goal. Norm Blaylott kicked it, straight and true, but no one celebrated.

An official's flag lay on the turf. "Offside, kicking team."

Tony Ross, acting as captain with Gardner off the field, was on top of the referee immediately. Blaylott paced around, disgusted with everything he saw. Three men, including Ben Kennedy, were restraining Gardner.

Lindy Eaker knew the call wasn't going to be changed, so he moved five yards farther back and formed the huddle. Eventually the rest of the offense did the same as the Warriors and the crowd settled down at last, with seven seconds remaining.

No one had bothered to pay attention to the thirty-second clock, though, and just as the Warriors took their place at the line, the referee's whistle blew again and more flags fell.

"Delay of game, kicking team."

The second penalty moved the ball back to the forty-two, and Ben Kennedy signaled for a time out. A fifty-nine yard field goal would be at least eight yards longer than anything Blaylott had even attempted before, so the coach considered putting his offense back in and throwing a long pass.

He knew Gardner couldn't throw it that far, and he had no faith in Eaker, so he decided to let Blaylott try again. Eaker set up on the forty-nine, and Blaylott stood behind him, breathing deeply as he waited for the snap.

When Eaker turned the laces and put the ball down, Blaylott stepped forward and kicked the ball as far as he could. He felt a rush of excitement when he realized he had hit it well, and that the ball was heading directly toward the goal posts.

He heard the gun sound to end the game, and then he saw nothing. A Boston defender, who had broken away from his blocker, ran at Blaylott and knocked him to the ground.

It didn't matter. The roar of the crowd was enough to let Blaylott know that he had successfully kicked the longest field goal in the history of the Washington franchise.

The officials couldn't risk a third consecutive penalty, and the Warriors had a 10-7 victory.

65

Dave stared across the room at Herb, who was staring glumly at Ben Kennedy, who was alternating staring at the two of them.

"Are you absolutely certain?" Herb asked. "Is he definitely out for the season?"

"Mr. Rojas, there are two weeks left in the regular season. The playoffs, should we be fortunate enough to get that far, will last an additional four weeks. That makes for a total of six weeks, and in case you are unaware of certain facts about the human anatomy, it usually takes at least that long for fractures of that nature to heal."

Herb looked over at Dave. "Reese is out for the season."

Dave picked up a pencil and rapped it against his desk.

"Well, we'll replace him. Waller's doing pretty well ..."

"Yeah. We replaced Jenkins. We replaced Gullotta."

"Mr. Rojas, replacing wide receivers is not that difficult. You may recall we have not been able to replace George Greenblatt, or the Adonis brothers ..."

"I get your point, Coach."

"So," Dave asked. "What are we going to do?"

"About Reese? I have already taken the liberty of contacting Morris Young."

"Hey, I remember him," Herb said. "He wasn't half bad!"

"That's a very succinct analysis, Mr. Rojas. The half that isn't bad is that he is a large man who can block. The half that is bad is that he cannot run at all."

"What about receivers?"

"Luke Talbot and Jeffrey Jones are performing well enough. They are managing to keep the defenses from double-covering Ross."

"For how long?" Dave asked.

"Until the other teams realize Ross is the only one who can catch the ball!" Herb said.

"I disagree, Mr. Rojas. Both Talbot and Jones are capable receivers. They will perform according to my directions."

"They're not Jenkins or Greenblatt, though," Dave said, sighing. "How the hell did we get into this? I mean what are we doing sitting here trying to piece together a football team?"

"Is it not a little late in the game to be asking that?" the coach asked sternly.

Dave smiled sadly. "I guess so."

"Damn it!" the coach shouted as both Dave and Herb sat straight up instantly. "I cannot believe that I am sitting in this office listening to you spout such inane drivel!"

He stood and started pacing around the room. "I would not stand for this from one of my players and I certainly will not stand for it from you! What do you think this is, a lark? There are people who have put their faith in you -- fans, players ..."

He pointed at Herb. "... your father."

"Now hold on a damn minute, Coach. We never said we weren't going to make mistakes. We had some ideas and we worked on them. And if you don't mind, we brought a winning team to this city, so don't talk about us letting people down!"

Kennedy looked at them sternly. "You brought me to this city, and I brought it a winning team!"

The sound of the intercom broke through their argument. "Yeah, Bridget, what is it?"

"There's someone on the way to see you."

"Yeah, well, tell them to stay away ..."

"It's too late. They're already on their way ..."

Dave, Herb and the coach all turned and looked as the door opened. "Greenblatt!"

"Hello, everyone," he said sheepishly. "I'd like to introduce you to my wife, Lisa."

They all stared, glancing from Greenblatt to the petite brunette at his side. As silly as it seemed, Herb thought that the two of them almost glowed. During the conversation that followed, they never stopped holding hands and casting sideways glances at each other.

"Sit down, George," Dave said. "I'd have to say you have a lot of explaining to do."

Kennedy turned to address his player.

"Son, I am not the least interested in hearing your reasons, or your excuses, for deserting your teammates as you did. I will leave that to Mr. Krause and Mr. Rojas, but once they finish with you, if you wish to return to the team, I will expect you at the practice field immediately."

Kennedy turned toward Dave. "I will expect Mr. Krause to telephone me as to the time of your departure. so that I will be able to accurately gauge your commitment to the team by the time it takes for you to show up at practice. Is that understood?"

Greenblatt nodded. "Yes, sir."

"Normally I would not even consider allowing someone to return to the team in a situation like this, but we have not been able to replace you. Assuming you have not allowed your talents to wither away, I will give you one opportunity to prove yourself."

The coach turned and marched out of the office, almost bowling over Herb.

"What the hell did you say to him?" he asked Dave as he set the chairs down.

"I told him to get his ass back to Oxon Hill and let us run the team."

Herb's eyes bugged out, and Greenblatt and his wife smiled at each other. "Well, George," Dave said as they all settled in. "What do you have to say for yourself?"

"The whole story," Herb said. "From the beginning."

"Herb, you sound like that damn district attorney."

"That's all right, Mr. Krause. I ... we do have a lot to explain. First, I want to say I returned because I felt I had ... have ... a duty, an obligation, to play for this team."

"Because you signed a contract," Dave said.

"I prefer to think of it as giving my word."

"Whatever," Dave said, signaling that he should continue with his story.

"Anyway, I do feel I should play for the team, and in addition, I want to play for the team. My only hope is, as the coach said, that my talents have not withered away. And with any luck, they haven't."

"That's all well and good, George," Herb said. "But that still doesn't explain ..."

"... why I disappeared? Well, it all started here, when Mr. Krause left me in his office. What he said struck me right where I lived."

"What I said?"

"When you told me to stop and think about what I was running out on, and from ... from someone who might care very much about me."

He glanced over at Lisa and squeezed her hand. "I left here, not to run away from the team, but to find Lisa. I had realized I was running away because I was scared."

"Of a stock market crash?" Herb asked drily.

"Of falling in love."

"Love? What the hell has love got to do with football? I mean, what do you want me to do, crank up the violins?"

"You may choose not to believe me. That is your privilege, of course, but I have no reason not to tell you the truth."

"Except that maybe you think if you feed us some happy horseshit reason for walking out, we might not think you were just a chicken-shit coward who lost his nerve."

Greenblatt looked over at Dave, almost pleading. "All right, Herb, lay off. Let the kid tell his story. Then we'll decide what he really is."

"Thank you. I came to the realization that I really cared about Lisa, and that perhaps she cared about me. If that were true, then I would have been going against everything I have learned and try to live by if I left without attempting to find her."

"I will assume you found her," Herb said.

"Not that it was easy. At first she refused to see me, and when she did, she refused to listen. But finally, after long and strenuous effort, more than I had ever put forth on the playing field, I might add, she began to see things my way. I convinced her to open her eyes to the one true way."

"He saved me, Mr. Krause," Lisa said. "He showed me where I had erred, where the true path to salvation lay."

"So he took you to Lippmann," Herb said.

"No!" they both said at the same time.

"You mean you did this on your own?" Dave asked.

"Well, it was mostly George. At first I was put off, but he made me realize there are men in this world who are sincere."

"I'm afraid I don't ..."

"Mr. Krause, I have been with men nearly all my life. I had my first affair when I was fourteen. He was in the Air Force, and he shipped out without telling me ... After that I went from one man to another, giving myself to every amorous desire, every sort of carnal activity imaginable. There was nothing I wouldn't do, and no one I wouldn't do it with ..."

I'm not sure, Dave thought, that I really want to hear this.

"... I took part in all sorts of perversions. I was involved with married men, married women, twins, triplets, midgets, foreign exchange students ..."

Midgets? Herb was suddenly curious. This I'd like to hear more about, he thought.

"... until finally, the inevitable happened. After an evening of wanton lust, I found myself alone the next morning. The man I had spent the night with was gone, but he had left a twenty dollar bill on the dresser."

She paused to catch her breath. "I remember thinking that this was an interesting way to make money. After that, I started charging for my services, and I found one thing ... when they pay for you, they respect you. And the more you charge, the more respect you get."

"She was up to five hundred dollars a night when I met her," Greenblatt said.

"That's a healthy amount of respect," Herb said.

"George?" Dave asked. "Exactly how did you meet her?"

Greenblatt looked suddenly solemn. "It was ... arranged."

"Like a blind date?"

"No, more like blackmail. Lisa should tell that part of the story, though."

Herb and Dave looked over at the girl, who paused for a moment as if trying to decide exactly how much she should tell. She looked over at her husband, who nodded serenely.

"I was sent up here, along with two other girls, girls named Cindy and Amy ..."

Greenblatt interrupted. "The same two ladies who caused so much trouble for Mr. Gardner and Mr. Ross."

"I was supposed to get involved with George."

"All right," Dave said. "But who sent you to do this?"

"I was under contract to Peace, Inc."

"Which is ..." Dave waited for the other shoe to drop.

Lisa looked at Greenblatt again, and he nodded again.

"Peace, Inc., is a subsidiary of the Lippmann Foundation."

Herb's jaw dropped.

"You mean, you were sent here to keep an eye on George."

"Exactly."

Dave exhaled loudly. "This is ... I mean, I knew Lippmann was an unscrupulous character, but this ..."

Herb jumped in at that point. "And then Lippmann was supposed to hit us up for cash to talk George into coming back."

"I don't know anything about that. I was just supposed to get George feeling guilty, and naturally he would call Mr. Lippmann ..."

"But George messed that up by taking off," Herb said.

"Wonderful," Dave said. "And we lost him for five weeks as a result, just because we wouldn't pony up half a million ..."

"Half a million!? I didn't think I was worth that much!"

"Well, you're not," Dave said. "Unless you get your tail out to practice."

"And in the meantime," Herb said, rubbing his hands with glee. "I'm going to place a few calls to our friends in the media ..."

George stood up immediately. "I'd ... we'd prefer it if you didn't do that."

"You can't want to protect that little crumb, can you?"

Greenblatt thought for a few moments before responding. "No, not really, but the entire episode might prove to be embarrassing. While the story of Lisa's redemption is certainly inspiring, she has had a past that might well be called ..."

"Checkered?" Dave volunteered.

Greenblatt nodded. "That would describe it. There are more than a few prominent personalities who would not appreciate Lisa's history becoming public knowledge."

"As I said, Mr. Krause, I've been with a lot of men, and some of them have become rather well-known."

She smiled slightly. "Actually, I wouldn't mind seeing the looks on their faces ... George was the first man I ever met who was truly sincere in caring about me. The rest of them ..."

"What about them?" Dave asked.

"They're slime. All of them. The high and mighty, they're the worst. Up there telling people they believe in law and order and the decent values Americans hold dear. Policemen who take freebies in the back seats of patrol cars. Judges and lawyers who look the other way. District attorneys who arrange deals ..."

"Really?" Herb asked, leaning forward. "Tell me more ..."

66

"Mr. Rojas, Mr. Warner, I'm glad finally to meet you." Thomas R. Banion stepped out from behind his desk to shake their hands. "Please sit down."

Banion's office looked like every lawyer's office Dave had ever seen in movies or television shows, from the paneled walls to the huge desk. It was an office clearly designed to enhance the stature of the man who occupied it.

District Attorney Banion was one of the most powerful men in the city government, with the power to investigate and humiliate anyone he wished. He used that power freely. He had investigated fraud in the school lunch program, corruption in the police force and drug trafficking among Congressional pages.

That last investigation was the one that had brought him national prominence, and had lifted his stature to the point where he was considered the front-runner in the next year's mayoral election.

The investigation of the Warriors was merely icing on the cake, something to keep his name in the papers while he positioned himself for the run.

Banion had worked hard for his success and he gloried in it. He had developed a reputation as an urbane, dashing man, a far cry from his adolescence, when he had been known as a boy who wore white, short-sleeved shirts and black bow ties and carried a briefcase to school every day.

Banion dispensed with further amenities and got right to the point. "I understand you gentlemen wanted to meet with me to arrange some sort of deal."

"So to speak," Dave said. "We'd like you to call off the grand jury."

Banion was momentarily stunned, but he recovered quickly and laughed.

"That, my friends, is the funniest thing I've heard in days. Why would I give up such a productive investigation just because you asked me to?"

"We feel it would be to our mutual advantage. After all, this investigation is wasting the taxpayers' time and money."

Banion laughed again. "So you think I'm wasting time and money? That's very interesting, coming from the two men who perhaps have wasted more money than anyone in the District of Columbia this side of Congress."

"Mr. Banion, we're not here to discuss our record."

"Perhaps you should be."

Dave shook his head. "We're just here to reason with you."

"And I am telling you quite reasonably to go screw yourselves!"

Dave shrugged and got up as if to leave. "Very well, then. We'll just have to let the chips fall where they may. By the way ..." He smiled at Banion. "... Lisa Greenblatt says hello."

"Who?" Banion asked in an irritated voice.

"Oh, excuse me. That's her married name. You probably knew her as Lisa Lyons. Here, I have a photograph of her."

Dave handed a snapshot to Banion, and the attorney looked at it. It was amazing how quickly the color left his face.

"Gentlemen," he croaked. "Please sit down."

67

"Welcome back, everyone, to NAFA Sunday Morning," Greg Fishbeck said. "It's time for our good friend Andre O'Connor and Andre's Angles."

"Thanks, Greg, and hello, folks."

"It's week number thirteen, Andre, traditionally the hard-luck week in the Association. A lot of strange things have happened in past week thirteens."

"Well, that would fit in perfectly with the rest of this very strange season. We've seen the ascendancy of the Chicago Trojans, the Cincinnati GoldStars and the Washington Warriors, although the Warriors seem to be slipping back late in the season. They did manage to beat Boston last week, but the Warriors still have lost four of their last six games after winning their first six. They're losing more players every week, with last week's loss of star running back Roxy Reese perhaps the most devastating."

"It certainly is, Andre. Reese rushed for well over a thousand yards, and they'll miss him."

"You bet, Greg, and things don't get any easier for Washington this week. The Warriors have to play the Wave in Miami, and revenge will definitely be a factor for the home team."

"That's right. Washington came from behind to beat Miami, 31-28, earlier this year."

Andre nodded. "This one's my lock of the day. Miami by fourteen."

"Andre, what's been the biggest surprise to you this year?"

"Well, two things. Cincinnati was the second-worst team in the league last year, but the GoldStars are rolling toward a first-place finish. Then there's the collapse of the New York Comets, who sleep with the fishes at the bottom of their division."

Dave Krause turned down the sound on his television in the visiting owner's box at Wave Stadium, not wanting to hear any more.

"Daddy?" Kim asked him. "Did that man really say 'sleep with the fishes,' or was I hearing things?"

"I'm afraid he did."

"I thought they only said things like that in gangster movies."

"Yeah, well, I think Andre believes that sort of thing. Say, how are your mom and Pinello getting along?"

"Oh, that's over. He moved out yesterday."

"Really?"

"Yeah, he said he had something to do in New Orleans, and I think he just got tired of ..."

"I had a feeling that wouldn't last very long."

"Is that why you never said anything to mom?"

"Hey, Kim. Your mom's a grownup. I don't have any right to tell her what to do. I'm just sorry you had to live with the creep."

"I didn't mind. It actually got to be fun after a while."

"Fun?"

Kim smiled. "Well, he was acting like such a big shot, so I started asking him for a lot of stuff ... a TV for my room, some new clothes, a VCR ..."

"You didn't let him have a moment's peace, did you?"

Kim smiled slyly. "Look, daddy. The game's about to start."

The Warriors, contrary to what Andre O'Connor and other pundits had said, were more than ready for Miami. Ben Kennedy had practiced the team hard, and had spent hour after hour reviewing film.

He had designed a game plan that took good advantage of what few weaknesses the Wave had. When the Warriors took the field, they were fired up, certain they could hold their own.

Of course, Miami was equally well-prepared and much more talented. Washington managed to score the first touchdown of the day, but after that, the game was all Miami.

As the game clock slowly ticked away the final moments of the fourth period with Miami ahead, 24-7, Jimmy Gardner stood on the sideline and kicked at the turf.

"We are doing the best we can, Mr. Gardner," Kennedy said. "I don't think I could have asked any more from this team."

"I know, Coach. I just don't like losing. Never have. Especially when we're getting killed by the refs like this."

"Do not blame our defeat on the officiating, Mr. Gardner. Miami is a far superior team."

Gardner looked at the coach with amazement. "Don't you ever get mad at all of this?"

"Of course I get mad. There are some nights I cannot sleep at all, I am so angry. I lay awake, grinding my teeth so loud it awakens my wife. But I have learned, with God's help, to control my temper, to channel my anger into more productive emotions. I might even say ... that it has made me a better coach."

Gardner didn't say anything, but he smiled.

"You see, Mr. Gardner, what good would it do for me to vent my anger? It would be nothing but an inexcusable expenditure of energy, and at this point in the season we should be conserving our energies as much as possible."

Kennedy let Gardner think about that one for a moment and then added, "If I do lose my temper, you had better hope you are not the target of it."

The coach turned away and gazed at the scoreboard. Gardner stared at him for a moment. He decided he was not looking forward to the day the Iron Irishman did lose his temper.

68

The call had taken Stan Pinello by surprise. Pinello had been in his office, tying up loose ends, confident that the season was over and his job was done. He was thinking about his upcoming two-week vacation in Bermuda when the call came from the commissioner's office ordering him to report to Ray Martini in Chicago.

When he arrived, he was more than a little surprised to find the commissioner waiting with Martini in his Daley Stadium office.

"Sit down, Pinello," Martini said without even the charade of amenities.

"Pinello, I wanted to bring you here to Ray's office because I wanted your help for the game," the commissioner said.

Pinello nodded. "Whatever I can do, Commissioner ..."

"I wanted you to participate because I want you to see how Ray does things. I think it would be beneficial to your future in the Association."

"But, Commissioner ..."

"Stan," he said, his tone softening somewhat. "Don't take this as a reprimand, or as some sort of punishment. The only purpose of this is to help you grow as a league liaison."

"But ..."

"After all, because of some of the mistakes made in Washington this year, we have lost our entire margin of error within the System. If the Warriors were to beat Chicago this weekend ..."

Martini interrupted. "Never happen, Commissioner."

"I know, Ray," the commissioner said, smiling. "With you in charge, I have no fear at all of that happening. But if it did, the Warriors would be in the playoffs and the Trojans would not. You are aware of that, aren't you, Stan?"

Pinello nodded.

"The Trojans were supposed to be closing out their schedule against a team with a record of three and ten. Instead, they are playing a team that is eight and five. Where should we place the blame for that, Pinello?"

"Commissioner, it's not my fault! We had equipment failures! We had uncooperative referees! And when they beat Boston ..."

The commissioner raised his hand. "Save it, Pinello. That is all in the past now. With the Warriors' fate in the hands of Ray Martini, their season is all but over."

Pinello sat and said nothing.

"I want you to watch this man. He is a complete professional. He has been in control this entire season, something, I'm afraid, that cannot be said for you. That's why I wanted you here this week, to see how a pro works. Every single game involving Chicago has gone precisely according to plan."

Pinello gritted his teeth. "Yes, sir."

In Washington, the coaches arrived early for one final day of preparation for the final game of the season. Roland Keene had been at Ben Kennedy's side since his college days. In his freshman season at Rayford College, he had tried out for the team only to be beaten by larger, stronger players.

He wanted so much to be part of the team that he volunteered to work as one of the team managers. The next year he didn't bother trying out, he just showed up for the manager's job and was given a clipboard.

Keene had been with Kennedy ever since, first as a graduate assistant and then as a paid assistant coach, a position he had held with every team the Irishman had coached. He was well aware of his talents, and knew that he had neither the temperament or the flair for strategy necessary to be a head coach.

Every time Kennedy had been hired, fired or had resigned, Keene had followed suit, happy to be working for the man he most admired in the world.

On this particular Wednesday, he was copying plays to be added to the game plan for the Chicago game when he heard a strange noise coming from the locker room down the hall.

Keene went to investigate, and the sound seemed more and more ghastly the closer he got. At first he thought it was one of the players pulling a practical joke, but then he had a horrible thought.

What if a wild animal had crept into the locker room unnoticed and then somehow had injured itself?

Keene turned the corner and found the source of the noise. The Adonis brothers were curled up on the floor, sound asleep and snoring softly. Keene awakened them carefully, got them breakfast and drove them downtown to meet with two ecstatic general managers.

"You slept on the floor all night?" Dave asked them.

Alphonse and Romeo nodded.

"Why?"

"We didn't have anywhere else to go," Romeo said.

"Why didn't you get a motel room?" Herb asked.

"No money," Alphonse said.

"How'd you get into the locker room?" Dave asked.

"Through the back gate."

"The gate? But the gate is locked at night ..."

"It is?"

Dave made a mental note to have the back gate repaired. "So you just came in and slept in the locker room?"

"That's right, Mr. Krause."

"We wanted to be here in time for practice."

"You wanted ... does that mean you're here to play football?"

"Hey, Dave," Herb said. "I hardly think they're here to reminisce over old times."

"Yeah. We want to play football. Are you going to let us play football?"

"Hold on a minute," Dave said. "What about Romano?"

"What about him?"

"I mean, what about your contract with him?"

Both Adonis brothers answered at once. "We just want to play football."

"He wouldn't let us play football."

"That's because the two of you had a contract with him," Dave said patiently. "You had to wrestle for him."

Romeo and Alphonse were not amused. They stood up together and stared down at Dave. "We want to play football."

"Uh, who am I ... Look, we want ... Damn it, guys, we've still got to do something about that contract or you can't play!"

Alphonse growled deep in his throat.

"Contract?"

"The piece of paper you signed," Herb said.

"Oh, that. That doesn't count anymore."

Dave was seriously perplexed, but he couldn't remember a time when dealing with the Adonises hadn't perplexed him.

"We told Mr. Romano we didn't want to wrestle anymore."

"We told him we wanted to play football."

Dave tried to keep his patience. "And what exactly did he say when you told him that?"

Alphonse shrugged. "He said no."

"He said we had to wrestle."

"But we didn't want to wrestle ..."

"I know," Dave interrupted. "What did you do then?"

"We changed his mind."

That stopped Dave cold. "You changed his mind?"

"We changed his mind."

"And how did you do that?"

"What do you mean, Mr. Krause?"

"Did you change Mr. Romano's minds the same way you change quarterbacks' minds?"

"About throwing passes?"

"Right."

"Well, sort of."

Dave swallowed hard. "Now, Alphonse, Romeo, I want you both to think real, real hard. All right?"

"Sure!"

"Is this a game, Mr. Krause?"

"Sort of. When you finished changing Mr. Romano's mind, was he still breathing?"

"Yes."

"Could he still walk?"

"Yes."

"Could he still talk?"

"He didn't talk much."

"Did you hit him?"

"Oh, no," Alphonse said. "Our daddy told us never to hit men who were that little."

"Good," Dave said. "What did you do?"

"We just told him we didn't want to wrestle. And then ..."

"Then?"

"Then we broke the door."

"You ... broke ... the ... door? How did you do that?"

"It was easy. We pulled the door off the, uh ..."

"Hinges?"

"Right. Hinges. And then we broke it into pieces."

"Little pieces."

"Tiny little pieces."

"And right after that, he tore up our contract into pieces."

"Little pieces."

"Tiny little pieces."

"Then he told us to go away and leave him alone. We did, but we made him say 'please' first."

"That's the magic word."

"Boys, have you got the pieces of your contract with you now?"

"Sure."

"Let me see them."

Romeo pulled several scraps of paper out of his pants pocket and put them on the desk. "Here they are. I can put them back together, if you want ..."

Dave shook his head. He could see that all the important parts were there.

"Do we win the prize?"

"You bet. You get to play football."

It was just what the Adonis brothers wanted to hear. They started clapping their hands and hopping up and down with joy. Dave realized he had better check one more thing.

"Uh, boys, could you wait in the outer office for a minute?"

"Sure, Mr. Krause."

As soon as the Adonises were out of his office, he dialed Carmine Romano's number in Wheeling. "Mr. Romano ..."

"I don't want to talk to you!" the man practically screeched.

"Mr. Romano, there's no need ..."

"I don't want anything to do with them! You can have them!" Romano was screaming so loud Dave had to pull the receiver away from his ear. "Those people are animals! Did they tell you what they did to my office?"

"Well, they said ..."

"They broke my door! It's all over the place ..."

"We'll be glad to give you some sort of compensation ..."

"No! No! No way! Just keep those animals the hell away from me!"

"If you want them in the off-season ..."

"Not a chance! Let some other fool handle them. I'm sticking with actors."

With that, the phone went dead.

Dave jumped up and shouted with joy as Herb looked at him quizzically. "We've got our defense back, Herb! We've got our defense back!"

69

By Sunday, the defense was back at full strength, and Dave and Herb hoped it would be enough to overcome the team's offensive problems. When they and Roy arrived at Daley Stadium Sunday morning, they were trying hard to keep calm. They knew that a victory would put them into the playoffs and a loss would end their season.

"Boy, you really get a great view from this box!"

"Dad, you say that every time we get to one of these places. You haven't been in a box you haven't liked yet!"

"So? They're all great, do you mind?"

"Hey," Dave said. "We have had a great time, haven't we?"

"Dave, you're talking like the season's over," Roy said.

"It might be. We could lose, you know."

"Yeah, but we're not going to! We're going to whip these Trojans and then get into the playoffs and ..."

"Say, dad, isn't that Coach Kennedy down there on the field?"

By eleven thirty, half an hour before the scheduled starting time of most of the games played in the Central Time Zone, the stadium was nearly full.

The television crews were making their final preparations and the business people who leased most of the luxury boxes were already halfway through their buffets.

Dave felt a tap on his shoulder and turned around to see a large man hovering over him.

"Excuse me, are you Herb Rojas?"

"Not quite, but close. I'm Dave Krause. Herb is over there."

"Hello, I'm Duncan Charles. I own the Trojans."

"Nice to meet you, Mr. Charles."

"It's Duncan. Everybody calls me Duncan. My father was Mr. Charles."

"Well, Duncan, it's good to meet you."

"You too. You know, with all of the damage you've done in the Association this year, I was expecting some sort of sleazy individual. But you guys, why, you look just like normal people."

"Thanks, I think."

"There you are, kid. Jesus, don't walk away like that!"

"Sorry, Ray. I just thought I'd come over and meet those infamous guys from Washington ... Dave Krause, this is Ray Martini, our league liaison and one heck of a guy."

"Good to meet you, Mr. Martini."

"Yeah, thanks ... Look, kid, I've told you not to wander off like that."

"I'm sorry, Ray, but we always introduce ourselves before the games ..."

"You'll introduce yourself when I tell ... Look, Krause," he said to Dave. "We've got to be going. Nice to meet you."

"Maybe we'll see each other after the game."

"Yeah, sure," Martini said as he led Duncan away by the elbow. For the first time all season, Dave was thankful that all he had to contend with was Stan Pinello, who irritating as he might be, at least did not lead him around like a small pet.

The game started, as all NAFA games did, at five minutes past the hour. Ray Martini, with Pinello looking on, signaled to the head linesman to signal for the kickoff.

As everyone expected, the game seemed exactly even at first. The two teams were grinding each other into the artificial surface, with neither giving an inch. The first quarter was scoreless and without penalties. It was finished in an astonishing twenty minutes.

The Trojans scored first, early in the second quarter, driving into field goal range and kicking a forty-yarder. That seemed to spark the Washington offense, which finally started moving the ball.

The biggest difference was the play of Willis Waller. He seemed to have adjusted well to his new role as the Warriors' prime running back, playing with a grim determination. He got two or three yards on his initial burst each time and then added two or three more after being hit.

Reese, who was on crutches on the sidelines, found his way over to Kennedy. "My boy's getting it done out there, isn't he?"

"I will assume by the nature of your question that you had something to do with Mr. Waller's sudden rejuvenation."

"You bet, Coach. I had a few words with him."

"And you said ..."

"I told him to get off his fat ass and start running, that if he did, there was no son of a bitch in the league that could stop him."

Kennedy thought about it for a moment and then smiled.

"Interesting, Mr. Reese. Vulgar, but effective. Perhaps you should consider coaching."

"Who, me? No way, man. When I'm finished here, I'm on my way back to Hollywood."

Ben Kennedy snorted as he redirected his attention to the field, where Gardner was having more fun than he had ever had in a football game. He felt five years younger. Everything he did seemed to work. His passes, while short, were sharp, and he was handing the ball off with crisp precision.

After a long drive, Gardner handed off to Waller for a short touchdown run that put Washington up, 7-3. The Trojans used the rest of the half in much the same way, but were able only to get a field goal for their efforts.

Steve Schulte, the Chicago kicker, was perfect from thirty yards as time ran out with the Warriors ahead, 7-6.

There was no place Association referees hated working more than Chicago's Daley Stadium, primarily because it brought them into contact with Ray Martini. While most of the NAFA's liaisons were obnoxious bullies who nagged, whined or threatened to get their way, Martini was an entirely different breed.

There was an undercurrent of violence in him that frightened officials. They constantly worked with the fear that he might one day get so worked up that he would actually do physical harm to someone. It was with that sense of apprehension that the referees met with the Chicago liaison at the half.

Martini, for a change, was well under control. "I want to commend you gentlemen on a finely crafted game. Things are going precisely according to plan. Now it is very important to me that everything go perfectly in the second half. Remember, this is an A priority game, and if there was such a thing as an A-plus game, this would be one."

The officials nodded almost in unison.

"So do precisely what I tell you. Do not do a single thing out of the ordinary without checking with me first. Not one penalty, until you get the word from me. Is that understood?"

"Yes, sir."

Martini stood and headed toward the door, but he stopped before exiting. "By the way, if you boys fuck this up, I'm not going to bother taking it to the commissioner. Your asses are mine!"

The third quarter was a replay of the first. Both defenses had stiffened, and while Gardner was moving the ball effectively, he couldn't get close enough for Blaylott to attempt a field goal. The Warriors' defense was every bit as determined, and the quarter ended without any scoring.

Martini turned to Stan Pinello as the teams switched sides to begin the fourth quarter. "Now you see, Stan, this is an exciting football game. The crowd's about ready to jump out of its seats."

"But Washington's ahead."

"By one point, but don't worry, Stan. Late in the fourth quarter, the Trojans are going to put together one last-ditch drive, one that's going to win them the whole season ... What the fuck?"

Duncan Charles was pushing his way past the security guards outside the door. "Get the hell out of the way! I own this stupid place!"

He was loaded down with three glasses, a bucket of ice, a bottle of tonic and a half-filled bottle of vodka. From the look of things, it was apparent that the other half of the bottle was inside Duncan.

"Out of my way! Coming through! Remember, buddy, I sign your paycheck!"

"It's all right," Martini told the guard as he pulled Duncan into the booth and pushed him into a chair. "What the fuck do you think you're doing, kid?"

"We're losing, Ray!" Duncan wailed. "We're losing!"

"Aw, I know ..."

"You told me we'd win, so you'd better get off your ass and get my team a score!"

"Sure, kid," Martini said in a soothing voice. "No sweat. Now why don't you high-tail it back to that nice big box of yours and watch the rest of the game."

"No way," Duncan said, shaking his head violently. "No way! I'm going to sit right here and watch. If you've been telling me the truth, I want to watch!"

The officials were waiting for a sign from Martini to start the fourth quarter, and the crowd was becoming restless. "All right, all right. You can stay, but don't move a muscle or I swear I'll flatten you. Understand?"

"Sure, Ray." Duncan held up the bottles he was carrying. "I've got plenty. Brought some extra glasses for you, too. Want a little drinkie?"

"No thanks, kid. Alcohol dulls the senses."

"How about you?" he asked Pinello, who shook his head, grateful for the first and only time all season that he worked with Krause and Rojas and not with this sloppy lush.

Gardner came out throwing in the fourth period, and the Warriors started moving for what might well turn out to be a clinching score, the way the defense was playing.

The Warriors moved inside the Chicago thirty, but suddenly started drawing penalty after penalty. Holding. Illegal motion. Another holding and an illegal procedure left them with third and thirty-two back on their side of midfield.

Gardner called an out pattern to Greenblatt designed to pick up twenty yards and get the Warriors back into field goal range. Desperately trying to prevent a completed pass, the Chicago defender tackled Greenblatt a split second before the ball arrived.

The Warriors screamed in protest when no flag was dropped.

Gardner was up in the official's face before the ball was spotted.

"What the hell do you think that was over there?" he screamed. "Haven't you ever heard of pass interference?"

"Back off, Gardner. The way I saw it, the ball reached your man before the defender."

"Like hell!"

"Play football, Gardner. Unless you want me to throw a flag for delay of game."

Gardner looked over to the sideline, where he saw the coach standing impassively. He cursed and ran off the field as the punting unit came on. Lou Andrews, as calm as usual, kicked a beautiful punt that sailed for the corner. It flew out of bounds before hitting the ground, and the official ruled the ball had carried into the end zone.

The Trojans started from their own twenty and worked their way slowly down the field. Three times they were stopped on third-down plays, but on all three occasions, penalties gave them first downs. They chewed up all but the final two minutes of the game and scored a touchdown to go up, 13-7.

"Hooray!" yelled Duncan Charles, jumping to his feet and almost spilling his drink.

Martini grabbed him and forced him back into his seat.

The kickoff carried into the end zone, and Rusty Price responded with one of his best returns, twisting and weaving his way through the defense all the way to the Chicago thirty-five. A clipping penalty, signaled by Martini, brought it back to the Washington forty.

Gardner called three plays in the huddle. Waller went off tackle for six yards and a screen to Ross yielded five more and a first down just across midfield. A quick out to Ross gained five more yards, and Gardner called a time out with forty-three seconds remaining.

Kennedy gave Gardner two more plays, and they worked well enough to get the Warriors down to the thirty with fifteen seconds to play. Kennedy called a late pass over the middle to Greenblatt, and Gardner was stunned to see his tight end breaking free. He lofted the ball right into Greenblatt's hands as the Chicago defense stood flat-footed.

Greenblatt caught the pass at the ten and took off for the end zone when he heard the whistle blowing the play dead.

"Offensive pass interference. The receiver pushed off to get clear."

The official found himself swarmed under by the entire Washington offensive unit. Gardner and Greenblatt were shouting at the top of their lungs, joined soon after by Ross and Gullotta. In the confusion, no one paid any attention to Benjamin Kennedy.

The coach had thrown his clipboard down in disgust and had marched up and down the sideline. Suddenly he stormed onto the field.

His intention at first was just to keep his players from getting thrown out of the game. With every step he took, though, he became angrier and angrier. He thought of all the calls that had been made that day, and all the calls that had been made all season.

By the time he reached the referee, he was beyond speech.

"What the ..." The official said as the coach pushed his players out of the way. "Get the hell off the field, Kennedy, or ..."

He never finished the sentence. Kennedy broke his jaw with one punch.

It was ten minutes before the officials were able to get play started again. Kennedy was ejected, the referee was carried off the field and the Warriors were penalized twenty-five yards -- ten for pass interference and fifteen for unsportsmanlike conduct.

It was first down and forever, with seven seconds left, when Gardner reformed the huddle. He hadn't called a play all season, but since the coach hadn't left instructions, he knew what he had to do.

"Hail Mary. Left. With one change." Gardner looked at Ross. "They know I can't throw it farther than thirty yards, so we'll set everything up at the twenty-five. Then you sneak away and break for the end zone."

He gulped and looked at his linemen. "Give me some time, guys."

"But, Jimmy ..."

"Shut the fuck up, Rossie. Just do what I fucking tell you."

In the other huddle, All-Association middle linebacker Eddie Carruthers was calling signals.

"This is it," he said. "They might have time for two more plays, but probably not. Just keep them in front of you, but remember, Gardner can't throw it any farther than thirty yards, so don't get caught too far downfield."

Every one of the one hundred thousand fans in Daley Stadium was standing when Gardner stepped up to the line, crouched behind his center and called for the snap. He took it and dropped back into the pocket.

The Trojans dropped eight men back into pass coverage, and the Warriors' offensive line easily picked up the three rushers.

Greenblatt, Gullotta and Waller broke to the left to set up for the traditional Hail Mary tip play. They set up at the twenty-five and seven defenders were in the vicinity.

Only the free safety followed Ross as he sneaked downfield.

Gardner faked to the left, drawing the coverage even tighter to his three receivers. Then he looked back to the right, where the defender was forty-five yards away and Ross was five yards behind him.

Fuck it, Gardner thought. Here goes. He reared back with every ounce of strength he had and released the ball. It was a long, spiraling pass that floated gracefully down the field.

The lone defender realized the ball was heading over his head and made a desperate attempt to recover.

In the liaison's box, Duncan Charles leaped to his feet and fell forward.

"NO!" he shouted, knocking his drink off the arm of his chair and onto the console in front of Martini. There was a sizzling sound, a puff of smoke and then the machine went dead as the ball fell just past the outstretched fingers of the defender into Tony Ross' arms.

Ross was one step from the goal line, and he lunged across it as the stadium clock ticked down to triple zero. The head linesman waited for word from Martini, and when none was forthcoming, he signaled the touchdown.

Forty-two Warriors crowded around Ross, wrestling him to the ground and pummeling him. The only Washington player who wasn't part of the celebration was Jimmy Gardner.

Ross noticed first. He spiked the ball and raced upfield to his friend, followed closely by the trainer.

"Well, Tony," Gardner said as he climbed to his feet. "I guess you caught the damn thing."

"Yep, you underthrew me a little, but I adjusted perfectly. Is it the arm?"

Gardner winced. "I think that one did me in. Feels like I've got spaghetti hanging from my shoulder."

In the booth, Ray Martini was pounding furiously on his console, trying in vain to beat it into working condition. Pinello had started running toward the field as soon as he realized what had happened, but both their efforts were in vain.

Norm Blaylott, as if he had been born to the moment, confidently kicked the ball through the uprights for the extra point that gave Washington a 14-13 victory and a berth in the NAFA playoffs.

Duncan Charles and Ray Martini sat in stunned silence and watched the Warriors celebrate on the field. Finally Duncan stood and stared drunkenly at Martini.

"You lied, Ray."

Duncan Charles turned with exaggerated dignity and walked out of the box.

70

Fred Reynolds' column, the Washington Tribune, December 14:

"If two gentlemen named Krause and Rojas are serving up crow these days, I'm ready to eat.

"I'll be the first to admit that no one was more shocked than I when the Washington Warriors won their first six games this year. And no one was more surprised when their late-season slump didn't become a total collapse.

"And I've got to admit to total astonishment that the Warriors beat a Chicago team that was markedly superior on paper.

"I'll make you a promise. Nothing the Warriors do the rest of this year is going to surprise me.

"Granted, they aren't going to have an easy time of it in Houston. The Lonestars aren't on the same level as Philadelphia or Miami, but they were strong enough to lead their division all year long.

"With Woody Rollins at quarterback, the Lonestars have an extremely potent attack. They led the league in scoring for the third straight year, so the Washington defense will be in for a major challenge.

"Of course, Houston's defense is every bit as bad as its offense is good. The Warriors didn't have much trouble moving the ball in their 28-26 victory at the Hoove in October. That was the win that gave the Warriors a 6-0 record.

"That game showed us one thing -- this is a team the Warriors can beat, if they can answer two questions.

"First, of course, is the unfilled coaching position. There is no way the NAFA will ever allow Benjamin Kennedy back on the field after the coach viciously assaulted an official. Our boys need a coach and they need one fast.

"Second, and far more pressing, is the need for a quarterback. Brian Rider has missed almost the entire season with an injury, so the only problem here is what his timing will be like. I think he'll be fine, and the Warriors should be able to adjust easily to a man who is actually mobile and can throw the long ball.

"It won't be easy. The fact that the game is in Houston gives the Lonestars an edge, but the Warriors have a good shot at victory. And should they win, they likely will be facing Miami at Wave Stadium, where the Wave is practically unbeatable.

"Stay tuned."

They knew it would be the most hectic week of their lives, but Dave felt he and Herb should take time out to make the trip to Oxon Hill. When they arrived, Ben Kennedy was packing his things into a cardboard box.

"He suspended you," Dave said.

"I am well aware of that, Mr. Krause. I received a telegram last night."

"They didn't say officially, but the word I get is that you'll never be allowed back in the NAFA."

"You'll be lucky if they sell you a ticket," Herb said.

"There's really no precedent. No one's ever punched an official before."

"Except for Bubblegut, and he got a year in prison."

"I am sorry I did it. It was a stupid, futile act."

"Hey," Herb said. "At least you broke the guy's jaw."

Kennedy sighed. "I have spent years in prayer, trying to control my temper. Now I have to start all over again."

"Coach, what will you do now?"

"Mr. Krause, I do not have the slightest idea. I will probably relax for a little while. Beyond that, I do not know. Perhaps there is a college or high school somewhere that would be interested in my services."

Herb shook his head.

"Why the long face, Mr. Rojas? Your team is in the playoffs. Surely you cannot be mourning the end of an old man's career."

"But ..."

"It was inevitable, and quite frankly, I have lost much of my desire to coach in this league. The game at this level has become entertainment more than sport, with petulant players and petulant owners fighting over the division of billions of dollars."

"But you love the game! I always thought you lived, ate and slept football."

Kennedy shook his head. "I would be a sad, sad example of a man if that were so."

Herb and Dave could think of nothing else to say. "One question," Kennedy asked. "If you don't mind, I'd like to know who'll be replacing me."

"Well, Keene already resigned ..."

"I expected that. Mr. Keene, I am afraid, is a man blinded by loyalty. I have been taking advantage of that loyalty for many years, and I suppose I will continue to do so."

"... and none of the other assistants wanted the job."

"All are men who specialize in certain areas. I selected them for their expertise, not their ambition."

"We needed someone familiar with your offense," Dave said. "So we couldn't go outside for a coach."

"That seems reasonable."

"And we needed someone who could call plays," Herb added.

Kennedy thought he knew what was coming. "Yes?"

"So we offered the job to Jimmy Gardner," Dave said.

Kennedy closed his eyes, looking for all the world like a man in pain.

"Can we assume by your reaction that you don't approve?" Herb asked.

"My approval is not necessary."

"And anyway, the only other person who volunteered for the job was my father."

"Please, Mr. Rojas, not even in jest!"

"Well," Dave said, extending his hand. "Thank you, Coach. You did one hell of a job."

"Yes, I did." He did not accept the extended hand. "I will instruct my staff to assist Mr. Gardner in whatever way possible."

He turned to leave and then stopped. "Gentlemen, one final word of advice.”

“Go ahead,” Herb said.

“You have had your fun. Now get out and leave the game to men who know what they are doing.”

“Thanks loads, Coach. We’ll miss you, too.”

71

The visitors' locker room in Houston was silent as the Warriors waited to take the field for their first-round playoff game with the Lonestars. The players sat and watched as Jimmy Gardner, his arm in a sling, paced in front of a chalkboard at the end of the room.

Gardner looked at the faces of his former teammates and tried in vain to think of something inspirational to say to them.

"Aw, shit, let's go play some football."

With an emotional roar, the Warriors stormed out of the locker room, followed closely by Gardner, Roxy Reese and the assistant coaches.

Actually, it had been an easier week than Gardner had expected. The staff had done the necessary scouting, and had all but developed the game plan. The assistants had conducted practice and run the meetings. Mostly, Gardner just sat and watched. He worked some with Brian Rider, but Rider was a four-year veteran who knew what he was doing.

As Gardner took his place on the sideline, one of the assistants handed him a clipboard with the offensive game plan. Gardner looked down at it and a shiver of fear ran down his spine.

He didn't recognize any of the plays.

He knew it was just nerves.

After all, he had been an NAFA quarterback for years, and as he had once told Ross, there wasn't a single thing in the world that frightened him.

Except coaching.

He tried to regain his composure, but he couldn't. He signaled to Rider to come over and join him.

"Brian," he said, draping an arm across his quarterback's shoulders. "I've always thought a quarterback should call his own plays. I always thought the man on the field had the best feel for the game, and that he needed to call plays to be a true leader. Do you know what I mean?"

"Sure, Jimmy."

"I always wanted to call the plays when I was out there, but Kennedy wouldn't let me ..."

"Hey, say no more, Jimmy."

"So you understand?"

"Sure. You want to call the plays now, and I couldn't agree more."

"Huh?"

"Jimmy, I can't call plays. I've never once called plays, even back in junior high. My coach always called the plays for me, so of course I want you to ..."

"Thanks, Brian. I appreciate that."

Rider smiled and walked away, and Gardner could feel his heart racing. He turned and stumbled over to his offensive assistant.

"Larry," he said. "I spent the whole season letting the coach call the plays, so I'm a little out of practice. I'm gonna need your help today."

"I'll do the best I can to help you, Jimmy, but I've never called plays before."

"You what?"

"Nope. Coach Kennedy made all the decisions himself. I never called any of the plays."

"Thanks, Larry."

Now Gardner thought he was having a stroke. He walked over and sat on the bench for as long as he could, hoping the Warriors would lose the coin toss to give him more time to gather himself.

They did, and in the visiting owner's box, Roy Rojas reacted the same way he had eight other times.

"It's an omen!"

This time it was. The Lonestars rolled down the field, with Woody Rollins brilliantly mixing his plays, and scored a touchdown after only four minutes.

As the kick-return team took the field, Gardner huddled with Rider and his offensive assistant.

"I'd like to establish the run," he said. "Larry, give me a couple of running plays."

"That depends on where we get the ball, Jimmy, but if you want my opinion, we should be passing against this defense."

"Yeah, we'll get to that. But let's show off the run first."

Larry Jackman pointed out a couple of runs, and Rider noted them.

"That all, Jimmy?" the quarterback asked.

"Get out there."

The two running plays lost five yards, and the third call -- a draw to Willis Waller -- lost three more. Andrews punted the ball away and Gardner went back to studying his clipboard.

As Houston started another drive from its own thirty-four, Tony Ross confronted Gardner.

"Jimmy, what the hell kind of plays are you calling!? Don't you remember anything? We've got to pass to beat this team!"

"What's the matter?" Gardner snapped. "Mad because I didn't call anything to you?"

"What?'

"We've got the whole damn game to throw to you, Rossie! Just keep your pants on!"

Gardner went back to studying his clipboard and Ross gave him a disgusted look and walked away.

The Lonestars scored twice more before halftime and led, 21-0, at intermission. It was only a prelude to a horrible second half. Every time Gardner did manage to call a successful play, the league liaison had the Warriors called for a penalty, and the Washington defense was spending far too much time on the field.

Scott Trent pulled up lame chasing a wide-open receiver on Houston's fourth touchdown, and Romeo Adonis pulled a hamstring trying to get to Rollins on a bootleg that turned into the fifth score.

By the fourth quarter, the Warriors were beyond hope. The league liaison was still pouring it on, though. He had been given strict instructions not to let up on the Warriors until the final gun, and he was following those instructions to the letter.

An interception return with eight seconds remaining was the seventh and final touchdown for the Lonestars, who won the game by a 49-0 margin to advance to the second round of the playoffs.

The Warriors' season was history, and the Washington contingent in the upper boxes was in shock. They had spent the game in silence, watching their team get massacred and making more and more frequent trips to the well-stocked bar.

None of them discussed the game until the flight from Houston was half an hour from landing at Washington's Dulles Airport. Roy Rojas was the one who finally broke the silence. "All right, so we lost. Big deal!"

"Huh?" Herb asked.

"Think about it. How many people thought we'd ever accomplish this much? Damn! The Warriors made the playoffs for the first time in thirty-one years!"

"Yeah," Dave said. "And lost the second most lopsided game in playoff history."

"So what?"

"Come on, dad. Cut the pep talk."

"No, I won't stop, Herb! You listen to me. Think about all the stuff you went through! Signing players no one else wanted, hiring a coach who knew his ass from a hole in the ground ..."

"I assume you're talking about Ben Kennedy and not Jimmy Gardner," Dave said drily.

"Gardner wasn't that bad."

"Come on, Roy. He didn't even watch the game, he was so busy reading his clipboard!"

"Yeah, dad. The man went for it on fourth and twelve."

Roy sighed an exasperated sigh. "You guys ..."

"Wait a minute, Herb. Your dad might have a point. I don't think we have anything to be ashamed of ..."

"We didn't win."

"So what? Eight teams go into the playoffs and four of them lose in the first round."

"Yeah," Roy chimed in. "And you know that old saying -- winning isn't everything."

"Shut up, dad."

"Come on, Herb, lay off the old man ..."

"Dave, you haven't had to listen to this rah-rah stuff all your life, like I have."

"Seems to me it was some of this rah-rah stuff that got us involved in this thing in the first place. I remember someone making a pretty emotional pitch last January."

"It seemed like a good idea at the time ..."

"It was, too!" Roy said. "Look what you managed to do!"

"Hey, dad, give me a break. A billion Chinese couldn't give a shit about what we did."

"I think you'll be surprised, son."

"Oh, really?"

"Well, not about the Chinese. I don't think they follow football, but I'll bet there'll be a crowd at the airport waiting to welcome the team home."

"Yeah, with tar and feathers."

"No way. They'll be there to thank us for giving the town a winner for once. I'll bet when we get to Dulles, there'll be a hundred thousand people with signs and banners, wanting to thank us for an exciting season."

Dave shrugged. "Anyway, Herb, it's not over yet. We've still got those two all-expense-paid weeks in New Orleans, compliments of the North American Football Association."

That settled Herb down a little. He had been looking forward to the Championship Bowl all year, whether or not the Warriors were involved. He had never been to a Championship Bowl, and the idea of the commissioner paying for his two-week vacation was enough to bring a smile to his face.

And while Roy Rojas had overestimated the crowd by a factor of twenty, there were about five thousand fans waiting to welcome the Warriors home.

Herb and Dave picked up their luggage and went straight to Cliches, where they spent the remainder of what had turned into a very long day consuming large quantities of alcoholic beverages. By the time Herb finally poured Dave into a taxi, the two of them were having trouble remembering their own names, let alone those of Jimmy Gardner, Tony Ross or the rest of the Washington Warriors.

NORTH AMERICAN FOOTBALL ASSOCIATION
League Playoffs

ROUND ONE

Miami Wave	40	San Francisco Kings	17
Houston Lonestars	49	Washington Warriors	0
Philadelphia Bulldogs	20	St. Louis Archers	3
Cincinnati GoldStars	16	Jacksonville Stingers	14

ROUND TWO

Miami Wave	21	Houston Lonestars	20
Philadelphia Bulldogs	31	Cincinnati GoldStars	7

ROUND THREE

The Championship Bowl At NAFA Stadium

New Orleans, Louisiana

Miami Wave vs. Philadelphia Bulldogs

72

After the merger with the United Football League had been consummated, the Association had gone shopping for a permanent home, where both the offices and a stadium for the Championship Bowl would be located.

It was decided early in the process that no city already represented by an NAFA franchise would be allowed to submit a bid. In addition, the commissioner made it clear that the city selected would never be considered for an expansion franchise.

Still, nearly every major city in the United States and Canada that didn't already have a franchise submitted a bid, as did Mexico City, Tokyo, Rio de Janeiro and Kingston, Jamaica.

The choices had finally been narrowed to Tampa, San Antonio and New Orleans, although the commissioner was fascinated by the thought of playing the Championship Bowl in Jamaica.

New Orleans won the competition by offering to build a one hundred thousand seat stadium with a retractable dome on city land, with a state-of-the-art hotel, shopping mall and office complex adjacent to it. The deal was clinched when the mayor agreed to sell the entire project to the NAFA for one hundred dollars.

His political opponents were apoplectic   at the thought of a hundred million dollar project being given away like that, but they were silenced by the revenues raised by the first Championship Bowl. It brought ten million dollars into the city's economy, a figure that increased with each and every year.

"Champ Bowl Week," as it had grown to be called, was a festival that rivaled and sometimes even surpassed Mardi Gras. People from the opposing teams' cities started arriving in town as early as a week ahead of time, and they were always ready to spend lots of money.

Championship Bowl tickets started at one thousand dollars each, for the upper two rows of the stadium. The prices increased as the seats got closer to the field, with the most expensive ones selling for fifty thousand dollars.

The luxury suites, most of which were leased by corporations when the stadium was built, went for one million dollars a year. They were equipped with closed-circuit television, full kitchens and bars and complete valet service.

The game always sold out months in advance. It had become the ultimate status symbol to possess tickets to the Championship Bowl. In years when the matchup was particularly attractive, scalpers had been known to get ten to fifteen times face value on the day of the game. And while the Association officially disapproved of ticket scalping, the commissioner took secret pride in the amount of money people were willing to pay to see the league's showcase game.

The Association was almost legendary in its generosity to franchise operators during Championship Bowl week. Teams were given twenty tickets and twenty hotel rooms to reward valued staff members, and the Association paid to transport everyone to New Orleans for the two weeks prior to the game.

Dave, Herb and Roy were not about to miss their chance. They endured the week of the final playoff games, thinking of little else than what they would be doing in New Orleans. Dave was planning to spend as much time as he could with Tracey Cagney, whose team would be playing, while

Roy had already made several dinner dates with Sally Adler.

Herb had planned to take Bridget with him, but he had returned from Houston to find her gone.

"She just quit, Mr. Rojas," one of the other secretaries said.

"Did she say why?"

The secretary shook her head. "She got some phone calls, and then she spent a lot of time at the copy machine. She told me to tell you goodbye."

He thought about finding someone else to take with him, but he realized that he really liked Bridget and decided to go alone.

There was one meeting to attend, ten days before the game. It was strictly a formality, a way to legitimize the expense of bringing so many employees to New Orleans. Most of the important decisions would be made at the Winter Meetings four weeks after the game.

An Association limo picked up the Washington contingent at the airport, and as it approached the complex, Dave, Roy and Herb all took a deep breath at their first glimpse of NAFA Stadium.

"Awesome, isn't it?" Herb asked.

"It makes you proud to be an American," Roy said, tears in his eyes.

"What's on the itinerary, Dave?"

Krause studied the schedule the limo driver had given them. "Well, there's a big cocktail party -- black tie -- at the hotel tonight, and then there's nothing to do after that until the meeting on Thursday."

"The hell with that," Herb said. "Let's blow it off and hit the town!"

"Say, guys. I might pass on tonight."

"Don't tell me you're tired, dad?!"

"Hell, no. It's just that ... I've got a date with Sally."

"No problem, Roy."

"So, Dave, it's just you and me, then."

"Actually, Herb, I was hoping to get together with Tracey."

"Great," Herb said sarcastically. "We'll stick around until the Dragon Lady tells you to take a flying leap. Then we'll hit the town together."

The Operators Party was the unofficial opening of the annual Championship Bowl festivities. It was restricted to invited guests. There had never been a reporter present, but there had been rumors, never confirmed, that the customary decorum associated with the management of the NAFA was dispensed with early.

The evening started with a sumptuous feast. Dave and Herb were handed glasses of Dom Perignon when they entered the ballroom, and they looked around with awe at their surroundings. The table appeared to be a mile long, covered with a buffet that would rival any state banquet in any country in the world.

There was roast duck and suckling pig, pheasant, caviar and escargot. There were lobsters and steaks, and huge roast beefs being carved by waiters. There was a dessert table dominated by a huge ice sculpture of the Championship Bowl Trophy. Beautiful hostesses in evening gowns were serving food and drink.

Dave and Herb had never seen so much wealth. Every finger seemed to boast a diamond, every neck a pendant or necklace of gold. All the women seemed to be wearing minks or sables.

"Where's the action?" Herb asked. "Where are the dancing girls, the mad, passionate women ready to make love on table tops?"

"Uh, maybe later," Dave said. "Do you see Tracey anywhere?"

"No. Maybe she won't be here."

"You heard what they said. Attendance here is *de rigeur*. I've heard they take your franchise away if you don't show up."

"Well, well, well! Look who's here!"

Duncan Charles obviously had been imbibing lots of the free champagne. "Dave Rojas, right?"

"Close enough," Herb said. "Herb Rojas."

"And Dave Krause," Dave said, extending his hand.

"How could I forget? How the hell could I forget? You're the guys who stole the Championship Bowl from me!"

"Well," Dave said, smiling. "I think our team had something to do with it."

"They had nothing to do with it!" Duncan said drunkenly.

"Well, if you say so ... Listen, Duncan, it's been a thrill seeing you, but ..."

"Hey, no way! You're staying right here! You stole my championship, the least you can do is have a drink with me!"

Duncan grabbed two glasses of champagne off a tray carried by a passing waiter.

Dave was searching the room for Tracey Cagney, so he paid only the smallest amount of attention to Duncan, leaving Herb to handle the conversation.

"Anyway, Duncan, we didn't steal it from you. You don't see our team here."

"They led me on the whole time! The whole damn time!"

"Led you on?"

Dave finally saw Tracey coming into the room. He waved to her. She seemed surprised to see him at first, but then she waved back.

"They told me it was gonna be mine. They lied to me!"

"Lied to you?"

"Yeah, so I wouldn't screw up their precious System!"

Dave was still trying to communicate with Tracey. He mouthed the word "later" to her, only to have her look back at him with a puzzled expression.

"What System?" Herb asked.

"Oh, cute! Act like you don't know about it!"

"I don't!"

Duncan sighed. "You mean they didn't tell you that you were going to the playoffs? They didn't tell you it was all set? They didn't tell you about the System?"

"Should they have?" Herb figured something was going on, and he wanted to make sure Dave was listening, too. "Dave, do you realize what this guy is saying?"

"Do I ... what?"

"Haven't you been listening? Pay attention!"

"I'm sorry. What ..."

"Look, we've got to get out of here. This guy's got one hell of a story ..."

Herb didn't wait for Dave to answer him. He grabbed Duncan by the elbow and led him out of the room. Dave, with a final wave to Tracey, followed.

It was well past midnight when Dave and Herb sat in the hotel's twenty-four hour coffee shop waiting for Fred Reynolds to join them. They had ordered an early breakfast, but neither of them had much of an appetite. Finally their guest entered the room. Herb stood and waved to him.

"Thanks for coming, Fred," Dave said when the reporter reached their table.

Reynolds, all bulk and horn-rimmed glasses, plopped down into an empty chair. He looked terrible.

"This had better be good," he growled. "I was just getting into bed when you guys called."

"It is, Fred," Dave said. "It's the biggest story since Watergate. Bigger, even."

"Then why in the hell don't you call the Post?" Reynolds asked sarcastically. "Woodward and Bernstein can get the band together again."

"Look, Reynolds," Herb said. "We're about to give you the biggest story of your career. Can we have a little cooperation?"

"Fuck cooperation. You two pinheads have been jerking me around all season and now you want cooperation. You finally get the team into the playoffs and then you hire a moron for a coach. Even when you do something right, you fuck it up. You guys could screw up a wet dream."

"Well then, Reynolds, to hell with you and your silly column, and your silly radio show, and ..."

Dave put his hand on Herb's wrist and interrupted him. "Fred, we wanted to talk to you, we wanted to give this to you, because we think you're the best reporter in the country and we think you'll know the best way to handle this."

"All right," Reynolds said with exaggerated dignity. "If you put it that way, I'll listen."

"All right," Dave said. He took a deep breath, but Herb spoke first.

"The season's fixed."

They let it lay there for a moment, watching for a reaction from the portly reporter sitting across the table from them. Reynolds maintained what they assumed was a journalist's impassive manner and said, "Yes? And?"

"That's it," Dave said. "The season's fixed! The whole damn thing from start to finish! They decide who they want in the Championship Bowl each year and they set up the whole season!"

Herb jumped in and picked up the story at that point.

"We just found out about this tonight, and we don't know all the details, but they run some kind of survey before the season and find out who people want to see in the playoffs and Championship Bowl. Then they work out the whole schedule ..."

"They've got a guy in the stands," Dave said. "The league liaison, who controls every game. Am I making sense?"

Reynolds indicated with a casual wave of his hand that they should continue.

"They decide before the game how it's supposed to go," Dave said. "The liaison guy is hooked up to the referees on the field by ..."

"... by radio." Reynolds finished Herb's sentence. "They control the game by having the referees call penalties at certain critical moments. Should I continue?"

Dave and Herb stared dumbstruck at the reporter.

"Gentlemen, you have just described the System, perhaps the worst-kept secret in professional sports."

"You mean you know about it?" Dave asked.

"Everybody knows about it! Oh, the Association thinks it's some big secret. They've sworn everyone to blood oaths not to tell, but it's been common knowledge for years."

"Huh?"

"Do you really think something that big could possibly be kept secret?"

"You mean all the reporters know about it? Sally Adler ..."

"Adler's a bubble-headed broad who wouldn't have a career if it wasn't for spandex, but yes, she knows. We all know."

"Then why haven't you told anybody about it?" Herb asked. "How the hell can you call yourself a journalist when you don't write about this thing?"

"Because we're not stupid, Mr. Rojas."

"What?"

"Come on, gentlemen, do you take us for fools? What's the most popular sport in the country?"

"Football," they chorused.

"You bet your ass. Even in the middle of the winter, when we're supposed to be covering basketball and hockey, you see stories about football on the front page. And when training camps start in July, kiss baseball goodbye. Nobody cares about America's so-called pastime until the World Series."

"All right," Dave said. "So football's popular, but that doesn't explain ..."

Reynolds raised his hand. "Suppose some poor slob did write about the System. What do you think would happen?"

"It'd destroy the Association," Herb said.

"Probably. And if you destroy the Association, you destroy pro football, right?"

"Well, yeah."

Reynolds smiled. "And without pro football, what would there be to write about?"

"What about college football?"

"Boring," Reynolds said. "How many college teams do you know of that have a national following?"

"Well, Notre Dame ... Southern Cal ... Oklahoma ..."

Dave chimed in. "Alabama ... Ohio State ..."

Reynolds shook his head. "Maybe, but let's face it. Outside of the town or the state a college team is in, the rest of the country couldn't give two shits about college football. But you go to the tiniest town in North Dakota and there are people there with their favorite NAFA teams. And all those people read newspapers and watch television, and if you destroy the NAFA ..."

"They stop buying newspapers and watching television," Dave said, beginning to catch on.

"Especially television," Reynolds said. "I'm sure newspapers would continue to exist, but I doubt the sports pages would be so thick without the NAFA. And gentlemen, I am well-paid for what I do. I'm not about to threaten my livelihood by destroying the very thing that supports me, and I seriously doubt any of my colleagues will, either."

"That's just great!" Herb shouted angrily. "You do that! You sit on your fat ass and ignore us, but Dave and I will go out there and get somebody to listen to us!"

Reynolds smiled patronizingly. "No one will believe you."

"What the hell?"

"To begin with," the reporter said with the air of a teacher trying to make a point to a particularly slow student. "The NAFA has done a spectacular job of public relations. Professional football has been promoted as the fairest, most honest, forthright, God-fearing sport ever created. It is run by men who love their wives and children, small dogs and apple pie. And last but certainly not least, they love America."

Herb snorted.

"These are men of character," Reynolds continued. "Men who would not do a dishonest thing is you held guns to their heads. If you were to appear out of nowhere and start telling people about the System, they flat out wouldn't believe you. You will be written off as crackpots who concocted a story to draw attention away from your own ineptitude."

Reynolds stared at Dave and Herb, who were once again speechless. "And so, gentlemen, I really must be getting to bed. If you come up with a real news story, such as your resignation, feel free to call me."

73

"Good afternoon, Mr. Krause, Mr. Rojas. Please sit down."

They had been expecting an audience with the commissioner. He made a habit of meeting with the operators of every franchise during the two weeks leading up to the Championship Bowl, and they knew their turn would come.

They had thought they would meet solely with the commissioner and one or two assistants, so they were more than a little surprised to find the entire executive committee sitting around a conference table. All of them were staring at the two guests as if they had just discovered them under a rock.

Dave and Herb had decided not to tell Roy about the System, because they knew what it would do to his belief in football. For that same reason, they hadn't told him about their impending meeting with the commissioner.

"Mr. Krause, Mr. Rojas, I'd like to introduce you to the members of the executive committee of the North American Football Association."

The commissioner started with the man on his right and went around the table. "On my immediate right is Dr. Ralph Pierson of the Cincinnati franchise. To his right is Lester Turkel of Los Angeles, Winston Spencer of Toronto, Louis Shoemaker of Minneapolis and Garrison Constantine of Denver. And of course you know our employees, Ray Martini and Stan Pinello."

They nodded as each man was introduced to them. When Pinello was named, Dave grinned.

"Hi, Stan. How's Muriel?"

Pinello glared at him.

"Of course there are normally six members on the committee, but our sixth position has not yet been filled. Perhaps you would like to know something about the duties of the committee ..."

"You take care of the System," Dave said in a matter-of-fact voice.

The commissioner shuddered, and Martini looked at them with total disgust.

"Well," Martini said. "Looks like we're going to have to play hardball with you boys."

"Please, Ray," the commissioner said. "No baseball metaphors!" Then he smiled, regaining his composure. "It appears you two have learned our little secret, so there's no sense in denying anything. Yes, gentlemen, there is a System, and yes, this committee administers it. In normal years, that is an easy task, but this has not been what you would call a normal year."

He stared hard at Dave, who tried to stare back.

"You ... gentlemen ... have made this one of the most trying years of my entire tenure."

"Glad to oblige," Herb quipped, but no one in the room even smiled.

"You have taken our carefully laid plans and thrown them into the trash bin," he said. "We had planned the most exciting season yet, guaranteed to attract the largest audience in history! The upstart Chicago Trojans taking on the mighty Miami Wave! David and Goliath! Egypt and Israel! What a classic matchup that would have been!"

"Sorry," Dave said.

"Of course, Philadelphia and Miami should provide a wonderful game," the commissioner said. "Granted, they are the two best teams in the Association. Still, it is not the game we all wanted to see."

The commissioner took a deep breath and continued.

"Of course, it was not all for naught. A great deal of good will come of this. You have pointed out several weaknesses in the System, and starting next season we will correct all of them."

"What are you going to do?" Herb asked.

"To begin with, games will no longer be ranked according to priority. It was actually a silly practice. Beginning next season, every game will be treated as an A priority game, tightly controlled from start to finish by the Association liaison. That should eliminate the possibility of teams taking us by surprise."

He smiled coldly at Dave.

"We also plan on installing backup communications systems in every stadium. That should eliminate equipment problems, and it was equipment failure ..." He glanced at Pinello. "... that gave the Washington franchise two of its victories."

"Huh?" Herb asked.

"In addition, we will alter the regulations concerning draft rights to players. If a team fails to sign a player it has drafted within six months, he will go into the next year's draft. That should prevent a repeat of the Willis Waller situation."

"Let's face it, boys," Martini said. "You'd never have been able to sign Waller if we'd had that rule this season."

"Oh," the commissioner said. "One more thing. We're eliminating the retired list. From now on, teams wishing to sign retired players will have to acquire them from their last team. And so, gentlemen, as you can plainly see, you have not managed to defeat the System. If anything, you have strengthened it."

"And it got you in the end, didn't it?" Pinello said.

"At Houston?" Herb asked.

"Yes, at Houston. It worked very well, didn't it?"

"I guess so. We lost."

"So what's the deal?" Dave asked. "You brought us in here just to tell us how much harder it'll be for us next season?"

"Not exactly," the commissioner said. "There are certain other events pertaining to your franchise I wanted to make you aware of. In fact, even as we speak, one of my press relations officers is holding a briefing announcing the very things I am telling you now."

Dave and Herb both sat up straight in their chairs.

"Yes," the commissioner said. "It would be to your advantage to listen carefully. To begin with, your friend Duncan Charles has been relieved of his franchise."

"You fired an owner?"

"Franchise operator, Mr. Rojas. There are no owners in the NAFA, which is why we were able to dispose of young Mr. Charles so easily."

"God, you sound like the KGB!"

"Hardly, Mr. Rojas. Duncan Charles was more than adequately compensated for the loss of his franchise. In fact, I believe he received one billion dollars."

Herb gulped.

"Exactly. That should help assuage the pain."

"It was that easy?" Dave asked.

"Yes, it was. He was declared an inefficient operator, relieved of his franchise and replaced on this committee by Mr. Turkel. It was that easy."

"And who gets his franchise?"

"That's none of your business!" Pinello said.

"Mr. Pinello, I am conducting this meeting," the commissioner said coldly. "The Chicago franchise has been sold to a consortium of Japanese investors."

"What about your rule?" Dave asked. "One man, one franchise."

"Rules are made to be broken. The amount of new money our foreign operators bring to the Association will help us build for the twenty-first century." Dave shrugged. "But we still were left with one other problem."

"Us," Herb said.

"Yes, Mr. Rojas. You. What were we to do with the Washington franchise? Despite our best efforts, you managed to overcome nearly every obstacle we put into your path."

"Hey," Herb said. "You can't keep a good man down."

"What obstacles?" Dave asked.

"We were responsible for nearly everything bad that happened to you. Randy Jenkins, Nick Gullotta ... both were achieved through our connection with Earl Spring."

"Spring was your boy?"

"Bought and paid for, Mr. Rojas. Bought and paid for. He is now living, I might add, on an island in Micronesia."

"So Spring found religion?" Dave asked drily.

"Actually, he has bought it. In truth, we bought it for him."

"He sends his love, by the way," Pinello said, smirking.

"So Lippmann was on your payroll, too?" Dave asked.

"Very much so," the commissioner said. "He plays his part rather well, don't you think?"

"Plays his part?"

"Yes. Mr. Lippmann comes across as a very successful man, doesn't he?"

"Comes across?"

"Certainly," the commissioner said. "William Peace Lippmann was born Vincenzo Morelli, in the Little Italy section of New York. He made his bones at the age of fifteen ..."

"You're kidding!" Herb exclaimed. "He was a Mafioso?"

"We helped him to go legitimate, such as it were, and our inside knowledge of his ... prior activities ... has enabled us to have a hold over him that has been very useful."

"What's to stop us from revealing all this?" Dave asked.

The commissioner smiled.

"There is no evidence anywhere, Mr. Krause. No one would believe you. William Peace Lippmann is one of the most respected men in the country. He meets with presidents, he appears on the Tonight Show, he ..."

Dave groaned. "What about Banion and his investigation?"

"That was us, too. In fact, Banion never thought of investigating you until Mr. Pinello suggested it."

"What about the Adonis brothers?"

The commissioner actually laughed. "I'm afraid we can't claim responsibility for that. Mr. Romano came out of nowhere, but he didn't hurt our cause."

"He certainly didn't," Dave said.

"So the Association was at the root of all our troubles," Herb said.

"Certainly. We were watching you all the time." The commissioner was interrupted by a buzz on the intercom. "Well, it appears that our next guest has finally decided to show her pretty face."

All eyes turned to the door as Tracey Cagney breezed into the room. "Hello, everybody," she said. "I'm sorry I'm late."

Dave jumped to his feet. "Tracey!"

"Hello, Dave," she said as she moved to the empty chair at the table.

"Tracey, what ... who ... what..." Dave sputtered.

"I told you she was trouble," Herb muttered.

"Tracey, are you a part of all this?"

"Yes."

"All along?"

"All along."

Something inside Dave seemed to snap. "Why, you lying little bitch! How the hell could you lead me on ...”

“Dave, honey, it was fun, but this is business.”

The commissioner raised his hand. “If I might interrupt this ... lovers’ quarrel.”

He smiled coldly at Dave and Herb. “We used Miss Cagney. We didn’t want her to be a part of this Association. The thought of a woman operator is something no one connected with the NAFA ever considered.”

The commissioner shuddered. “Football is a man’s game.”

Dave looked over at Tracey, expecting an outburst. She sat there quietly, although she seemed tense.

“We were going to take away Miss Cagney’s franchise after her trade with you.”

“Which one?”

“The one I vetoed. That showed me that a woman couldn’t possibly run a franchise. She was willing to trade three of her best players simply for ... revenge.”

“I made a mistake,” Tracey said.

“Yes, you did. And so, Mr. Krause, we put Miss Cagney on a sort of probation. We told her there was a way to get back into our good graces.”

Herb caught on first. “You put her on the street.”

The commissioner smiled coldly. “So to speak. We encouraged her to start a relationship with Mr. Krause.”

“Thanks, friend,” Dave said coldly to Tracey.

“We had a good time, sweetheart. That’s all it was.”

"But you knew they were doing this to us!"

"If I'd told you, they would have done the same to me."

"Most assuredly," the commissioner said when Dave turned to him. "Of course, it was her decision."

Dave looked at Tracey, but said nothing.

"You two can talk later," the commissioner said. "But there is one more item of business we must cover before you leave. As I was saying before Miss Cagney arrived, you were able to overcome most of the obstacles we placed in your way, and I must assume you would continue to do so. I am just as certain you would not accept the place we have in the System for the Washington Warriors."

"Doormat?" Herb asked.

"Something along those lines. And because the stockholders of the Washington franchise would probably look at your performance this season, no matter how inept it actually was, and return you to another term in your current positions, we feel we have no choice but to revoke the Washington franchise."

"WHAT!" Herb and Dave were both on their feet.

"You can't do that!" Herb shouted.

"The decision already has been reached. It is being announced at this very minute. We will be rid of you, and of your ..."

"Hold on a minute," Dave said, trying hard to remain calm. "How are you going to get away with that?"

"Easily. We have a codicil in our bylaws that allows us to revoke the franchise of any city that fails to draw seventy-five percent of capacity over a five-year period."

"But we doubled our attendance this year!" Herb said.

"I'm very sorry, Mr. Rojas, but that wasn't anywhere near enough to make up for four extremely poor years prior to this one."

"But what about progress? What about the fans?"

"The fans will survive. They survived the loss of two baseball teams. Those who really want professional football can travel to Philadelphia, or New York, should they so desire."

"How can you possibly justify ..."

"That will be the easiest part of all. There is a gentleman in Tacoma, a Mr. Albert Willis, who has amassed a sizeable fortune in the aerospace industry. Mr. Willis has been pursuing a franchise for the last five years, and all our surveys have shown that putting a team in the Pacific Northwest would be a bonanza for us."

"But ..."

"And what state is Tacoma in, gentlemen?"

"Washington," Dave said.

"Very good, Mr. Krause," the commissioner said. "In fact, we're thinking of making the Warriors a regional franchise. If we were so inclined, we could continue to call the team the Washington Warriors."

"You wouldn't dare!"

"We certainly would, Mr. Rojas, but we probably won't. We will probably try to remove any taint in people's minds connected with your unfortunate franchise and its unfortunate history."

"But Tacoma?"

"Yes, Tacoma. The city has promised a domed stadium within two years, and existing facilities will be adequate until that time. Of course, there will have to be a slight geographic realignment in the Association, but that is a minor detail and a very small price to pay for replacing a weak franchise with potentially a very strong one."

Herb collapsed into a chair. Dave glanced over at Tracey, who shrugged.

"Of course," the commissioner said. "You gentlemen will be free to enjoy yourselves and attend the Championship Bowl, courtesy of the Association. We are happy to have you as our guests." He smiled at them coldly. "Never let it be said that the NAFA has no concern for the unemployed. Now if you'll excuse us, we have business to conduct."

Dave and Herb didn't say much of anything until they were downstairs in the hotel bar. "Got any ideas, Herb?"

"Just one. I'm going to have one helluva good time for the next week and a half. I'm going to drink more booze and have sex with more women than I ever have before, and I'm going to let the God-almighty North American Football Association pick up the tab for my fun. What do you say, pal? What do you say we cost this damn league a bundle?"

Dave couldn't help but smile. "Why not? We already have."

They ordered doubles, and they were about to start drinking them when they heard the page. "Will Mr. Herbert J. Rojas please pick up the white courtesy phone?"

Herb looked around and didn't see a white phone, so he asked their waiter.

"It's outside in the lobby, sir."

"I guess I'd better go take the call. Probably some damn reporter. Don't get too far ahead of me."

"You'll catch up," Dave said, lifting his drink. It was five minutes before Herb returned, and Dave was finishing his second drink at that point. He was starting to feel pleasantly fuzzy, but he wasn't too fuzzy to notice the strange look on his friend's face. "Well? Who was it, Reynolds?"

Herb shook his head.

"Your dad?"

Herb shook his head.

"Well, are you going to tell me or do I have to drag it out of you?"

Herb sat down hard and drained his drink. "It was Bridget."

"Bridget?"

"Yeah, my ... assistant. The one who quit last week."

"Oh, yeah. How did she know you were here? And where was she calling from?"

Herb gave him a strange look. "She's here in the hotel, and she says there's someone we ought to meet."

"Maybe later, man."

Herb shook his head. "That's what I told her, but she said it's got to be now."

"What the hell," Dave said, sighing. "I guess we can always get back to this. Where is she?"

"The penthouse."

~"The penthouse? That thing goes for six thousand dollars a night. How'd she afford something like that?"

"Damned if I know."

It took them ten minutes before they were knocking on the door of the penthouse, but it was only another ten seconds before Bridget Russell opened the door. "Hello, Herb. Dave."

"Bridget," Dave said, nodding.

"Where have you been?"

"All in good time, Herb. All in good time. First I'd like you to meet my father." She led them across the huge living room and into a second room that was far more intimate. As they entered the room, a tall man uncoiled himself from a sofa and drew himself up to a height Dave guessed must be about six-foot-four.

"Daddy, this is Herb Rojas and Dave Krause. Guys, this is my dad, Jack Russell."

Russell shook hands with both men. He had a handshake that nearly overpowered Dave. Herb tried to squeeze back and regretted it.

"I've been wantin' to meet you boys," Russell said. "Bridget's told me a lot about y'all."

"Really?" Herb seemed a little nervous.

"Hey, Herbie, don't worry. Bridget's a big girl."

Herb looked relieved, but Dave was more curious than anything else. "Mr. Russell ..."

"Call me Jack, Dave. Down where I'm from, we try to keep it on a first-name basis."

"All right ... Jack ... Tell me, exactly where are you from?"

"San Antone."

"Texas?"

"You know of any other San Antonio?" Herb whispered under his breath.

"You're probably wonderin' why I wanted to talk to you boys, aren't you?" Russell asked them.

Dave and Herb both nodded. "Well, I've been havin' my little girl keep an eye on you. My Bridget's really sharp. In fact, in another ten years or so I figure I'll probably turn my companies over to her."

"Companies?" Herb asked.

"Daddy's in oil," Bridget said proudly.

"Then you're not really a ..."

"Secretary? No, Dave, I'm actually more of a ..."

"Spy?"

Bridget smiled sweetly. "I prefer to think of my job as well, a sort of ... shall we say ... talent scout."

"Talent scout?"

"That's right, boys," Russell said. "When I heard about what y'all were doin' in Washington, I wanted to get a look at you."

"Why?"

"All in good time, Mr. Rojas. All in good time."

"You see, daddy's a real football fan. Always has been."

"Yep, I've been tryin' to buy into the Association for ten years or so."

"You must be pretty well-fixed then."

"Herb!"

"That's all right, Dave," Russell said. "Never did mind a man who was impressed by money. Yep, Herb. I do all right. Started out with a coupla l'il oil wells in east Texas back about thirty-five years ago. Last year my accountants told me I was halfway to my second ten billion."

Herb gulped. "B-b-b-b-b ..."

"Billion, sweetie," Bridget said.

"Anyway," Russell said. "Back when the bottom dropped out of the domestic oil market, I diversified. Got into lots of things, more stuff than I could keep track of. Did all right, too, but what I really wanted was a football team."

"Why didn't you buy one?" Dave asked. "I seem to remember Dallas was up for sale about five years back."

"I tried, but that danged fool of a commissioner wouldn't let me move the team to San Antone, and I'll be danged if I'm movin' up to Dallas."

"So?"

"So, Herbie, I got together with a couple of my buddies from the oil bidness a year or two back, and they brought in a couple of their buddies. By the time we were finished shootin' the bull, we were talkin' about startin' our own football league."

"You're kidding," Dave said.

"Not at all. We're just a bunch of rich ol' boys with more money than we know what to do with, and we figgered it'd be a challenge to take on them boys in the NAFA."

"You're right about that," Herb said. "It'd be a challenge."

"I don't think you know just how much of a challenge it'd be," Dave said. "Those guys are tough, and the commissioner, hey, that guy's the fucking prince of darkness."

"Daddy's pretty tough, too," Bridget said.

Russell just smiled. "I'll take my chances," he said.

"Excuse me, Jack," Dave said. "But you still haven't told us why you called us in here."

"Like I told you boys, we're gonna take on the NAFA. It's all a secret now, but we're goin' public next week with a big press conference in New York. Eight franchises startin' play in three years and four more two years after that."

"What cities?" Herb asked.

"Well, we figgered we had to be in some of the big ones the NAFA's already got, like New York, L.A. and Chicago, but most of the rest of the ones we're goin' after are open cities. We're startin' out in Orlando, Salt Lake, San Diego, San Antone of course, and ..."

"And?" Dave asked.

Herb knew the eighth city, or at least he thought he did.

"Washington," he said, grinning.

"You've got it," Russell said.

"And you want some advice from us, right?"

Russell laughed. "Shit, no, Herbie! We've got all the advice we need. We've had consultants workin' on this for six months, and we know exactly what we're doin'."

"Then what ..."

"Dave, good buddy, I thought you might like to meet with our Washington owner. I know you boys need jobs."

"Your Washington owner?" Herb asked. "And who is he?"

"Well, it ain't exactly a he ..."

"Then who?"

"Well, Herbie, I think you know her pretty well."

Once again, Herb caught on. "Bridget?"

"That's right, sweetie. Want to come work for me and help run a football team?"

"What about Dave?"

"Hey, you don't think I'd break up a winning team, do you?"

"What about Roy?" Dave asked.

Bridget rolled her eyes. "We'll talk about it."

"No System, right?" Dave asked. "All the games will be played straight?"

Bridget looked at her father, who didn't say a word.

Jack Russell just winked.

THE END